ERIN HAWKINS

UNEXPECTEDLY IN LOVE SERIES BOOK FOUR

Surprisingly Us

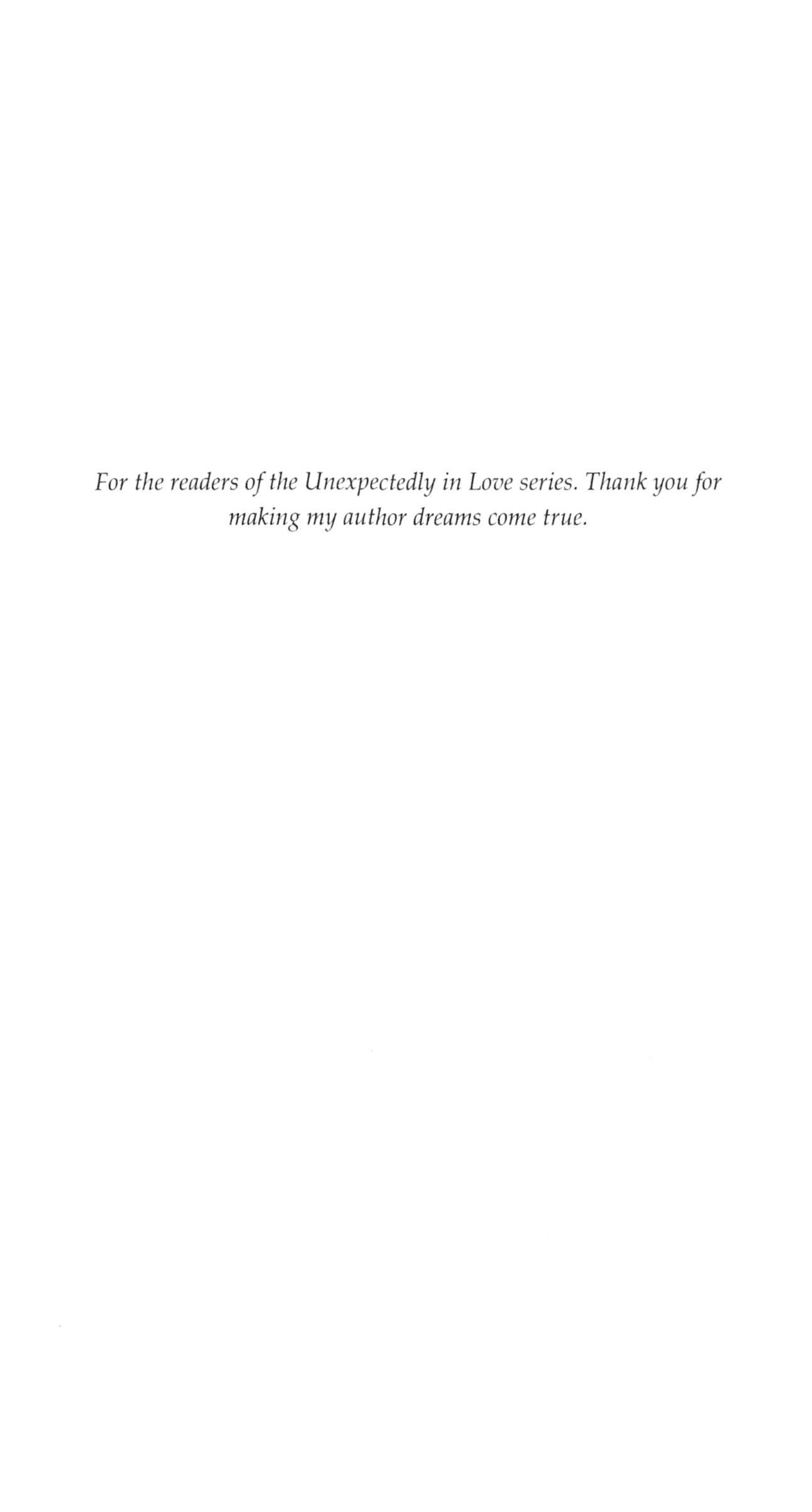

For the readers of the Unexpectedly in Love series. Thank you for making my author dreams come true.

979-8-9897817-1-3

Cover design by Cover Ever After covereverafter.com

Edited by Chelly Peeler inkedoutediting.com

Titles by Erin Hawkins

Reluctantly Yours
Unexpectedly Mine
Accidentally Ours

Best Laid Plans
Not in the Plans

Author's Note

*Surprisingly Us is the fourth book in the Unexpectedly in Love series. This book is a **standalone**, and does not need to be read with the series. However, there will be spoilers for previous books.*

*Please be advised this book is an **open-door** romance, with **on-page** sexual content. Mature readers only.*

Content warning: Some aspects of the professional ballet world have been adjusted for your reading pleasure

Also, content includes mention of past parental deaths, anxiety, childhood cancer, and divorce.

CHAPTER 1

Colette

A bead of sweat rolls down my sternum and into the front of my leotard. As it slides, it tickles the sensitive skin between my breasts, but I don't move. I hold my position and wait. My quads are burning, my calves are screaming, but I don't flinch.

"That's all for today," Alexei, our choreographer, calls in his thick Russian accent from his chair at the side of the practice room.

Slowly, I lower my heels, my left big toe relieved that my body weight is no longer bearing down on it. I take a breath, and press the heel of my hand to the sweat slick spot between my breasts, letting the material of my black leotard absorb the moisture gathered there. I look around at my fellow dancers. Sweat dripping down the sides of Sebastian's face. Isabella taking a deep breath as she makes her way over to grab her water bottle. Dimitri at the point of tears while he limps over toward a trainer to get some relief for his cramping calf muscle.

On stage, we make the moves look effortless, but in rehearsals, that's where blood, sweat and tears are shed.

This isn't even an official rehearsal.

The spring session ended a few weeks ago and the company is on a break for the summer.

I make my way over to the group of dancers on one side of the room, catching the conversation that's already in progress.

"That was a reminder of why I'm going home for six weeks. I need a break." Dimitri towels off his sweat-slick face.

"You still planning on Greece?" Sebastian asks.

Dimitri nods, flexing his foot as he works through the cramp in his calf. "Yeah, I'm going to wait tables at my uncle's restaurant and soak in the sun." He eyes the group. "I'm always up for visitors."

"You know I'm coming to visit." Isabella grins. "I'm going to help my sister with her kids for a few weeks, then I'm there."

Dimitri's already beaming smile gains an extra watt with her confirmation. They're both flirtatious by nature, but I've noticed it tick up a notch recently.

Isabella turns to me. "What are your plans, Colette?"

"Um, I'm going to stick around the city."

"Colette doesn't take breaks," Sebastian teases, wrapping his arm around my shoulder. "She's a machine."

Dimitri shakes his head. "I don't know how you do it. Everyone needs a break. It's part of the process."

The off-season is an eight-week period when dancers from the company disperse to take time off, work side jobs like waitressing and nannying, or pick up other paid dancing gigs. You can use the time however you want, but I don't travel or take time off. I use it to train and stay in shape for the next session.

My routine gives me comfort. I'd be lost without it.

Besides, the fall session's shows were announced this week and *Rubies,* a brand new, original piece by Alexei, caught my attention.

Fiery, raw, and deeply sensual.

Those were the words used to describe Alexei's new piece.

It's exactly the kind of role that would elevate my dancing and put me in a position to be promoted to principal, the highest rank a dancer can achieve in the company.

"Should we grab a celebratory drink at Chancy's Bar?" Dimitri asks.

The others nod and agree as they start to gather their bags.

"I can't. I've got plans."

"It better not be a date at another barre. B-A-R-R-E. Get it?" Dimitri's laugh fills the practice room.

I laugh with the others. It's a routine joke that while everyone else is out having fun, I'm drilling away in the practice studio.

The truth is, I couldn't stay today if I wanted to. "I have Hannah's rehearsal dinner tonight."

"That's right. Have fun at the wedding." Isabella closes her eyes and crosses her fingers. "I'm manifesting a hot groomsman for you to walk down the aisle with."

"Thanks." I don't bother to burst her bubble that I already know who I'm walking down the aisle with and while he is very handsome, he's also very married. All of Hannah and James's wedding party is either married or in a committed relationship. All of them except me.

"We're on for practice next week? For the Leg-Up fundraiser showcase?" I ask Sebastian.

As a volunteer and advocate for Leg-Up, a non-profit dance collective that focuses on providing free dance classes to financially challenged students, I've asked Sebastian to perform with me in the dance showcase at their fundraising gala in a few weeks.

He nods. "Sure thing."

"Great. I already confirmed the studio times and sent you a schedule before practice today."

"You're on top of it, as always." He picks up his bag. "You sure you can't come for a drink?"

"I really can't. My bridesmaid to-do list is too long."

My best friend, Hannah Cartwright, is getting married tomorrow and while she isn't a bridezilla, I'm her maid of honor, and taking my duties very seriously.

"Okay, I'll see you next week, doll."

"See you." I start gathering my things when Alexei calls out to me from across the room.

"Colette, a word." He motions me over.

Crap. It's never good news to be called over by the choreographer after practice. My mind combs over today's practice, wondering what I must have done wrong. Trying to anticipate Alexei's feedback.

I've been dancing since I was seven years old, and with The City Ballet Company for the last eight years. Over that time, I've worked my way up the ranks of the corps de ballet to a soloist, and I know that principal dancer is within my reach. It's what I've been working toward. It's what I desperately want.

Alexei motions for me to sit.

"How are you feeling about today's practice?" he asks.

I hate when he asks how I'm feeling. It doesn't matter how I *feel* if he thinks my dancing wasn't good enough.

I struggle to pick out a section of footwork that I could improve.

I chew on my lip before finally answering. "I know I could sharpen my pirouettes in the middle."

He nods silently, but doesn't look satisfied with my answer, so I attempt to find something else I can work on.

"The ending needs work?" It's a question because I'm trying to pick apart what felt like was a flawless routine.

"Colette, there is nothing technical with today's routine to improve. Your grace as a dancer is unmatched."

My heart soars at his praise. It's what I live for.

"Your technique is flawless. Alignment, turnout, port de bras. There's nothing I can critique you on there." Even though I can hear the 'but' coming from a mile away, I still flinch. "But where you're excelling with your technique, you're lacking in passion."

He sighs. "It's not enough to execute the moves, you must connect with the audience. Let them feel the emotion of the dance; joy, anguish, lust, rage," he emphasizes each one with a balled-up fist. "Dancing is storytelling. It's clear you know all the words, but you have to give them a voice. Dive deep into your emotions and let them pour out of you on the stage."

I nod, taking in what he's saying.

He must see something on my face, or a lack of something because his lips press together ruefully and he sighs. "Even as I'm advising you to find more passion in your dancing, I can see your mind whirring, trying to make sense of it. Trying to find a technical aspect to improve. But that's not what I'm after."

I nod, but I'm quiet, still processing what he's saying.

"I noted your interest for the lead in *Rubies.*"

"It sounds amazing. And so different from anything I've danced before."

He nods. "It is." His thumb and index finger slide over the meticulously groomed salt and pepper hair at his jaw. "The dancer I'm looking for will need to strip away perfection. This performance will be messy and raw. It focuses on the desire and passion that one experiences with a new love. Vulnerability and uncertainty, joy and contentment. All the emotions that come with a person finding love for the first time. It's an awakening that will require every raw emotion to be at the surface."

At his words, my stomach sinks. I'm a confident dancer. I

didn't get this far in the company by being timid, yet there are things that I haven't experienced and they happen to be everything Alexei just mentioned.

"As dancers, we get caught up in this world," he motions to the practice room, "but it's out there," he points to the door, "where we find what brings our performances to life. Real connections. Real emotions. Love, heartbreak, betrayal, loss. All of life's messiness is what molds a technical dancer into a breathtaking performer. To bring your performance to the next level, you must be able to deliver that. It's what sets a principal dancer apart from the rest."

I swallow thickly and nod. "I understand."

He pauses, then sighs. "You have all the potential in the world, Colette, but if you want the lead role in *Rubies*, you need to find a way to bring more passion into your performance," his fingers rap against the left side of his chest, in emphasis, while his gaze bores into mine, "or this role is not meant for you."

I swallow thickly, Alexei's reference is to my evaluation this past spring session. And the fall session before that. They were my best technical performances, yet they weren't enough to land me the lead and promote me to principal dancer in the company. There was something missing.

According to Alexei, that something is passion.

"Evaluations for *Rubies* are in eight weeks. You'll need to make every effort to give a passionate performance, or you won't be considered for the lead role. And I'm afraid a promotion to principal will be off the table."

Over the years, it's been hard watching other dancers advance to principal while I stay at soloist.

Soloist is an amazing accomplishment. I know this. But if I were satisfied with soloist then his words wouldn't have such a soul-crushing effect.

"I understand," I tell him, my voice even despite my thundering pulse and tightening chest.

He nods. "Enjoy your weekend, Colette."

All I can do is nod and watch him leave, the metal practice room door banging shut with a heavy thud at his exit.

Somehow, I find the strength to push up and out of the chair, gather my things and walk out of the room. I sit on the bench outside, trading my ballet slippers for trainers Mr. Rogers style, while trying to collect my thoughts.

My life outside the studio isn't non-existent. I do have friends. I socialize with the other company dancers, our rigorous lifestyle bonding us together. Though I could make more of an effort to see them outside of the studio.

There's my best friend since childhood, Hannah. And most of her friends have become mine by association. My philanthropic work, making tutus for visits at the children's hospital, and my recent collaboration with Leg-Up, a non-profit dance school. And I've got Maxine, my sometimes sweet, but mostly grumpy Maltese cat.

My life is busy and full.

Yet, even as the thought forms in my brain, I know it's not completely true. I know what's missing.

What Alexei has found lacking in my dancing.

Passion.

I do a quick dictionary search on my phone just to make sure there's no confusion.

An object of desire or deep interest. Ardent affection. Sexual desire.

A group of dancers from the ballet school walking by pull my attention from my phone. They're huddled together, looking at one of the girls' phones and giggling. The middle girl suddenly drops her phone in her bag, then splits from the pack to run up to a guy. She leaps into his arms and wraps her legs around his waist. Their lips crash together and soon I'm blushing watching this young couple make out in the middle of the building.

Young love. Or lust. I'm not sure what it is for them, but

they've clearly got chemistry. My heart kicks up a notch at the thought of what that would feel like. The excitement of leaping into a man's arms and having him kiss you passionately. It's such a foreign idea, my skin starts to tingle. Because you can't get to the leaping into someone's arms part without the dreaded D word.

I will my brain not to think it. It knows my body has a mind of its own and will retaliate with a very visible skin reaction.

I'm staring intently at the couple when my phone buzzes in my hand.

The text isn't from a guy. It's from my best friend, Hannah, reminding me to bring my overnight bag to her rehearsal dinner tonight because we'll be going straight to the hotel after.

Hannah's a few years older than me, but it's still a reminder that I've got friends who are getting married while I've yet to *date* anyone.

Oh, no. Now I've done it.

Date. Dating. Dated.

Every form of the word causes an adrenaline spike in my veins. My nails immediately find the itchy patch of skin that's starting to bloom across my chest.

I've danced onstage for thousands of people before, so why does the idea of sitting in front of one person and sharing a meal with them make me break out in hives?

Maybe it's not just the meal sharing thing, it's all the things that come after that.

I pull my water bottle out of my bag and press it against my red, splotchy chest.

Dating.

I've never been in love, never had my heart broken, never allowed myself to be vulnerable the way people in love do. Because all of that would require dating and putting myself out there to meet someone.

It's not that I don't want those things. I do. I simply haven't had time for them. I've been drilling technique, pushing myself to be the best technical dancer I can be, and now I'm learning that the one thing holding me back from becoming a principal dancer is the fact that I haven't lived my life outside the studio? Instead, I've been living and breathing ballet for eighteen years.

Well, that and the small issue that I'm allergic to dating.

It's a medical condition, really.

An unexplained phenomenon that I can't control and therefore have decidedly chosen to avoid its trigger.

Dating.

The red bumps start to spread down my arms.

The couple catches me staring and my cheeks warm with embarrassment. I hadn't even realized I'd still been watching them.

I pull my gaze from the young couple and throw my bag over my shoulders.

Okay, time to go.

Walking through the complex, t, the spring session posters are still hung in the presentation boxes outside. Ava Wilks and Zuri Moore, two of The City Ballet's principal dancers, gracefully captured by the company's photographer. The three of us have been dancing together since we were young.

As a friend, I'm happy for them, but I want more for myself.

I don't want to only be known for being a flawless technical dancer. I want to move people with my performance. Ignite passion and emotion. And be promoted to principal.

It's not even a want at this point, it's a necessity. Principal is the pinnacle of my hopes and dreams as a dancer and I wouldn't be able to look myself in the mirror in the morning if I wasn't giving one hundred percent effort to reach my goal. Landing the lead in *Rubies* is a vital step toward that goal, and in turn finding passion in my life to influence my dancing is what I need to do.

If dating is what I need to do to unlock the passionate dancer within me, then I'll have to push past this mental block and physical reaction. And I'll figure out how I'm going to do that right after I get a hydrocortisone cream on this rash.

CHAPTER 2

Rhys

The tie around my neck is suffocating me. I reach up to loosen it, then glance around the large mahogany table at all the unfamiliar faces.

I'd ask someone to open a window if we weren't on the eightieth floor.

I avoid stuffy boardrooms if I can help it, but today is necessary.

After being away for nearly five years, I'm back in New York City for the annual meeting for The Spencer Foundation. While I usually attend these meetings virtually, line-item number two on today's meeting agenda, *Rhys Spencer trust fund installment,* is the only reason I made the effort to show up.

As I wait for the rest of the suits to filter in, I scroll through the flood of texts I've received since my return to the city was announced.

Party invites and friends looking to catch up.

Acquaintances wanting to meet about investment opportunities.

And women texting me to meet up. Lots of women.

My phone buzzes with another text. This one a picture of a

woman from the neck down. Glorious tits. Her legs crossed, teasing the triangle between her legs. With a body like hers, I should remember, but the fake tits, spray tan and tiny lace thong are not unique. She looks like most of the women I've fucked.

Unknown number: *Hi! It's Cassidy from Palm Beach. I'm in the city this weekend. Call me!*

Normally I'd save her contact information, but today I'm just not interested.

That's not true. It isn't just today.

A week ago, I was on a yacht in the Caribbean. The alcohol was flowing. The women were topless. Yet, I was bored out of my mind. Restless. Not even the orgy taking place on the yacht's upper deck could pull me out of my funk. I've been feeling that way for a while now.

I'm about to delete the message when a hand claps me on the shoulder.

I look up from my phone to find my cousin, Jerrod, staring down at me, a shit-eating grin on his face as he looks from me to my phone screen. The woman's nearly nude photo is still visible.

"Rhys, good to see you, buddy."

His use of buddy is ironic. We're not friends. Not even close.

He extends his hand to me, so I pocket my phone and meet his firm grip.

"Jerrod."

Our clasped hands remind me of all the arm wrestling matches we did as kids.

As we shake, his grip tightens and I follow suit, not to be outdone.

We've been competing against each other since I can remember. From who lost their training wheels first to who had the best grades in prep school. Sports, academic success, even whose facial hair was more abundant in puberty. It was always a competition.

Where Jerrod excelled in academia, I was better at sports. He was the quiet book worm, where I was the life of the party. Not much has changed. Jerrod's a high-level executive at Martin, Breaker, Short. He's done well for himself and even has an attractive, successful girlfriend.

The one thing he doesn't have, and never will, is the Spencer name. A fact that, for some reason or another, drives him mad.

I turn to the man next to me and point to Jerrod. "Have you met my cousin, Jerrod Grossweiner?"

The man's mouth opens to respond but I'm not listening for his answer. My question was only posed to poke fun at Jerrod's last name. Jerrod's mouth twitches. He knows exactly what I'm doing. It's what we do.

"Over the years, I've gotten used to seeing you as a tiny head on a computer screen." Jerrod looks me up and down, taking in my appearance. "I like your pink suit." His lips press together like he's stifling a laugh.

My mouth twists into a restrained sneer. "It's salmon," I bite out.

"Yeah, okay." He pats me on the arm. It's a consoling gesture. He's placating me.

I like fashion, so fucking sue me if I want to look good. Expressing myself with clothing is something I enjoy.

The wild thing about it is I'll get questions about my fashion choices and people questioning my sexuality, and in the next breath be accused of being a manwhore who hooks up with hundreds of women. There's no pleasing people. So, I don't bother.

That's exactly how I'm handling it right now with Jerrod, because he wouldn't know fashion if it knocked him on his boring navy-suit, silver-tie-wearing ass.

"Your tie is crooked." Before I can react, Jerrod reaches out to straighten my tie, and it takes everything in me to not smack his hand away.

When he's done, I brush an invisible piece of lint off his shoulder to satisfy me instead.

I'm easygoing. It's not often someone gets under my skin, but Jerrod does. Just his presence has my blood pressure spiking. That's why I make it a point of not seeing him if I can help it.

"I'd love to hear about all your adventures," he says.

I shake my head. "There's not much to tell."

"That can't be true. Even without your presence in the city, you've been keeping us entertained."

"How so?" I ask, eyes narrowing.

"Social media has been very informative." He winks, but it's not friendly. "It's like they've got a tracker on you. Everything that's going on in your life laid out for all to see."

Ramsey, my assistant, has mentioned a few articles circulating. Some are true, some aren't. Photos on social media that were taken out of context. I've never bothered to set the record straight because it doesn't matter to me.

Jerrod's goading me, hoping I'll engage, but I'm not going to take the bait. I'm here for one thing. The final installment from my trust fund.

My eyes shift to the movement around us. All the board members have arrived. My grandfather is at the head of the table now talking with his assistant.

I cover up the unease of being in this environment by giving Jerrod a lazy grin. "You shouldn't believe everything you read on the internet."

"That's true, but where you're concerned, it's known to be a reliable source." He leans in. "Don't worry, you'll be out of here in no time. Then, you can go play and leave the work to the rest of the grown-ups."

His condescending tone grates at me. We're the same age, yet he's talking to me like a child. What a fucking dick. I want to remind him of the time we got lost in the woods and he cried like a baby while I carried him for miles until I found a way out.

I shouldn't let him get to me. It gives him too much satisfaction.

Ignore Jerrod, get the money, and get the hell out.

I'm relieved when my grandfather asks everyone to be seated and he starts the meeting.

My fingers itch to retrieve my buzzing phone from my pocket and zone out by scrolling, but I force myself to focus on my grandfather's words.

"Now to the matter of Rhys Spencer's trust disbursement." He clears his throat before continuing. "On his thirtieth birthday, Rhys Spencer will receive his final trust installment of two hundred fifty million dollars."

My gaze moves to Jerrod. He's playing at being unaffected, but I can see the way his jaw ticks.

While his parents provided him a comfortable upbringing, the business deals and investments my father made in his twenties and thirties are unmatched. His ingenuity and financial savvy grew The Spencer Foundation—and the large sum that is my trust fund—into what it is today.

I breathe a sigh of relief at how smoothly that went. I half-expected my grandfather to deny me the money. For there to be a character clause or some bullshit stipulation that I didn't know about, leaving me blindsided and desperate to fulfill it.

Two hundred and fifty million dollars.

That's the second installment. The first was when I was twenty-five. It was a smaller sum then, only a hundred million. I invested half of the money and have been traveling and living off the rest ever since.

I should be pleased, but the knot in my gut that took hold the moment I arrived back in Manhattan doesn't release.

"Now to the next order of business." Around the room,

board members straighten in their chairs, as if to say the real meeting has finally started.

My grandfather leans back in his chair. "I'm stepping down from my position as foundation board president."

The room is silent for a beat before panicked whispers start circulating.

Jerrod's gaze flicks to me, a hint of a wolfish gleam in his eyes, before his attention returns to our grandfather who has held up a hand to quiet the room.

"It's time to usher in a new generation. I never planned to stay as long as I did, but with the situation we found ourselves in, it was necessary."

He's talking about my parents' death. The fact that Ward Spencer became the president of The Spencer Foundation board when my parents died and I was too young to take the position.

My grandfather motions for Macintosh, the board's legal advisor, to speak.

"As specified in the foundation bylaws, it is required to have a family member as the board's president." He continues, "A formal vote will be required, and the conditions met, as one must be thirty years old in order to become the board's president."

Another nod from my grandfather and Macintosh closes his binder.

I'm still processing when Jerrod speaks up.

"I'm very much looking forward to the opportunity to provide my service to the foundation."

My grandfather nods at Jerrod.

What the fuck?

Jerrod's taking over as the foundation board president?

"Wait. When was this decided?" I motion to Jerrod.

My grandfather's mouth draws downward. "It hasn't been officially, but there's been no indication that there were other candidates." He looks pointedly at me. I'm the only other candidate that would be eligible. Jerrod's mom, my dad's sister, would be the only other blood relative candidate, but she divorced Jerrod's dad years ago then moved to Costa Rica with a surfer named Rodney.

He's right. I haven't been involved with The Spencer Foundation, but the thought of handing over *my* parents' legacy to Jerrod makes my stomach turn sour.

"May we speak privately?" I ask my grandfather, nodding to the door of the conference room, needing to get away from all the sets of eyes on me.

He gives a half-nod in response, and we stand to exit the room, only to find Jerrod has followed us. Clearly, he doesn't know what the fuck 'privately' means. I ignore him and focus on my grandfather.

"I want the position." The words are out of my mouth before I can fully weigh their implications.

"Hmm." His fingers pinch his lower lip before he releases it. "It's good to see you taking interest, but it's not my decision to make."

"Can't you choose your successor?" I ask.

"I have influence, but ultimately the board will vote. That's how the foundation has been set up."

I look through the glass door where the board members are still seated. Jerrod had entered the room earlier, making the rounds, shaking hands, and easily conversing with the foundation's board members.

I should know who the other board members are, recognize their faces and know what is going on in their lives, but I don't. I'm suddenly ashamed I don't know much about them or the foundation. That I've distanced myself from the one thing my parents valued outside of spending time with our family.

"The minimum requirement is that you're thirty years of age, which both you and Jerrod will be in three months' time."

Our birthdays are only a day apart. I'm older by sixteen hours. A fact I used to rile him up more than once when we were kids.

"Are there other requirements?" Jerrod speaks up from beside me. "Anything that would help us understand the candidate they're looking for?"

"The foundation has always prided itself on its upstanding character and morally conscientious board. Board members exemplify and follow a code of ethics."

My grandfather's gaze shifts to me.

"It is important to remember that the care one shows in their personal life is a direct reflection of their character and how they will handle themselves as the president of the foundation. The Spencer Foundation is highly regarded, and its board president must be as well. It's more than handing out checks. The president is the face and the moral fiber of the foundation."

I swallow thickly as my mind recalls the past five years. It's been an endless string of parties and wild adventures. My sex life could be likened to the montage from *Wedding Crashers*, falling into bed with a different woman every night. The woman who texted me her tits earlier is only one of many.

Jerrod's comment about the articles circulating about my exploits. Even while I've been abroad, every club spotting, every woman on my arm has been relayed by the media, establishing a reputation that is nothing like the one my grandfather mentioned.

My grandfather's voice draws me back to the conversation.

"With two candidates, there will need to be a vetting process. The board members will want to get to know you better," he nods to Jerrod, "and your significant other, as the president and their partner are often seen as the embodiment of the foundation."

My stomach sinks again. Jerrod's girlfriend, Corinne Marks, is not only gorgeous and successful but her family owns one of the country's top grocery store chains. She's exactly the kind of woman that would be the board president's girlfriend or wife. That's his advantage. And he knows it.

The more my grandfather talks, the more uneasy I feel.

All my past exploits are flashing before my eyes and it's not pretty. Not to say the women weren't gorgeous, because they were fucking knockouts, but it's the amount of them that's an issue. And there were a lot.

My phone buzzes in my pocket. Likely another DM or text from some hookup I can't remember.

"I will let the board know you are both interested in the position, and I'll be in touch with the details of the selection process."

I'm watching my grandfather return to the conference room when Jerrod claps a hand down on my shoulder.

"You don't have to do this, Rhys. When I'm president I'll still support Wesley and Abigail's causes. Your mother was a fan of the visual arts. She loved the ballet, right?"

My gaze narrows. I hate that he's talking about my parents like he knew them well. Anger rushes through my veins, hot and thick. There are no words coming from my mouth, but there's a rumbling sound. It might have been a growl.

He sees my reaction and I swear his lips turn up in delight.

"I don't want you getting upset. You've got your trust fund. Why don't you hop on a plane and go have fun?"

Fuck that.

If Jerrod thinks I'm going to move aside while he takes what is rightfully mine, he's dead wrong. I push the anger and shutter my face to gain control of my emotions.

A smirk splits my lips. "You're right, Jerrod. I do have my

trust fund *and* I'm going to be the president of The Spencer Foundation."

He's quiet a moment.

"Did you miss Grandfather's speech? Where he said one's personal life is a direct reflection of their character?" He shakes his head, mock sympathy settling over his features. "Yours is a mess, Rhys. You're a tabloid's wet dream, and because of that, you'll never get the board's approval."

My jaw tightens. He's right, and I hate it.

It's going to take more than a charming smile to win the board over. To get them to see me as the best candidate for the position. But I've got three months until we turn thirty, until my grandfather steps down and the board votes.

Three months to do what? Find a girlfriend? Make my life look like a carbon copy of Jerrod's?

It sounds like a nightmare. But the reality is if I don't do it, if I don't try, Jerrod will be president of The Spencer Foundation.

As if I feel someone watching me, my gaze shifts to the framed family portrait hanging above the mantel. I was eight or nine and we were on vacation in Italy. We had to stand still for hours. Jerrod and his family were there, too, and he spent the entire time running around making faces at me, trying to get me to move and react. At the time, I'd hated that he was free and I had to sit for the portrait.

My dad pulled me aside after and told me he was proud of how I'd handled the distraction. That sometimes life is distracting but keeping focus on your goal, on family, and what is most important is the key to success.

I've been distracted. Unfocused. But right now, in this moment, I know what is most important.

"Corinne and I are having a dinner party in a few weeks. The board members will be there so it's only fair I invite you. Level playing field and all." He moves to head back into the conference room but turns back again. "Oh, and feel free to bring a date. If you can narrow it down."

I give him a patronizing smile. "Looking forward to it."

Determination floods my veins as I turn toward the foundation's office exit.

"May the best man win," Jerrod calls as I stride down the hallway.

I'm tempted to flip him off, but instead, I throw him a backhanded wave.

Outside, the early summer heat hits me and all the bravado I mustered in front of Jerrod starts to slide off like a melting ice cream cone. A moment ago, I was certain, but now, I have no idea what I'm supposed to do.

What the fuck did I just get myself into?

Ramsey, my assistant, is waiting by the black SUV.

"To the airport?" he asks.

That was the plan before I walked into that meeting.

I hesitate.

I could leave.

Forget about what I told my grandfather, and all about The Spencer Foundation. Let Jerrod be president. Let him *win*.

It's what I've done so many times in the past. Bowed out because I didn't care. Didn't see the value in competing with Jerrod. The wins weren't celebrated and the losses were rubbed in my face.

A heavy weight settles across my chest. I care about this. About the foundation. My parents' legacy.

I shake my head. "No, we're going home."

"Home?" he asks, as he slides into the vehicle beside me.

It's a good question. For a long time now, home has been wherever I feel like being for more than a few days at a time. But in New York City, I have one residence.

"Yeah. We'll be staying in Manhattan."

"And why is that?" he asks.

Ramsey's used to my restless ways. Never in one place for

long. He's been with me since I left New York City the first time and for efficiency, he always has his suitcase packed.

"Jerrod was there."

We exchange a knowing glance.

Ramsey groans, before adjusting his glasses. "What did you get yourself into?" He reaches for his neck. "I refuse to participate; my neck still isn't the same after that tandem bike race three years ago."

It had been a silly bet between me and Jerrod, his friend Smith, and Ramsey, who by default as my assistant got roped into being my partner. A wager gone too far after too many beers in an Amsterdam bar.

"Nothing I can't handle."

"I love your optimism." He pats my cheek. "It's precious."

Recalling what my grandfather had said about the board president's character, I tell him, "I need to clean up my image. No more parties, no more women."

Ramsey's brows shoot to his sandy-blonde hairline, his brown eyes light with intrigue. "No arguments here, but how does that involve Jerrod?"

I tell him about my grandfather stepping down from foundation board president and Jerrod's desire to take the position. How I refuse to let that happen.

"It's competing against Jerrod, which I fucking hate, but I hate the thought of him running The Spencer Foundation even more."

Ramsey nods, he's my assistant, but he's also a good friend, and the voice of reason in my chaotic life. I don't always listen to that voice, but he knows he's free to give his opinion either way.

"All right. Let's do this." He adjusts his glasses, then reaches for his phone. "I'll set up an appointment with my cousin Percy at Bergman's. He'll get you a grown-up wardrobe."

I scoff. "What does that mean?"

"Your clothes are," he eyes my suit, "how should I put this nicely? Loud."

"They're an expression of me," I argue.

"Exactly."

That's all he says. No elaboration. The point is to be less like I am now.

"Fine. I'll pick out a few things."

"And you'll need new friends."

"What's wrong with my friends?" I ask.

Ramsey's brows climb higher on his forehead. An inch for each confounding statement that comes out of my mouth.

"Do I really need to elaborate?" he asks. "Because I've got a PowerPoint presentation worth of material."

"They're a little wild," I concede.

His eyebrows don't budge.

"Okay, a lot wild. That's what we do together. Have fun. Let off steam. Get a little crazy."

"You see how you're proving my point."

Now I'm thinking about my friends in the city and all the crazy shit we've done. Most nights we were together, we made scenes from *The Hangover* look like a Disney movie. So much debauchery.

My phone buzzes with a text.

Vulcan: *Party last night was lit! Don't be sleeping on it tonight, bro*

I scroll to a picture of my friend Matt, with two women sitting in his lap as the club lights flash behind him.

Ramsey squints at my phone screen.

"Who's Vulcan?"

"That's not his real name."

"So he purposely requests people call him that?"

"It's Matt, you know, Bryce's cousin that's in the grunge band, Flaming Torpedo? Vulcan's his stage name."

"Flaming Torpedo?" Ramsey cringes. "That sounds like what happens in the bathroom after I eat spicy food."

Ramsey's right. If I'm going to turn over a new leaf, I'll need to ditch my old friends. It doesn't have to be forever, just while I'm being evaluated for the board's president position.

"Okay. I'll keep a low profile."

Jerrod's dinner invitation resurfaces, along with his jab about bringing a date.

"Jerrod's having a dinner party for all the board members in a few weeks. I'll need a date."

Ramsey shakes his head. "You're going to need more than a date to convince people you've changed your fuckboy ways."

I can easily drop a fortune on looking the part, and stay away from old friends and bad habits, but the real issue is finding a woman that could measure up to the board's standards. The women I typically fuck are not the 'meet the foundation board' type.

Exhibit A, my phone being bombarded with sexts and nudes.

I doubt Corinne sends Jerrod nudes. Maybe she should. It would probably help with the stick that's permanently up his ass.

I scroll through my phone, hoping a gem will pop out at me. Some demure, emotionally-stable woman that could impress the foundation board members and make me look good. A woman that could compete with Corinne's success and flawless image.

No woman I've hooked up with fits that description.

While I'm thinking, my eyes snag on the pile of mail next to Ramsey.

"What's this?" I ask, taking notice of a fancy gold envelope among the rest.

"Mail I picked up from your PO box. Most of it is old. With all the traveling, I've made everything paperless that I possibly can."

I slide a finger under the sealed gold envelope and pull

out the contents. As I suspected by the weight of the premium paper and the hand-painted floral design, it's a wedding invitation.

I find the names in the center in an elegant script font.

Hannah Cartwright and James McKenzie.

For the first time since I walked into the board room this morning, a genuine smile pulls at my lips.

"What's that?" Ramsey asks.

"An invitation to the Cartwright-McKenzie wedding." I hold it out to him. "Reply yes."

He glances down at the invitation, his eyes widening. "The wedding's tomorrow. It's bad form to RSVP this late."

I shrug. "I didn't get the invitation until now. And I need to be at that wedding. It'll be the perfect way to reintroduce myself to New York City's elite and most respected families. And possibly find a high-caliber woman I can date to impress the board."

He sighs but nods, then picks up his phone to type something out.

I stare out the window as we pass the tree-lined streets of the city I grew up in. Everything looks familiar, yet so much has changed. I'm not the person I was when I left the city five years ago and I'm nothing close to the man my father was. But that's not going to stop me from making sure Jerrod stays off The Spencer Foundation board.

CHAPTER 3

Colette

There's a knock on the door. "Twenty minutes, ladies," Johnathan, Hannah and James's wedding planner calls, before looking around the room. "Where's Sophie?"

"I'm here!" Sophie rushes in behind him, out of breath, and a bit disheveled in her one-shoulder gown.

Sophie skirts by Johnathan, giving him a quick kiss on the cheek as she passes.

Johnathan eyes Sophie with amusement. "Soph, do not be the reason we don't hit the aisle at four o'clock sharp." He taps his watch, his tone mildly scolding.

Sophie and Johnathan used to work together at Marion Adler Events where Sophie had a paid internship before she left to pursue her Sustainable Wedding Chic blog and her own wedding planning business. She's also engaged to Hannah's brother, Hunter.

"Cut her some slack, Johnathan," Hannah, the bride and my best friend, teases. "She's a mom of two five-month-olds. *My nieces*."

Johnathan's lips twist into a smirk. "You know it wasn't those precious babies that made her late."

Sophie's cheeks flush pink, but the color looks good on

her. "I'm sorry I'm running late. And Johnathan's right; Hunter and I lost track of time."

Hannah pulls Sophie in for a hug. "I love you and Hunter together, but it's my wedding day, let's not talk about my brother's sex life."

Sophie giggles. "I think we agreed to *never* talk about it."

"Exactly." Hannah laughs.

Emma Hart, Hannah's wedding gown designer and the owner of Emma Belle Bridal, bends down to make a quick adjustment on Hannah's train. Emma is married to Sophie's brother, Griffin Hart. And Griffin works with Hunter at the Cartwright's real estate company, Premier Real Estate.

It's kind of wild how this group is connected.

"I found the other shoe!" Chloe exclaims, holding one of Hannah's Christian Louboutin heels in her hand.

"Thank you, Chloe!" Emma reaches for the shoe before helping Hannah into it.

Chloe is an assistant editor at St. Clair Press and married to Barrett St. Clair, who is good friends with Hunter.

Sophie and I are two of Hannah's bridesmaids. With a few cousins and other friends, there are seven of us total. Emma and Chloe are Hannah's personal attendants.

As we count down the minutes to walking down the aisle, the other women are circling Hannah like a prized fighter about to enter the ring, making sure everything is in place. Her makeup artist swoops in for a last-minute touch up, while Hannah's mom, Katherine, is furiously taking pictures in the background alongside the wedding photographer.

As Hannah's best friend and maid of honor, I'm trying to be here in this moment with her, but with everyone around, I haven't the faintest clue what I should be doing. Sending good vibes?

It doesn't help that Alexei's words from yesterday's practice keep repeating in my head.

It's outside the studio, in our personal lives, that we find what gives us passion in our dancing.

I've been desperate to talk to Hannah about my conversation with Alexei, but it's her wedding weekend. There's no appropriate time to pull the bride aside and lay out all my problems. I did start researching dating websites yesterday before the rehearsal dinner until a bout of hives took over and I had to stop and place ice packs on my chest.

Sophie snaps me out of my fog. "Hey, Lettie, I know you're in charge of the bridal suite set up, but I got a few things for the welcome basket so I left those with Johnathan's team. Also, I didn't know if it would be helpful but I got pictures of the room and emailed you a few setup ideas."

Sophie's a wedding planner, so I shouldn't feel inept, but it's hard when I have zero experience with these kinds of events and everyone else around me is literally a professional.

"That's great. Thanks, Sophie."

"You bet. If you need any help with it, just let me know."

"I will." But I know I won't ask her. For her, it's a night off, one where she can spend time with Hunter and get a break from motherhood. I want her to enjoy it. And I desperately feel the need to be helpful with something.

She nods, giving me another radiant smile before moving toward the door where the florist is handing out bouquets.

I'm about to do the same when Hannah clasps my hands in hers, a giddy smile on her face.

"Lettie, I'm getting married today. Can you believe it?" Her glossy brown hair is pulled back and pinned neatly in an intricate chignon.

"Yes." I laugh, rubbing my thumb over her vibrating hands. "And you look gorgeous. The most beautiful bride there ever was."

"You have to say that, you're my best friend."

"I get to say that because I'm your best friend."

"Remember all those times we dressed up in princess gowns and pretended we were getting married?"

I recall the memories and smile. "Lots of tulle and sequins on those dresses. I'm glad our taste has changed."

Her sweetheart neckline and mermaid style dress is elegant, yet sexy. Emma captured Hannah's playful sophistication perfectly with her design.

Her eyes rake over me. "You look gorgeous, too. I love the hairstyle you chose."

"It's always up in a bun of some kind so I thought I'd go for something different today. And," I finger the teardrop earrings dangling from my ear, "it shows off these beautiful earrings."

The earrings are a bridesmaid gift from Hannah. They're part of her new jewelry line at Facet & Filigree, her SoHo jewelry store that opened last year. It's been a big year for her and as her best friend, I've loved cheering on her successes.

She beams. "I love seeing everyone wearing them."

"They're a perfect complement to the dresses."

The champagne-colored silk dress Hannah chose for us is fitted in the bodice with a mid-thigh slit. Each bridesmaid was able to pick the most flattering neckline. Me and my small breasts opted for a deep V-neck.

"I know the night is going to fly by the moment we walk out that door. The last ten months have been a whirlwind and I know the wedding activities have taken up a lot of your time, so I want to say thank you for everything. And, I love you."

She starts to sniff, tears forming in her eyes.

I point a stern finger at her, hoping it will ward off my misty eyes as well. "Do not cry, it'll ruin your makeup."

"My makeup is waterproof; you know I'm going to be crying all night."

Hannah is emotional, but anyone would be on their wedding day, I'm sure.

I pull her in for a hug, careful not to smush the front of her delicate dress. "I love you, too, Hans."

We start to walk toward the door when Hannah turns back to me. "Oh, I almost forgot. I have a huge favor to ask."

My heart flutters with anticipation. I'm desperate to be helpful. While twenty-some years of friendship secured me the role of Hannah's maid-of-honor, I've found this last year that having zero relationship experience doesn't lend itself well to planning bachelorette parties and bridal showers. Thank god for Pinterest, and for the other ladies, whom all are either married or engaged.

"Of course. What can I do?"

"I wasn't going to make it a big deal, but I want everything to be perfect today, so while I don't think there's anything to be concerned about, I want to put it on your radar because that would help put me at ease."

As an only child, Hannah's like a sister to me. She has her older brother, Hunter, and they're close now, but their seven-year age gap meant they weren't playmates growing up. Hannah and I were the princess costume-wearing, Barbie-playing, six and eight-year-olds when Hunter was a hormonal teenager that wanted nothing to do with us.

My answer is automatic. "Of course, I'll do anything."

"Will you keep an eye on Rhys tonight?" she asks.

At the mention of our childhood friend, my body starts to tingle. His name brings up so many memories. Summers spent at Lake George with our families. Lots of laughter. He could always make me laugh. And tiny spark of something else.

"Rhys Spencer?" I confirm, just in case she's talking about another Rhys. One that might not be a devilishly handsome or wildly intimidating man.

"Johnathan informed me he RSVP'd yesterday so they're shifting a few things around to put him at a table with Chloe and Barrett." She sighs. "Who RSVPs to a wedding the day before?"

It's a rhetorical question but in this case, the answer is Rhys.

"My parents said it would be a nice gesture to invite him since he's back in the city, so I did. I didn't actually think he'd come. But now that he is, I want to make sure he's on his best behavior."

She doesn't need to elaborate. Or mention the gossip about his reputation for partying and hooking up with women. And it's not all rumors. There's been plenty of photographic evidence. Social media can be a blessing and a curse.

I press my lips together, letting my mind wander to the man I've seen gracing many tabloid articles and social media posts.

It doesn't matter if you approve of his smooth charm or bad boy reputation, there's no way around it, Rhys is beautiful. His dark hair, wild and rebellious, just like his soul. Hazel eyes that I swear alight with flecks of yellow when he's being mischievous, at least that's how they appeared when we were younger.

I never knew exactly what Rhys and I were. Friends, I guess.

When we were younger, he was my protector. Both the only children in our families, we were paired together, and often people thought he was my older brother. As we aged, and puberty hit, I started to see him differently. His effortless charm, his knowing smirk, and the way his presence made my body feel boneless. It was confusing.

Our five-year age difference meant we were always in different stages of our lives. When he was eighteen and doing god knows what with girls his age, and even older, I was a gangly preteen with braces and a training bra.

"Is he bringing a date?" I ask, hoping that would ease Hannah's concerns.

"No. Which now that I think about it, maybe I shouldn't have denied him a plus one. It would be better if he brought his own date instead of hitting on my family and friends."

I can see the stress on her otherwise flawless face. Hannah, like me, is a perfectionist in everything she does. She wants today to be perfect, and Rhys is a wildcard.

"Of course, I'll take care of it." Even as I say the words, I'm uncertain what I mean by that. I haven't seen Rhys in years and I'm not sure he'll even recognize me. But it's Hannah's day and I'm here to support her in whatever she needs.

"Thank you." She pulls me in for a quick hug.

"Don't worry about anything. I've got it under control."

Famous last words.

The ceremony was beautiful. At least what I remember from it. I was distracted looking for Rhys in the audience, wanting to get a visual on my target before the reception started, but I had no luck finding him.

Dinner has been served. Speeches have been given—I crushed mine, there was laughter and tears—and the dancing part of the reception is in full swing.

Still no Rhys.

In a room of nearly five hundred guests, I'm starting to think if he is here, I'll never find him.

I'm making the rounds again when my mom finds me.

"There you are." She pulls me in for a hug. "You look beautiful."

"Thank you." I take in her blue eyes, same as mine, except hers are a bit puffy and she looks tired. "You look pretty, too."

"You're being kind."

"I haven't seen Dad since the ceremony. Is he still here?"

My eyes search the crowd of guests around us, expecting my dad to not stray too far from my mom.

She glances around. "He was. I thought he'd find you before I did."

"No, I haven't seen him. Well, if I don't catch him, I'll see you both on Tuesday night for dinner."

"Oh, I was going to call you. We need to cancel dinner. Your father had a meeting come up." My dad is a professor of economics at NYU. He's got tenure and has been instructing there for nearly twenty years.

"Okay." I smile, attempting to hide my disappointment. Outside of Hannah, my parents are my support system. After the week I've had, I really could use a family dinner. They always boost my confidence and make me feel better when I'm stressed.

"I'll look at our schedules and we'll figure out another time that works."

"Okay. That sounds good."

My eyes shift over my mom's shoulder and snag on a man in a light purple suit.

Who's that?

But another glance and my heart rate kicks up a notch.

The man is at the bar ordering a drink. From the back, all I can see is his dark messy hair and broad shoulders, but then he turns.

Seeing his face is like a punch to the ovaries. It's like the man's square jaw and perfectly sculpted nose have been chiseled out of granite. His hazel eyes flash with mischief, as a lazy grin pulls at his lips, exposing his charming smile.

Rhys.

Upon closer inspection, I was wrong, the suit isn't purple. Not like Barney, anyway. It's more lavender with a hint of blue. And unlike most of the guests who are wearing ties, Rhys's crisp collared shirt is unbuttoned at the top, exposing a few inches of smooth, golden skin. A paisley print pocket square in hues of pink, purple and blue, and tan suede loafers complete his look. And boy it is one hell of a look.

I'm so captivated by his appearance; I've completely forgotten my mission.

I blink, allowing myself to return to the present where my mom is still gushing about the light fixture she found for the real estate broker's penthouse she's been hired to redecorate all while tracking Rhys's gaze across the ballroom where it lands on Becky, James's redheaded cousin.

Alarm bells start going off in my head.

This is the moment I've been waiting for.

Gotcha!

"Mom, the lights sound amazing. I've got to go take care of something. Can we catch up later?"

"Of course, honey." She nods and gives me a thoughtful smile. "If I don't see you later, we'll talk this week."

"Love you." I press a kiss to her cheek before beelining it to the bar.

CHAPTER 4

Rhys

While I'm waiting for the bartender to pour my drink, I turn back toward the reception and scan the area. A room full of New York City's upper crust society and wealthy businesspeople is exactly what I expected from Hannah Cartwright and James McKenzie's nuptials.

I've yet to speak to the bride or groom. I missed the ceremony, intentionally, because witnessing Hannah and James's love declaration isn't why I'm here.

My eyes settle on a sexy redhead over by the cake table. Her eyes lift to mine and a seductive smile pulls at her lips. She selects a piece of cake. With her eyes still on me, she dips her fork in the frosting, then temptingly swirls her tongue around the end of the fork. Some frosting gets stuck on her upper lip, so she removes it with the tip of her tongue.

Fucking hell.

The redhead is giving off one-night-stand vibes, which would have been an easy yes for me in the past, but that's not why I'm here. I divert my gaze to keep my dick from leading me astray.

When I step away from the bar, I nearly collide with someone.

"Excuse me," I say, quickly stepping to the side to move around, but the person matches my move, and blocks me.

My eyes drop to the woman who's put herself in my path. Long, dark hair styled in loose waves around her shoulders. Heart-shaped, bubble gum pink lips and the bluest eyes I've ever seen. Her fair skin stands out in a room full of bare-shouldered women with faux tans and sun-kissed skin from the height of summer.

She's stepped between me and the redhead like a body-guard blocking a bullet. And from the somewhat menacing look on her face, it appears I'm the bullet she's trying to intercept.

Wait a minute…I know those eyes.

They're as blue as the waters of Lake George that I used to swim in as a kid.

And the way that nose wrinkles when she's determinedly set her mind on something.

That's when it hits me.

The woman staring me down like she's got a bone to pick is none other than Colette Davenport.

"Lettie spaghetti?" My lips twitch as the nickname falls from my lips.

Her jaw drops before she clears her throat and crosses her arms over her chest. "No one calls me that anymore."

My grin widens at her defensive positioning. "That's a shame."

"Not really. No one wants to be referred to as a limp noodle."

My eyes drop between us. Toned, lithe muscles shape her arms and her trim waist is accentuated by the A-line fit of her floor-length gown. She's nothing like a limp noodle. Not that she was before. The name was mostly generated out of the fact that spaghetti rhymes with her nickname, Lettie, and she was extremely flexible. Her body, not her temperament.

No, Lettie has always had a streak of stubbornness and

determination, as she's demonstrating here by the stern look she's fixing me with.

"You can call me Rhys's pieces." I smile down at her, loving the way her button nose wrinkles at my suggestion. "It's still your favorite candy, right?"

"I don't eat candy."

"Hmm, that's too bad."

Lettie eyes me, suspicion darkening her gaze. "We need to have a little chat."

I press my lips together. She's so serious, it's adorable. "Yeah, about what?"

She drops her arms to her sides and sighs. "I know what you're up to eyeing the redhead over there."

My smiles widens. I'm suddenly glad I came tonight. "Oh, yeah? What am I up to?"

She clears her throat. "All right, I'm going to be honest with you."

My brows lift in amusement because this is Lettie and if there's one thing I can count on from her, it's the truth. She was never good at lying, whether it was about us sneaking cookies before dinner or admitting to the adults if we used the old rope swing that was off limits due to safety concerns.

"As if I expected you to lie to me?" I tease.

Glancing around, she draws closer like she's going to share a secret. As she leans in, a soft, feminine scent, sweet yet sensual, surrounds me. It's jasmine, I think.

I blink, momentarily sidetracked by her proximity.

What were we talking about?

"She's James's cousin and she just went through a terrible breakup."

That's right. The redhead, who I couldn't care less about.

"The thing is, she's in a very vulnerable emotional state right now. She thought she was going to marry the guy, so imagine how being at a wedding makes her feel?"

I blink. "Not following."

She swats my arm. "She's devastated. Absolutely traumatized by the whole thing."

I glance over at the redhead. Her eyes are still on me, her mouth still making eating cake look like foreplay. She doesn't look traumatized at all.

"Then why'd she come?" I ask.

"Because it's for family and that's important."

I shake my head. "You're losing me again."

Lettie sighs. "You've seen *Wedding Crashers*, right?"

I smirk. "One of my favorites."

"Of course, it is."

"Remember when Vince Vaughn hooks up with the bridesmaid and she turns out to be a real nut-job?"

"Yeah?"

She motions toward the redhead.

"Now I'm confused. Is she vulnerable from a breakup or a clingy basket case?"

"Um, both! Her vulnerability makes her attach to guys really quickly. That's not your style, so you should definitely avoid her."

I take another look at her defensive stance and my smile widens. I have no intention of talking to the redhead. In fact, tonight is an exercise in will power. To prove that I can fight against my baser urges, and not fuck a fellow guest.

"I see. You're eliminating the competition because you want me all to yourself."

Lettie's nose scrunches up again. "What? No."

"Come on. You saw me across the room and you thought, *now there's a man who could show me a good time.*"

"I did see you across the room and I thought, *that man in the purple suit needs a friend.*"

I chuckle, but I can hear the hint of defensiveness in my tone. "It's periwinkle."

Her eyes drop to scan the full length of me. "Okay, sure."

"And it's Dolce & Gabbana."

"That's great."

"A June wedding is the perfect occasion for this suit."

While most of the men at this wedding are wearing black or navy, and the groom and groomsmen are in tan suits, I like that I stand out in this suit. And I know I look good.

Ramsey wanted me to wear a navy suit, but I figured if I'm going to give up my style for the foundation board, I'm going to have one last hurrah. Besides, this ensemble is tame compared to others. This one says, I know how to dress so I'm going to show you.

Lettie's lips press together, then she smiles up at me. "There's no need to get defensive. I like your periwinkle suit."

Her hand reaches up to my lapel, her thumb sliding over the material there while her fingers press against the fabric beneath. She's not touching me, but that simple movement has me entranced. Our eyes lock and I remember what it's like to be in her presence. The way she always made me feel grounded. Even when my world felt overwhelming.

I inch closer and she abruptly drops her hand.

"So, we're good? No trying to sleep with Becky?"

"Who's Becky?" I ask, still a bit woozy from Lettie's presence.

"The redhead."

I nod. "Sure, I'll keep my distance."

"Great!" She glances around the ballroom. "Let's see. Just a few more."

"You're losing me, Princess."

Her gaze darts back to mine. "Princess?"

"New nickname since you didn't like the old one."

She scoffs. "I don't like that one either."

But I love the way her cheeks pinken when I call her princess, so I'm going to keep calling her it.

Her gaze drifts over to a group of women. I can see it written on her face. She's not talking to me because she had a burning desire to reconnect. I get it now. She's on a mission.

If I'm understanding this correctly, Hannah has sent Lettie to keep an eye on me. To prevent me from hooking up with anyone at the wedding. Lettie is here to cock-block me. Trouble is, she's the prettiest cock-blocker I've ever seen.

"Hannah asked you to keep an eye on me." My lips twitch.

Her eyes widen but she nods. "She doesn't want you sleeping with any of the guests."

With my reputation, it's a valid concern. Funny thing is, I'm on my best behavior now. But Lettie doesn't know that. And there's something about the fact that she's been tasked with the chore of babysitting me that is amusing.

"Sure. I understand."

Relief washes over her face, and her beaming smile is back.

"Thank you, Rhys." She places her hand on my arm. Her touch is light, yet I feel the spark of it through both my shirt and jacket. "It was nice to see you."

"Likewise." So very nice.

She turns to leave and I already feel the loss of her presence. That's when it occurs to me, it would be too easy to agree and let her go, so I opt for messing with her instead.

I take a sip of my drink, not letting her get far before I add, "I'll behave myself, if you dance with me."

CHAPTER 5

Colette

Rhys's request to dance has me stopping in my tracks.

I turn around to meet his gaze. Those hazel eyes surrounded by flecks of gold. His dark brows raised in challenge.

"One dance?" I ask.

In response, he sets his lowball glass on the table nearby, then takes my hand to lead me toward the dance floor. The band is playing a cover of an upbeat pop song and the guests on the dance floor have made a large circle where they're taking turns dancing out to the middle to display their moves.

Rhys and I join the group, watching on the periphery as Hunter pulls Sophie out into the middle for a sweet, two-step move. In preparation for their wedding in a few months, they've been taking dance lessons and now they're showing off their skills. They look so good together.

Hunter and Sophie finish their move and dance over to rejoin the crowd. Rhys tugs on my hand, but before we can make it to the center, the song fades out and the band immediately transitions into a slow ballad.

Using our joined hands, Rhys spins me to face him.

"May I have this dance?" he asks.

"Do I have a choice?" I quip.

"Of course. You have all the power. And with great power comes great responsibility." His hazel eyes light with amusement.

"This one goes out to all the single women at this wedding who could easily be charmed by Rhys Spencer tonight," I say before placing my hand on his shoulder.

With his hand clasped over mine, his other hand drops to my waist. Immediately, I feel the weight of it there. Foreign, yet not uncomfortable. His fingertips press lightly against the silk of my dress to draw me closer. My other hand lifts to his shoulder, again taking in the smooth texture of his designer suit.

I'd been teasing him about his purple suit, hoping to affect him the way he'd annoyed me with an old nickname, but of course, he was too confident to be upset.

"Are you single, Lettie?" Rhys's voice is low, a husky edge to it as he murmurs in my ear.

"Of course," I blurt out.

He laughs. "What does that mean? *Of course*?"

"Yes, I'm currently single." I don't bother to mention that has been my permanent status.

"And no date tonight?" he asks.

"No, I'm focused on other things right now."

I've been focused on other things my entire life, but that's not relevant information to this conversation. Besides, there's no need to tell Rhys that I've got zero dating experience or that there's a half filled out dating profile sitting on my laptop at home.

Let's not think about any of that right now or I will break out in a red splotchy rash.

"I see."

Over Rhys's shoulder, my eyes meet Hunter's. He's dancing with Sophie, holding his fiancée close, but he's eyeing me and Rhys with concern.

"Your dance career," Rhys says. "That's what you've been focusing on?"

"Yeah." I nod, letting him lead us around the floor. "What about you?"

"My dance career never quite took off, so I've had to settle for crashing weddings and tricking beautiful women into dancing with me."

"But, seriously?"

He flashes me a cocky smile, then shrugs. "I had a few business meetings."

"How long are you staying in the city?" I ask, wondering if he'll disappear again after tonight.

"I might stick around a while."

That's Rhys. Aloof. Keep things vague. Never able to commit.

He's been like that since the accident. Since his parents died.

I decide now isn't the time to get into the past. Right now, all I need to do is finish this dance with Rhys, then I'll be able to get on with my night knowing that he will be keeping his hands to himself.

The lull of the music and the magic of the female singer's airy voice has the whole dance floor floating. Rhys and I are no exception. We sway, our bodies pressed together, and it's just easy. I take in a breath, and it feels like the first in this whirlwind of a day.

As the song comes to an end, Rhys spins me out before gently pulling me back to him.

I'm a moment away from asking where he learned to move so easily when I remember.

His mom. She loved to dance and would make Rhys practice with her.

It's a fond memory, Abigail forcing a moody teenage Rhys to lead her around the patio. He'd pretend he was annoyed, but by the end of their dance, he was grinning ear to ear.

The memory fades as my watch buzzes with a notification and I pull away to silence it. It's the alarm I set to remind myself to decorate Hannah and James's suite.

"What's that for?" Rhys asks, pointing at my watch.

"I've got to go."

"It isn't midnight. You've still got a few hours until the carriage turns into a pumpkin," he teases.

"Very funny."

"Come on, Princess. You can't leave me or I might get into trouble." He flashes me a wolfish grin and I instantly believe him. He looks like trouble.

"One dance," I remind him. "You promised."

"I did say one dance, but I didn't promise that was all it would take."

My eyes narrow trying to recall our conversation. Darn it. He's right. I didn't make him promise that would be it.

"All right, Princess. What's the plan?"

The new nickname isn't my favorite, but I'll let it slide tonight because it's probably the last time I'll see Rhys for another ten years and there's no point in getting into a fight over it now.

My lips twitch. Invite Rhys along to decorate Hannah and James's hotel suite?

He is tall, which might come in handy for hanging things up.

And if he's with me, I'll be assured that he's not going back on his word.

"If you come with me now, then you promise to not hit on any of the women here tonight."

"I promise."

I hold up my pinky.

With a smirk, he hooks his pinky around mine. "Now it's a promise."

"All right. Let's go."

"A little to the right," I instruct from where I'm standing in the middle of Hannah and James's bridal suite.

Rhys sighs, his arms still stretched above his head as he turns to look at me. "This is lame. I don't think they need a banner to know that they're married now."

That's what he says, but he completes the task anyway, shifting the custom gold and ivory Mr. & Mrs. McKenzie banner to the right before tying it to the other side of the drapery pole.

"It's ambiance," I say, setting the personalized champagne flutes that Sophie ordered for James and Hannah on the tray along with the monogrammed ice bucket, 'M' for McKenzie, that is currently chilling the Veuve Clicquot.

"What's this?" Rhys points to the basket of honeymoon goodies me and the other ladies collected for the newlyweds.

"A welcome basket."

There's water and some snacks in case they were too busy at the reception to eat much and are still hungry. Massage oil and scented candles. Some lingerie for Hannah and a few sex toys.

He holds up the mini vibrator, still in its plastic packaging. "Looks like Hannah and James are in for a wild night."

"Put that back," I order.

It's like I'm hanging out with a toddler. He's into everything, and making it impossible to get this job done. When he doesn't, I yank it from his hand and set it back into the basket. "I'm regretting bringing you."

I pull up the room layout and décor ideas Sophie emailed me to see what else needs to be done. I'm studying it when Rhys appears over my shoulder.

"Holy shit. There's a diagram?"

"Yes." I narrow my gaze at him. "Would you please be helpful?"

"What are you talking about? I'm helpful. I hung that banner."

I ignore him and do a final check on what's left to do.

"Okay, now let's do the petals."

From the bag of supplies, I find the pack of red rose petals and open it.

I lift Rhys's hand from his side and dump a pile of petals into it.

"What am I supposed to do with these?" he asks, staring at the petals.

"Start at the door and scatter them in a path toward the bed."

His brows shoot up. "Seriously?"

"Yes. Like this."

Rhys watches as I scatter a trail of petals from the door toward the bed.

"Why do they need rose petals? Or any of this shit? Aren't they just going to fuck?"

I'm aware of Rhys's reputation, but nothing could prepare me for the way the word 'fuck' rolls off his tongue. It's like a lick of heat to the back of my neck. It's crude and completely unnecessary, but for some reason it's also kind of hot.

"Language," I warn. My parents had a strict no cursing policy growing up. Even now that I'm an adult, I still can't imagine cursing in front of them.

"Come on, we're adults now. No one is going to chastise you for an F-bomb." He lifts his brows in challenge.

I open my mouth to say that simple four-letter word, but nothing comes out. I know I can say it, it just feels unnecessary.

"Whatever." I motion for him to keep spreading petals.

"Stick with me, Princess, and I'll have you saying all the four-letter words."

"No, thank you."

That's what I say, but my brain has already enrolled in Rhys's school of dirty words and is reciting today's lesson.

Fuck.

Dick.

Cock.

Rhys.

I swallow thickly, trying to remember what his question was. Oh, yeah. The reason for all this stuff.

"It's their wedding night, this is romantic and it makes it special." I sigh. "Haven't you ever done anything romantic for someone?"

He pauses, a thoughtful look on his face before his lips split into a grin. "I've given a lot of orgasms."

"That's not what I meant."

"Orgasms are romantic. It means that you care about the other person finishing."

All I can do is shake my head and try to not think about Rhys handing out orgasms. He probably uses the word 'fuck' a lot when he's doing it. The baby hairs at the back of my neck dampen with sweat just thinking about it.

I motion to the second bag of petals on the table, suddenly anxious to complete this task and get out of here. "Hand me those, please."

"More rose petals?" he asks.

"I've got a second bag. I'm going to use them." Sophie will kill me if they go to waste. As the owner of Sustainable Wedding Chic blog and wedding planning service, her goal is to minimize waste associated with weddings and events. I've been instructed to return all the packaging as it needs to be properly composted.

"Come on. You can't tell me that a guy giving it his all to get you off isn't a romantic gesture."

I'm thankful that I am faced with the task of sprinkling the petals into the shape of a heart on the bed right now so I can appear not to be affected by Rhys's comment. Meanwhile, my cheeks are turning as red as the petals in my hand.

"It's personally what I live for."

"We all have to have goals, I guess."

Where Rhys appears to have all the experience, I've got none. I've never been touched that way by a guy before but there's no way I'm telling him *that*.

"All done," I say, tossing the last of the rose petals onto the floor before gathering the bag of supplies up.

"That was easy." Rhys dusts his hands off like he's satisfied with the job.

"Says the man who hung a banner."

"I hung the shit out of that banner."

"Yeah, okay. Let's go before your head gets too big to fit out the door. Hannah and James will not be excited to see you in their suite on their wedding night."

He ignores my comment.

"And look," he points to the bed, "I made a design."

I stare at his design and my eyes bulge. The heart I had perfected a few minutes ago is nowhere to be seen.

"Is that a vulva?" I ask.

He bursts out laughing. "Wait, what's a vulva?"

"You know. All the parts that make up female genitalia." I motion toward my lower region.

His lips twist with confusion. "I thought that's a vagina."

"No," I shake my head, "it's called a vulva. The vaginal opening is only a part of it. Clearly, it's the *only* part you care about," I murmur under my breath, still staring at Rhys's rose petal design.

"It's lips, and not the vulva kind. The red petals are the outline, the pink is the filler." Rhys smirks at me. "Geez, Princess, get your head out of the gutter."

I stare at him for a moment. Wondering how I ended up here, discussing vulvas with Rhys.

Then, I reach forward and scatter Rhys's design.

"No lips. No vulvas. Just sprinkled rose petals, please."

"You're the boss."

"Exactly," I say, moving toward the door, now that everything is in its place.

"So, what now?" he asks on our way to the elevator.

I shrug. "Back to the reception."

"That's boring. Surely there's something more fun we could do." He wiggles his eyebrows and I'm wondering if this is a continuation of the conversation we were having in the suite. Or at least Rhys was having it while I worked diligently and tried to ignore the way his words made my lower belly flutter.

Rhys is not hitting on me. That would be ridiculous.

"I'm the maid of honor, I can't ditch out on the reception. There's still an hour left."

We exit the elevator at the lobby, and start making our way back to the ballroom when we find Hannah's Aunt Maggie draped over a chair.

I stop to address her.

"Maggie. Hi. What are you doing out here?" I ask.

"Oh, Connie." Her head lulls to the side to look at me, a lazy smile on her face. "How are you?"

"It's Collette. And I'm good. How are *you*?"

"That's right, dear. Colleen." She pats my hand, her eyes attempting to close, but then they widen when she sees Rhys. "And who do we have here?"

"Maggie, this is Rhys. Rhys, do you remember Hannah and Hunter's Aunt Maggie?"

"It's been a while. Good to see you again."

He extends his hand to her, but she uses his arm to pull him down to her for an awkward half-standing, half-sitting hug instead.

"You smell divine." Maggie sniffs Rhys's neck. "Doesn't he smell divine, Colleen?"

I ignore her question and look around for her driver.

"Maggie, is Arturo with you?" I ask.

She shakes her head. "I lost my purse."

Rhys and I share a look. Aunt Maggie is drunk as a skunk.

"Your driver, Arturo?" I repeat.

"Oh, I gave him the night off." She waves at Rhys. "I like a man who knows how to dress."

"She likes my suit." He brows lift, a satisfied smile on his lips, like he's getting validation against my teasing from earlier.

"Now's not the time." While still staying close to Maggie, I pull Rhys aside. "She needs to go—"

"I've got a car outside," Rhys offers before I even finish. "I'll help her get to it."

I smile up at him, relieved. "Thanks, that would be great."

"You can thank me later," he whispers in my ear before pulling back to reveal a flirty wink.

That lower-belly flutter is back and I'm suddenly understanding the phrase 'panty-dropping smile.' Rhys has one and the purpose is clear.

"And here I thought you were being nice."

"I'm always nice, Princess, especially to you."

I shake my head, tempted to refuse his help just to not have to deal with his smugness, but he's already helping Maggie out of the chair.

"Maggie, I'm going to go look for your purse," I say. "Rhys is going to take you to the car."

"Oh," Maggie lights up when Rhys puts his arm around her, "you have very nice arms."

I roll my eyes because that's the last thing Rhys needs to hear.

I expect him to throw it in my face or smirk as he walks by with her, but instead, he's engaged in conversation as he helps her toward the door.

"There are a few steps here, but I'll help you down them, okay?" I hear him say.

I'm tempted to watch them all the way out the entrance to the hotel, but then I remember I need to get her purse.

Luckily, I find it at her table, then move as quickly as I can in this flowy dress out to the front of the hotel.

A few feet away, Rhys is guarding the open car door where Aunt Maggie appears to already be loaded inside.

"Got it!" I wave the purse as I rush toward him.

Rhys smiles and all the signals in my brain get confused.

I'm normally light on my feet and graceful, but these three-inch heels don't care about my reputation as a dancer. Their thin ankle straps are not the supportive laces I'm used to and the moment I step down onto the sidewalk, midstride, I lose my footing and launch forward.

For that split second, I'm free falling, and my stomach nosedives. My body braces for the hard concrete landing, but it never comes. A strong arm wraps around my waist, pulling me upward.

"I got you, Princess." His husky words tickle my ear.

He lifts me up and spins me around to face him, but he doesn't let go of his hold on my waist. His body is firm and warm, his scent spicy and luxurious. Those intense hazel eyes of his drop to my lips. With his arm still around me, holding me close, Rhys's hand lifts toward my face.

Is he going to kiss—

His fingertips brush away a loose strand of hair that I didn't realize was stuck to my lips.

"Your hair—"

"Thanks." It comes out more breathless than I intended.

After what feels like forty-seven minutes of staring into his gorgeous face, Rhys releases me.

I clear my throat and press my hands against my dress to make sure everything is in order. "How's Maggie?"

"She's already passed out," he says.

"Oh, no. Is she breathing?"

"You tell me."

I duck my head inside the car to find Aunt Maggie sprawled across the seat, snoring loudly.

When I move to get in the car, I realize with Maggie lying down, the three of us won't fit across the seat.

"How should we—" I begin, but Rhys scoops me up around the waist and pulls me into his lap. I make an elegant *oof* sound as I crash into his hard body.

"Problem solved." He shuts the door before I can protest.

"Seatbelt?" I ask.

"Is that necessary right now?" He motions to our shared seat.

"Yes. Safety is always important. And if we get in an accident, I'm your human shield."

He pulls the seatbelt over his shoulder, then across my body, where I take it from him to buckle it.

"There," I say, satisfied, until I realize that now I'm strapped to Rhys. Rhys's hard, muscular body that's warm and like Aunt Maggie confirmed, smells divine. *What have I done?*

But the driver is already pulling away from the curb.

"Lettie, this is Wanda, one of my drivers. Wanda, this is Colette Davenport."

"How do you do, Miss Davenport?" Wanda asks.

"I'm great. Just great." I clear my throat, trying to rid my voice of the high-pitched tone it has taken on since I strapped myself to Rhys. "Thank you for the ride."

"You're most welcome."

"Wanda's my favorite driver in the city."

Wanda laughs. "I've seen a lot."

My lips twitch. "I'm sure you have."

I reach for my clutch, which Rhys had brought to the car when he walked Maggie out, and pull out some lip balm.

"Stop moving so much."

"Maybe you should have sat up front," I argue.

"Maybe you should watch where your a—"

"We're here!" I call, hitting the button on our seatbelt before reaching for the door handle.

Wanda helps us get Maggie out of the car, then Rhys lifts her upper body while I carry her legs.

Thankfully Maggie's purse has the keycard we need to access her building and her apartment. Inside her apartment, we shuffle down the hallway, then take a sharp turn into her bedroom.

"Watch her—"

Rhys knocks Maggie's head into the door.

"Head," I finish, too late.

"I'm doing my best." He groans. "She's not a small woman."

"Maybe you need to increase your weight training."

"I'm fucking ripped under this suit; I'll have you know."

"I don't care what it looks like. Let's see it in action."

"You got the easy part."

"Yeah, because I'm half your size."

By the time we get Maggie onto her bed, we're both sweating.

"Can we just leave her like this?" I ask.

Rhys motions to Maggie's sequin dress. "I'm not undressing her, are you?"

Maggie rolls over, a sigh escaping from her lips right before she murmurs something about blue cheese olives.

"Nope. I think she's good."

We leave her purse on her nightstand, then quietly exit her apartment.

I don't want to bother Hannah tonight so I text Katherine, Hannah's mom, to let her know that we helped Maggie get home.

When I look up, Rhys is eating a chocolate chip cookie.

"Where'd you get that cookie?" I ask.

"Maggie's lobby. They were complimentary. You want a bite?"

"No thanks." Sugar-laden baked goods aren't a part of my diet.

"More for me then." With one more bite, he devours it. "Where to now?"

Now that Maggie is home safe and the adrenaline has worn off, I'm exhausted.

"To bed." I yawn around the words.

"Is that an invitation?" Rhys wiggles his brows.

"You're relentless."

"It's in my nature."

This time when we get in the car, I get my own seat. My body shivers against the cool leather and Rhys pulls off his suit jacket to drape it over my arms.

"Thanks."

I give Wanda my address and a few minutes later, we're pulling up to my apartment building.

"Tonight was fun," Rhys says, a playful smile on his face.

I laugh. "Yeah, it was." I take off his jacket and hand it back to him. "Let's do it again in another ten years."

He nods. "Sure."

"Okay, well, goodnight."

I watch his tall, muscular frame jog down the stairs, then dip back inside the car. I expect him to drive away but instead, he rolls down the window.

"I can't leave until you go inside."

It's a thoughtful gesture, but it makes me flustered because now he knows I was watching him leave.

I give a quick wave before pushing through my apartment building door.

"Goodnight, Princess," I hear Rhys call as the glass-paneled door shuts behind me.

CHAPTER 6

Rhys

"Are you decent?" Ramsey calls from the other side of the door.

I stretch my arms overhead, letting out a guttural groan as my muscles contract, then relax.

"You know I'm alone," I call.

If I'm home, I'm alone. I never have a woman in my bed.

"That wasn't the question." His voice is muffled next to the door frame. "It was are you decent?"

I lift the covers to find I'm in boxer-briefs.

"Yes."

Ramsey opens the door carrying a tray of my favorite hangover remedies. And he's wearing white gloves.

"How are we feeling today?" After setting down the tray on the side table, he throws open the window shade with the zest of a Regency period servant.

"Jesus, what's with the gloves? Have you been watching *Bridgerton* again?"

"It's customary to rewatch the previous season before the new one comes out."

Sometimes Ramsey likes to pretend his life is different

than it is. Meaning, he would prefer to have lived in the Regency period. He puts up with my shit, so whatever gets him through the work day, I don't care.

"And when's that? You know you can't start the new season without me."

He chuckles. "I got you hooked, didn't I?"

I neither confirm nor deny his allegations.

Ramsey holds up the detox recovery supplement I usually take after a night out, but I didn't drink much at the reception. With all the running around Lettie and I did, there wasn't time to.

"I don't want any of those."

"Is it that bad? Do I need to have the IV service come?" he asks.

"No, I feel great. Not hungover at all."

I pull on a pair of jeans, leaving the top unbuttoned, then reach for the pack of cigarettes on the counter. I pull one out before making my way onto the top deck. Ramsey follows, shooting me a dirty look as I light up.

"I have one a day. Give me a break. It's my one indulgence."

"Yeah, right. So, the women and booze, those are necessities?"

"I'm working on that. I hardly drank last night and there weren't any women."

Not exactly true. There was Lettie and we had fun, but not the kind I'm used to.

I take a deep inhalation of my cigarette, loving the way the nicotine hits my blood stream, when I spy a woman and her two kids walking down the dock.

"That man doesn't have a shirt on. And he forgot to button his pants."

The woman glares at me while covering her child's eyes.

Ramsey sighs. "Why do you insist on antagonizing the neighbors?"

"I'm in my house and it's not like I'm naked."

"Technically it's a boat and the deck is equivalent to a balcony, so you're not *inside* your house."

"Semantics." I lean against the deck railing and close my eyes, loving the warmth of the sun on my face.

While a hundred-foot yacht isn't the most practical living space, it's the only one I've kept in the city and I like being able to sit outside to enjoy the fresh air.

Ramsey dramatically waves his hand to fan a puff of smoke away, indicating that the air isn't technically fresh.

He clears his throat. "There's a picture from last night."

My head jerks in his direction. "What do you mean? I was on my best behavior." Okay, maybe pulling Lettie into my lap instead of moving up front with Wanda wasn't gentlemanly, but if that's my only indiscretion then I deserve a fucking gold star.

He extends his phone out to me.

I stare at the photo on the screen. It's me and Lettie leaving the wedding. It must have been taken after I'd put Hannah's Aunt Maggie in the car. Lettie had been rushing toward the car and tripped, but I'd caught her.

I use my fingers to zoom in on the photo.

My arm wrapped possessively around Lettie's waist. My fingers brushing the loose hair off her face. That's the picture they published.

I shake my head. It's the perfect example of a photo being taken out of context. She'd only been in my arms for a few seconds, tops. That photographer must have gotten every moment leading up to that shot and every moment after, yet this is the one that they posted.

"Another woman was with us."

"There were *two* women? Jesus, Rhys, I thought you were going to stop that shit. What about the foundation board?"

"Calm down. The other woman was Hannah's Aunt

Maggie and we were taking her home. She had too much to drink at the wedding."

"You're lucky they didn't get you with the other woman, too. That would have been an easy story to spin."

"I only had that one threesome. You make it sound like it's been a common occurrence."

"You know as well as I do, it's never about what actually happened, it's what others believe could happen." He waves a hand at me. "When you've had mischievous fuckboy written on your face in permanent marker for the last five years, it's not exactly easy to get it off."

I exhale, then rub my thumb along my bottom lip. "What's the damage?" I ask.

Ramsey lifts his brows. "Surprisingly, none. In fact, social media is abuzz with speculation in a good way for once."

He scrolls on his phone and shows me another picture. It's Lettie and I dancing at the wedding. We're not the focus of the photo, just two people dancing in the background. It must have been taken and posted online by another guest. Social media did its thing and somehow connected the two.

"It's assumed she was your date."

Seeing the picture of us dancing, I recall how it felt to hold Lettie in my arms. Familiar, yet new. Looking into her blue eyes transported me back to those summers at Lake George, remembering how young and innocent we were then, but her lithe, muscular frame beneath my hands, the way her tongue unconsciously brushed over her full pink lips, piqued the interest of the man I am now.

But I shouldn't think of Lettie like that. And if I'm going to have any chance of cleaning up my reputation, I need to keep my dick in my pants for the next few months. Until the board votes.

I hand him back the phone. It had been easy with Lettie last night. She was sharp and witty, and gorgeous. And exactly who I should be spending my time with. She'd be the perfect girlfriend to help me win favor with the foundation board.

But why would she date me?

That's the million-dollar question. Or in this case, the billion-dollar question because that's the value of The Spencer Foundation. While its main purpose now is philanthropic efforts, investments, and partnerships with global companies, the entrepreneurial efforts made by my parents when they started it has grown the foundation to a billion-dollar entity.

And Jerrod wants control.

The memory of his smug face sends a fresh wave of anger coursing through my veins.

Ramsey waves the phone. "Jerrod texted as well. Corinne needs to confirm a head count for their dinner party, so Jerrod wants to know if you're bringing a date."

"Of course he does."

I stamp out my cigarette butt on the railing, then toss it over.

Ramsey's jaw drops. "You can't just throw those overboard. That's littering."

I push my hand into my hair. "Shit. I forgot."

He sighs, grabbing the net nearby. "I'll go fish it out…again."

"I'll remember next time. Promise."

"Or you can just quit smoking. That would work, too."

I ignore his comment, my focus returning to Jerrod's text. I can't show up alone to that dinner party. Not when he and Corinne are going to be playing happy couple dinner party hosts and all the board members and their significant others will be there.

I need a date.

More than a date.

A girlfriend whose reputation and grace will make me look like a reformed man.

Ramsey drops the wet butt in the trash can.

"Tell him I'm bringing a date," I say, moving toward the sliding door that leads to the living area.

"Do you actually have a date?" Ramsey calls.

"No, but I'm working on it."

CHAPTER 7

Colette

While Sunday is a day of rest for most, it's typically my busiest. Running errands, meal preparation for the week, laundry, and cleaning. There's something so satisfying about getting organized for the week ahead. With all the time I devoted to Hannah and James's wedding events this past week, I've got even more on my plate to put my life back in order.

My to-do list is long, and I just added another item to it.

Find more passion in my life.

This morning when I woke up, I went straight to my laptop and started filling out a profile on one of those sites where you want to meet people and hang out. I'm not even going to say the four-letter word.

Then I got overwhelmed and took a break for my traditional Sunday morning yoga class. Now, I'm all Zen and hoping it will make finishing my profile less intimidating.

I'm walking down Sixty-Ninth Street, on my way home, when Hannah calls.

"Good morning, Mrs. McKenzie," I answer playfully, and she squeals with delight. "How are you this morning?"

She sighs. "Happy, but exhausted."

"I can only imagine."

"For future reference, I don't recommend inviting five hundred people to your wedding. I didn't want to leave anyone out, so I think I spent thirty seconds with each guest."

"Wow. I only talked to about twenty people last night and I was ready to find a quiet, dark room to recharge in."

Her laugh is light and airy, then she says, "Hunter said he saw you dancing with Rhys. Thank you for taking one for the team."

With her mention of Rhys, my thoughts easily drift back to my time with him last night.

Rhys was not what I had been expecting. Neither was the dream I had about him.

Strong, firm hands wrapped around me. His deep, husky voice whispering in my ear. *Fuck.*

Even thinking about it now is making me sweat.

But when I woke up, all hot and bothered from the dream, I refused to reach for my vibrator. I didn't want to have Rhys on my mind when my orgasm hit. It felt weird, like somehow, he would know.

I don't know why, because after last night, it'll probably be a decade before I see him again, but I didn't want to risk it.

"It was no problem. He was easier to distract than I thought he'd be," I say, stopping at the 'no walk' signal at Amsterdam Avenue.

"Yeah? That's good to hear. Maybe I had nothing to worry about. The suite was beautiful, thank you for making it special."

"I'm happy you liked it. Sophie helped me get organized with a lot of it."

"You both are so sweet. I was so tired, my feet were killing me and all I wanted to do was sleep, but I told James I refused to be in a sexless marriage, so we had a quickie before we passed out."

I think of Rhys's words. *They're just going to fuck, then pass out.* He might have been right, but at least Hannah thought the decorated suite was a nice touch.

"We're at the spa now, James is recovering from having too many signature Manhattans, and then we're off to the Maldives tonight."

A sharp twinge pulls at my side. I close my eyes and imagine a beach and a lounge chair, the clear calm waters, the warmth of the sun's rays on my skin. My legs dangling off a ledge into a pool, letting my sore feet push through the cool water.

The peace. The rest.

My body shivers with delight.

"Lettie, you there?" Hannah's voice cuts through my fantasy.

"Yeah, sorry. I'm here."

I open my eyes to find the walk signal on and people filtering around my still stationary body. I step off the curb.

I try to remember the last time I took a vacation. A weekend off. Even a day.

I can't rest until I become a principal dancer.

It's the thought that has been pushing me forward since I can remember. Embedded at a ripe age of seven when Nana Rose, my mom's mother, took me to the ballet for the first time. I'd been awestruck by the dancers' grace and strength, and that had quickly turned into determination. I wanted to be just like the dancers I'd seen on stage, and make it look effortless.

My Nana Rose had beamed ear to ear when I'd proudly declared that I wanted to be a principal dancer someday. She had been a ballet dancer, but didn't have the feet for it; my mom had the feet, but no desire to pursue it. Nana Rose had been thrilled to discover I had the feet and the heart.

She passed away two years ago, and even though she never said it, I'd felt the heavy weight of disappointment that she didn't see me reach the goal we'd shared. But over the last two years, I've been more determined than ever to reach it.

I shake the memory of Nana Rose and refocus on my conversation with Hannah.

"You're going to have such a good time. Send me some pictures."

"I will, but James wants us to keep our phones off for the next two weeks. That's a stretch for me, I'm still so plugged into everything that's happening at the store, but I'm going to humor him if I can."

"I think that's great. It'll give you two a chance to unwind from all the wedding craziness and really enjoy your time together." It's what I want for her, but selfishly I'm dying to talk to her about my conversation with Alexei. I hold my thoughts in, though, because now is not the time. Still, a sigh manages to escape, and it comes out heavier than intended. "I'm going to miss you."

"Well, even though I won't be back for a few weeks, you know you can call Sophie or Chloe or Emma to hang out, right?"

Hannah is my best friend, but she's also the one that keeps me in the loop with social events. Without her, my already lacking social life would be nonexistent, and I don't think I'd have any other friends besides Sebastian and Isabella. Though, I have gotten to know Sophie, Emma, and Chloe better through Hannah's wedding events and started to form my own friendships with them. It's a slow process. I'm not easy to get to know. I'm aware of this and so is Hannah.

"You'll be back for the Leg-Up fundraiser, right?" I ask.

"Of course, I wouldn't miss it."

"I love you. Have so much fun."

"Love you, Lettie."

The call disconnects and I take a long pull of my athletic greens through the straw in my cup. I used to think it tasted like dirt, but I think all my tastebuds have shriveled up, so now it tastes like nothing. I suck it back, knowing the benefits it's giving my body.

I open my phone's notes app and add a few items to my list.

Reschedule dinner with my parents.

Call Chloe, Emma, and Sophie to make an effort.

I lift my gaze just in time to see a pair of loafers peeking out from the sandstone staircase leading to my apartment building.

Hmm.

I hope it's not my neighbor, Ricardo's, ex-boyfriend. He's been known to cause drama and I really don't want to deal with him today.

As I inch close, I find it's not Jimmy. No, the man sitting on my apartment building stairs is dressed in light blue shorts and a short-sleeve button-down with two large flamingos on it. One on each side of the placket. My eyes are immediately drawn to his left arm where black ink is covering nearly every inch of his skin.

Trees. Mountains. A lake. All woven beautifully together.

There's something about that tattoo that makes my stomach clench.

The sight of the majestic landscape in addition to the muscular forearm and bicep it's etched onto.

When my gaze finally connects with his face, even with the designer shades covering his eyes, I recognize his chiseled jaw and wickedly handsome smile.

I hadn't expected to see them again this soon. I also didn't expect the way my body tingles at the sight of him there.

"Rhys?"

CHAPTER 8

Rhys

I check my watch. I've been waiting on the stairs of Lettie's apartment building for an hour. It's nine o'clock on a Sunday. I can't imagine where she'd be. My only saving grace is the iced frappuccino I'm sucking down.

A legging-clad set of legs stop in my line of sight. I'm tempted to lower my sunglasses to get an unobstructed view of those toned cheeks, but they turn too quickly.

"Rhys?"

The leggings are talking to me. My eyes jolt up to meet their owner.

It's Lettie.

She's dressed in a gray cropped tank top and the ass-hugging leggings, of course, her hair is tied back into a ponytail, the waves from last night still evident. She's got a backpack over her shoulders and a clear jar with a straw and some thick, dark green liquid in it.

"What are you doing here?" she asks.

"Good morning to you, too." I stand and extend the paper cup to her. "I was in the neighborhood. I brought you a coffee."

"I don't drink coffee." She shakes the cup of green sludge

in her hand as if that explains why she doesn't need caffeine. "Athletic greens."

She takes a long pull from her straw, and I watch as chalky flecks in twenty different shades of green fight their way up the clear tube.

"Okay. More for me, I guess." I take a swig of the rejected black coffee and nearly choke. Disgusting. I pull the packets of raw sugar I'd taken from the coffee shop in case they were needed. They're needed.

Lettie watches me dump the packets in then pull the straw out from my iced coffee and stir it.

"Where are you coming from?" I ask.

"Yoga class."

"That explains the leggings."

"Leggings aren't just for yoga. I wear them most days."

My eyes drop to her legs. Last night, they were hidden by her long, flowy dress. She's a professional dancer, so it's expected that she's fit, but seeing the smooth, supple curves of her muscular thighs and the way the tight material grips her firm ass is causing an unexpected reaction. I'm used to looking at women I'm attracted to this way, but I'm not used to directing these thoughts at Lettie.

Until last night. My brain reminds me of all the ways I'd noticed Lettie last night. How the familiarity of the girl I'd known growing up morphed into a rush of excitement at the woman she'd become.

"Um, how was yoga class?" I ask, reminding myself why I'm here.

"Good." She shrugs. "It's what I do every Sunday morning." Her eyes run the length of me, stopping on my shirt. "Flamingos, huh?"

My shirt has two large flamingos on it. It's fucking obnoxious and I love it.

As part of my quest for acceptance by the foundation board, Ramsey went through my clothes and deemed most of them unwearable. I agreed to a temporary makeover, so he banished most of my clothing to the spare bedroom, but I kept this shirt because I like pink and flamingos are cool.

I push my sunglasses into my hair so I can see her better. "It felt like that kind of Sunday."

Her eyes drop to my left arm again. To the black ink sleeve tattoo that covers my skin. I'd noticed her gaze on it when she first saw me here waiting.

"And this?" Lettie reaches out to grip my forearm. When her fingertips settle on my skin, it sends a jolt of energy through my body. My eyes lift to find her blue orbs wide with surprise.

Did she feel it, too?

She releases my arm and steps back, her free hand nervously teasing into the hair of her ponytail.

"So, what are you doing here?" she asks.

"I thought we'd chat. Catch up a little."

And I'd ask you to pose as my girlfriend at Jerrod's dinner party next week.

The bridge of her nose wrinkles. "Isn't that what we did last night?"

I shrug. "I wanted to see you again. We didn't get to talk much last night."

Lettie looks hesitant. "I've got a bunch of stuff to do. It's not the best time."

"That's cool. I can hang."

"It's really boring. Cleaning and meal prep. Nothing you would want to do."

I stare down at her face. She doesn't want me here. I can see it so easily in her features. But Lettie's my best option for a woman that could impress the board. I've got to shoot my shot.

I pin her with a warm smile. "Nothing about you could be boring."

Her face softens with my sincerity. It's true, I'm fascinated by Lettie and am curious about her life now. Also, I need to figure out how to approach her about the whole girlfriend thing and I know standing out on the street to ask her isn't going to work.

"Fine." She starts climbing the stairs to the front door, so I follow her.

Lettie takes out her keycard to unlock the door but before she can swipe it, a woman on the other side opens the door for us.

"Thanks, Mrs. Donahue." Lettie holds the door for the woman, offering a hand to her as she slowly walks over the threshold.

The woman, who must be in her eighties, looks me up and down.

"Who are you?" She pushes her dark-framed glasses closer to her eyes as she leans in to inspect my shirt. "My husband Marty had a shirt like that."

"I'm Rhys," and because I'm trying things out, "I'm Lettie's boyfriend."

Lettie's mouth drops open, but it's a few seconds later when she finds the words. "No, Mrs. Donahue, he's not."

"Not yet, but I'm working on it." I toss a wink in Mrs. Donahue's direction.

"Don't say that," Lettie hisses. "It will only encourage her."

A wide smile spreads on Mrs. Donahue's face. "Oh, you're a charmer. I've never seen Colette with a young man. This is a wonderful development." She pats me on the arm as she passes. "Colette, make sure your boyfriend knows he needs to ensure the main door latches when he comes and goes, it sticks sometimes."

"Noted." I wave to Mrs. Donahue as she descends the stairs.

When she's gone, Lettie jabs me in the ribs. "What are you

doing? I thought you just said you wanted to catch up. Now, you're telling my neighbor that you're my *boyfriend*?"

"It slipped out. I am technically your boyfriend, though. I'm a friend that's a boy."

She glares at me but holds open the door. "That's not how you made it sound."

I follow her to the elevator and place my arm over the door while she enters.

"I like Mrs. Donahue. She seems nice."

"She is nice, but sometimes a little senile. She refuses to move out of her apartment and into an assisted living situation. I do my best to keep an eye on her."

"That's nice of you. You're such a good person, Lettie. Such a good friend who helps others when they're in a difficult situation."

I give her my most charming smile, but her features stay wary as she punches the button for the third floor.

"Thanks. I guess."

A quick ride later, she's opening her apartment door and I follow her in.

"So, this is your apartment." I glance around, taking everything in.

It's clean and tidy, decorated in neutral tones. There's a dry-erase calendar on the side of the refrigerator that needs a key to decode. Over by the living room window, there's a cat climbing tower positioned perfectly for outdoor viewing and lounging by its furry gray occupant.

"You have a cat." A warm sensation floods my chest.

Lettie finally got her cat.

"That's Maxine. I've had her for two years."

"Remember when I tried to give you the cat that belonged to the Jenkins'?"

Her lips twitch. "How could I forget?"

Lettie was five and I was ten. She wanted a cat so badly, and my ten-year-old brain thought it was logical to give a cat to a young girl when its current owners were older and might not be able to take care of it any longer. It was poorly thought out and when my parents found out what I had done they made me return the cat to its home and Lettie was heartbroken. The next day, I used my allowance to buy her a stuffed cat as a replacement. She named it Whiskers and carried it around everywhere she went.

I scan the kitchen. Everything neat and tidy. Nothing out of place.

Lettie toes off her sneakers and lines them up by her door.

There's a decorative bowl of fruit on her counter. A shiny red apple calls to me, so I pick it up and take a bite.

"Did you just come over to eat my food, because that's annoying. I was going to eat that later with some almond butter."

"Oops, sorry." I extend the apple now with a huge bite taken out of the side to her.

She waves it back to me. "Well, I don't want it now."

My eyes drop to her laptop on the counter. I tap the spacebar and it wakes up. There's no password or pin to put in. It opens directly to the website Lettie was on last.

"Do you mind?" she asks, rushing over.

"Not at all." I shift the computer to get a closer look, blocking her from taking it. "What's this?"

"Nothing," she answers quickly.

But if it's nothing, then why is her voice two octaves higher than usual?

She moves to skirt past me and reach for the laptop, but I snatch it up and out of her grasp. I take another bite of the apple while my eyes scan over the screen.

It's a dating profile. One she's currently in the middle of filling out.

Interesting.

"This doesn't look like nothing."

I lift the computer higher so I can keep reading.

"Must love cats," I read aloud. "Or at least not be allergic."

She's hanging on my forearm trying to pull the laptop back within her reach. She's a strong woman, but I'm stronger and even on her tiptoes, I've got the height advantage.

"That's not for you to see, Rhys. Give it back."

I'm trying to focus on reading her dating profile, but my body registers the feel of Lettie's body pressed against me, jumping up and down, and it's a real distraction.

"Rhys, give me my computer!"

When my gaze drops to hers, I'm overwhelmed by the desperation in her big blue eyes, by the vulnerability I see there. It has me immediately lowering my arm and handing her the computer.

Her throat works to swallow. "I think you should go," she says tightly.

I think I should tell her why I'm here before she throws me out.

"Did you see the *Online Social* post from last night?" I ask.

She shakes her head. "I don't even know what that is."

"A social media gossip account followed by millions of people that puts out news about celebrities, and it's speculating that we're dating."

Her gaze snaps to mine. "What?"

"You haven't seen the pictures?" I ask.

She shakes her head. "I'm not on social media."

I hand her my phone, the post already loaded.

"How are you a celebrity? What are you famous for?" she asks.

"My charming personality." I wiggle my brows, but Lettie just rolls her eyes.

"Because of my family. And my money. And who I'm friends with. Let's just say I've given them a lot of material over the years and now they won't leave me alone."

She drops her gaze to my phone screen to study the photo.

After which, she promptly laughs. It's light and airy. No trace of the irritation from earlier.

"We both know that wasn't a 'passionate embrace.'" She quotes the caption. "It's ridiculous what people make up. Definitely fake news." She hands the phone back to me. "The good news is that it's so far-fetched no one will believe it."

"Why is it far-fetched?" I ask, even though I already know the idea of me and Lettie together might not be an easy sell.

"Because we're not together. At the very most, we're friends. And before last night, we hadn't seen each other in years."

She's right, but no one else knows that.

I nod to her laptop. "What's with the profile?"

"It's something I'm looking into." She drops to the couch, then pulls her legs in cross-legged. "It's come to my attention recently that I'm lacking passion in my dancing. It's holding me back from getting roles I want that could ultimately promote me to principal dancer at the company."

"Passion, huh?" I take another bite of the apple while considering this. "You were pretty passionate last night when you were trying to keep me away from other women."

"That was determination. There's a difference."

"So you're looking to date?" I ask.

She clears her throat. "Um, maybe." Then she nods. "Yes. That's why I'm filling out the profile."

Her hand drops to her chest where she promptly starts scratching. In real time, I'm watching an angry patch of red start to spread up her neck.

"Are you okay?" I point to the red splotches. "Jesus, are you having some kind of reaction?"

"Oh, no!" She jumps up and rushes over to the freezer. I follow her to find she's pulled out two large ice packs and is holding them against her chest.

"What is going on?" I ask.

"Don't say the d-word."

"D-word?" I wrack my brain for what that could be.

"It's four letters. And it's really hard."

"Dick?"

She closes her eyes in frustration. "No, what you said earlier about the profile."

"Oh, date."

I follow her back over to the couch where she leans back with the ice packs on her chest and closes her eyes.

"Hold on." My eyes drop to the angry red splotches that are working their way up her neck. "This reaction is to the thought of dating?"

She groans. "Stop saying it. It's stressing me out."

"Lettie, look at me."

Slowly, she opens her eyes to meet mine.

The vulnerability in those blue gems framed by dark lashes pull me in. She's got no makeup on her face, and I can make out a light dusting of freckles over her nose. Damn, she sure is pretty.

But that's not why I'm here.

"What about dating is stressful to you?" I ask.

"Um, let's see, what isn't stressful about it? Sitting across from a guy you know nothing about and interviewing each to find out if you have any shared interests. The whole concept is terrifying."

I'm shocked by this discovery. "You're a professional ballet dancer. You perform in front of thousands of people on a regular basis, but going on a date is terrifying?"

She laughs. "Dating is nothing like dancing. Whenever a sequence is giving me trouble, I practice it until it's second nature. It's repetition, muscle memory. How does one train for dating? How do you practice something that involves other people? Conversations that can't be anticipated? Situations that can't be predicted? It's madness and it's overwhelming."

That's the moment everything clicks together. The lightbulb goes on. The key turns in the lock. Whatever metaphor you want to use. My question from earlier is answered.

Why would Lettie want to date me?

Lettie is looking to date but she's clearly got anxiety about it.

I can be her practice. The guy that she already knows to guide her through the overwhelming parts of dating.

A wide smile pulls across my face.

"Why are you looking at me like that?" she asks, ponytail swishing with the shake of her head.

I clear my throat, "Because I think we can be of help to each other."

"What do you mean?"

"You want to practice dating and I need a girlfriend with a good reputation."

Her eyes narrow and her nose does that cute scrunching thing it does when she's thinking hard. "Why do you need a girlfriend?"

"Clean up my image." I explain the situation to Lettie. How my grandfather is stepping down from president of The Spencer Foundation and how my cousin, Jerrod, could take the role if I don't prove to the board that my former playboy image won't tarnish the foundation's good name.

She presses her lips together.

"I don't know."

I need to sell this better.

"I'm cleaning up my act. I'm Rhys 2.0. No partying, no shenanigans, and no women. Besides you, of course."

"What's the difference between partying and shenanigans?" she asks.

"Shenanigans is doing stupid stuff."

She squints at me. "Like what?"

"Like seeing who can knock down a row of empty beer cans with their pee stream."

She makes a disgusted face. "That's what you do in your spare time?"

"Not all the time. I do other stuff."

She's quiet, waiting for me to elaborate. *What other stuff?*

"I like to be outside as much as possible. Listen to music. And I like to make sandwiches. I make a mean Reuben on rye. Oh, and I collect designer loafers."

Lettie presses her lips together. I can tell she's trying not to laugh.

I'm positive I could come up with better things but she's putting me on the spot.

"That's great and all, but I don't think we have anything in common."

Over on the climbing tower Maxine stands to stretch before jumping to the ground and making her way over to us.

"I have a cat."

Her face softens. "You do?"

Mental note. Get a cat. And like Ramsey advised, some new hobbies. Ones that Lettie would find interesting.

"Yeah, we should get Maxine and…" I wrack my brain for a good cat name, "Mo together sometime."

"Mo?"

"Short for Maurice." I'm really committed now.

"That's cute."

"He's a cute cat. Lots of stripes and fur."

"How did you come up with that name?" she asks.

"Maurice was my grandfather's name. My mom's dad. He's who I was named after, just shortened to Rhys."

"You named your cat after your grandfather?"

I shrug. "Why not?"

Before I tell anymore white lies, I steer the conversation back to the task at hand. Getting Lettie on board with dating me. *Fake* dating me. Because it won't be real. It's a mutually beneficial transaction between two friends.

"Come on. It's perfect. You already know me. We're

friends. The anxiety about meeting a new person will be a non-issue with me." My gaze falls back on her white board calendar. The one that is jam-packed with a daily schedule, various notes, and appointments. It's another selling point. I stand up and walk over to the calendar. "Look at this schedule. There's no time for online dating. I'll have a few events for us to attend, and some social media posts to make it look authentic, but other than that, you can determine how much or little you want to see me. However it fits into your schedule."

I can see it in her eyes. The way her forehead softens and her shoulders lower from where they've been lifted to her ears.

"Come on, Lettie," I cajole, giving her my best smile, "will you do me the honor of being my fake girlfriend?"

CHAPTER 9

Colette

I can't believe Rhys's proposal. Me and him, fake dating? The idea, on its face, is absurd. Yet, the more I look between him and my unfinished dating profile, I wonder if it really could be an option.

A *safe* option. One that doesn't involve hives and awkward conversations.

It would eliminate having to finish answering all those profile questions and I wouldn't have to weed through the responses or purchase stock in hydrocortisone. All the time-consuming online chatting before eventually exchanging numbers, then finally meeting in person. And if the guy is not a fit, back to the drawing board.

What Rhys is proposing is adaptability.

He'd make it fit.

I mean *us*. He'd make *us* fit. Mutually beneficial fitting.

Okay, that's not making it better. My brain's already flipped tracks, no course-correcting can keep my eyes from dropping to his crotch.

His shorts are tailored, probably custom, and while I'm sure he doesn't have a boner right now, I swear I can see the outline of his dick a bit left of center.

My eyes snap back up to his face.

Back to the point.

We already know each other; I wouldn't have to spend precious training time getting to know someone new. I wouldn't have to change my routine because I'm trying to fit someone else into my life. Rhys would know my priority is dancing and everything that entails. Outside of the events and dates we would be going on; we wouldn't need to interact.

The part of my brain rooted in efficiency is jumping up and down. *Problem solved! Look no further!*

But this is *Rhys*.

My eyes drift back over to him. He's got Maxine cradled in his arms like a baby, a satisfied smile pulling at her mouth as he rubs between her ears, and under her chin.

I don't blame Max. Rhys is walking, talking catnip.

His reputation precedes him, and it's BIG.

In comparison, I was kissed and felt up when I was sixteen at the junior dance academy after which the boy promptly informed me that he was in fact gay and appreciated me helping him come to that conclusion. That's the extent of my physical experience with guys.

That's right. V-card still intact, but I'm not a prude. I know how to take care of myself. Or at least how to purchase battery-operated devices to help me.

Hydrocortisone and a good vibrator. That's really all I need to survive.

But that's what has gotten me into this situation. I have zero dating experience and therefore a lot of anxiety about dating. Or is it that my anxiety about dating has left me completely inexperienced with guys?

What came first? The anxiety or the lack of experience? It's a chicken or the egg type question. I'm not sure I'll ever know.

Now, Rhys is proposing a solution. And it might work. But I need to know how. I need details.

"How would this work?" I ask. "Logistically?"

Rhys's lips curve up. "Logistically, I'll let you know the dates of events I need you for. We'll plan some social media posts for authenticity, and the rest is up to you. You let me know when you're free for dates, and I'll arrange them."

My gaze drops to his fingers again. To those big hands massaging Maxine. The veins and corded muscle that bulge beneath the ink on his forearm and bicep. Those hands will need to touch me. Even more intimately than last night when he wrapped one around my waist to dance. I swear I can still feel the weight of it imprinted on my lower back. The way that heaviness made everything below my waist dull and achy.

Don't think about Rhys and sex. We won't be doing THAT. I'm not saving myself for anyone or any reason, but I can't imagine that we would even fit together like that. I mean, I'm sure things would *fit*, but I need someone who won't mind my inexperience. I'm sure Rhys is used to women who have a repertoire of bedroom tricks. That use their sexual prowess to garner the attention of a man like him.

"We'll need to touch," he says.

My eyes snap back to his. It's like he can read my mind.

"Yeah, I know."

"And kiss."

I suck in a breath because now I'm thinking about kissing Rhys.

Wondering how soft his lips are. How warm and firm they'd feel pressed to mine.

Now I'm looking at his lips. They're full and expressive. His mouth twists into a lopsided grin.

When my eyes return to his, he wiggles his brows. My cheeks immediately flame because he must know what I'm thinking.

I let the knowledge that he's likely kissed hundreds of women douse the fire attempting to spark in my belly. Hundreds of beautiful, *experienced* women, I'm sure.

But I need to stop beating myself up about my lack of experience. To get experience, I need to take the first step.

Dating Rhys would be a starting point. A way to dip my toe into the dating pond. The other stuff…*sex*…will come later when I've met someone I'm more compatible with, and fake-dating Rhys has helped me become less likely to break out in a head-to-toe body rash at the thought of spending time with that person.

"Like in public to make it believable?" I finally ask.

"Yeah."

"Tongue or no tongue?" I do better when I know specifics. When there's a plan in place. I can't be thinking we're going to be giving each other gentle pecks on the cheeks and then get surprised by a full mouth kiss.

He's watching me closely. "You tell me."

"What would you normally do with a woman you're dating?"

"First of all, I don't date. Not like this." He motions between us. "I've hooked up in public restrooms. Women have sucked me off in front of my friends and an entire room full of people. I don't remember that one as much as the pictures someone took." My eyes are bulging when he glances back at me. "You're going to need to tell me where the line is."

I swallow down the butterflies that threaten to emerge when I think about doing any of those things with Rhys. "Yeah, we won't be doing any of that." I make a waving motion, like I'm sweeping those thoughts away. *All those dirty, delicious thoughts. Goodbye!*

He nods. "Agreed."

"So, touching and kissing, but only in public under the ruse of fake dating. You'll send me the dates for events you need me to attend and I'll send you some open times for practice dates." I nod, satisfied with the parameters I've laid out for this fake-dating arrangement.

Rhys stands, setting Maxine down gently on the couch, then extends his hands to me.

I take his hand and stand.

We're facing each other, inches apart, yet it feels like I'm inside his shirt. His warm, masculine scent washes over me and it makes my knees weak.

I'm tempted to sit back down, but Rhys slips a hand around my waist, holding me there. My body immediately goes rigid with nerves.

It's not much different than the way he held me last night while we were dancing, yet alone in my apartment it feels a whole heck of a lot more intimate.

"What are you doing?" I ask.

"We'll need to touch. And it will need to be natural. If we're dating, you can't turn into a cardboard cut-out when I put my arm around you."

I roll my shoulders back, trying to ease the tension there.

"What are *you* doing?" he asks, a teasing smile on his face.

"Getting comfortable," I say, leaning away from him.

"Yeah, you look really comfortable right now." He drops his arm.

"Sorry, I'm just not used to having guys touch me like that. I mean, when it's necessary for choreography, sure, and I'm super comfortable with Sebastian, but this," I motion between us, "is new."

"Who's Sebastian?"

"He's a soloist at the company and a good friend. We've been paired together in a few roles."

He nods then places his hand on the side of my waist. His fingers tickle the space between my waistband and my cropped tank and I start to squirm and giggle.

"Jesus, okay." He runs a hand through his messy hair. "Let's try something else."

He releases me, then moves to sit down on the couch.

"Come straddle me."

"I'm sorry, what?" I can't help the nervous laughter that escapes. "I don't see how *that* is necessary. No one's going to be straddling anyone in public."

"It's a strategy. You go past the point you need to be comfortable with. Pushing you into a more uncomfortable situation now, when we're alone, will make it easier for you to relax with simple touches when we're in public."

I want to see his logic but my body is doing that tingling thing again.

Maxine stands to stretch, then starts moseying her way over to Rhys, his vacant lap her target.

"Come on, before she beats you to it."

He leans back into the couch cushion with his hands interlaced behind his head, looking perfectly self-assured. Like he knows what he's talking about.

I decide not to think about it. It's like ripping off a band-aid, right? Except it feels like it's going to be one of those really sticky ones that does its job and then some, vowing to seal that cut up like a vault by sacrificing the perfectly unharmed skin around it. Not to mention if there's any hair in the vicinity. *Ouch.*

My thoughts on bandages gives Maxine the advantage and she's already nearing Rhys's lap.

It's now or never.

Okay, Lettie, just do it.

I rush over to where Rhys is seated on the couch, lean forward to place my hands on his shoulders for balance, and bring my knees onto the couch to straddle his lap.

Okay, this isn't that scary.

"You have to sit down, Lettie."

Oh, that's why my thighs are shaking. I'm still holding up all my body weight.

"Right."

I lower my butt onto Rhys's thighs, but there's still as much distance between our chests as I can manage without falling backwards.

"We're going to stay like this until you relax."

I exhale, trying to let out the tension in my body.

Closing my eyes helps shut out all his charm and sexy smirks, but there's still the matter of the warm, sensually scented body beneath me.

It's just Rhys.

Charming, sexy, body of a Greek god, Rhys.

No. I need to think of childhood Rhys. The sweet, easy-going boy who was my friend and protector. I recall his goofy smile with braces, the way he cried when he skinned his knees falling off his bike, the way he would patiently wait for me when I was slower and couldn't keep up with the older kids, and the intimidation slowly fades.

Finally, I'm leaning forward to lay my head on his shoulder.

Okay, this is nice.

With the idea that I've got this dating situation under control and the relief that comes with knowing I won't be scouring through dating sites, I'm finally able to relax.

Rhys's hand comes around to my back. His lips press, warm and firm, against my neck.

I barely have time to register the sensation when I hear it.

Click.

I pop my head up to find Rhys's free hand with his phone in it.

"What's that for?" I ask.

"Social media. We'll want to post consistently. Make sure we look happy and content."

Well, I was before he took that photo.

"It'll be more convincing that way."

I climb off his lap while he starts typing something out on his phone. When he's done, he turns the phone screen toward me.

A cozy Sunday with my <red heart emoji>

There we are, cuddled together on the couch. Rhys's hand splayed against my back, his pinky finger teasing at the waistband of my leggings like he doesn't have a care in the world. My face is partially hidden behind his head, and my eyes are closed, but I'm smiling. He captured the moment where his lips pressed to my neck and I smiled. It doesn't tell the story of my unsettled nerves but one of a woman clearly comfortable snuggling with her boyfriend on the couch.

"Can I post it?" he asks. "If I do, it will be official. The answer to everyone's burning questions after last night's photos. And the start of our arrangement."

I gulp. This is it.

Are we really doing this?

What's the worst that could happen?

I don't follow my brain down that rabbit hole, but instead focus on what I want. Dating experience. Getting out of my comfort zone and experiencing new things sans hives. I've already managed that by straddling Rhys on the couch without so much as a red splotch surfacing. Imagine what more there could be.

Oh, god. Imagine what more there could be!

Alexei's words come back to me. *It's what you experience outside the studio that elevates a dancer's performance.*

That's what I need. And with Rhys's help, I'm determined to get it.

"Let's do it." I nod.

I watch as he hits post.

It's official. Rhys and I are (fake) dating, and we just announced it to the world.

CHAPTER 10
Rhys

"Why are we here?" Ramsey asks, opening the door to one of the city's feline rescues, before following me inside.

"I'm getting a cat."

His eyes widen. "Why?"

After Ramsey and his Bergman's personal stylist cousin, Percy, spent three hours outfitting me with a new wardrobe full of boring clothing, I'm looking forward to doing something fun.

"I told Lettie I had a cat."

"Again…why?"

"I don't know. It just came out of my mouth. Now I need to adopt a cat or Lettie will know I was lying."

"Can you tell her the cat ran away?" he asks.

I give him a withering look.

"You know you live on a boat, right? And cats hate water."

"It'll be an indoor cat."

"Okay, but you're supposed to be focused on cultivating new interests and hobbies."

"A cat is a new interest. I think I've always liked cats, just never gotten one until now."

He sighs. "Could it possibly be because they don't travel well?"

"Taylor Swift takes her cats everywhere. Even the *TIME* magazine cover shoot."

He eyes me with skepticism. "Since when do you know anything about Taylor Swift?"

"I read the *TIME's* article."

"You read?" His jaw drops in mock surprise.

"Hilarious." I throw a sardonic look his way. "And, since you asked, her music is badass. You should listen to it sometime."

"I've been a Taylor stan for years. 1989 TV is lit."

"What's TV?" I ask.

He rolls his eyes. "Taylor's Version. How do you not know that?"

"I'm learning, okay? It's a new interest."

"I thought you'd take up a sport or do some volunteer work." Ramsey grabs a brochure off the wall. "Maybe you can volunteer here and take a bunch of pictures with a cat and show them to Colette so she thinks you weren't lying, then you don't really have to adopt one."

"I'm getting a cat," I say firmly.

After filling out the appropriate paperwork, we're let back into the large area where the cats are kenneled. I've been instructed to let them know which cats I'd like to invite into the free room to pet and cuddle.

"So, what's your plan with Colette?"

I informed Ramsey that Lettie and I agreed to fake date for both our benefits. He really didn't see how I would be benefitting her, until I explained she was inexperienced and wanted to practice dating.

You're not going to sleep with her, are you? he'd asked.

I'd immediately explained the rules Lettie and I decided on. Only touching and kissing that is appropriate in public. Which seemed like a gray area since I've hooked-up in semi-public places, but Lettie was content with it, and that's what matters.

After I left Lettie's apartment, I immediately texted Jerrod to tell him Lettie and I would be attending his dinner party later this week. He responded with a thumbs up which is a passive-aggressive 'fuck you,' so it seems like we're on the same page.

We walk by the cages to check out the cats and my heart sinks.

"This is depressing. I want to adopt them all."

Ramsey shakes his head. "You get one."

"This one's cute." I point to a white cat with the prettiest blue eyes. "No stripes, though."

"Does the cat have to have stripes?" Ramsey asks, bending down to check out a black cat on the lower shelf.

"I told Lettie his name is Maurice and he's furry with stripes."

"What cat wouldn't be furry?"

"I don't know, I was getting deeper into the lie and I panicked."

Ramsey rolls his eyes. "Step aside."

"We've got our first date tonight," I say, glancing into a cage with a brown tabby. I stick my finger through the metal door and it nuzzles up against me. The sheet taped up next to the cage indicates he's a male brown tabby and three years old.

"Where are you taking her?" Ramsey asks.

"Wherever you get us a reservation."

He rolls his eyes. "Thanks for the advance notice." But then, because I pay him an insane amount of money to put up with me, he pulls out his phone to start calling for a reservation.

It's a simple date. After learning about Lettie's dating anxiety, I figured it was best to keep things chill. Not overwhelm her with too much action. Zero action, in fact.

"This one," I say, pointing to the brown tabby that has mischief in his green eyes.

It only takes a few minutes in the cuddle room to decide that this cat and I are going to be a good fit. He's playful and a good cuddler. What more do you need in a cat?

I hold him up and he paws at my face before nuzzling my chin. "I'd be more open to keeping your name, but you've got to be Maurice when Lettie's around. I'll explain everything to you later."

Ramsey shakes his head, but I can tell by the way he scratches under Mo's chin that he's smitten, too.

I can't bring Mo home yet; he's got to have a check-up and the vet that provides their services to the shelter isn't working today. Also, they've got to approve my paperwork.

We exit the shelter and Ramsey calls Manny, one of my drivers, to pick us up.

"He's parked down the block." Ramsey motions toward Second Avenue.

"Cool, let's go."

We're a few steps down the sidewalk when I hear the click of a camera. I look up and immediately recognize the guy. Dressed in a plain green ball cap and cargo shorts with a goatee and glasses, it's one of the photographers who I've seen lurking around since I got back to the city.

He's probably the one that took the photos of Lettie and me at Hannah and James's wedding.

Ramsey shakes his head as we both get into the car, ignoring the continuous click of the man's camera.

"Fucking pap." Ramsey curses inside the car. "You know he's waiting for the next juicy story."

"He'll be waiting a while. I'm on my best behavior now."

He nods, scrolling through his phone.

"That photo you posted yesterday with Colette was a good strategy." He pulls it up to show me the likes and comments, all I can do is stare at the photo and remember how perfect Lettie felt in my arms.

To distract myself from the memory, I glance at one of the comments.

"Wait. What does that say?" I ask.

But Ramsey doesn't need to read it because I have eyes.

Run, sweetie. A man like that will ruin you.

Cute couple, but it won't last.

He's a player. He'll break your heart.

"I thought you said the photo was a good strategy. These comments are fucking shit."

"I didn't say the comments were good, but having a photo of you two that isn't staged at an event makes it more believable." He points to the photo. "You'll need more of this to legitimize the relationship."

"I told Lettie I would only need her for a few dinners or events. She's busy with training and doesn't have time for dating, that was the beauty of the arrangement."

He shrugs. "You'll need to spend some time together doing normal couple things. That's what's going to sell this."

"Yeah, I'll figure it out."

"Maybe that photographer following you could be a good thing."

"What do you mean?" I ask.

"Good press."

"That's not what that guy's after." He makes his living off making me look bad.

"But if that's all you give him, what can he do? He'll either post it or lose interest. It's a win-win."

Ramsey has a good point. If bad press is what built my reputation, then maybe some good press is what could fix it.

CHAPTER 11

Colette

***Rhys:** Pick you up at eight.*

I stare at his text message. Eight? That seems late for dinner. I usually eat at six when I get home from my day at the studio.

After practice, I'd showered and dried my hair, which took forever because it is deceptively thick, and now I'm standing in the ladies' dressing room trying to figure out what to wear. Planning for efficiency, I'd packed up everything this morning so I could save time and change here. But with Rhys not picking me up until eight, I've got nearly three hours to decide what to wear…three hours to overanalyze everything.

Isabella walks into the dressing area and looks around at the clothing options strewn about. "Hot date tonight?"

"Um, yeah. Kind of."

"Seriously?" Her mouth opens in shock, but she quickly recovers. "Not that you wouldn't have a hot date. It's an expression, and I wasn't expecting you to say yes."

I laugh because while Isabella feels bad for insinuating I have no personal life, it's the exact reason why I'm doing this with Rhys. To put myself out there. Kind of.

"He's a friend. We grew up together. Our parents are—were—friends. His parents died in a boating accident fifteen years ago." As I'm saying it to Isabella, I can't believe it's been that long since Wes and Abigail died.

"Is it casual? Like a hook-up?" she asks.

"No. Not a hook-up. There won't be any hooking up, just dating as two people do."

She laughs at my awkward answer. "Okay, so what's his name?"

"Rhys Spencer."

Isabella's eyes go wide. "You're dating Rhys Spencer?" It's the shocked expression from before but mixed with confusion.

"Do you know him?" I ask warily.

"Yeah."

Oh god, now I'm wondering if she *knows him* knows him.

"Everyone knows who Rhys Spencer is. He's one of NYC's wealthiest bachelors." She presses her lips together, then continues. "Okay, don't take this the wrong way, but I don't see you two together. He's a total bad boy and you're so sweet and wholesome."

I really should take this opportunity to practice making me and Rhys as a couple believable by telling her how sweet he is and thoughtful and kind, and hot, except that can be observed by anyone with eyeballs, but the reality is with Hannah on her honeymoon, I need someone to talk to about this entire situation.

So, I tell her everything.

"So, you're not really together." Isabella nods in understanding. The worry line between her brows fades and her smile returns as if the balance has been restored to the universe. "Okay, that makes more sense."

"I don't know what to wear."

Isabella eyes my choices and promptly wrinkles her nose.

"I don't like any of those options." She lifts one of the blouses I brought. "What even is this?"

"You really tried to hold that one in, huh?" I laugh.

"I know." Her face lights up. "Here." She pulls a silky slip dress out of her bag.

I frown at the gunmetal gray fabric. "How is that not wrinkled?"

"It's designed to be wrinkle resistant."

"Okay." I hold up the midi-dress by its spaghetti straps. "Where's the rest of it?"

"You go out on stage in less than this."

She's right, but hundreds of faceless people are far less intimidating than Rhys Spencer's one striking face. *It's just practice*, I remind myself and that eases my nerves somewhat.

I strip out of my spandex shorts and cropped tank, then work the silky material down my body.

I lift my hands out to the side. "Well?"

She studies me a moment. "Lose the bra."

"Excuse me?"

"That's the whole point of the dress. Free the nipples."

I unclasp my bra and yank it out from under the dress. The silky material settles against my bare skin, *ahem*, and nipples, causing a tingling sensation.

"I'd suggest that it looks like I'm in a nightgown, but I wouldn't even wear this to bed, let alone outside the house."

"You look great. We need to normalize the nipple and utilize its full potential as a fashion statement."

"Since when are nipples a fashion statement?"

"Since Kate Moss. Everything from the 90s is back."

Do I really want to free my nipples around Rhys? For some reason that feels dangerous. Like I'm already out of my depth with this whole dating thing, and now I'll be one slip of a strap away from a wardrobe malfunction.

"You're trying to get out of your comfort zone, right?"

She's got me there.

"Okay, let's work on a nice smokey eye to go with it. And we'll want to do a neutral lip, to keep it balanced."

"How do you know all this stuff? Did I miss the day in academy when fashion and makeup were discussed?"

Isabella laughs. "You know my mom is a stylist, so there's that, but everyone has different interests. Besides dancing, I love clothes and makeup."

She motions for me to close my eyes so she can begin working on my eye makeup.

My only interest has been dancing. Everything in my life has revolved around that, and while I don't want it to change completely, I know in order to grow as a dancer, I need to find balance. That's what I'm doing with Rhys.

When Isabella is done with me, I look in the mirror.

Dark, smokey eyelids, pastel pink lips and whatever she did to highlight my cheekbones. I look like a different version of myself. To the point that I wonder if it's too much.

Isabella reads my uncertainty. "You look gorgeous. Like a woman going on her first date."

"It's technically my second date. I went with Hannah's cousin to a wedding one time."

She points to my white sneakers.

"Wear those. It'll be a good balance of sexy and casual." As a fellow dancer, she knows how beat up our feet are. I barely managed to wear the heels for Hannah's wedding, so knowing I can wear my tennis shoes tonight gives me some comfort.

"I took your clothes. What are you going to wear home?" I ask.

She looks through my pile of clothing and selects a tank top and skirt combo.

"See, that's cute," I say when she's got it on.

"Yeah, but this date doesn't call for cute." She swats me on my butt. "Now, go get 'em, tiger."

It's only six o'clock, so I go home and wait for Rhys.

By the time Rhys picks me up, I'm so hungry I could chew my arm off. I thought I could adjust to this later dinner time by having another snack. But afraid I wouldn't be hungry for dinner, I kept the portion size small and by the time I realized I should have eaten more, I was already hangry. Now it's too late and I'm crossing over into risky territory.

Maybe it's the low blood sugar, or the silky slip dress that keeps teasing against my nipples, but the moment I open the door to find Rhys standing there in a dark suit jacket, t-shirt and jeans, I'm nearly delirious. He looks good enough to eat.

"You look…" Rhys starts.

"Famished?" I respond because food is all I can think about.

And because my body can only handle one crisis at a time, I've completely forgotten to be paranoid about being braless.

Rhys leans forward to peck me on the cheek and his scent envelops me. He's citrus and spice and everything nice. My nipples reach out to get closer.

"No." Rhys pins me with one of those panty-melting smiles of his. "Gorgeous."

For a moment, my heart trips over itself, but then I remind it to get back into rhythm.

Look away, my body warns. *We don't want to be completely naked under this dress.*

"Okay, great, let's go."

I motion him toward the elevator where we find Mrs. Donahue has just gotten off.

Her eyes light up when she sees Rhys.

"Hello again." She smiles coquettishly at him.

Rhys gives her a casual nod, barely acknowledging her existence, and Mrs. Donahue swoons. Her eyes go hazy. Rhys has triggered something in her and she's no longer with us in this hallway but in a faraway time fantasizing about a past lover, hopefully the late Mr. Donahue, but if it's not, I won't judge.

"I think Mrs. Donahue has a thing for you," I whisper.

"I only have eyes for you, Princess," he teases.

A few minutes later we're out on the curb and I'm staring confused at a large hunk of metal with tires. Rhys hands me a helmet.

"What's this for?"

Without saying a word, he takes the helmet from me and pushes it onto my head.

I can practically feel the foundation sliding off my face. Isabella would be so mad to know her makeup work is being mistreated this way.

"There you go," he announces, satisfied that my head now weighs twice as much as it did before.

"Gee, thanks."

"Safety first."

He climbs on, making it look effortless.

"You actually want me to ride on that thing?" I whine.

"Yeah, how else are we going to get to dinner?"

"In a car. The *normal* way?"

I catch his smirk before it disappears under his helmet. "You should know by now, that's not my style."

"Well neither is this dress, but I'm wearing it, aren't I?" I motion to the dress that will make it impossible to straddle this motorcycle without showing my underwear.

"Oh, I didn't think about that."

"A man in pants wouldn't, now, would he?" With this new obstacle, the restaurant and dinner feel even further away. I really should have had that banana and peanut butter smoothie.

He gets off the bike and studies me a moment like this is a brain teaser. How to get the girl on the bike without showing her butt to the world.

"I got it." He pulls a pair of gym shorts out of the storage compartment. "Put these on."

"Are these clean?" I ask.

"Don't ask a question you don't want the answer to."

"But I do want to know the answer."

He sniffs them, then sighs. "Do you have a better idea?"

"Yes. We can get a cab. Or walk."

"That's not as fun. You said you wanted to try new things. New experiences." He motions to the motorcycle.

"This dress is a new experience," I argue, but Rhys just lifts his brows in challenge.

He's not going to let this go. I can see it in that impish smile of his.

"Fine," I relent, pulling his gym shorts over my shoes and up to my waist under my dress. Rhys helps me get on the back of the bike, then he joins me.

Because my dress is slim through the hips, I had to bunch it up at the waist and pool the material between me and Rhys.

"Wrap your arms around me."

I snake my arms around Rhys's waist. After yesterday's lap straddling, this feels easy. Either his theory about doing more challenging stuff so other things feel easy was right or holding onto him is far less scary than the idea of falling off the back of this motorcycle.

He's warm and solid and okay, I see why this has appeal.

He lifts his phone up to take a photo of us. I lean into him and let my chin rest on his shoulder.

We look cute. A surge of pride rushes through me.

Look! I can do this.

Then, Rhys starts the engine and my stomach lurches. With my arms wrapped around him, I'd forgotten that we need to drive this thing somewhere.

"Hold on tight."

"Like my life depends on it?" I ask, because that's what this moment feels like.

"Come on, Princess, I'd never let anything happen to you."

"Did you get reassurance from every driver in the city? Because that's who I'm worried about."

I wince as we take off onto the city street, nervous that we'll be clipped by a car speeding by.

We take the side streets south to Chelsea and I gain confidence in Rhys as a driver. He doesn't take off at top speeds like I've seen some motorcyclists do. The only thing hotter than a bad boy on a motorcycle is the fact that he obeys traffic laws.

We're stopped at a light and I think I'm going to make it and everything is going to be okay, but then his hand drops from the handlebar to his side and grazes my knee.

Okay, it was only his pinky finger, yet that one simple touch is sensory overload.

"Hands on the handlebars!" I yell.

"You okay back there?"

"Yeah, I'm good. Just don't crash."

"We're already here," he says, dismounting. The light we were stopped at is really a parking spot near the restaurant.

I bend forward to pull the shorts off, then straighten to hand them to Rhys.

Rhys puts the shorts back in the storage compartment along with our helmets.

"Maybe don't lean forward like that again." He eyes the top of my dress.

My mouth drops open and I automatically press a hand to my sternum where the dress was gaping. "I don't have a bra on."

"I'm highly aware now."

"So, you saw my breasts?"

"Only the tops of them. It's cool. I'm your boyfriend, remember?"

I nod, still trying to get into my role as Rhys's girlfriend.

As we approach the restaurant, I notice several men with cameras. At first, I think they're tourists, excited to capture their time in the Big Apple on their fancy cameras, but then they raise their cameras at us.

"Rhys, are you back in the city for good?"

"Colette, how long have you and Rhys been dating?"

I'm so confused by what is happening that I can't even react.

Rhys possessively wraps his arm around my waist and without a word to the cameramen, he guides me into the restaurant.

"What was that about?" I ask once we're inside.

"Nosy photographers."

"I mean this in the kindest way, but why would they be following you?"

He gives me a cheeky grin. "Gee thanks, Princess. You really know how to deflate a guy's ego."

I lift my brows, ready for him to answer the question.

"I honestly don't know. I'm entertaining, I guess."

After checking in with the host, they take us to a table toward the back of the restaurant. It's quiet and secluded. The moment I sit down across from Rhys, the heat starts crawling up my neck.

"It's happening." I wave a hand over the hot rash flaring up on my neck.

"Okay. Don't stress."

My eyes widen in disbelief. "That's easy for you to say."

"We can figure this out together."

"There's nothing to figure out. I can't do this this. We should leave before my body turns into one giant splotch."

"You were fine when I picked you up and although a bit nervous, you were okay on my bike, so what was the trigger?"

"I don't know? This situation." I gesture between us. "Me sitting across from you. I don't know why I thought it would be different with you. Clearly, my body doesn't know the difference between fake dating and real dating. It's stressed about this either way."

"So, it's because I'm sitting across from you?"

"Yes! No! I don't know. Maybe."

"Okay," he looks around the restaurant, "we can figure this out."

"Let's just go."

Rhys stands up and takes my hand. "Come on."

But we don't walk toward the exit. Instead, he points us toward the bar where there are a few stools open next to each other.

"Can we sit here?" he asks the bartender, pointing at the open seats.

"Help yourself."

He pulls out one of the low-back stools for me, then takes the one beside it.

"Problem solved. Now I'm not staring at you from across the table."

I lean against the back rest and press a hand to my chest. It's still red and splotchy, but I'm already more at ease. I turn to glance at Rhys's profile. He studies the menu before he sets it down to take a drink of the water the bartender set down a moment ago.

"Thank you."

"There's always a solution, right?" He winks at me, his perfect lips sliding across his face in a dangerous smile.

CHAPTER 12

Rhys

"And that's why, to this day, Ramsey refuses to ride a bike."

Lettie laughs, and I drink it in. It's a great laugh. There's a robustness to it that I find surprising, maybe because it doesn't sound like it belongs to such a demure, petite woman.

Lettie's laugh disappears into a yawn.

I motion to where she's covering her open mouth. "You were just humoring me with your laugh."

She props her elbow up on the bar top then rests her chin in her hand. "Not at all. I'm just tired from the day." She glances at her smart watch. "It's past my bedtime."

"It's nine-thirty."

"I'm an early riser, so I like to get to bed at a decent time."

"I'm a night owl."

Her lips twitch. "Not a surprise, Mr. I'll pick you up at eight."

"Late dinners are a habit I picked up in Italy." I study her tired eyes. "Why do you wake up so early? Isn't the company on a break right now?"

"Yes, but I'm not taking a break. I'm keeping my training routine and I've got rehearsals for a fundraiser showcase for Leg-Up in a few weeks."

"No break?" My brows raise. "Doesn't your body need rest?"

"I like to stick to my routine."

She lifts a shoulder and my eyes are drawn to the movement there, to her toned yet delicate arm, and the way the thin strap of her dress is begging for fingertips to tease it down. The knowledge that she's not wearing a bra makes it even more enticing.

That's more than once tonight that I've forgotten that the strikingly beautiful woman next to me is the same girl who used to make mud pies on the beach of Lake George.

It's Lettie spaghetti. Stop staring at her tits.

My eyes snap back to her face.

"What's Leg-Up?" I ask, hoping I'll be able to focus on her answer and not the way her nipples are taunting me through the silky material of her dress.

"It's a community dance studio that offers free or reduced-price classes to families. We're raising money to clean up the studio. It recently got damaged with a flood from old pipes that were leaking. It needs new drywall and flooring, then once that's complete, there will be a community day where we can paint the studio and get it ready for classes to resume."

The excitement that lights up her eyes as she tells me about it has my attention focused on her face.

"It's a passion project."

"I can see that. You're very passionate as you talk. It's almost like you're awake now," I tease.

She laughs and it's the sound I didn't know I was missing in my life. It's light and airy, like a delicate flutter of infectious warmth.

"I think I'm deliriously tired, but also I just love that those who otherwise wouldn't be able to afford classes have the opportunity to be exposed to the art of dance in many forms, not only ballet."

"That's really cool." It reminds me of my parents' work and the reason they started The Spencer Foundation.

"Well, between cross training, and practice for the showcase, and assisting with a summer class at the academy, I've got a full schedule." She motions between us. "That's why this arrangement is helpful."

"I'm glad."

She takes a sip of her Pelligrino and the bartender clears our plates.

I've never cared about my lack of career before but hearing Lettie list off all the things she's involved with, all the ways she's contributing to projects she's passionate about, I'm suddenly embarrassed I have nothing to offer in return.

Lettie's not the type of woman who'd be impressed simply by my wealth and status. She's got goals and none of them is riding my dick or asking me to buy her expensive shit.

"Oh, I completely forgot I had some ice breaker questions for first dates." She pulls out her phone.

I smile. "We've already been talking for an hour."

"I know, but it's easier to talk to you because we already know each other. We have history. I can't rely on this comfortability with future dates."

My brows raise at her use of the d-word. "Careful, we don't want to bring back the hives."

Her eyes widen as she brushes a hand against her chest.

"You're good, Princess." I grin before taking a drink of my whiskey. "Okay. Shoot."

"They're either-or questions. Do you prefer winter or summer?"

"Easy. Summer."

"I'm a winter gal. I love when the city is decorated for the holidays and snow is falling. Cozy blankets and hot tea in front of a fireplace." Her face turns all dreamy and it makes me wish she could have all those things right now.

"You make it sound so appealing."

"That's because it is." She scrolls on her phone. "Okay, next question. Beach or ski vacation?"

"Ski."

"You just said you prefer summer, so why a ski vacation?" she asks.

"During the summer, the beach is great, but if there's a chance to go skiing, then I'm there."

"Hmm. It's the beach for me. I don't ski."

"You never learned?" I ask.

"It's a liability. I don't want to get injured on the slopes and risk my dancing career."

"So, the beach it is."

She sighs. "Yeah, if I ever took a break, I would lie on the beach all day. Maybe read a book. Swim. Just relax."

"Sounds like a good time to me."

Her expression is wistful. "It's not happening anytime soon, but maybe someday."

She takes a drink of charged water, then turns back to her phone.

I nod for her to continue questioning.

"Guacamole or salsa?"

I shake my head and press my lips into a firm line. "Tough question. Guacamole if I'm having tacos, salsa if I'm having nachos."

"You're not answering the questions correctly. It's one or the other. You can't have your cake and eat it, too."

"Mmm. I love cake. Is that a question on your list?"

She scrolls on her phone. "Yes. Cake or Pie?"

"That's a tough one. Depends on the kind. I'll go with chocolate cake and cherry pie."

She frowns at my inability to play this game correctly. "You can't have both."

"I can because you're going to say neither so I can have yours."

Her eyes meet mine, and I raise my eyebrows in challenge, before she rolls her eyes to the side and back to her phone.

"Oh, that reminds me. We should know each other's birthdays. Mine's April second."

I nod. "August tenth."

"That's right. I remember celebrating it at the lake. Your dad always made you the best cakes. He had a knack for decorating. The fire engine with Oreo tires was one of my favorites."

"That was a good one. The snake was cool, too."

"That one freaked me out. The red velvet cake mix he used for that one made it look like it was bleeding out. I had to close my eyes to eat it."

Our eyes catch and a wave of sadness and longing rolls over me. Sometimes it's hard for me to connect with people who knew my parents. While memories of them are wonderful, they're always laced with sadness.

Lettie clears her throat. "Sorry. Back to the questions. Here's a good one. Lose sleep or skip a meal?"

"I already know your answer," I say.

"You're right, food intake is important, especially for athletes."

"I'd skip a meal. I need my beauty rest."

She sits up taller, like she's excited to be getting the hang of this thing. Asking questions to get to know someone. Dating. Hell, I haven't done anything like this myself in years. It's almost comical that I'm the one she's practicing dating with when my experience in that area is barely greater than hers. Now sex, that's a different story.

"Tattoo or piercing." She eyes the ink on my left arm. "I don't know why I'm asking. It's clear which one you would pick."

"Hate to disappoint you, Princess, but this one I can't choose between."

"What do you mean? You clearly would choose tattoo."

She does a quick scan of my face and ears. "You don't have any piercings."

My brow quirks up. "No?"

Her eyes drop to my chest. I know what she's thinking before she speaks.

"You have your nipples pierced?" she asks, surprise registering in her voice.

I shake my head. "Guess again."

Her eyes drop lower, to my crotch. As she processes this information, her jaw goes slack, her lips forming a perfect circle, and it's all I can do not to think about how they would look wrapped around my cock.

"You pierced your penis?" She gapes, her eyes widening as she continues to stare at my crotch in disbelief.

But now it's all I can think about. With the power of suggestion, my brain has drawn up a detailed visual of Lettie on her knees for me. My hand in her hair guiding that sweet mouth of hers. Watching my cock sink between her lips, smooth and wet.

I immediately clear the image, discreetly adjusting the bulge in my pants with one hand as I reach for my water glass with the other. This whole night has been different than I thought it would be. I was already enjoying myself more than I ever have with a woman and now this conversation has taken our innocent first date into a territory I am strictly trying to avoid.

"Yeah." I clear my throat.

She's curious. I can see it in her eyes.

"I think that's enough for tonight, don't you?" I ask.

"Yeah." She nods, tucking her phone back into her purse. "I guess it's getting late."

I pay the bill, then we walk back out to my bike, cameras flashing as we climb on. It's a quiet ride to Lettie's apartment. I'm almost concerned she's falling asleep and will forget to hold on when I feel her arms tighten around my waist.

At her apartment, I help her off the bike and put the extra helmet in the storage compartment.

She hands me the gym shorts and I throw those in with the helmet.

"What do you do at the end of a date?" She looks up at me, blue eyes wide with uncertainty.

Anything I would normally do after taking a woman out is off limits with Lettie. I've already gone too far with her in my head. Planted thoughts that will make it a challenge to not think about her later.

She wants to practice dating, but this is going to be the textbook version, not hands on.

"Walk you to your door," I say, leading her up the stairs to her apartment before turning to face her. "And a kiss on the cheek."

I lean down to press my lips against her soft skin and her scent, floral and sweet, yet sensual, has me lingering there. *Fuck. She smells amazing.*

When I pull away, I notice her lips twitch before they split into a grin.

"Liar."

"Fine. But this isn't what would Rhys do, it's what would Lettie's gentlemanly date do. There's a difference."

"You're saying the guys I would be going out with are gentlemen and would kiss on the cheek?"

"Most likely."

She considers this a moment before asking, "Is that because of who I am or because of who they are?"

"Both."

"Okay, so a kiss on the cheek and a promise to call me tomorrow?"

"If the date went well."

"Did the date go well? How would I know?" she asks.

Because I don't want it to end.

"It's a feeling you get. It takes practice to read another person's body language."

She holds a hand up to her mouth to cover a yawn.

"And yours is telling me you need to get some rest."

She nods. "You're right."

I watch as she opens the front door and slips inside, turning to give me a small wave.

"Goodnight, Rhys."

"Goodnight, Princess."

CHAPTER 13

Colette

My watch buzzes, alerting me to the distance I've gone. Three miles.

I slow to a walk and take a deep breath.

Running, weight training, Gyrotonics, and yoga; they're all a part of my cross training during off-season.

My pace is slower than usual. I stayed up way too late last night, and I can feel the drag of my body today. But as a tradeoff, those few hours of sleep I missed for my time with Rhys was progress toward the challenge Alexei tasked me with.

I practiced dating with Rhys and it wasn't as stressful as I thought it was going to be.

Sure, there were moments, like when his fingers brushed my leg or I learned that he has a hidden piercing, that I was slightly overwhelmed, but then Rhys would make a joke or flash that charming smile of his and it would give me comfort.

His piercing is something I shouldn't be thinking about. I don't even know what kind it is, only the general vicinity that it's located.

His dick. It's somewhere on his dick, my brain chimes in.

Despite it being late when I crawled into bed last night, curiosity got the best of me. That reminds me, I should probably clear my search history or *types of male genital piercings* is going to be at the top.

Before I can follow the steps to clear it, my phone buzzes with an incoming call. It's Rhys. My face flushes as if he's calling because he knows that I was thinking about him and his piercing. I calm my heart by telling myself it's only a coincidence. Rhys is a lot of things, but there's no way he's telepathic.

"Hi," I answer brightly, banishing the dirty thoughts of him from my brain.

"How's your day going?" His voice is like butter melting on a hot biscuit. Not that I eat carbs, but if I did, I'm sure that's what I would compare it to. It's so smooth, it makes my stomach flutter.

"Good. Busy. How's yours?"

"Good, but I've been distracted thinking about you."

My eyes widen at his seductive tone.

"You have?" My heart rate picks up, so much so that my watch beeps with an alert, asking me if I'm working out again. I tap the button to deny the suggested workout. The only thing working out is my imaginative brain.

He chuckles. "This is Rhys." There's a short pause. "From last night. I'm calling to let you know I had a great time."

Oh, right. We're practicing.

"Thanks. Thank you. Yes." I palm my forehead. I sound like a bumbling idiot. I clear my throat and start again. "I had a good time, too."

"I'd like to take you out again," he says, charm oozes from his voice and it's practically hypnotic.

Somehow, I manage to respond. "Okay. Sure. Let's do it."

"Too enthusiastic," he says, trading his velvety tone for his usual husky one to give the critique. "You need to make me work for it."

"Really? I thought the point was to go out again so I can get more experience?"

"With me, but we're practicing what you would say to another guy. One who's calling you up after a first date. You don't want to be easily available."

"I'm not." I huff. "I'm super busy. That's why I'm fake-dating you."

"How about dinner and a movie tomorrow night?" he asks, his tone changing again to indicate he's not Rhys, but some future guy asking me out.

I pause, taking in the feedback he's given me. If it isn't Rhys asking me, but another guy, I'd say no. With the exception of last night, I don't like events that take place on weeknights. It interferes with my schedule.

"I'm busy tomorrow night."

"Okay. How about Thursday?" he asks.

"Um, I'll need to check my calendar and get back to you."

"That's perfect." His voice is back to normal but I'm not certain if the conversation with random future date guy is still happening.

"Are we still practicing?" I whisper as if that will keep us in character.

"No, Princess. You did good. Not committing right away leaves a guy wanting more."

I beam with pride.

"Real talk. There is a dinner party next week at my cousin Jerrod's. He's invited all the foundation board members and their significant others. It's a good opportunity for me to get some face time with the voting members, so I'll need you to attend with me."

"When is it?" I ask.

"Next Thursday night."

The Leg-Up showcase and fundraiser are Friday night.

Attending a dinner party the night before isn't ideal. I'd like to be snuggled up in bed by ten at the latest, but the dinner is fulfilling my side of the agreement so I'll have to make it work.

"That reminds me, I've got an event the following night. Remember I was telling you about Leg-Up? The showcase and fundraiser are next Friday night, and I guess I can bring a date."

It hadn't occurred to me before, but since I'm fake-dating Rhys, I should take full advantage of practicing in as many situations as possible.

"I'm at your service."

"Okay. Good."

That's when it occurs to me. Our date last night went well, but it was practice. Other than the photographers that were nosily waiting outside the restaurant, we weren't under a microscope. But, this dinner party, the one at Rhys's cousin's is meant for us to display our relationship to The Spencer Foundation board members, and convince them Rhys is capable of a committed relationship. It's the part of the arrangement where we'll need to act like a real couple and make it believable.

That overwhelming feeling I had when Rhys proposed this plan is back. *What if I can't pull off the ruse? What if they don't believe we're together and it ruins his chances at becoming board president?* I don't know if I can handle that kind of pressure.

"I can hear you freaking out through the phone."

"You can? I didn't say anything."

"It's the silence that tells me you're overthinking."

"Huh. Well, you're right. I am. I feel unprepared to pose as your girlfriend in front of a bunch of people. And the fundraiser is going to have family and friends there. We'll have to convince the people closest to us that we're dating."

"You want to come over later and we'll strategize?"

It occurs to me I don't even know where Rhys lives. I forgot to ask him last night.

"Okay, sure."

"I'll have Wanda pick you up around six."

"Sounds good."

CHAPTER 14

Colette

I would normally have a quick, light lunch before I head over to the Leg-Up studio for the Elements of Ballet class I teach on Wednesdays and then practice with Sebastian, but I told Chloe, Emma, and Sophie I would meet them for lunch today.

When I arrive at the bistro, the ladies are already seated. We exchange greetings and hugs before I sit down to check out the menu.

"I have to tell you all. I just finished the best fake-dating romance manuscript I've read in a long time," Chloe says. "The agent who pitched it found it in their slush pile. I'm obsessed with it. God, it was so good."

"That's really saying something because we all know how much fake dating is near and dear to your heart." Emma smirks.

"It is?" I ask, confused by the conversation. I also have no poker face, so I'm hoping my forehead doesn't have an *'I'm fake-dating Rhys'* neon sign flashing on it.

"Chloe and Barrett were fake dating before they got together for real," Emma says.

I blink. "Really? I didn't know that."

Chloe smiles, like she's recalling a fond memory. "Oh yeah, Barrett and I did not like each other."

"That's oversimplifying it. Barrett liked you but didn't know how to express his feelings so he was grumpy and that made you think he hated you, so you hated him back. Then you fell in love."

"Now who's oversimplifying it?" Chloe teases, turning from Emma back to me and Sophie. "She's skipping the part where Barrett walked in on me throwing an unauthorized bachelorette party in his mother's penthouse apartment and blackmailed me to fake date him if I didn't want him to tell his mom."

"Wow. Then what happened?" I ask.

Chloe laughs. "I was so annoyed with Barrett because he didn't tell me all the information before we met Fred Hinkle, the businessman he was trying to win over to land a deal. I didn't know our backstory and I was caught off guard."

Her comments have me thinking about the situation with Rhys.

"Did you and Barrett have to touch and kiss to make it believable?" I ask, wondering if I should be taking notes.

"Yes, which I was annoyed by at first because I thought he was a cold-hearted asshole. But then when I got to know him, he wasn't like that at all." Chloe pauses for a moment and her cheeks start to pinken. "And that's when things started to heat up between us."

Chloe points her fork at Emma. "I think Emma would agree that pretending to be in a relationship definitely ratchets up the sexual tension."

Emma smiles. "It's true. I wanted Griffin the moment I saw him, but getting drunkenly married in Vegas didn't seal the deal. It was much later, after we fell for each other, that made sex even more intense because we had waited so long."

These ladies are a wealth of information. And I had no idea that's how Chloe and Emma's relationships started.

"How did I not know this?" I ask, looking between them.

Emma shrugs. "We're all happy and settled now. I guess how our relationships started is only a fraction of the story."

Sophie laughs. "While I don't really want to talk about your and Griffin's sex life, I will admit, I wish I had been here to witness both of you ladies falling in love with your husbands."

"You were still in Las Vegas?"

"Yeah, Griffin came to New York with Emma for a few weeks while I was at a senior conference for my event planning degree."

I nod, remembering that Hannah had told me Sophie moved here after she graduated from UNLV. That Sophie and Hunter had hooked up in Las Vegas when he was there for work and she was out celebrating her graduation, and had been shocked when they were reconnected through Hannah's wedding planner and because Griffin was working with Hunter.

"Chloe, how did you and Barrett get to know each other when you were fake dating?" I ask, intrigued that I have a friend who has been in a similar situation that I am with Rhys, minus the blackmail part.

"We didn't. At least not at first. I thought we were going on one dinner date, but he blindsided me by telling Fred that we had been dating for six months and were in love. I was frazzled to say the least."

My heart rate ticks up a notch. While I'm fully aware of the board member dinner next week and the stakes our fake relationship holds for Rhys, Chloe's story has me again questioning if I can pull off our fake relationship in such an important setting.

"After that, it was a crash course. Sometimes I wonder if I should have made flash cards. You know, for background on each other, likes and dislikes, hobbies, and favorite things. So I would have been more prepared. But I'm a nerd like that."

Emma laughs, affectionately patting Chloe's arm. "Griffin and I played games and did a bunch of personality tests to prepare for the interview I had with Kandi Kline at *The Dress* magazine. Oh, and the Target date night scavenger hunt ended up being one of the favorite things we've ever done."

I'm mentally cataloging all this valuable information.

Emma sets her fork down and wipes at her mouth with her napkin. "But ultimately, we got to know each other by spending time together."

With my busy schedule, I don't have a lot of time, so flash cards might be the way to go. I discreetly pull my phone out and add index cards onto my list of things to pick up before I go over to Rhys's place tonight.

"Speaking of romance, I'm starting a book club."

Emma giggles. "I'm surprised it took you this long."

"I've been busy, but now that Barrett and I have been married for a year and our two pups are trained," across the table, Sophie snickers, and Chloe shoots her a look, before continuing, "well, for the most part. Anyways, this is something I've been wanting to do."

Chloe opens her e-reader and extends it out for the rest of us to see.

A gorgeous, shirtless man with a six-pack—no, an entire case of abs—arms covered in tattoos, with a seductive smile winks back at me. *Sweet baby Jesus.*

Fake Dating the Bad Boy. That's the title. *How is that the title?* And why is it making my palms sweat?

Oh, because that is my life right now.

I am literally fake dating a bad boy.

"That's the e-book cover." Chloe reaches into her St. Clair Press tote bag to pull out a stack of books.

"I love that you have your e-reader on hand," Sophie says.

Chloe smiles. "It's my emotional support e-reader."

Emma laughs. "I didn't know that was a thing."

"I bet you have a travel sewing kit stashed in your bag." Chloe nods to Emma's oversized purse.

Emma's laugh trails off. "Okay, yeah, I get it."

"Not everyone is into man chest covers, so I have discreet paperbacks for everyone." Chloe passes a book to each of us. "I want to share my love of reading romance with all of you."

"Thank you." I accept the book from Chloe and glance down at the cover. It's a pretty shade of lavender with a sweeping font scrolled on the front. It's in complete opposition to the sexy man chest cover Chloe just showed us.

Around me, the other ladies are celebrating the gift, eagerly examining its contents.

"You're my best friend, Chlo. Did you know that?" Emma grins, reading the back cover.

Sophie sighs. "I don't know if I can do this. I have a full-time job and twin baby girls."

"Book club is also girl time. You're still invited even if you don't read the book."

"It's not necessarily the time to read the book. It's what happens after. The last book you gave me made me incredibly horny. I'm already insanely attracted to Hunter. We have a lot of sex. When I read these books, it's like I'm insatiable. Hunter loves it, of course, but I find it impossible to control myself around him and I end up getting nothing done."

Hearing Sophie talk about her relationship with Hunter, their chemistry and clearly, very active sex life, makes me wonder what that would be like. Sex in general, but also sex with the man of your dreams. An image of Rhys pops into my brain. Clearly all the time we've spent together and this whole fake dating thing has tricked my brain into associating him with any talk of relationships and sex.

Emma giggles. "That's not a bad problem to have."

"It is if you're trying to plan multiple weddings, not to mention my own."

Chloe smiles. "Like I said, no pressure. Even if you don't read it, book club will be a fun time to catch up and talk."

"Is there anything we can do to help?" Emma asks Sophie.

"At this point, it's tasks like final meetings with vendors and tracking RSVPs." Sophie turns her attention to me. "Speaking of, you sent yours back a while ago with no plus one, but I'm curious if you would like to amend that now."

"Wait, why?" Chloe asks, turning to look at me. "Who is your plus one?"

Sophie shoots Chloe a look of surprise. "Have you been living under a rock?"

"More like living under a stack of books," Emma quips.

Chloe pins Emma with a teasing glare, but Emma pats her arm. "You know I love you for it."

"She's dating Rhys," Sophie says.

"Rhys Spencer?" Chloe asks, her jaw dropping. *"Oh my god.* I must have been so wrapped up with work and Barrett, I missed this exciting news."

With three sets of curious eyes all trained on me, I swallow a bite of my salmon and quinoa salad, then take a sip of water.

"It's new," I say, finally. "We reconnected at Hannah and James's wedding and we're seeing where it goes."

I want to pat myself on the back for how casual I sound. See, maybe I can be convincing.

Sophie sets her fork down. "Hunter's not one to get involved in other people's relationships but he was concerned when he saw you two dancing at the wedding and when it was confirmed that you two were dating, he had some opinions on it, that's for sure." Sophie doesn't have to elaborate on Hunter's opinions for me to know what was likely said. It's the same reason why Rhys needs me to be his fake girlfriend. His reputation for sleeping around and partying doesn't exactly make him great boyfriend material.

I nod, not surprised by Hunter's apprehension about me

and Rhys. "Hunter's like a brother to me, so I can see how he might be concerned."

"I'm curious what Hannah thinks." Emma takes a bite of her chicken sandwich, then washes it down with Diet Coke. "Have you talked to her?"

Since Hannah left for her honeymoon, I've gotten one text from her. A picture of her and James arriving at their resort, drinks in their hands, and tired, but blissful smiles on their faces. Maybe it's a blessing that Hannah is out of the loop right now. That she isn't calling or texting me asking about the new relationship between me and Rhys that came out of nowhere.

"No, not yet. I didn't want to bring it up before she left for her honeymoon. The timing didn't feel right."

When I'd agreed to the fake relationship with Rhys, I hadn't given any thought to needing to explain the relationship to friends or family. I'd been solely focused on how the act of dating could help me find passion in my dancing in time for fall evaluations and the role selection for *Rubies*. But after this conversation, it's clear I need to work on my enthusiasm for our relationship.

Chloe's already got the picture of me and Rhys pulled up. The one he took of us on my couch to confirm we were dating. "Aw, I think you two are cute together."

Emma reaches forward to show her phone screen.

"Forget cute. This picture is hot," she says, her jaw dropping as she glances back over to me. "The way he looks at you."

My face flushes.

It's the one from our date. Rhys's hand possessively wrapped around my waist as we walk inside. My nipples pebbled beneath the silk of the slip dress. When Isabella told me to make my nipples a fashion statement, I didn't realize they'd actually be hitting the tabloids.

"You two look so freaking good together." Sophie fans her

face. "The sexual tension in that photo alone is making me sweat."

"How many dates have you been on?" Emma asks at the same time Chloe starts talking. "Are you officially in a relationship or is it casual?"

Sophie's eyes widen. "Have you always had feelings for him?"

My mouth hangs open trying to sort out their rapid-fire questions. Before I can respond, my phone buzzes with the notification that I've got class in thirty minutes. *Saved by the buzz!*

"Oh, shoot. I've got to get to my class." I take one last sip of water before I start gathering my things, pretending like I didn't just sidestep their questions.

Sophie checks her watch. "I've got to get back to work, too."

Chloe waves the paperback at me. "Don't forget your book!"

"Thanks!"

After hugs goodbye and promises to join the group chat to discuss the book, I toss the paperback in my bag and leave the restaurant for my class at Leg-Up.

On the walk, I think about what Chloe shared. How she'd wished she was more prepared for playing her part as Barrett's girlfriend. Preparation is my middle name, so I take it as a sign that Rhys and I need to spend more time practicing for the dinner party next week and tonight, that's exactly what we'll be doing.

CHAPTER 15

Rhys

"You live on a boat?"

Lettie stands on the dock, squinting at me from under her pink New York Yankees hat. She's in black spandex shorts and an oversized white t-shirt with her long, dark hair spilling over her shoulders. A jean jacket folded over her arms and a beige tote bag hangs from one shoulder.

The answer is obvious, I do live on a boat, but Lettie's question runs deeper than simply being surprised by the idea that someone has chosen a home on the water. It's because as a man who lost both his parents in a boating accident fifteen years ago, it's an interesting choice.

"Yeah, this is home. For now."

"Until you decide to sail off into the sunset?" she asks, a curious smile on her lips.

"Something like that." I extend my hand to her. "You want to come aboard?"

"Yeah." She slips off her tennis shoes, then takes my hand to step on. I can't help but check out her ass when she bends over.

"I feel overdressed." She eyes my naked torso as she passes into the main living area, her gaze following the ink of my tattoo from my forearm to where it wraps over my shoulder and the left side of my chest.

Whether Lettie's in a silk dress or a t-shirt and leggings, she always looks good. And the spandex biker shorts she's wearing right now are no exception.

"This is boat life attire. Clothing optional." While I like to get dressed up to go out, when I'm at home or out on the water, I'm used to being shirtless and dressed down. It's all those shirtless summers I spent at Lake George. It's ingrained in my blood.

"Hmm." She glances around the space before her eyes settle back on me. "You missed a button." Her finger waves in the direction of my jeans where the top button is undone.

I shrug. "That's how I like it. It's comfortable."

"Like a woman taking off her bra after a long day?" she asks.

"Be my guest, Princess. No bras required here."

Her eyes skate over my naked torso again. "Yeah, I'm good."

She sets her tote bag down on the coffee table, and glances around the space.

"I thought Wanda was messing with me when she dropped me at the boat slip entrance."

I would have joined when Wanda went to pick Lettie up from practice but I picked up Mo from the shelter today, so I was getting him settled in. It didn't help that as soon as I opened the cat carrier door, he bolted and I've spent the last hour looking for him.

Lettie looks around. "Where's Maurice?"

"He's around here somewhere," I say, yanking the tag off the brand-new cat bed before I casually toss it onto the couch. "He's being shy."

When I invited Lettie over, I hadn't anticipated that Mo would need some time to adapt to his new surroundings. I figured he'd be as cuddly and playful as he was at the shelter, but after making one round of the main-level living room, he bolted. All the doors have been shut, so I'm certain he's hiding inside somewhere.

"Oh my gosh. Is that a Litter Robot 4?" Lettie points to the self-cleaning litterbox Ramsey set up for Mo earlier.

"Um, yeah. I think so."

"I'm jealous. I love Maxine, but god, I hate scooping her poop."

"I'll buy you one." I've got unlimited funds so a two-hundred-dollar self-cleaning litterbox is nothing, but the way Lettie lights up at the suggestion has me immediately reaching for my phone to text Ramsey.

"I can't let you do that."

"Of course you can, Princess. And it's already on its way." I wave my phone to show her that it's been ordered before setting my phone back on the counter. "Besides, when I bring Mo over, he'll use it, too."

Lettie laughs. "Nothing says romance like fresh cat litter."

"Do you want a tour?" I ask.

"Sure."

I show her around the main living and dining area, then downstairs to the state rooms, the galley, and crew quarters.

She looks around the crew quarters which is made up of three small sleeping cabins and a galley kitchen. "Does anyone stay here with you?"

"My assistant, Ramsey, does. But he's in one of the state rooms. He has too much stuff to fit in one of these cabins."

"Do you cook?" she asks, taking in the spotless, and mostly bare kitchen.

"I have most of my meals catered by a chef, or I go out."

I lead her down the hallway, past the three guest state rooms, one of which is Ramsey's, to the master stateroom.

"And this is my room."

I chuckle watching her stand in the doorway craning her neck to look in.

"You can come in."

"I don't want to pry. Bedroom spaces are private and I wasn't sure if there was anything you didn't want me to see."

I glance around. Like the rest of the yacht, my bedroom is spotless. Dark wood headboard and nightstands. Navy bedding.

"I am capable of picking up after myself."

"Where's your closet?" she asks.

I motion toward the open door. When she takes in all the clothes, her eyes widen and she laughs lightly.

"It's like you crammed your entire personality into this one room. There's nothing out there, but in here," she pulls out a plaid Valentino suit, "it's so vibrant."

Seeing the space through Lettie's eyes makes me realize that while this is where I'm staying, I don't *live* here. There's nothing personal besides the clothes in my closet. I could pick up and leave at a moment's notice if I wanted to. Even though I own the yacht, I've never made it a home. It's temporary, like my time here in the city.

"Yeah, that's my typical wardrobe, but this," I motion to the section of the closet that is now filled with the charcoal, navy, and beige suits and solid-colored dress shirts, "is what I need to wear now to prove I'm serious about the board position."

"Sounds like you're not happy about that."

She turns to find me leaning against the island in the middle of the closet.

"It's part of the role I need to play."

Her eyes drop to my bare torso for a moment before lifting back to mine.

"Like us fake dating?" She asks.

"Yeah."

Lettie's eyes drop again and this time she motions to my still undone button. "That button is making me twitchy. It's like an unfinished task. I don't like it."

I laugh as her gaze drops to the button again.

"It reminds me of eating too much on Thanksgiving and needing to unbutton the top button of your pants. But you don't look like you overate." She waves toward my stomach. "You're all muscly and toned with your six pack."

I place my hands on my hips and give her a cheeky grin. "Are you checking me out?" I tease.

She scoffs but I can see the way her cheeks pinken at the idea of being called out on it.

"There's so much skin. I can't *not* look." Her gaze skims over my left arm. "I had no idea your tattoo went all the way up to your shoulder and chest. Is that Lake George?" She points to the inked body of water and surrounding trees across my left pec.

"Yeah." I nod. "Want a closer look?"

When she steps closer, I immediately regret offering. Her feminine scent floods my senses, but instead of wanting to pull back, I have the strongest desire to bury my nose in her hair and breathe her in more.

"It's beautiful." Her hand lifts to hover over my skin. She's not touching me, yet I can feel her all the same.

"Yeah."

She's staring at my tattoo, but I'm looking at her.

"When did you get it?" she asks.

"I started it a few years ago. Did the lake first on my chest, then kept adding to it from there."

"For your parents." Her eyes lift to mine and seeing heartfelt sympathy in those pools of blue nearly knocks me off balance.

I nod, my throat suddenly constricted with emotion. I don't talk about my parents. There's no one to talk about them with. My grandfather has never been the type to get emotional or reminisce, he's more of the mind what's done is done and move on. While I did therapy early on to address the trauma of losing them, I was a teenage boy who didn't want to open up and felt more comfortable pushing down my emotions. Out of sight, out of mind.

Lettie's fingertips dance over the ink on my bicep and immediately my skin turns to gooseflesh. I didn't expect her touch to affect me this way. Featherlight traces on my skin as she makes her way over the curve of my shoulder and across my collar bone. I remember how intense the pain had been when my tattoo artist had done that part. How the physical pain had brought up so much emotion that I'd immediately pushed it back down again.

Even as I watch Lettie's fingertips make their way down toward my chest, her destination clear, I'm not anticipating the reaction. Her fingernails trace lightly over the trees and my nipples tighten in response. Then, her hand splays out over my left pec, her palm pressing gently into my skin that is covered by the inky water of Lake George, right above my heart.

A sharp pain pierces my sternum and radiates through my chest. Beneath Lettie's palm, my heart thumps wildly. Erratically.

What the fuck is happening to me?

My reflex is to grab her wrist. To make her stop making me feel whatever the hell this is.

She steps back, but my hand is still holding her wrist, keeping it at a safe distance, like it's a branding iron that's going to burn me.

"I'm sorry," she says.

I drop her wrist. "It's fine. I—"

Before I can attempt to explain what just happened, a loud meow sounds at our feet, cutting the tension between us. It's Mo. He's been coaxed out of hiding and is now rubbing his body against Lettie's legs.

"Aww. There you are." Lettie scoops the brown tabby up and snuggles him to her face. "Hi, Maurice. Or do you prefer Mo?" she asks, cuddling him to her chest.

I'm relieved that Mo came out of hiding, even more so that he helped break the tension in the room. I watch them for a moment, then turn away to open a drawer and pull out a t-shirt, still trying to understand what just passed between me and Lettie.

Many women have touched me there before, explored my skin and my tattoo, but Lettie's hands on me felt different. It ignited something in me that I'm not ready to address. And while my tattoo has been healed for years now, it's what's underneath that is still wounded and scarred.

She saw *me.*

The longing. The loneliness. The hurt.

I pull the t-shirt over my head, letting it serve as a barrier between me and Lettie and these unwanted thoughts. This moment is a reminder that I need to keep my relationship with her in the shallow end, close to the shore, and not wade out to deeper water.

I need to keep things light and fun, and that's what I plan to do.

CHAPTER 16

Colette

I give Mo's back another stroke before he walks off. He sniffs along the carpet as he tentatively explores the rest of the space. His behavior reminds me of when I first brought Maxine home to my apartment, like he's seeing everything for the first time.

"What's in the bag?" Rhys asks, entering the living area pulling my attention from the brown tabby.

He's wearing a shirt now. *Thank god.*

Being around a shirtless Rhys is not for the faint of heart. And that undone button on his jeans? Ridiculously hot, yet also unnerving because why wouldn't you finish fastening your pants? It's utter madness.

And speaking of things that are irrational, I wonder if I was imagining that there was something crackling between us a minute ago in his closet.

I'd been exploring his tattoo. Taking in the way the artist had perfectly captured the dreamy summertime landscape of our youth. The only major difference being the black ink and its various shades of gray that muted the typically vibrant colors of Lake George.

When my palm spread over his smooth skin, I'd felt his

heart beating rapidly beneath it. I'd been surprised to witness the rest of his body respond to my touch. The way his nipples pulled tight and his breathing became shallow and uneven. Then he'd grabbed my wrist and it had felt like I'd encountered an electric current.

Dangerous yet exciting. *Alive.*

It had me wanting more.

I distract myself from the thought by reaching into the bag to pull out the set of markers and the notecards I started making earlier. "Notecards for our likes and dislikes, interests and hobbies."

"And why do we need those?" Rhys asks.

Because I refuse to be in a situation where I don't have control.

I ignore the pesky thought and give him a less vulnerable answer.

"So, we can get to know each other more quickly. Appear to be a real couple. Chloe told me that's what people do when they're fake dating."

"You told Chloe St. Clair that we're fake dating?" he asks.

"No, I just asked about her and Barrett. How they navigated the fake dating thing. She was an excellent resource."

"She told you to make flash cards?"

"No, this is my own process. I like that they're small and can fit in my purse." I hold one I've already cut up for him. "And be easily referenced."

He takes the notecard.

"I color coded them. Yellow for me. Blue for you."

"Why do I get blue?" he asks.

"Yellow is my favorite color. Blue is yours."

Rhys shakes his head. "Blue isn't my favorite color."

My brows lift. "It was when we were younger."

"I liked blue back then, but I'm older and more mature now."

"So, what's your favorite color now?" I ask.

A sly grin spreads across his face. "Pink."

I laugh because it's unexpected. "Seriously?"

"Yes. Men can like pink."

"Yes, of course they can." I can't help but smile at his insistence. "And why do you like it?"

He laughs. "Because someone once told me I couldn't and I thought fuck that. Now, it's my favorite color."

"A rebel without a cause."

He nods. "I wore a salmon-colored suit to the board meeting last week. My cousin, Jerrod, was personally offended so it was worth it."

"Fine. I'll make note of that here." I hold up the favorites card, which includes color, food, drink, scent, movie, musician, and book. "But I'm not changing your color scheme. I already made the cards."

"Aren't these all things we'll learn as we go?" Rhys asks.

"This speeds up the process."

He takes the stack of cards I've made for him to fill out. The mention of his cousin has me wondering exactly what has been going on between them.

"What's the situation with you and Jerrod? I thought you two were close growing up."

Rhys scoffs. "Close competitors."

"I do remember there being some tension between you two but I thought it was teenage boy stuff. Hormones and egos trying to best each other."

"Unfortunately, we didn't grow out of it, he wants the president of the board position to spite me. To take something that is rightfully mine. It's the same shit that I dealt with when we were younger."

The words are stated matter of fact, but a flicker of hurt crosses his face.

"I'm sorry." I don't know what else to say.

"It doesn't matter. What matters now is that I win."

The look of determination on his face is intense. I've

always seen Rhys as a laid back, go with the flow, nothing gets under his skin kind of guy.

Rhys takes the notecards I've outlined for him and starts filling them out.

I watch him for a moment before returning my attention to the notecard I'm filling out, more curious than ever about his relationship with Jerrod. It's clearly contentious if Rhys feels like he must compete with Jerrod for the presidency of the foundation that his own parents created.

While the Spencer family has always been known for their wealth and entrepreneurial undertakings, Wes and Abigail put The Spencer Foundation on the map because of who they were as people. Yes, money is necessary, especially with non-profit organizations, as I'm learning with my work at Leg-Up, but it was the way they showed up and were a part of the community that made the difference.

I see that in Rhys, but it seems right now he's too caught up in the competition with Jerrod to realize what he truly has to offer.

"What else do you think we should know about each other?" I ask.

"I've got a whole list." He waves his phone at me.

My face lights up, excited he's taking this seriously. "Is it another 'this or that'?"

"Sort of."

"Okay." I nod for him to proceed with his question.

"Shower or bubble bath."

"Shower. It's efficient. I have trouble relaxing in a bath."

"Probably because you haven't had a bath in my tub before." He winks. "I'm a bubble bath man all the way."

I picture Rhys surrounded in bubbles in his giant bathtub and laugh. "Next."

"Neck or lips?"

I blink, confused by the question.

"In what way?"

"Where you liked to be kissed."

"Oh." I clear my throat while my mind races.

Do I have a preference? Only one guy has ever kissed my neck and he's currently pinning me from across the coffee table with his wildly expressive hazel eyes.

"What kind of questions are these?" I ask.

"Spicy 'this or that' for couples."

"Why would we need to know that?"

"We're working on our intimacy. Young, hot couples like us would be fucking a lot, exploring each other's bodies, so since we're not doing *that*, this is the next best thing."

"Is it?" I gulp. I don't know what to focus on first. The fact that he called us a young, hot couple or that he said we would normally be fucking a lot.

"Okay, we'll skip the 'this or that' spicy edition."

"Great. Thank you."

"Let's try something else."

I glance over to find Rhys staring at me. If I'm not mistaken, his eyes are studying my lips.

"Who was your first kiss?" he asks.

I swallow thickly, feeling the same wave of heat I'd experienced with Rhys in his closet slide over my body. "That's a random question."

"Is it?"

"I doubt that's going to come up in conversation at Jerrod's dinner party."

He lifts his brows. "Do you want to be prepared?"

My eyes narrow warily, but he's got me there. Of course I want to be prepared. And if I apply his same reasoning for the lap straddle, that if we talk about these more intimate details now, then surface level topics will be easy to pull off later in public, then it makes sense.

"I was sixteen and it was a boy from junior dance academy. Jeremy Castle. What about you?"

"Fourteen. A girl from school." His eyebrows furrow like he's struggling to recall her name.

"You don't remember her name?" I ask.

"Let's say there have been many since. Was he also your first?"

"First what?" I ask, my growing suspicion of what he's asking starting to make my hands sweat.

"Hook-up. Sex. Fuck."

My brain short circuits. I bolt upright from my seat on the floor banging my knee on the coffee table as I go. When I reach for my knee, I knock the glass of water off the table and Mo scurries across the room, running for his life.

It's pandemonium. It's chaos. And I think I've avoided the sex talk, thank god. But just for reassurance, I start collecting my stuff.

"I'm hungry. I think we need to go get some snacks. Where's the nearest Trader Joe's?"

"We don't need to go to the grocery store." He reaches for his phone. "I can order in dinner. It'll take two minutes."

My shoulders deflate. I know I should push through the anxiety and discomfort, but it's like a really challenging rehearsal, I need a short break to regroup.

"I need to get some other stuff for practice tomorrow. I'm not a good hangry person, you know this."

He stares at me a moment, then starts to nod slowly.

"Sure. Let's go."

Whew. That was a close one.

CHAPTER 17

Rhys

I could have had food delivered, but Lettie insisted we go out because she needed to pick up a few snacks for the rest of the week. Part of me thinks it was a distraction technique she employed to avoid the conversation we were having.

I know I was pushing it with asking those spicy 'this or that' questions, especially after I'd felt that connection with her in my closet, but it's hard to hold back because the more I learn about this grown-up version of Lettie, the more I want to know.

I'm aware that Lettie has anxiety about dating, but until we were discussing those intimate topics, it hadn't occurred to me that she is inexperienced with all aspects of relationships, including sex. I've never been much of a dater. Relationships have been non-existent, yet I've had a lot of sex. One doesn't always equal the other, but in Lettie's case, I'm wondering if it does.

I wonder if she's a virgin.

As we walk through the grocery aisles, Lettie randomly stops to place items into the cart I'm pushing. It's very domestic. Ramsey would cackle if he saw me right now. I'm almost tempted to take a photo to prove that I do know where food comes from and how to obtain it.

Lettie sets a bag of trail mix in the cart.

I pick it up to study the contents.

"I thought you said you didn't eat candy."

"It's not candy. It's trail mix."

"With candy in it." I verify the ingredients and to my absolute horror, she's right, there is some fake chocolate substitute trying to pass as a beloved candy. "You gave up the delicious goodness of Reese's Pieces for generic candy pieces?" I ask.

She laughs. "I had no idea you'd be so passionate about it."

"And this bag is full of raisins. You hate raisins."

She blinks, staring up at me with surprise. "How do you remember that?"

I shrug. "I remember a lot of things." A memory surfaces, causing a smile to pull at my lips. "Like how Hunter and I convinced you and Hannah that raisins were shriveled up squirrel nut sacks."

A laugh bursts from her as we turn the aisle into the produce section.

"That was disturbing on many levels, but it's not the only reason I don't like them. They get stuck in my teeth. I don't like most dried fruit for that reason."

The raisin discussion only sidetracks my brain for a moment, then it's right back to thinking about Lettie and sex.

On one hand, I really shouldn't push her on it. It's her personal business.

But we're friends and if it helps our relationship be more convincing, I think we should talk about these things. Also, now I'm beyond curious if Lettie is a virgin. I shouldn't care, I shouldn't have thoughts about it, but now that my brain has gotten hold of it, it's impossible to think of anything else.

I decide if I'm going to ask her, I've got to come out and

ask. Leading into things with Lettie only gives her more time to overthink and panic. I'm going to rip this off just like I used to do for her band-aids that got too sticky when we were kids.

We sidle up to the fruit section where Lettie starts inspecting the apples.

"You've had sex, right?" I ask.

At my completely random topic change, Lettie's already erect back stiffens. "We're in the middle of a grocery store," she whisper-hisses. "And what does that have to do with anything?"

That's a good question. Nothing, really, except my own curiosity.

I raise my hands in surrender. "Nothing."

We move to the other side of the produce case in silence, me following her as she selects a red bell pepper, the topic clearly dropped.

Or is it? My mind was already running wild and now that the question is out there, I'm even more curious.

Is Lettie a virgin?

Has she given head before?

I wonder if she's had an orgasm?

Lettie suddenly whips around to face me.

"I've had an orgasm before!" she shouts as if in response to the question I didn't ask out loud.

The woman shopping with her toddler in the cart on the other side of the produce case opens her mouth in shock, looking between us before promptly rushing away.

Lettie's eyes widen. "Oh, fudge."

I wave it off. "I'm sure she's heard worse." I lean closer to her and lower my voice since she's concerned about it. "And I'd fucking hope you've had an orgasm, but that wasn't the question."

My eyes drop to the white vegetable in front of us and pick it up. It looks like an oversized, white carrot. Not as dick-shaped as I would have liked for demonstration purposes but

I'm not sure where the cucumbers or eggplants are located, so this will have to do.

I lift it up between us, brows raised.

"Penetration."

Lettie sweeps one foot out to the side before bringing her foot to rest on the inside of her other leg. It's some kind of ballet move and also appears to be some kind of nervous twitch. "I've used a vibrator and a dildo before."

I'm starting to wonder if she's a figure skater, not a ballet dancer, for how much she's skating around this issue.

"Has a real dick ever been inside your pussy, Princess?" I ask.

She pulls her bottom lip between her teeth and shakes her head. "No."

I nod slowly, but my body's response to Lettie's confession isn't as I expected. A warm sensation floods my chest, and all the blood in my body rushes downward toward my dick. The appendage is swelling with the thought that it would be perfect for the task of deflowering Lettie.

All I can think about is how warm and tight she'd be. The thought of stretching her for the first time, filling her up until she's at the brink. Her snug pussy wrapped around me, constricting my cock as I pump into her.

My brain finally chimes in. *What the fuck, man? This is Lettie. No fucking way.*

Clearly my current state of celibacy is starting to affect my judgment.

"That doesn't change things, right?" Her big blue eyes stare up at me with concern.

It shouldn't change anything. We agreed there'd be nothing physical between us outside of keeping up appearances in public. Touching. Kissing. That's all.

But for some reason I'm struggling to look at her the same. To keep my filthy imagination from concocting a multitude of dirty thoughts about her.

If I thought she was flawless before, now that I know she's untouched, she's even more perfect. *And off-limits.*

Lettie doesn't have a big brother that would come for me if I teased her and played with her, then fucked her senseless before sending her on her way.

No, *I'm* the guy that used to be her protector. That's the role I filled in her life when we were growing up. I can't be thinking about her like that.

But she's not Lettie spaghetti anymore. She's this beautiful, talented woman who deserves the perfect guy. And I'm not that guy.

"Rhys?" Lettie breaks through my runaway thoughts.

I have to remind myself what the goal is here. To convince the foundation board that I'm the right person for the president position. Lettie playing my girlfriend is an important part of that, but her virginity has nothing to do with our fake relationship.

"Yeah. It doesn't change anything." I drop the overgrown carrot back onto the pile, but Lettie selects two and places them in her cart.

"What the hell are those?" I ask, trying to steer my mind away from our previous conversation.

"Parsnips."

I nod, listening as Lettie explains how they're a good starch substitute and are naturally sweet.

As we move through the remaining aisles and I help Lettie bag her groceries, I can't stop thinking about our conversation. Fuck. I wish I could go back and stop myself from asking her. From finding out that Lettie's a virgin, which has no relevance in our fake relationship other than to drive my imagination wild.

You know what they say, curiosity killed the cat.

CHAPTER 18

Colette

Sebastian stands behind me to get into position for the lift. It's a lift that Alexei has been working on with us over the last few weeks and we've decided to incorporate into the showcase for the Leg-Up fundraiser. He wraps me around his back before swooping me between his arms. At the final position my face is only inches from the floor. It's a trust fall at its finest. If Sebastian misses the cue, I'll be needing rhinoplasty.

We nail the lift then move into the last sequence before holding our final position.

Two breaths later, we stand and look at each other.

"Holy shit." Sebastian wraps me in his arms, and I laugh into his chest. "We nailed it."

"That was so good, right?"

"Fucking phenomenal. If I wasn't so sweaty, I'd give you a hug." He reaches for the towel hanging on the barre. "You want to celebrate with a drink at The Smith?" he asks.

"I would but I have plans with Rhys."

"Ah, that's right. The boyfriend." He says it like he's putting quotation marks around boyfriend. "Fine. Ditch me. See if I care."

"You'll have a million other people to talk to."

"I know." He sighs. "I'm very popular."

"Modest, too," I tease.

As I part ways with Sebastian at the women's locker room entrance, my mind wanders to Rhys.

It's been two days since we hung out. Since I told him I was a virgin in not so many words.

Has a real dick ever been inside your pussy, Princess?

The way he'd licked his bottom lip after he asked me that has been playing over and over in my mind.

I'd been self-conscious to tell him, but relieved at the same time. I wasn't sure what to make of his reaction. He'd gotten really quiet, bagged up my groceries and later, after we finished exchanging our finished note cards at his place, he had Wanda take me home.

I know it doesn't matter if I'm a virgin. I've explored my own body to know what I like, but just like a pas de deux, I'm sure sex with a partner makes things more fun, more *rewarding*. And hopefully someday, I'll find a guy that I want to take that step with.

The warm water in the shower feels so good, I linger for a few extra minutes. The additional practices to prepare for the showcase have left my body sore and exhausted, even more than usual. After I change and gather my things, I collapse on a bench outside the practice studio while I'm waiting for Rhys.

I'm surprised when Sebastian sneaks up behind me and lightly squeezes my shoulder. "Last chance for drinks."

"Ow." My muscles are tender and I wince with the contact.

His brows knit with concern. "You okay?"

"Yeah, I changed up my cross-training routine and my shoulders have been super sore. I need to book a massage with Dani, I've been too busy to fit it into my schedule." I know self-care is important, but between my rehearsals for the Leg-Up showcase fundraiser and all the time I've been practicing dating with Rhys, it hasn't been my priority.

"Want me to give you a quick massage?" he asks.

A few summers back, Sebastian spent his off season in Costa Rica and took a massage therapy course. He's never formally practiced but he's a lifesaver when we're in a pinch.

I'd been planning to pull out my massage gun when I get home, but if Sebastian is offering, I'm not going to pass up a chance to get some relief.

"That would be great."

Under Sebastian's hands, my muscles melt. As he works the knots in my deltoids, it's a cross between pain and pleasure.

"It would be better if I had some oils."

With smooth strokes, he concentrates his efforts against the muscle along my shoulder blade.

"I don't know, this feels really good." I sigh, trying to relax as his hands work their magic. "But also, like I want to punch you in the face."

Sebastian laughs but continues to work his thumbs up the side of my neck.

I've got my eyes closed, but a familiar tingle across my skin, one that has nothing to do with Sebastian's massage, has them flying open.

Walking toward us like a young David Gandy on the runway is Rhys.

Underneath his tan suit, the top two buttons of his shirt are undone. My eyes drop to his shirt and as he gets closer, I can make out the floral print on it. It's subtle and not over the top like some of the outfits I've seen him photographed in. I smile at how it's so perfectly Rhys. Playful, and rebellious, not caring what other people think. Except he doesn't look particularly playful right now.

He removes his sunglasses and his sharp gaze lands on Sebastian.

"You can take your hands off my girlfriend now."

My brows reach for my hairline at his icy tone. That's not what I was expecting from him at all.

Sebastian lifts his hands off my shoulders. "No problem."

"Colette." Rhys's gaze warms when it lands on me, yet there's a boatload of intensity in that one word.

He sounds so serious; I'm half-expecting him to challenge Sebastian to a duel.

The thought has me biting my lip to stifle a laugh.

Rhys is never this stern.

It's confusing.

There's no reason for him to be giving off what Chloe would describe as 'touch her and die' vibes with Sebastian. He should save this acting for when we're with people that he needs to convince he's serious about me.

"Rhys, this is Sebastian." I motion between them and Sebastian extends his hand. "We're in the company together and he's my partner in the showcase for the Leg-Up fundraiser.

"Sebastian, this is Rhys," I continue, hoping to cut the tension that has settled upon us.

"Her boyfriend," Rhys says, smugness etched on his features.

Sebastian chuckles. "So, I've heard."

"Good." Rhys's perfect lips twist into a devilish smirk before he sets his sights on me again. "You ready, beautiful?"

"Y-yeah." I nod, reaching for my bag on the bench, which Rhys promptly takes and throws over his shoulder. "See you tomorrow, Sebastian."

"You bet. Let me know if you want to set up a session." He wiggles his fingers to indicate a massaging motion. "You're really tight and I didn't quite get all the way in there."

Sebastian's talking about my tight back and shoulder muscles but my face flushes at the way he makes it sound.

"That won't be necessary," Rhys answers for me, his clenched jaw making the words come out gruff.

"I can do full body as well," Sebastian calls, his teasing tone evidence that he knows he's gotten under Rhys's skin, and is enjoying it.

I attempt to scold him with a head shake but his wide, boyish grin makes it impossible to do anything but smile.

Rhys reaches for my hand and starts leading me toward the curb.

The way his hand firmly holds mine, commanding, yet gentle is familiar, yet it makes my stomach flutter.

I turn to look up at Rhys, his jaw still clenched tightly, his neck muscles straining under the associated tension. I've never considered a man's neck to be sexy, but I'm enthralled by the way his Adam's apple bobs as he swallows.

"What was that?" I ask.

"What?" He shrugs.

"Back there. With Sebastian? You were being rude."

"Rude?" He scoffs. "I wasn't the one with my hands all over someone else's girlfriend."

My brows lift. "All that because he was giving me a massage? Sebastian's my friend. We've been dancing together for years."

I laugh, but Rhys doesn't look amused. It's preposterous to think there would be anything between me and Sebastian. He's like a brother to me, supportive and fiercely loyal.

He stops suddenly, turning to face me.

"I didn't like seeing his hands on you. No boyfriend would want to see that."

"Not even a fake one?" I ask, trying to lighten the mood.

His jaw stays set like it was cast in stone.

"Besides, that was nothing. When we're dancing, his hands are all over me."

I mean for it to be comforting. To prove that Sebastian and I are comfortable with each other from being in one another's personal space all the time, but as Rhys's gaze narrows, and his eyes darken, I realize that he didn't find my comment reassuring at all.

Oops.

A deep rumble escapes from Rhys's throat.

Wait. Was that…a *growl*?

Oh my god. It was. Rhys just *growled*.

I'll have to tell Chloe and the other ladies.

I'm thinking about what they're going to say about this when I notice Rhys's hardened gaze is still pinning me into place. This time there's no conspiratorial smirk or knowing wink.

Wow. Rhys is really committed to playing the part of jealous boyfriend here.

Hmm, I wonder what a *real* girlfriend would do in this situation?

I'm thinking she'd try to comfort her boyfriend, make him feel appreciated and wanted. The thought of making Rhys feel that way does something funny to me.

I wrap my arms around his neck. With that singular move, his jaw eases, so I know it's a good start.

His scent surrounds me, warm and spicy with a hint of pine, like a hot summer day at the lake.

My eyes zero in on his lips. They're still in a flat line, but the pronounced dip in the middle of his upper lip gives him a pouty appearance. It's one of my favorite things about his mouth.

Is that weird? To have a favorite thing about your fake boyfriend's mouth? Especially since I've never felt it?

That leads to a whole slew of questions.

Should I kiss him? Does he want me to? This is technically public, right? Will he think it's part of the arrangement or just because I wanted to? Do I care?

While I'm analyzing, Rhys's hands move to wrap tightly around my waist. It's such a simple movement, yet when he puts his hands on my body, it feels possessive, like he's claiming me.

Arousal blooms in my core, and it scatters all the over-thinking thoughts.

"Does this make it better?" I whisper, before lifting onto my toes to deliver a soft kiss to his lips.

It's a sweet kiss. A peck.

When I pull back, I find that the clenched muscle in Rhys's jaw has softened.

"Yeah," he whispers, his hazel gaze dropping to my mouth.

The pressure of his firm lips on mine has me wanting more.

I want to know what he tastes like.

The thought comes out of nowhere.

Okay, not *nowhere,* it's been floating around in my brain since I saw him at Hannah and James's wedding, but it's the first time I'm acknowledging it.

I want to kiss Rhys.

There. I said it.

For practice. Besides, what's the point of having a fake boyfriend to practice with if I'm not taking advantage of all the features? He said we'd need to touch and kiss in public, yet the kissing part has been nonexistent.

"What about this?" I use the leverage of my hands around his neck to pull him down to me. This time, when our lips meet, I slide my tongue against his bottom lip. He welcomes me there with a lick of his own.

I start to pull back again, but he chases my mouth. His lips crashing down again as his arms tighten around my body, holding me to him.

"Fuck, yes."

A rumble finds its way out of his throat. It's the antithesis to the moody growl that escaped him earlier.

My heart hammers in my chest as Rhys's mouth devours

mine. I thought I was in control, but his skilled mouth is easily reminding me I have no business trying to seduce him.

It's practice, I reassure myself. And the sidewalk outside Lincoln Center is as public as it gets.

I'm planning to make this spot my new home when Rhys's mouth releases me. I'm immediately having withdrawals.

My eyelashes flutter open to find him staring at me. He looks confused.

I clear my throat but that doesn't stop the visions I'm having of repeating that all over again with Rhys pressing me against a wall. Good lord, Chloe's romance novels are filling my head with all sorts of ideas.

"That's what I would have done if we were really dating. Since you were upset about me and Sebastian," I offer as an explanation. "Also, I thought it was important to know what you taste like. In case there's a quiz or something. I'd hate to be unprepared."

He sweeps his thumb over my bottom lip, the evidence of our kiss still lingering there.

"What do I taste like, Princess?" he asks.

"Mint. Spice. A fever dream I don't want to wake up from." Did he slip me some truth serum or am I just that bad at not being completely transparent?

His mouth lifts at the corner. "That's very specific."

"What about me? What do I taste like?" I ask.

It's purely research. I'll need to know if my breath is bad or if there's anything I can improve on for future kisses. Not necessarily with Rhys, because that's not what I should be focusing on, but at this moment I'm having a hard time imagining kissing anyone else.

"Like you're mine."

I blink because I'm not sure what that means. I'm debating whether I should ask or if it will only demonstrate my inexperience even more when his hands glide up my back and my sore muscles tense again.

That's all he says as he guides me the rest of the way to the curb. After that scorching hot kiss, it takes me a moment to reacquaint myself. I'm staring at a black SUV.

Disappointment hits. "You didn't ride your bike?"

"I thought you didn't like my bike."

He's right. I'd been annoyed at first because it was big and scary and overwhelming. And the dress I had been wearing wasn't the right attire for a motorcycle, but I'm in leggings now.

I shrug. "I was going to give it another shot." Especially the way it felt to wrap my arms around his waist and hold on tight. And let's not forget that one time when we were at a stoplight and he placed his hand on my bare thigh, letting those long fingers tease the sensitive skin on my leg.

He opens the door for me. "I think you'll be happy once you're inside."

He's right. My eyes light at the sight of my favorite trail mix. It's packed in a small pink zipper pouch. One of those reusable ones that Sophie uses for her girls. It's a snack for a toddler and I love it.

"Dinner's not until later, so I figured you needed a snack."

"Thank you. I am famished."

I unzip it and start snacking.

"Why was Sebastian giving you a massage?" he asks.

"I've been really sore lately, a new cross-training program plus rehearsing for the showcase has made it harder for me to recover."

He nods, watching me devour the trail mix.

I'm a few bites in when I notice something. "This tastes different."

"Different how?" Rhys asks, lips twitching.

"The candy pieces are...better. Are these," I examine a candy-coated peanut butter piece, "real Reese's Pieces?"

"Maybe."

"And there aren't any raisins. Did you pick them out?" I ask.

He shrugs. "I made it."

"You made it?" I repeat, not fully understanding. "Like you bought all the ingredients and put it together?"

"Yeah." He nods.

"For me?" It's obvious, yet I'm still in shock.

It's a small thing, but I'm realizing that's the part of fake-dating Rhys I'm starting to enjoy the most. The little things he does. Picking me up from practice, planning dates that work around my schedule, and now, this sexy man in his designer suit is making me custom trail mix so I don't get hangry after a long day of practice.

The Reese's Pieces are delicious. They probably have more sugar in them than I want to think about but with the grueling workouts I've been putting myself through, I'm going to enjoy them.

I pick out a few candy pieces and toss them in my mouth.

Rhys grins down at me. "I knew you only liked the trail mix for the candy pieces."

"That's not true. I like the nuts, too."

I pop an almond in my mouth to prove it.

"Sure." Rhys presses a kiss to my head while I suck down some water to help the dry almond make its way down my throat.

"You're the best fake boyfriend in the entire world."

CHAPTER 19

Rhys

Beside me, Lettie's happily munching on the trail mix I made her. I should be satisfied that she's happy but right now, I'm losing my mind.

That kiss. It did something to me.

I hadn't been expecting it.

The jealousy I'd had when I saw her with Sebastian, his hands rubbing her down, had been real. And she thought I was faking it. Pretending to be overprotective and possessive. I'd surprised myself, but everything I said, every emotion I felt, hell, even when I growled, it was real.

I fucking growled. What is wrong with me?

My brain is stuck on a time-loop, replaying the kiss repeatedly, trying to make sense of what just happened. The moment Lettie's soft, plump lips were on mine, it was nothing like I imagined. I've kissed countless women, but I've never felt *that*—whatever was happening the moment Lettie's lips touched mine.

I turn to look at her, but staring at the soft pillows of her heart-shaped mouth only makes it worse. One glance and I'm easily remembering how right her lips felt against mine. How perfect she tasted. And fuck did she taste unbelievable. I'd been trying to play it cool, but when she asked me what she tasted like, I blurted out the first thing I could think of.

Mine.

But that's not right. What the fuck does mine even taste like?

Besides, she's not really mine. But fuck, after that kiss, I wanted her to be. I wanted to find any excuse to seal my mouth to hers again.

Still mystified by my reaction to Lettie's mouth on mine, I shake my head, trying to clear the memory, and this foreign sensation.

Pretending that my brain isn't racing with wild and inappropriate thoughts right now is the hardest thing I've had to do but somehow, in the middle of all of it, I'd managed to send a text to Ramsey to book Lettie a massage appointment.

When we pull up to the building, Lettie looks around.

"I thought we were going to grab dinner then go to my apartment?"

"You need a massage, so," I motion to the medical-grade spa Ramsey located moments ago when I texted him, "you're getting a massage."

"It's just that easy?" she asks. "With a snap of your fingers?"

"More like a text, but yeah, it's that easy."

"I don't want to complain, because I really do need a massage, but you should be using your powers for good."

"My powers?" I ask.

"Your resources. Not just monetary but I know you have a huge platform on social media of people following you, and you're influential. You've got...what's it called?" She snaps her fingers several times trying to recall the word. "Oh, charisma. You know, where people enjoy being around you and it gives you the ability to influence others."

I'm taken aback by Lettie's words. Maybe it's because I've always thought people wanted to hang out with me because of my wealth and parties. That still may be true, but Lettie seeing it another way makes me think differently.

While Lettie's getting her massage, I spend some time researching Leg-Up, the non-profit dance organization that she and Sebastian have been rehearsing for the fundraiser showcase next week. From what I can tell, it's a great organization but fundraising efforts have stalled out over the years. The fundraiser is a final effort to raise money that is needed to revitalize the studio and be able to offer more classes.

My mom loved to dance. She wasn't a professional like Lettie, but she was known for being the life of the party, and if there was music, she'd be up and moving to it. At fifteen, right before she and my dad got in the accident, we were at a barbecue with the Cartwrights and Davenports and some other friends at Lake George. I was being a typical moody teenager, embarrassed by my parents' actions, but she still demanded I dance with her. I'm thankful now that she did because it was one of our last moments together.

I think about how she would react to seeing an organization like Leg-Up needing funds and volunteers to keep its doors open. And how much effort Lettie has put into preparing for the showcase. Lettie's right, whether she meant I should specifically donate to Leg-Up, or was talking in generics, showing my ability to support organizations will help my stance with the board. Donating to Leg-Up is a no brainer.

CHAPTER 20

Rhys

Two days later, I'm still thinking about Lettie's kiss. For the first time since we agreed to this fake relationship, I'm second-guessing how this is supposed to work. Outside of the specific events I need her for, I'd told her she could let me know when she has time for dates, but with how busy she's been this week, we haven't seen each other much. I should be cool with my freedom, I always have been, but instead I find it's leaving me restless.

I play with Mo, using the laser pointer he loves so much until he gets distracted with the plastic bag the rest of his toys came in. Finally, I break down and text Lettie.

Rhys: *Want to hang out tonight? I can bring Mo over and some take-out.*

Princess: *I'm busy.*

Then a second later, another text comes in.

Princess: *For real, not trying to make you desperate for more.*

I'm remembering when I told her that she needs to say no to a guy's suggestion to hang out to leave them wanting more, but she's not supposed to use it on me. Not seeing Lettie tonight has a sharp pinch forming behind my ribcage.

Rhys: *You have plans? Should I be jealous?*

Princess: *Ha! I don't think so. I'm making tutus.*

Rhys: *Are you sure? Making tutus sounds like code for something. Is that code for something?*

Princess: *I make tutus and then me and other dancers distribute them at the children's hospital a few times a year.*

Rhys: *That's cool. I'll come over and help.*

Princess: *Are you sure? It's not glamorous work.*

Anything to spend time with you.

I stare at the screen, rereading my words before I press send. I'm going for casual and flirty, but that sentence has way too much truth to it, so I delete it.

Rhys: *Got nothing better to do*

Princess: *Okay, how about six o'clock?*

Maurice is spooning Maxine on the cat bed that I brought over to Lettie's. When they were first introduced, she barely tolerated him, but she's taken a liking to that bed, so if he climbs in, too, she doesn't bother moving.

While the cats are snuggled up, Lettie and I are on the couch making tutus. I'd brought over tacos for dinner, but Lettie had already heated up her chicken, rice, and steamed veggies, so she ate that instead. Though I did convince her to take a bite of the churro I brought for dessert.

When I told Ramsey what I was doing tonight he looked at me like I'd grown horns, then he smiled and told me to have a good night.

I toss another finished tutu onto the pile.

"You make that look easy." I motion to where Lettie's tying another knot, then hold my hands up. "Maybe my hands are too big, it makes tying the knots harder."

"Don't worry about it." She examines the tutu I finished before giving me a thumbs up. "I appreciate the help. That's two more tutus than I had before."

"I think my hands would be more useful doing something else."

Her eyes drop to my hands and I swear her cheeks go rosy. I love that I can see every expression on her face. Every thought.

She's surrounded by tulle, in her usual attire, a cropped tank and leggings, messy bun on top of her head and face free of makeup. I should be immune to the sight of her now. But unfortunately for me, Lettie isn't the kind of woman you become resistant to. Where I've always found the allure of women to fade with familiarity, it's the opposite with Lettie. Every time we spend time together, it only leaves me wanting more. At this point, I'd come over just to scoop Maxine's litterbox to hang out with her. In hindsight, I should never have bought her that self-cleaning one. My mistake.

"How about a foot massage?" I offer.

She blinks before refocusing on the tutu she's working on. "Um, no. You'd be horrified if you saw my feet."

I laugh, because how bad could they be? "Try me."

She lifts her brows in challenge. "Are you sure?"

I motion for her to extend her legs toward me. When she sets her feet in my lap, I pull off her slipper socks. I thought she was kidding, trying to scare me, but what I find is disturbing.

Her toes are curled. The knuckles bent, not by choice. Calluses line the sides of her big toes and pinky toes. Her toenails are purple underneath, housing blood blisters and bruises.

"What the fuck, Lettie?" I gently rotate her foot to get a closer look.

"What?" she asks. "You said they couldn't be as bad as I was making them out to be."

But they're that bad.

"I was wrong. And they're worse."

"It's part of being a professional dancer." She grins at me. "Giving up my dreams of being a foot model."

She's making light of it. It's what she's used to, but I'm still not over the shock.

I run a thumb over one of her big toes, lightly tracing the bunion there.

"That's been there for over ten years. I don't know what my feet would look like without it."

My finger continues to glide over each battered toe.

"This little piggie got smashed. This little piggie lost his nail. This little piggie has a bunion, and this little piggie—"

She grabs the decorative pillow beside me and smacks me in the face, putting an end to my ballerina feet rendition of *This Little Piggie*.

"I know my feet aren't pretty and I warned you."

"You know I'm just teasing you, right?" I ask.

I lift her foot to my lips and press a kiss to her big toe.

Her gaze narrows. "Okay, that's weird. Do you have a foot fetish? Is that what this is?"

"If I did, I wouldn't be turned on by yours."

She lifts the pillow again, but I hold up my free hand.

"Kidding." Gently, I brush my thumb over the callus on her pinky toe. "I can't believe you put yourself through such torture."

"It's not torture. I love dancing."

I shake my head. "I don't know what that's like. Loving something so much you'd make sacrifices for it."

I reach for the lotion in the basket next to the couch. It appears to be part of a self-care kit that Lettie keeps available. Bandages, lotion, nail strengthener, and other products.

"Isn't that what you're doing? Sacrificing the life you were living in order to be president of your parents' foundation?"

"I guess you could say that." But even as the words pass my lips, I know it's not true. Spending time with Lettie doesn't make me feel like I'm sacrificing anything. It feels like I'm being given a gift.

"Hannah's going to be home in a few days," she says.

"Have you told her about us?" I ask, pumping lotion into my hand then rubbing my hands together to warm it.

"No. She and James agreed to turn off their phones and enjoy each other on their honeymoon, so she has no idea that we're dating." She clears her throat. "Fake dating."

My hands wrap around her left foot and she jumps.

"Ticklish?"

She nods. "Yeah."

Using my thumbs, I work the arch of her foot with smooth, fluid strokes.

"I'll tell her at the Leg-Up fundraiser. She's less likely to freak out in a public place."

"You think she won't approve?" I ask.

"She asked me to keep an eye on you at her wedding so you wouldn't hit on any of her family or friends, and now we're dating? You tell me."

"You could tell her it was love at first sight."

"For whom?" she asks.

"You, of course. My periwinkle suit and paisley pocket square got you all hot and bothered."

She laughs. "She won't believe that for a second."

I continue massaging her foot while I think about what she said.

"Do you know why Hannah doesn't like me?"

She sighs. "I don't know if it's you specifically. She dated a guy before James that monogamy wasn't his strong suit, so she's skeptical about guys like you."

Guys like you. The connotation never bothered me before. I used to let anything negative easily roll off my back. Zero fucks and all that, but for some reason it's starting to get under my skin. It's burrowing deep, a layer that feels impossible to shed.

"I've never cheated."

"Because you've never had a girlfriend to cheat on?" she asks.

"Yeah." I glance back down at her foot, focusing my attention there so I can sidestep whatever unpleasant emotion is making my chest tight.

"Or she might think you're trying to take advantage of me." She sighs, tying another piece of tulle onto the waistband. "I'll tell her you aren't. That this is mutually beneficial. Although right now, I'm having a hard time remembering what I bring to the table. Your hands are absolute magic."

I can't help the grin that spreads across my face.

"That feels good."

I press my thumbs into the ball of her foot and she moans.

I rub circles around her ankle and she sighs again.

"Hmm. You're really good at this. It's almost like you've had practice."

"I asked your trainer to give me a few pointers," I admit.

Her eyes fly open. "What?"

"Just the basics. I'm not going to be a professional masseuse, but I thought it would be good to know how to make you feel good."

It's the only way I can give Lettie any pleasure without getting myself in trouble, but unfortunately for me, even rubbing her feet, hearing her sighs of relaxation, is a huge turn on.

"Is this because Sebastian was giving me a massage the other day?" she asks.

No. And yes.

"I'm your boyfriend. I'm the one who should take care of you. Give you what you need."

"I'm not arguing." She sighs into my touch, her eyes closing again. "And you're my fake boyfriend."

"Sure."

As I continue to massage her feet, switching from the left

to the right, Lettie's hands stop their progress on the tutu she's working on. Her breathing evens out and eventually she's asleep. I stare at her for a while. Perfect, pink lips parted slightly. Wild, messy bun pressed into the pillow. She's so fucking pretty, it hurts.

The fact that she easily fell asleep on the couch before nine o'clock is indicative of how hard she's been working. If this is how intense she is during off-season, how does she manage all of this when there are rehearsals and performances?

I scoop her up in my arms. I knew she'd be easy to carry, but I didn't know how good she would feel in my arms. Once I lay her on the bed, I settle her in and pull up the covers.

A deep sigh leaves her lips before she shifts onto her side, curling into the pillow and nuzzling her hands under her chin.

When I reach to turn off the lamp, the book on her night-stand catches my eye.

Fake Dating the Bad Boy

The cover is light purple with tiny read hearts all over it.

I pick it up and look through it. At first glance, the title suggests it's a How-To manual, but after further perusal, it's a romance novel.

My thumb stops at page one hundred and ten, the words cock and pussy jumping out at me.

That's interesting.

Lettie lets out a soft snore. I set the book back down on the nightstand and after turning out the light, exit her room.

Out in the living room, I stare at the pile of tulle and elastic waistbands. She needs the rest, but she's going to be frustrated that we didn't get the tutus done.

With one phone call, I could easily have this done, but Lettie emphasized that part of the magic is that they were made by the dancers. Hopefully they won't mind me being a stand-in.

Before I settle in to work, I box up the leftover food and put it in the refrigerator.

Lettie's near-empty refrigerator.

The white board hanging on the wall tells me tomorrow is grocery shopping day. Wednesday is laundry and a vet appointment for Maxine. Her to-do list and schedule that is never ending.

I send Ramsey a quick text, then get to work.

CHAPTER 21

Colette

"Does that feel good?" Rhys whispers. His hands massage my calf, one thumb pressing into the tender muscle on the outside of my shin.

"Yes." I sigh, relaxing into his touch.

He works his hands up the back of my leg, my aching muscles begging for attention.

"What about this, Princess?"

His warm palm skates along my inner thigh. His fingertips teasing the top of my leg as his thumb inches closer to the apex of my thighs.

A tingling sensation rushes between my legs. Suddenly, my clit is pounding like it has its own pulse. Throb, throb, throb.

With a devilish grin, Rhys bites down on his bottom lip, and looks up at me from between my thighs.

Jesus, I might orgasm from just looking at him.

Those fingers of his tease the edge of my underwear until one slips beneath.

"So wet for me, aren't you, Princess?"

I am wet. So, so wet. I can feel it on my fingertips.

Wait. It's his fingers, so why do I feel the slickness on mine?

My eyes fly open to discover I'm in my bed with my hand in my leggings.

The dream wasn't real, but the throb between my legs is.

I roll over and check my phone. It's just before six in the morning so my alarm hasn't gone off yet.

My dream was clearly inspired by Rhys's foot massage last night.

It had felt nice.

More than nice.

Had he really kissed the bunion on my toe? And rubbed my feet like he wasn't turned off by them?

No, he had to have been totally grossed out, but he did a decent job of hiding it.

I close my eyes, and snake my hand down past my waistband again, hoping I can return to the image and let dream Rhys finish his task.

I'm so achy. I need more than just my hand.

I reach into my nightstand and pull out my vibrator.

Typically, I don't masturbate in the mornings, but it's something I've had to do more frequently in the last few weeks. Undoubtedly, it's Rhys's fault.

Back to my dream.

Those big hands of his slide up my calves, thumbs teasing over my knees, then tracing along the inside of my leg.

A long, firm finger sweeps down my center before plunging inside.

I shimmy my leggings down far enough to gain access, then slowly work the shaft of the vibrator inside me. I'm so wet, it sinks in easily.

"So wet for me, aren't you, Princess?"

My muscles clench around the silicone shaft, giving me some relief. I line up the clit stimulator and turn it on.

Yes. Sweet relief.

Even though the walls of my apartment are thin, Mrs. Donahue is hard of hearing so I've never worried about the fact my bedroom wall is next to her living room and kitchen. Not that there's been any action coming from it beyond my solo endeavors.

Sometimes I can hear her television cranked up to a ridiculous volume but at least I have the reassurance that she can't hear me. But right now, it's too early for *Jeopardy* or the nightly news, so it's quiet on the other side of the wall.

Enough thinking about Mrs. Donahue. Back to Rhys.

My eyes flutter closed and my hips start to rock in time with the suction on the clit stimulator.

It's so good, a low moan escapes my lips. I'm so worked up from the dream it doesn't take me long before I feel my orgasm building. It's right there. Oh god.

"Yes, yes, yes," I chant, as I fall over the edge. My walls clenching tightly around the shaft of my vibrator.

Right as I fall, there's a sound on the periphery of my consciousness. It's a thump. Maybe a thud. My first thought is maybe Mrs. Donahue is rearranging her furniture again.

But I hear it again. And it's not on Mrs. Donahue's side of the wall. It's coming from my living room.

There's a knock at my bedroom door. "Lettie?"

Oh my god. *It's Rhys.*

"You okay?" he asks.

"J-j-just a second," I call, but post orgasm, it's weak and the sound of my voice doesn't travel far.

I flip the covers back and lunge out of bed.

With my leggings down to my knees, I trip. Bracing for the fall, my hand loses control of the vibrator. I leap to my feet and yank up my leggings, but a quick search for the vibrator has me coming up empty.

At that very second, Rhys opens the door.

"Did you fall out of bed?" he asks.

I'm panting. Out of breath. From my orgasm or the shock of Rhys still being here, I'm not sure, the two events have blurred together.

That's right. I just masturbated to the thought of Rhys while he was on the other side of the door. Oh god, I can't think about that right now.

What was his question?

"Um, no, must have been Mrs. Donahue."

His brows lift. "You think she fell? We should check on her."

He motions toward the front door.

"No, she's probably rearranging furniture. She does that."

He smiles at me. "Good morning. How'd you sleep?"

"Great. Good. Fine. Just a bit disoriented." I pat at my leggings, making sure I did in fact achieve my goal of pulling them up to cover my body.

He points to my clothes. "You fell asleep on the couch so I left you in your clothes."

I swipe a hand over the top of my head, trying to calm the wild hair there. What was a cute messy bun last night is now a chaotic mass of hair.

We stand there staring at each other until Rhys's gaze shifts toward my bed.

"What's that sound?" he asks. "Something's buzzing."

"Hmm?" Denial is the first step so that's where I'm going to start.

"Is that your alarm?" He looks toward my nightstand and I follow his gaze.

The panic in my chest eases when in fact I see that my phone is buzzing. It is my alarm. *Thank god.*

I walk over to turn it off, but when I silence the alarm, the buzzing continues.

My head jerks back in Rhys's direction. His shirt is rumpled from sleep. His hair is disheveled but somehow still sexy, and the way his lips twist with focused concentration as his head swivels around the room is adorable.

But enough about him because the buzzing is still happening.

And it's getting louder.

Shoot. I had the vibrator on the crescendo setting. It keeps building. And building. The vibrations getting more intense over time. I didn't need that feature this morning. I was all ready to go after dream Rhys teased me, but my vibrator doesn't know that and is still working hard…somewhere.

I rush toward the closet. Had I flung it all the way in there?

Nope.

My next target is the chair in the corner. Maybe it's lodged in a cushion, or vibrating against a wooden leg.

Not there, either.

With every failed attempt to locate the missing vibrator my heart has accelerated its rhythm to a thunderous pounding in my ears, making it difficult to track the buzzing.

"I think it's coming from under the bed," Rhys says, moving in that direction.

"Watch out! It could be a monster," I warn, hoping he'll be scared and give up the search.

No such luck. He gets down on his knees and lowers his head to look under the bed.

"I found it," he announces and I'm officially deceased.

The moment is an out-of-body experience, yet the warmth of my face flushing in anticipation of his teasing quickly brings me back to Earth.

He stands and the waiting is awful.

His back is still to me, but the buzzing stops, indicating he's turned it off.

It's not only what it is that's stressing me out, but the fact that I just *used* it. That there is most likely still evidence of my use on it.

My mouth goes dry. All the moisture is currently leaking out of the palm of my hands.

Maybe this is the dream. It could be a dream within a dream. I think that's a thing.

But it feels more like a nightmare, and I'm hoping to wake up any moment in a cold sweat. My flaming hot chest and back would agree that's preferable right now.

Somewhere, there's a woman much cooler and chill than me with zero self-consciousness and humiliation surrounding a situation like this. She'd laugh it off. And if she's a sultry vixen, confident and experienced, she might even ask the man to use it on her.

My knees go weak at the thought.

That woman is not me.

I was bracing for his teasing, and completely unprepared for this agonizing silence.

Why is he just standing there?

Finally, Rhys turns and walks toward me. With his hazel eyes locked on mine, he hands me the vibrator.

"You'll want to clean that."

I nod, because what else is there to say?

Then, he leaves, closing the door behind him on his way out.

When he's gone, I rush to the bathroom to collect my thoughts, but it's like herding cats.

What the heck just happened?

Don't think about it. It'll be fine.

I'll never be able to look Rhys in the eyes again.

Holy cow, that orgasm was intense.

After I've recovered from my mental breakdown, brushed my teeth, and fixed my hair, I wash said battery-operated device and return it to its home in my nightstand drawer.

I have to face Rhys eventually, might as well rip this band-aid off.

But when I walk into the living room, ready to embrace the discomfort of the situation, he isn't there. It's only Maxine lounging on her back in a patch of sunlight coming through the window.

"Where's Rhys?" I ask her, but she barely glances in my direction.

What had been a mess of loose tulle last night has now been organized into rolls of remaining tulle.

I appreciate that he picked up, but I still have so much work to do. I decide maybe I'll push weight training class an hour and see if I can get a few more tutus made. But first, I need sustenance.

I stop halfway to the refrigerator remembering today is grocery shopping day and there's only one browning banana left to eat. I open it anyways, hoping I can rummage up some yogurt, even though I know I finished the last of it yesterday in my smoothie.

I blink. Then, blink again.

My refrigerator is full. Practically overflowing yet in an organized way that would make *The Home Edit* proud.

Maybe this is still a dream. I grab out the ingredients to make a breakfast smoothie. Because they're all there. All my favorites. But how?

Rhys.

That's when I see the box.

Sitting next to the wall by my two-seater dining table is the box I use for completed tutus. And it's full.

CHAPTER 22

Rhys

I've just sat down on a lounger on the deck when Ramsey appears at the sliding door, a disapproving expression on his face.

"What?" I arch my brow beneath my sunglasses. "I'm fully clothed." I motion to the shorts and polo shirt I'm wearing. The same ones I was wearing last night when I went over to Lettie's apartment.

I'll shower and change later, but right now all I want to do is smoke and clear my head.

I inhale, then blow a puff of smoke into the balmy morning air. Seeking the satisfaction that this one cigarette usually gives me, I take another drag.

I'm waiting for that sense of calm to rush over me.

It doesn't.

"You slept at Colette's last night," he says, dropping his phone onto the side table before taking a seat on the lounger next to mine.

I wrap my lips around the paper and let my head fall back against the lounger. "Yeah."

His glare deepens while Mo saunters out onto the deck,

his body slipping through the small opening Ramsey left between the sliding doors.

"Nothing happened," I say, before Ramsey can berate me for corrupting Lettie. For being a foolish man who can't keep his dick in his pants.

That's not entirely true. Something happened. But it's not what he thinks.

I'd awoken to a sound coming from Lettie's bedroom. It sounded like a moan, but could have just as easily been a yawn or that satisfied groan she makes when she's stretching. It's what I'd assumed until I heard the thump and rushed in to check on her. She'd barely gotten her pants up before I opened the door.

I should have knocked, but in my sleep-dazed state I'd thought Lettie had hurt herself and took immediate action. Turns out, there was no emergency.

Just an unidentified buzzing sound that continued even when Lettie turned her phone alarm off.

And when I found Lettie's vibrator, still buzzing under her bed, I was shocked, not because she has one and uses it, but because I'd never anticipated her to use it when I was on the other side of the door. I never imagined she would be comfortable getting herself off when someone else was around. And the mortified look on her face told me exactly that.

Which means there's no way Lettie had known I was still out in the living room, curled up on her couch with Mo snuggled in next to me, while Maxine batted at my face because I was in her spot. Of course, once I vacated, Maxine lost interest in it, and went to lie on the sun-soaked rug instead.

And fuck, the moment I felt the wetness on her vibrator, still fresh from being inside her pussy, my brain short-circuited. I wanted to rub my thumb over it, then lick it. I imagine even the tiniest taste would have been so fucking good.

Now I'm thinking about her fucking herself with it. Pressing that vibrator inside her hot, wet cunt. Damn. I want to see it. But fuck, there's no way I can go there with Lettie. She's perfect and sweet, and she deserves more than anything I can give her.

Ramsey clears his throat, interrupting my runaway thoughts. "Something happened. You've got a guilty look on your face."

"Nothing. I swear." I take another drag but it tastes bitter, so I give up and put it out on the ashtray next to me. "When I texted you about the groceries, she was already asleep. I stayed up late making tutus, then slept on the couch."

"You mentioned the tutus. What are they for?"

"Lettie makes them for the children's hospital. It's some dream with a dancer thing where she makes tutus, then hands them out."

Ramsey's smile widens. "I don't know what you did in a previous life to deserve this, but the fact that you're even friends with a woman like that, practically a saint, is beyond my comprehension. And she's willing to play along with this fake relationship? Honestly, none of this makes sense."

He's right. I don't deserve Lettie. I'm lucky to have her, so I need to not think dirty thoughts about her and focus on our goals—getting Lettie dating experience and keeping Jerrod from taking over my parents' foundation board.

"Did she like the groceries? I added on a few other snack items that I thought she might like."

I didn't stick around to find out. After the vibrator incident, I had to get out of there. It was too dangerous to stay. Too tempting to fall back into my old ways and take Lettie with me.

If it had been a month ago and any other woman but Lettie, I would have stripped those leggings off so fast and buried my face between her thighs, then fucked her into the mattress until we were both spent.

"Yeah. That's great. Thanks."

Ramsey scrolls on his phone. "Let's see. You've got Jerrod and Corinne's dinner tomorrow night. Did you want me to select a dress for Colette to wear?"

"No, I'll do it."

He lifts his brows. "Okay."

My reasoning is if I pick it out, then I can select something that won't be distracting. But then, I think of Lettie's soul-crushing blue eyes, her pretty pink lips and her radiant smile. Oh, and the faint scent of her pussy that was on her vibrator this morning.

The dress is the least of my problems.

I tuck my hands behind my head, before turning to Ramsey. "Will you add the food delivery as a reoccurring order? Oh, and have Martin's pick up her laundry tomorrow."

"Is this part of the arrangement you made?" he asks.

"No, she didn't ask for it, but I can see she needs help. She's busy and I want to make her life outside of dancing as easy as possible."

"Interesting. It sounds like you actually care about her."

I shrug off his observation. "Of course, she's my friend." Who I desperately want to kiss again and can't stop thinking about when I'm not with her.

Mo jumps onto the lounger and starts to make his way over to my lap. I give him a long stroke down his back as he settles in. The calming sensation I couldn't find with the cigarette starts to paint itself over my body.

I nod to Ramsey. "I'm thinking of loaning your services to Lettie. You know, to help with anything she needs. You good with that?"

"I'd be offended but I'm certain she'll be more fun to hang out with than you."

"I knew you'd be pleased."

"Oh, and I got the information you needed from Leg-Up.

The wiring instructions are with Jason at the bank, ready to send when you give the word."

"Thank you."

"Just so we're clear, you're offering to anonymously match donations at the fundraiser up to ten million dollars?"

"Yeah." Mo lifts his chin toward me so I can scratch under it.

"But you're already donating five million, so you're going to match your own donation?"

I smile at Ramsey's befuddled look. "I never said it had to make sense."

My parents set me up for life, they made it easy for me to enjoy my life, but I know they never intended for me to do nothing with it. As a family we enjoyed our time together at Lake George, sailing and adventuring to new parts of the world, but they also knew hard work. That's the part I'm less acquainted with. Seeing how hard Lettie works, in her career and donating time to others, makes me think it's time to reevaluate what I'm doing with my life.

CHAPTER 23

Colette

Colette: *Thank you for the groceries and finishing the tutus. I still can't believe I fell asleep. Oh, and thank you for the massage last night. You're an amazing fake boyfriend!*

I reread the text message I sent Rhys an hour ago.

It's cool. It's casual. It makes no mention of vibrators or self-induced orgasms.

He hasn't responded.

Why hasn't he responded?

What is he thinking?

Why did he just leave this morning?

As my thoughts start to spiral out, I remind myself that Rhys and I are fake dating. He needs my help, and I doubt he's going to abandon his effort to gain control of his parents' foundation just because he found my vibrator and was slightly freaked out that I had just used it. Because as he had suggested, that's what soap is for. Right now, I'd like to wash the memory from my brain.

I drop my phone into my cross-body bag and vow not to keep checking it.

To forget it even happened.

That's not likely, but I'm going to try.

Since today's to-do list was cleared by Rhys, I've decided to use my free time before I have to be at the practice studio to visit my parents. They've canceled the last two weeks of family dinner nights due to conflicts in their schedules, so even while we've talked briefly on the phone, it's unusual that we've gone this long without getting together, and I miss them.

Their apartment is only a few blocks away. That's how ridiculous it is that I haven't seen them recently. It shouldn't be that hard to get together, but with my busy schedule and their work, it has gotten more challenging. Even more so over the last few months.

On my way through the lobby, I say hi to Micah at reception. He's on a phone call, but he waves as I enter the elevator.

We moved into this apartment when I was twelve. Once my dad had gotten tenure at NYU and my mom started taking on more clients at her interior design business. While Central Park West was an upgrade from our home in Brooklyn and it made my commute to the academy easier, I'd still been devastated by the move. My mom tried to cheer me up by making decorating my new room a fun event, but even pink walls, a canopy bed with sheer overlay and my own phone line was a hard sell.

Maybe it was my stubbornness, my resistance to change, or simply raging teenage hormones, but eventually, I grew to love the new place and it became home.

I knock but no one answers, so I use my key to let myself in.

I turn down the hallway and run straight into my dad and the box he's carrying.

"Colette, sweetie," he startles before shifting the box to one arm to embrace me. The familiar smell of his aftershave comforts me. It's like a hit of nostalgia I didn't know I needed so badly.

"What are you doing here?" he asks.

"I was in the neighborhood." I lift my arms up like it's a coincidence.

"You live in the neighborhood."

"Exactly. I haven't seen you since Hannah and James's wedding and that was for like five seconds, so I thought I'd stop by." I glance down at the box. "What's in the box?"

He makes a waving motion of dismissal. "Oh, just some old stuff."

My eyes snag on a framed photo of me from a dance recital when I was ten. Another of me and him when we did a father/daughter trip to San Diego over spring break one year.

"Aren't those the photos from your office?" I ask.

He looks down into the box, then back at me.

"Pam was helping me clean out the office and she must have put some things in here by accident. I'll go through those later." He sets the box down, then wraps his arm around me and walks me toward the living room.

My eyes scan the space, cataloging the walls and furniture to see what might have changed since I was here last.

As an interior designer, my mom loves to constantly change their furnishings. She changes her wallpaper like other people swap out seasonal dish towels.

It used to bother me as a child, especially when I got attached to a certain pillow or figurine and then *poof!* it would be gone to usher in the latest trend in home décor.

My mom used to tell me *it's not change, it's progress* because even at an early age I craved routine and order. Seasonal menus are all fine and good, but give me a restaurant where the menu doesn't change so I know my favorite dish will still be on it. And don't get me started on the stress of finding out the ballet tights company I ordered from for fifteen years went out of business.

"Is Mom doing another redesign?" I ask, taking note of the two sitting chairs that are no longer there.

"Something like that. You know how she is; I can't keep track." He laughs, but it seems forced.

"Is she home?" I ask.

"No, she had a client meeting downtown."

I nod. That seems to be how it goes lately.

My dad pushes a hand through his hair. It's still dark, like mine, but flecks of salt and pepper are starting to appear around his ears and at his hair line. He's a handsome guy. Tall, lean build and dark glasses that my mom always said made him look like a sexy professor. As his teenage daughter, that was something I did not want to hear.

I don't know if it's because in the last month I haven't seen him for longer than a few minutes at a time, but he looks different. A few more wrinkles at the corner of his blue eyes, maybe? He looks tired and stressed, the same way my mom had appeared at Hannah and James's wedding.

"I was wondering if we could find a weekend for the three of us to go to Lake George?" I ask.

Our house at Lake George has not been impacted by my mom's constant need to reinvent every living space. *It's timeless,* she said when I asked her about it. *No need to change it.*

Maybe that's why I love it there so much. It's a constant.

My dad winces. "That's going to be a tough one this year. Your mother and my schedules are completely opposite right now. I'm teaching an evening course during summer break and she's booked with client meetings during the day."

"Surely we can find one weekend that would work." I give him my best pleading look, lower lip pout and all.

"What about that boyfriend of yours?" His brows lift in question.

Oh, right. Somehow, I've managed to forget about Rhys. Not intentionally, he's just locked in a place in my brain for safe keeping so I don't keep ruminating over how he found my vibrator under my bed this morning and has yet to respond to my text.

My fingers itch to check my phone. *Don't do it.*

"Rhys?" I ask.

"Unless there are others?" He smiles.

I shake my head. "No, just him."

"He's a good kid."

I'm surprised by his nonchalant attitude about me and Rhys. I'd expect a dad, especially mine, would be more concerned about his daughter dating the bad boy with a big reputation. But I've never dated anyone. Never brought anyone home or introduced a guy to my parents, so maybe he's unfamiliar with how to handle the situation.

"You think so?" I ask.

"If a wonderful person like you is with him, he must have good qualities."

I smile at that because I'm finding Rhys isn't who everyone thinks he is. He's so much more.

"Does he make you happy?" he asks.

It's a simple question, but with me and Rhys's situation, it's not a simple answer. We're together for reasons that don't require happiness to be a factor, but when I think about our time together, his teasing and patience and thoughtfulness, then I guess the answer is yes.

"Yeah, he does."

"That's what is important."

We catch up, talking about his summer course and my upcoming evaluations for the fall session. I confirm that he and my mom will be at the Leg-Up fundraiser event on Friday evening, then he walks me out. As we go our separate ways, him heading south toward the NYU campus and me west toward Lincoln Center, I realize he never answered my question about Lake George.

As I walk, I pull my phone out to see if Rhys has responded.

Still nothing.

Is this dating? Waiting anxiously for a guy to text you

back? And stressing about why he's not? Well, screw that. I need to clear the air. And when I say clear the air, I mean have the extremely awkward conversation via text message so it doesn't require me to stare at Rhys's gorgeous face while we talk about my vibrator.

Colette: *Are we going to talk about this morning? <grinning and sweating emoji>*

CHAPTER 24

Rhys

My phone buzzes with a text from Lettie.

Princess: *Are we going to talk about this morning? <grinning and sweating emoji>*

I still haven't responded to her text from earlier.

After running into Hunter and his friends at the NYC Racquet Club, he invited me to grab a beer. I don't play tennis, but everyone who's anyone has a membership there. Most of the foundation board are members here, so making appearances here is important to my efforts to connect with them.

"Should we address the elephant in the room?" Hunter asks.

I glance up from my phone. "What?"

"You and Colette. Hannah comes home tomorrow, and let's just say my sister doesn't love surprises unless they're for other people."

"Lettie said the same thing, but I'm not sure what else there is to say. We're dating. It's that simple."

"Lettie's like a second sister to me." He motions to Griffin. "We already know how protective you are of Sophie."

From the way they're smirking at each other, I can tell there's a story here.

"What happened?" I ask.

"Griffin found out I was seeing Sophie behind his back and we ended up in a fight out on the terrace."

"It wasn't only the fact you were seeing her behind my back. She was twenty-two and pregnant, of course I was angry." Griffin's gaze softens. "Can't imagine not knowing those babies now."

He's referring to Hunter and Sophie's twin girls.

I look between the guys. "So you think Hannah's going to kick my ass?"

"Wait a minute." Hunter holds up a finger. "There was no ass kicking."

Barrett chuckles. "I was there. Griffin kicked your ass."

"I tripped and fell," Hunter insists.

Griffin smirks, pressing his lips together, but I can see the shake of his chest, holding in laughter. "Sure."

"We're not talking about me right now." Hunter turns his attention back to me and his face turns serious. "What are your intentions with Colette?"

The other guys go quiet, their eyes on their drinks in front of them.

"I've always had a soft spot for her, and now that we're older, it's more."

For a fake relationship, I'd expected my answer to require more thought to make it convincing, but like it's second nature, it easily rolls off my tongue. Even if my relationship with Lettie is fake, that statement right there holds many truths.

Hunter nods, considering it. "I know you were protective of her growing up, but as her official surrogate big brother, I'll have to make your life hell if you hurt her."

"Understood." I nod, before taking a sip of my beer.

When I get home later, I settle in on my couch and turn on the television to a rerun of *How I Met Your Mother.* It's one of my favorite shows, but I mute it because I know all the episodes, and I need to focus to respond to Lettie's text.

I hit the voice to text and speak into my phone.

Rhys: *I'm glad the groceries were helpful. And the tutus were easy once I figured out the knots.*

She's quick to respond.

Princess: *Thank you so much! You didn't have to do that.*

Rhys: *I wanted to.*

Princess: *Well, thank you. And the other thing…*

Right. The other thing. The thing I haven't been able to stop thinking about all day.

I hit the talk to text and say the first thing that comes to mind. No, make that the first thing that's appropriate that comes to my mind.

Rhys: *Pleasuring yourself is a natural thing.*

Princess: *You sound like a sex education teacher I had in middle school.*

Rhys: *Good. I think it's best if I keep it professional.*

Princess: *Why's that?*

This is a test. Repeat, this is a test. Do not engage.

I set my phone down and stretch out on the couch.

Because I can't stop thinking about what you must have looked like filled with that toy. How hard your pussy must have clenched down on it when you came. Your wetness dripping over the length of it. And that soft, breathy moan that I now know was you coming is etched in my brain forever. I want to hear it again with my fingers deep inside you. With my lips around your clit, sucking it hard until you come and beg me to stop.

I let the thoughts in my head run rampant, treating them like the drunk guy at a party who's annoying the fuck out of everyone, but if you just give him a minute, he'll eventually eat the pizza you ordered and pass out.

I hit the talk to text button again and give her the PG version.

Rhys: *Because I'm your fake boyfriend. It's my job to make sure you're not uncomfortable and I take it seriously.*

Princess: *Is that why you left this morning? So I wouldn't break out in hives?*

"That, and I didn't want you to see how hard I was thinking about you using your vibrator," I mumble. My spoken words immediately populate the text message box. Fuck. I hit the talk to text button but that's not what I wanted to send to her.

When the text shows up on the screen, I fumble to hit the X to delete it but end up hitting the arrow that sends the message instead.

Rhys: *That, and I didn't want you to see how hard I was thinking about you using that vibrator.*

"Fucking hell." I groan as my fingers quickly find the unsend message feature, but it denies me because she's already read it.

Those three dots appear indicating Lettie's typing. *Fuck. Fuck. Fuuucck.*

Princess: *Are you trying to make me feel less awkward by embarrassing yourself?*

I stare at her text.

She thinks I was kidding. Only trying to make her feel less self-conscious.

I could tell her it's the truth, but that cracks open a door that I've vowed to keep shut in this arrangement. If I agree, tell her I'm only trying to make her feel better, will she be convinced I wouldn't react that way toward her? That I don't see her as the beautiful, desirable woman she is?

It's better if I take the easy way out. Accept the get out of jail free card that Lettie is giving me after my texting fuck up.

Rhys: *Is it working?*

Princess: *A little. I appreciate that you aren't teasing me about it.*

Rhys: *Do you want me to tease you? Would that make it better?*

Princess: *No! I'm good. Let's just forget it. Please.*

Rhys: *Okay. I'm sending a dress over for the dinner party on Thursday.*

Princess: *Thank you. I haven't had any time to think about what to wear. I've got final rehearsal tomorrow with Sebastian for the Leg-Up showcase.*

Rhys: *You're going to do great. I'm sending positive vibes your way <winking emoji>*

Princess: *You're the worst.*

Rhys: *I couldn't resist. You know it's in my nature to tease.*

Princess: *I know, you could at least try not to.*

Rhys: *Anything for you, Princess. I don't want to be a buzzkill.*

Princess: *<smacking head emoji>*

Rhys: *Goodnight, Princess.*

Princess: *Goodnight*

I'm relieved that Lettie and I were able to clear the tension from this morning. With Jerrod's dinner party in two days, where all the board members will be in attendance, I need us to be solid. I need her to not be overwhelmed by playing her role of my girlfriend.

I toss my phone on the table and adjust Mo so he's snuggled up on my lap, then I reach for the binder that Ramsey assembled for me. It's a cheat sheet for the foundation members that will be in attendance Thursday night, so I can be knowledgeable about their families and the work they're involved in outside the foundation.

As I read through their bios, it becomes clear that I'm in way over my head. The board members are well-educated, artists, scientists and businessmen and businesswomen involved in many philanthropic organizations, just like my parents had been.

I turn the page to Jerrod's bio and scan through it. His work and accomplishments align perfectly with the other board members.

How can I compete with him? He's the golden boy who can do no wrong, while I'm the black sheep whose every mistake is captured and shared by the media.

Dread settles in my gut. This is exactly what I wanted to avoid.

The silver lining is that I have Lettie. She's my phone a friend. My golden ticket. Gorgeous, gracious, and talented.

I'm relying on Lettie to be a distraction from my reputation. Here's hoping I'm not the one getting distracted by her.

CHAPTER 25

Colette

"How cool is it that my dress is on this site now?" Isabella turns her phone screen in my direction.

She's referring to the celebrity spotter page that has a picture of me and Rhys from our dinner date last week. It's ridiculous. We're not celebrities, but apparently Rhys has been followed by the page for years. It's the same source that posted the photos of us leaving Hannah and James's wedding. And that captured us kissing outside the practice studio near Lincoln Center earlier this week.

"If they ask, I'll tell them you were my stylist," I say.

"Damn straight."

Isabella sets her phone down to finish applying my eyeliner, and I try not to blink. Since she did such a great job last week, I asked if she would help me get ready for the dinner party at Jerrod and Corinne's.

A few minutes later, she's done with my makeup and starts to pack everything up.

I smile when I see Rhys's photo pop up on my screen. I haven't seen him since the morning of the vibrator incident, but I'm trying to keep the nerves at bay because tonight is an important night for him.

"Hey." His smooth, seductive baritone flows through my phone speaker. At the sound, my heart rate immediately spikes.

I'm still getting used to the reaction my body has to Rhys's voice. I've developed a system to counteract the reaction and return my heart rate to normal.

It's a simple exercise really. Whenever Rhys's low timber registers in my ear, I take a breath, count down from five in my head and focus on slowing my heart rate. It's the same thing I did when I first started performing with the company and had nerves before going on stage.

I move the phone away from my mouth and exhale slowly, until I reach one.

Much better.

"You sent a whole rack of dresses. I only need one dress for tonight."

"I couldn't decide which one I liked best."

"You picked them out yourself?" I ask.

He chuckles. "Yeah, I like shopping. Retail therapy is good for the soul."

"Even for women's dresses?"

"Shopping for you was easy. You look good in everything."

I'm glad we're having this conversation on the phone, because my face goes hot and I can't stop smiling.

Instead of taking a breath again, I distract myself by thumbing through the dress rack.

"How am I going to decide which one to wear?" I ask.

"I'll help you. I'm outside your building right now."

What?!

"You are? Okay. I'll buzz you in."

The moment he steps inside, Rhys presses a kiss to my cheek, then promptly scoops up Maxine. She must have heard his voice on the phone because she's there, waiting by the door.

If she wasn't a cat, I'd scold her for looking so desperate.

"Sorry, Max," he rubs her head, right between the ears how she likes, "I didn't bring your boyfriend."

"Aww, you guys are too cute. I didn't know your cats were dating," Isabella teases. "Or are they fake dating, too? You know, for publicity on GossipCats.com?"

I shoot her a glance, but she just shrugs innocently.

Turning back to Rhys, I finally take all of him in.

Black on black suit, thick, dark wavy hair that somehow looks both tamed and unruly, and a clean-shaven face that accentuates the sharp edge of his jaw.

"You look nice."

He gives me that lopsided grin of his and it only adds to his intoxicating attractiveness.

Isabella and I exchange a look because yeah, Rhys looks more than nice. Nice is how you describe a lovely smelling candle, not Rhys Spencer in a black-on-black suit.

"Thanks. You look—"

"Half ready?" I fill in for him. I'm in a robe but my hair and makeup are done.

His eyes drag up the length of me. "Perfect." He hands me a bouquet of flowers. "I brought you these."

"Oh, you didn't have to do that."

"It's what a guy would do for you. Flowers before every date."

I can feel my cheeks heating, but his words remind me this is all pretend. Just practice. Like going into the studio to work on a tricky sequence or jump.

Behind me, Isabella clears her throat.

"Isabella, this is Rhys. Rhys, Isabella. She's a dancer with the company, too." I motion to Rhys. "You already know who he is."

"Your reputation precedes you," Isabella says, extending her hand for a shake.

Rhys smirks, then takes her hand and kisses it. Isabella's

natural glow deepens. When she gets her hand back, she waves it near her face.

"Lettie, your fake boyfriend is making me real swoon."

Of course, she says it loud enough for Rhys to hear. And his ego only gets bigger. I hope his head will be able to fit through the apartment door by the time Isabella's done fawning over him.

"Have the best time, you guys!" she calls, blowing me an air kiss as she throws her bag over her shoulder and walks out the door.

With Isabella's exit, Rhys turns to me again, looking me up and down in my robe before moving over to the rack of dresses.

With his back to me, I'm able to study him.

He is gorgeous in the black designer suit. There's no argument that his tailored jacket is perfectly cut for his broad shoulders and the slim fit of his pants accentuates his long legs and muscular thighs, but there's something missing.

He turns to find me staring. "What are you thinking?"

"Nothing. Brain is completely empty over here."

"You can't lie to me. It's written all over your face."

I'm not sure how he reads me so well. I make a mental note to practice my poker face.

I shrug. "Your suit. You look devastatingly handsome, but honestly, I like your old clothing better. Purple suits and flamingo shirts. Oh, and I thought the picture of you online in pinstripe pants and a patchwork button-down has to be one of my favorites."

"We already established that suit was periwinkle. And you've been checking me out online?"

My lips twitch. "I don't even have to search. You're everywhere and the headlines write themselves."

His gaze drops to his black suit. "Jerrod and my grandfather are subdued men. The goal is to fit in tonight."

I get it. I just wish he didn't have to change himself to fit in.

He pulls a red dress with a ruffled one-shoulder neckline from the rack.

"I like this one."

I was eyeing that dress earlier, and while it's gorgeous, I think it screams 'look at me.'

"Am I going to fit in with the other guests wearing that?" I ask.

"No, you'll stand out, but that's a good thing."

"Really?"

"Yes. Trust me, Princess."

I nod. "Okay, let me try it on."

Rhys settles onto the couch while I take the dress to my room. A minute later, I've got the dress on and it fits perfectly. Only problem is I can't get it zipped up all the way.

The sore muscles of my shoulders from weightlifting yesterday are restricting what is typically an easy reach for me. I contort myself a few different ways, until I'm heavily panting and a sheen of sweat breaks out on my forehead. It's no use. My fingers are just out of reach. Back-zip dresses are a single woman's nightmare.

But I'm not a single woman now.

"Rhys?" I call on my way to the bedroom door.

When I open it, he's already there.

"Jesus Christ, Princess." He rubs his thumb under his lower lip, assessing me.

"What?" I drop my eyes to my body where Rhys is currently staring. "Is the dress too much?"

"Not at all. You look absolutely stunning."

"Yeah?" I can't hide my smile, because even if he's said the same words a thousand times to a hundred different women, somehow, he makes it feel special. The way his eyes dance over me and his lips split into a satisfied grin is nice. "I can't get the zipper up. Can you help?"

As soon as I turn around to show him the issue, I remember I don't have a bra on.

The one-shoulder requires either a convertible strapless bra or to go without. My small breasts and I have never met a strapless bra we like so I'm going without. And the dress material is thick enough that nipple covers will do the trick.

I wait for Rhys to start pulling the zipper up, but there's nothing.

"Is it stuck?" Maybe that's why I was having such a difficult time.

He clears his throat, and finally there's movement. Up, up, up it goes until his fingers brush against my back when he fastens the clasp at the top. I hold stock-still, fighting the shiver that my body is desperate to embrace.

"You're good," he says, his voice husky and only an inch from my ear.

"Thanks." I turn around to face him. "That is until I have to take it off later tonight. I'll probably need your help with that, too. I'm sure you're even more skilled at taking women's dresses off."

It's supposed to be funny, but when I look up to find Rhys's eyes darkening, I realize how it sounded.

Heat licks at my cheeks.

"I'll make sure you're not stuck in it before I leave."

"Thanks."

On the way out the door, I notice that while I was getting ready, Rhys placed the flowers in a vase with water.

In the car, Rhys fills me in on the board members of The Spencer Foundation. Ramsey compiled a binder with the board members and their significant others, children, hobbies, etc.

I know our appearance tonight as a couple is going to have a big impact on the board's view of Rhys. While I can't be solely responsible for his character, I'm a piece of the puzzle. A way for him to prove that he's leaving his playboy persona in the past and ready to take on the foundation board president role.

The thing is, I see that in Rhys. With or without us fake dating. I know he could step into the role his father had wanted for him. He's smart and talented, a people person that could easily work with others. The issue is, he doesn't believe it.

But right now, we need to review our game plan for the evening.

"So, we're childhood friends who recently reconnected and are now dating."

He gives me an easy nod. "Yeah."

"So, what do you need me to do tonight? Any special requests?" I ask, hoping that if I have a task or purpose, it will help me focus on that and take the pressure off the situation.

His gaze skims over me, and I feel every inch of it. When his eyes reach mine, the intensity of his stare is like a punch to the gut. The hazel of his eyes, greenish gray with flecks of gold, has been pushed out by darkness. There's a good five seconds where I'm not sure I'm breathing. The air in the car is thick and hot. Then, Rhys's mouth splits into that devilish grin of his.

"Pretend you like me."

It's hard not to roll my eyes at his request.

"I do like you. I wouldn't have agreed to this if I didn't."

"You know what I mean."

The reality is I won't have to pretend. I'm attracted to Rhys. Whether I should be or not, when he's around, my body reacts. Maybe that's what is making tonight feel important.

"Just be yourself, but also be madly in love with me."

I scoff playfully. "All you said was I needed to like you."

He grins. "Just thought it would be the perfect opportunity for you to practice."

My brows lift. "Is this relationship one-sided? Or will you be falling over yourself, madly in love with me, too?"

"Is that what you want?" he asks, his gaze falling to my lips.

Rhys Spencer hopelessly devoted to one woman? That would be a sight to see. That woman being me? I can't see it happening.

"We should do whatever is best to make you look good with the board."

"In that case, all you'll have to do is stand next to me."

I shake my head, laughing again. "You should save this flattery for the board members."

"It's true." He slides his hand in mine. "Thank you for doing this with me."

I look down at our joined hands. A flicker of something pinches my chest. Pretending to like Rhys tonight won't be a problem, it's being able to tell the difference between what's fake and what's real that is starting to concern me.

CHAPTER 26

Rhys

When we arrive at Jerrod's place, I reach my hand out to Lettie to help her out of the car. My eyes make their way up Lettie's form. The dress she wore on our date last week was sexy, yet casual. But in this red dress, the way it hugs her ass perfectly and shows off her toned arms and trim waist, she's downright seductive.

It had been easy to shop for her, all the dresses I selected would have been stunning on Lettie.

I shouldn't be looking at her like this.

But looking isn't off limits, right?

No, the guilt isn't from appreciating her tonight in this dress, it's due to the other things I've done recently.

My conscience weighs heavy as I recall the way I stroked myself to the thought of her this morning in the shower. Thoughts of her pleasuring herself gave way to fantasies of what I would do if I'd walked in on her. That spiraled into imagining her on her knees for me. Full, pink lips stretched around my cock.

And that was all before I saw her in this dress.

The dress's higher neckline and ruffle across the bust is less revealing than her slip dress was on our date. Yet something about the red color, the way her dark hair sweeps over her bare shoulder, and how the short hemline shows off her toned legs will haunt me in my dreams.

When she'd asked me to help her zip it up, I'd thought it would be no big deal. I've unzipped many dresses in my life.

That was before my eyes devoured the sight of the smooth, flawless skin of Lettie's naked back and discovered she's not wearing a bra again tonight.

I shouldn't be thinking about Lettie in her dress, or out of it. I need to be focused on connecting with the board members tonight. Now, I know my previous thoughts of Lettie being a distraction are correct.

"Come on in." Corinne welcomes us into the penthouse apartment. "I'm Corinne Marks." She introduces herself to Lettie.

"Colette Davenport." Lettie extends her hand for Corinne to shake.

"I already know who you are and I'm a huge fan."

"Oh, thank you." A tinge of pink rises on Lettie's cheeks.

"You look gorgeous. I love that dress," Corinne gushes. "You look nice, too, Rhys."

"Thanks for having us, Corinne." I drop a kiss to her cheek.

"She's nice," Lettie whispers as we make our way into the living area where the other guests are gathered.

The few times I've been around Corinne, she's always been pleasant. She and Jerrod have been dating for years, yet I don't know much about her, other than that she's a bubbly, petite blonde and her family owns a national grocery store chain where she's recently been promoted to chief financial officer.

"There he is." Jerrod greets me with an aggressive one-arm bro hug. "The man of the hour. Glad you could make it. It wouldn't be a party without Rhys Spencer, am I right?"

Jerrod's antics grate on my nerves, but I'm highly aware of

the other guests around us. We're on display with many of the board members here, and no matter how obnoxious he is, I need to be civil.

"Jerrod, this is Colette Davenport."

"Yes, I remember. We met at Lake George years ago. I was visiting Rhys's family for a few weeks."

The last time Jerrod visited me at Lake George was a year or so before my parents died. We'd had a good time taking the boat out on the lake and cliff jumping to impress some girls. Doing stupid shit that fourteen-year-old boys think is cool. I thought it was a turning point in our relationship. Where we were becoming more friends than rivals. But shortly after my parents died, things got more competitive between us. I never knew why.

"That's right." Lettie nods. "It's been a long time."

Jerrod takes her hand and makes a show of kissing it. "Nice to see you again. And wow, you in that dress," a low whistle passes through his lips, "just stunning."

I wrap my arm around Lettie's waist and pull her close. *Mine.*

Lettie stiffens for a moment, but then she leans into me, her body fitting snuggly against mine. It's the best fucking feeling in the world. And damn, she smells so fucking good.

Corinne cuddles in next to Jerrod, but he's too focused on me and Lettie to notice.

"You make a beautiful couple." Corinne beams at us before turning to Jerrod. "Don't they look good together?"

She's oblivious to the way he's glaring at us. Either Corinne doesn't know how competitive Jerrod and I are, or she likes adding fuel to the fire.

"Yes," he eyes me suspiciously, "they certainly do."

We make the rounds; I introduce Lettie to the other couples there and as I'd predicted she fits perfectly into the group. With her by my side, I don't feel like an imposter. The square peg trying to fit into a round hole.

My grandfather and his second wife, Edith, are among the guests.

"Good to see you again, Colette." My grandfather gives Lettie a light embrace and polite kiss on the cheek.

Edith, on the other hand, embraces Lettie like a long-lost relative. She's so happy, she's nearly in tears. "When I heard that you and Rhys were together, I thought to myself, *oh, Edith, can we be so lucky to be blessed with some cute little ballet dancing great-grandchildren?"*

Lettie's eyes widen before finding mine.

I'd argue that Edith doesn't know when she's being inappropriate but after years of comments like this, I've realized she knows, but she doesn't care.

I squeeze Lettie's hip to let her know I agree Edith's mentioning kids is wildly premature. "I think it's a little too soon to be talking about babies."

"Yeah, Rhys, wasn't it only a few weeks ago you were photographed with another woman on your arm?" Jerrod's lips twitch, a sly smile pulling at the corners. "No offense, Colette, but monogamy isn't Rhys's strong suit. And babies? He'd be cutting you a check faster than you could say 'baby daddy.'"

Corinne pinches Jerrod in the side.

"What?" Jerrod shrugs. "I'm not wrong."

I should have known Jerrod's agenda tonight was to make me look bad. Even with Lettie on my arm, the evidence of my reputation is damning. For a moment I wonder if any of this will matter? If even with Lettie's help I won't be able to disengage myself from who I was. Who everyone still thinks I am.

My fingers tighten into Lettie's hip, anger and frustration getting the best of me.

Then, her hand is there, covering mine. Her fingers gently easing between mine and I relax.

"You're right, Jerrod. That was Rhys before we were together. And it may be crazy but once we reconnected,"

Lettie looks up to catch my eyes, "everything fell into place. It's hard to explain, but it felt like it was meant to be."

"That's how it was with Jer. I was wild and didn't want to be tied down, but then he looked at me with those puppy dog eyes and I just knew that was it."

"It's good to see both my grandchildren happy." My grandfather nods. "Now, let's have a drink to celebrate."

Jerrod and Corinne went all out, even hired a bartender for the evening. While I'm getting me and Lettie a drink, Jerrod finds me at the bar.

"Colette sure is something." I follow his gaze across the room to where Lettie and Corinne are talking with Sasha, one of the board members, and her partner, Alana. "Now, the question is, why is she with you?"

"Fuck off, Jerrod," I murmur before plastering a smile to my face, so no one is the wiser.

He makes a tsking sound which only annoys me further.

"Make it make sense, man. She's too good for you." He shakes his head. "Unless you're paying her?"

His insinuation isn't far off. Maybe that's why it gets under my skin.

"We were friends, and now we're more." My lips twist into a sneer. "I guess it's hard for your tiny brain to comprehend that."

"Don't worry, Rhys." He pats me on the chest. "I'll figure it out."

Before I can get another word in, he clinks his glass to let everyone know that dinner is being served.

At dinner, the seats already have place cards, and Lettie is at the opposite end of the table. There's an empty seat beside me, leaving me disconnected from the group and I wonder if Jerrod did that on purpose. Now, not only do I not have Lettie in my corner, but it's harder to engage with those a few seats down.

I'm taking out my aggression on my dinner salad when a man walks into the dining room.

"I apologize for being late," he says.

"Don't worry about it, Sandeep." Jerrod stands to greet the man I recognize as one of the board members and my dad's old friend, Sandeep Patel. "We've just started."

"Don't get up." He motions to those who have stood to greet him, but they ignore him and he makes his way around the table saying hello and giving a handshake or a quick hug before he finally takes the empty seat next to me.

"Rhys," he says, dropping his napkin into his lap, before extending his hand to me, "I was hoping to be seated next to you."

I shake his hand, surprised by his confession. "You were?"

"You bet. We need to catch up." He turns to the dark-haired woman next to him. "Aditi, have you had a chance to talk with Rhys?"

With a polite smile on her lips, she shakes her head no.

"Well, we need to rectify that."

Over the five-course dinner, Sandeep engages the table, telling jokes one moment, then posing a thoughtful question for discussion the next.

It's clear now, Sandeep is the life of the party, but also highly respected among the board. He's the guy that makes everyone feel welcome and in an environment like this where Jerrod is constantly trying to poke holes in my parachute, I'll take all the help I can get.

By the end of dinner, I've gotten to know Sandeep, Aditi, and several other board members better. And I think they've gotten to know me.

When there's a break in conversation, my eyes settle on Colette at the end of the table. She's talking with Corinne and Trisha, one of the board members, and her husband, Antoine.

"Your girlfriend, I presume." Sandeep nods as he works his way through the decadent chocolate cake that was served for dessert.

"Yes, Colette Davenport. She's a ballet dancer with The City Ballet."

"Impressive. And what about you, Rhys? What are your aspirations?" he asks.

I had a whole list of things of intelligent things to say, things I figured the board members would want to hear from a prospective board president candidate, but looking into Sandeep's kind eyes, I find it impossible to embellish.

I've got nothing, I might as well own it. "I don't know."

He smiles. "You're in good company. I don't know a lot of thirty-year-olds, or almost thirty-year-olds that do. The cool thing is, you've got time. And from what it sounds like, an open mind to figuring it out."

After Sandeep's reassurance that I'm not completely hopeless, I finally let myself relax.

Later, once dinner is cleared, and the group is having after-dinner cocktails in the living room, I notice Lettie heading for the bathroom and follow her there.

"Hey," she says, when she finds me standing outside the door.

"Thank you for being here tonight. I had no idea we wouldn't be sitting together."

"It was nearly impossible, but I survived one meal without you," she teases. "Jerrod was asking a lot of questions about us, but nothing I couldn't handle."

Her response fires up my blood again. I should have known Jerrod was playing games by separating us, but now hearing he was questioning Lettie about our relationship has me livid.

Lettie must see how tense I am. "Don't worry. I defended your honor and told them what an amazing boyfriend you are, and that we're madly in love." When I don't laugh, she reaches out and places a hand on my chest. "You'd do the same for me, right?"

"Yeah, but I wouldn't have to justify being with you or explain what an amazing person you are. Everyone knows what kind of person you are. It's easy to stand beside you. The hard job is standing next to me. Rooting for a guy that doesn't have anything going for himself."

"That's not true. And, yes, your reputation has been built on behaviors that don't serve you anymore, but that doesn't mean it's the kind of person you are. The kind of person you want to be."

I'm caught up in Lettie's kind words. The way she's helping me in this moment. How even though we haven't been beside each other most of the night, she's been on my team.

My eyes drop to her lips. I want to kiss her, but no one's around. I have half a mind to drag her back to the living room and kiss her there so it's allowed.

I do the next best thing and wrap my arm around her waist to pull her into a hug. She wraps her arms around my shoulders, closing the space between us. The way her body feels pressed against mine should be illegal. And she smells fucking amazing.

I take a long inhalation to trap her scent in my lungs, hoping our proximity will have me smelling like her later. I've never wanted a woman's scent to linger, to have it settle on my clothes and my skin, but with Lettie, I want to wrap her scent around me like a security blanket and take it with me wherever I go.

I pull back an inch, leaving our faces only inches from each other.

I'm this close to saying fuck it and kissing her when I hear a woman's squeal of excitement coming from the other room.

Lettie pulls back. "What was that?"

"Didn't even hear it," I lie.

She shakes her head, then lifts on her toes, pressing a light kiss to my lips. It's so soft, there's barely any pressure to it. I'm desperate to chase her retreating lips, but she grabs my hand and pulls me toward the living room.

"Come on, let's get back in there."

With Lettie's hand in mine, we make our way down the hallway and into the living room.

We find Corinne buzzing around the room, a mega-watt smile plastered to her face as she wipes at her eyes. Everyone's cheerful and talking. The energy of the party has shifted for some reason.

"Congratulations!" I hear Edith say as she pulls Corinne in for a hug. Then Edith turns to my grandfather. "See, Ward, great-grandbabies aren't as far off as you think."

Is Corinne pregnant?

Then, Corinne's right in front of us, all pink cheeks and glossy brown eyes.

"Can you believe it?" she asks before extending her left hand out to me and Lettie. "We're engaged!"

With the movement of her fingers, a large diamond twinkles up at us. No, large is an understatement. This diamond is massive.

"Congratulations!" Lettie drops my hand so she can hug Corinne. "That's wonderful news."

"Thank you. I wasn't expecting this. I mean we've been dating for years and we've talked about it but I always thought we'd wait longer, so this is a huge surprise."

My eyes find Jerrod across the room. He's surrounded by my grandfather and Edith, Aditi and her husband, John, Eileen and her partner, Gwen. He laughs at something Aditi says, then bringing the champagne glass to his lips, his eyes meet mine and his brows flex.

The good mood I was in evaporates with one glance at his smug face.

"Congrats, Corinne." I pat her arm then leave her and Lettie standing there to make my way over to Jerrod.

"I heard the exciting news," I say as I approach.

He hands me a glass of champagne from the table nearby.

"Congratulations," I say tightly. That's code for w*hat a fucking joke.*

"Thank you." Jerrod nods, his silent message clear. *You liked that, eh?*

When we clink glasses, I squeeze the stem between my fingers, channeling all my frustration there so I don't use too much force and end up smashing our glasses together.

From an outside perspective, it probably looks like two cousins exchanging pleasantries. Me congratulating Jerrod on his engagement. I would be happy for him if that's how it was between us, but that's not our relationship. He always wants to win and while I've stepped back in the past, deciding it wasn't worth it to compete with him, I can't do that now, not with The Spencer Foundation and my parents' legacy at stake.

"Corinne looks happy." I nod across the room where Corinne and Lettie are still talking.

"She's been waiting four years."

"The timing was convenient."

"I like to think of it more as strategic. Something that would have happened eventually but has an even bigger impact at this moment. But you don't know much about strategy or you would've spent the last five years building relationships with the board members." He takes another swig of his champagne. "The gun went off years ago, and you're still back at the starting line, Rhys."

I know he's right but I can't let him see my panic. That his engagement only further proves that he's been on the right path all along while I've been lost and fumbling around. I try to take comfort in Sandeep's words earlier.

It's okay not to know.

But Jerrod pulls me back into the arena, this battle ground that we've built around the two of us.

"You can't win, Rhys. Not if we're being appraised on our character and values."

My eyes lock with Lettie's across the room.

I see the concern in her blue eyes. *You okay?* The silent message calms me. I have to leave before I say something in front of the board that I'll regret.

"Congratulations, Jerrod." I hand him my untouched champagne glass and walk away.

CHAPTER 27

Colette

As promised, after he took me home, Rhys unzipped my dress. Then, he kissed me on the cheek, gave Maxine a quick pet, and left. He'd been quiet on the ride back to my apartment, clearly frustrated with how the dinner party ended. I know he felt that the traction he made with the foundation board members had been overshadowed by Corinne and Jerrod's engagement, but I had no idea what to say or do to make him feel better.

After I change into pajamas, I wash my face and put on moisturizer. Maxine is already snuggled up on her side of the bed. I'm about to crawl in to join her when my phone rings on my nightstand. At this time of night, I have my do not disturb setting on except for letting a few people, my parents and Hannah, bypass it for emergencies.

It's Hannah.

"Hey! You're back," I answer, excited to finally talk to her. It's only been ten days, but it feels like so much has happened in the short time since she's been on her honeymoon.

"Hi! I'm downstairs."

"You are?"

"Yeah, will you buzz me in?" She asks.

I scramble off my bed and rush toward the front door.

I hit the button to unlock the front door, then open the door and wait. I'd be paranoid about standing in my apartment hallway in my tiny sleep shorts and tank top, but I know Mrs. Donahue has to be asleep already and Ricardo, my neighbor across the hall, works nights as an ER doctor.

A minute later, Hannah steps off the elevator and rushes toward me.

Her newly tanned skin has her glowing like a Grecian goddess, making her sapphire-blue eyes pop.

"Welcome home!" I throw my arms around her, nearly knocking her backwards. "It's so good to see you."

"Same." She laughs, squeezing me tight. "Sorry, I know it's late, but tomorrow will be hectic with the Leg-Up fundraiser, and I wanted to see you."

Normally, I might be stressed by the fact that it's after ten and I'm not in bed yet, but I'm too wired from the dinner party with Rhys and now Hannah being here has me nearly bouncing off the walls.

"You look amazing! How was the Maldives? And being officially married?"

"Thank you. It was amazing. Sun and surf and lots of sex."

"Sounds like it was perfect."

"It was."

I move toward the kitchen.

"Do you want something to drink? Sparkling water? Tea? Decaf latte?"

I don't have the last one, but I could probably run down the block to get her one. Or across the city. That's when I realize all this energy I have right now is nervous energy. While I'm excited to see Hannah, I'm also anxious to tell her about Rhys and the fact that we're dating. Fake dating.

"Water is good. And I can get it." She laughs, taking a glass out of the cabinet and filling it up with the refrigerator's filtered water. "You're wired. Did you have caffeine tonight?"

I move to take a seat on the couch and she follows me.

"No, but I did have a glass of wine."

Her brows lift. "Yeah? What did you do tonight?" She sets her water glass on a coaster on the coffee table, then leans back into the couch cushions.

I pull my legs in cross-legged, take a deep breath, and tell her everything.

She leans forward and calmly takes a sip of water.

"As soon as I got to the airport last night, I checked socials and saw everything online."

I wince. Even though she has to know I didn't intentionally not tell her, I feel bad that's how she found out.

She laughs. "It's ironic that I asked you to keep an eye on him at my wedding and now you're dating him."

"Fake dating. Don't forget the fake part." Even as I emphasize it to Hannah, I know I'm reminding myself as well. Maybe it's the fact that we'd been preparing all week for tonight, but it felt different between us. Like we were more connected. That we understood each other on a deeper level than just our goals in this fake relationship.

And then there's the tiny issue that I wanted him to kiss me in the hallway even though it had nothing to do with our fake relationship. There would have been no witnesses, yet when his eyes dropped to my lips, I was fully ready to participate in any behind-the-scenes activities. When we were interrupted by Corinne's squeal of excitement, I gave him a quick peck. It wasn't even a ghost of a kiss, yet I'd felt it all the way down to my toes.

"You're not breaking out in hives, so something has changed."

I smile. "You're taking this better than I thought."

"Oh, that's because I love you and I'm a supportive friend.

But Rhys? When I see him, let's just say he's going to get an earful."

"Come on. He's not the guy we thought he was and I think you should give him a chance."

She arches her brow. "I'm not familiar with the best friend protocol for fake relationships. Do I have to pretend I like him, too?"

"I'm new to this as well, but I think you smile and pretend we're the cutest couple you've ever seen."

"Hmm. I guess I'll have to take your word for it."

"Did you know that Chloe and Barrett fake dated?" I ask.

"I think I heard that from Emma." Her lips twitch. "Does anyone else know about you and Rhys?"

"Only Isabella and Rhys's assistant, Ramsey. And now you." I pause remembering Sebastian knows, too. "Oh, and Sebastian."

She nods. "Okay. Does the relationship have an expiration date?"

"After The Spencer Foundation board votes on its new president in a few months. That will be after evaluations so hopefully we'll both have gotten what we wanted."

We spend the next hour catching up on her honeymoon and what has been happening between me and Rhys the past few weeks. I'm thankful that when she's gone, I'm able to crawl into bed and fall asleep. I need the rest because tomorrow is a big day.

CHAPTER 28

Rhys

"Let me see that one." I point to the ring that first caught my eye. The one that immediately called to me because I could see how it would fit perfectly on Lettie's finger. How elegant and sophisticated it is, just like her.

Pascal, the jeweler, takes it from the felt insert and hands it to me.

Jerrod and Corinne's engagement had been a surprise. I guess when you've been dating someone for four years, it could happen at any moment, but the self-satisfied smile on Jerrod's face gave him away. He couldn't help but throw it in my face. That's what he gets off on, not only the competition, but winning.

On the way home, Lettie tried to assure me that Jerrod and Corinne's engagement wouldn't be a factor in how the board votes, but the feature article that accompanied their photo and engagement announcement online today made me think otherwise.

The article was more than speculating that Jerrod would be taking the board president position at The Spencer Foundation. My grandfather was even quoted in the article, confirming that Jerrod was an exceptional candidate and that the engagement to Corinne was evidence of his commitment to the foundation's strong family values.

In the past, I would have brushed this off. Not let Jerrod's antics affect me, but every decision I make up until the board votes is critical. I've got to start thinking like him. Scheming. Strategizing. It's the only way I'll be able to compete with him.

Holding the delicate platinum band between my fingers, I inspect the ring at every angle. The princess cut diamond shimmers as I rotate it under the light. The small diamonds surrounding the center stone only add to its brilliance.

For a moment, I let myself imagine this ring on Lettie's finger. How it would feel to hold her hand with the solid gem beneath my fingertips. *Mine.*

The ring is perfect. It's what I would pick out for Lettie, if this was real.

I'm caught off guard by the thought, and the rush of satisfaction it gives me.

Clearly, I'm losing my mind. The idea that I would be proposing marriage at all is wildly entertaining, but to have the woman be Lettie is even more absurd.

A woman like her would never hitch her wagon to mine. Not for real.

My chest aches as I hand the ring back to Pascal, but an engagement between me and Lettie would only be for show, so I don't need to consider what kind of ring she would want. My only focus right now is to demonstrate to the board that, like Jerrod, I am serious about commitment and family. And to do that, I need to propose to Lettie.

"I'll go with the first one," I tell him, clearing my throat. Doing my best to ease the tightness that has worked itself there.

He nods, then places Lettie's perfect ring back in the case before taking the ring I've selected to the back for polishing.

It's a beautiful ring. Flashy and over-the-top, like the one Jerrod put on Corinne's finger.

I lean back in the chair. With so much attention on me and Lettie lately, I'd opted to come in the back door of Pascal's jewelry store and use a private room. As Ramsey had suggested, I thought the publicity would be helpful with showing the public, and especially the board, that Lettie and I are in a strong, committed relationship, but Ramsey has shown me several posts and photos that felt intrusive. Not just of us as a couple, but of Lettie on her own, walking to practice or leaving her apartment.

The back door clicks and I look up from my phone.

Ramsey walks in and with the biggest shit-eating grin on his face, he saunters over to where I'm sitting.

A moment later, Pascal appears with the ring box. "You're all good to go, Mr. Spencer." He moves to hand me the velvet box but Ramsey intercepts.

"Oh, let me see what you picked out."

He opens the box and his jaw drops to the floor.

"What the hell is this?!" he exclaims.

Pascal turns the box back toward himself, clearly wanting to make sure that he put the right ring inside. He doesn't know that Ramsey's reaction is because he had no idea I was looking at rings today.

When I asked Ramsey to make me the appointment, I didn't tell him what it was for.

His reaction is the reason why.

"I thought you were getting her earrings. Some nice two-carat diamond studs to commemorate the fundraiser show-case tonight. You know, like a good billionaire fake boyfriend would do." He gestures to the ring, which he's removed from the ring box and is waving around wildly. "This isn't earrings, Rhys."

"I know. I—" I start to explain, but he cuts me off.

"I can't believe that Lettie is going along with this. You

know, she is one of the best humans I've ever met, but agreeing to a fake engagement so you can upstage Jerrod is another level."

My mouth opens to speak, but I don't know what I'd say. I haven't mentioned anything to Lettie yet. Picking out a ring is more than premature, it's ridiculous. But I can't tell Ramsey that. Besides, I'm planning to talk to Lettie, to ask her, but with her fundraiser showcase tonight, I haven't had a chance.

"Look at my baby all grown up," Ramsey teases, he hands me the ring box, then holds up his phone to take a picture of me. He sniffs and pretends to wipe a tear. His panic from a moment ago nowhere to be found. "I never thought this day would come."

"Fuck off," I growl.

"So touchy." Ramsey opens the ring box again; this time his shock is replaced by awe. "How many carats?" he asks Pascal.

"Six point one four," Pascal responds.

Ramsey lets out a low whistle. "Damn. I need a fake boyfriend who wants to shower me with lavish gifts."

"You're coming to the fundraiser tonight?" I ask, hoping to change the subject.

"Lettie invited me personally, so of course I'm coming. And, I have a little bit of a crush on Sebastian so that's fun."

"Sebastian?" I ask.

"Yeah, Lettie's dance partner."

"He's gay?"

"Um, yeah." Ramsey shoots me a look of annoyance. Like I exhaust him.

He's one to judge.

"Huh, I didn't realize."

"It was probably hard to see through all that jealous rage."

"What are you talking about?"

"Lettie told me you were jealous of Sebastian giving her a massage. You even growled. That's so not like you."

"That's a normal boyfriend reaction."

Ramsey wiggles his brows. "A normal *fake* boyfriend reaction?"

He's trying to get a reaction out of me, but I won't give it to him. "I've got to play my part, don't I?"

Ramsey moves the ring box side to side.

"It's so sparkly. When are you popping the question?"

"I don't know."

"Normally, I would say you should opt for a romantic candlelit setup, but if you're going for publicity that's not going to give you as much bang for your buck."

"When do you think I should do it?" I ask, hoping he'll laugh in my face like I would expect anyone else to and tell me I'm an idiot for even concocting this plan.

"If Lettie's on board, then I think tonight is the perfect opportunity."

He's right, but there's no way I'd be able to discuss it with Lettie beforehand.

Ramsey follows me out to the vehicle waiting out back. With the small velvet box tucked away in my pocket, I text Lettie.

Rhys: *Good luck tonight, Princess.*

The text goes unanswered, as I expected it would. She's already at the theater preparing for tonight.

Later, when I'm dressed in my suit for the fundraiser, I stare at the velvet box on my dresser before shutting off the light and leaving. I'm halfway up the stairs when I decide to run back and get it. There's no downside to being prepared.

Watching Lettie perform is not how I imagined it would be. I knew she'd be graceful and make it look effortless, but I had no idea how strong she is. How fierce and determined.

I've been to the ballet many times. My mom was a lover of

the ballet. She had been a dancer into her teens, but didn't have the talent to continue professionally. When I was younger, we'd go to performances as a family and by the end she'd be misty-eyed. I had always thought she was sad about her dance career ending, but watching Lettie and Sebastian onstage, I get it now. The performance is more than the dancer's movement, it's the way they use their bodies to express emotion and connect with the audience.

Lettie's magnetic onstage. As I watch her, I think about the hard work and grit she puts into a career like this. I wish I was half as passionate about something as Lettie is about ballet.

One moment I'm caught up in their movements, the next I'm trying to reconcile that the same woman who was having an anxiety attack about dating is flawlessly pirouetting in front of a packed theater. It's hard to believe she has any insecurities at all for the way she moves. And she and Sebastian are spectacular together.

Knowing Sebastian has no romantic interest in Lettie puts me at ease. It allows me to enjoy the performance and not take note of every time he touches her and where, though I'm still highly aware.

His arm around her waist, I want it to be mine.

A hand cradling her thigh or her calf, I want to be the one feeling her smooth skin beneath my palm.

I'm not jealous of him, yet by the time the performance is done, I'm on edge thinking about all the ways I'm dying to touch Lettie but can't.

Lettie and Sebastian take their bows to a standing ovation. There are hundreds of people here, so I'm not expecting any acknowledgment, but then Lettie makes eye contact and throws me an enthusiastic wave before blowing me a kiss.

Ramsey elbows me in the ribs. "Did you see that?" He gestures to Lettie. "That was for you."

"Yeah, I saw her."

Sebastian flashes a flirtatious smile in Ramsey's direction, and I nudge him back. Ramsey swats me with his program and I flick his ear. We're acting like a couple of tweens teasing each other about their crushes.

Once the curtain drops, the audience starts to filter out to the theater lobby where the rest of the night's festivities will take place.

It's just my luck that Ramsey and I run into Jerrod and Corinne on our way into the lobby.

"Rhys, your girl really knocked it out of the park," Jerrod says.

"She's so talented." Corinne sighs, emotion still filling her eyes from the performance.

"She's amazing. I'm so proud of her." The words fall easily from my lips. They'd be the same even if I wasn't her fake boyfriend. Lettie is a talented dancer and I am proud to know her. I know she wants more. That's the motivation behind dating and finding more passion in her life, but based off what I saw on stage tonight, in my opinion she's already there.

There's a bottle neck at the theater door, leaving us stuck next to Jerrod and Corinne. While we're standing together, another couple that I don't recognize exits the row in front of us. The woman, an energetic redhead in a pink dress, nearly flings herself at Corinne.

"Corinne!"

"Diem!" Corinne exclaims with matched enthusiasm.

"Oh my goodness. I heard about your engagement." Diem hugs Corinne tightly while bouncing on her toes. "Let me see that ring!"

When Diem pulls back from their embrace, Corinne extends her left hand.

"It's breathtaking." Diem pats Jerrod on the arm. "You did good."

A satisfied smile spreads across Jerrod's face. "I did, didn't I?"

"It's so big. And look at that clarity." Diem examines it.

Jerrod's gaze flits to mine. He's loving this moment. I have the urge to whip out the engagement ring in my pocket and show him up, but I refrain.

"Peter, good to see you." Jerrod shakes the guy's hand.

"You two are having one hell of a year," the guy who must be Peter says. "Corinne's promotion. Now an engagement."

"Things always come in threes," Diem proclaims, her enthusiasm building. "Oh! I bet Jerrod will get the board president position. That's number three!"

Diem must feel my hard stare on her because it's after this declaration that she finally shifts her gaze from Corinne and Jerrod to Ramsey, then me. Her eyes widen when they meet mine and I think she's just realized who I am, yet she doesn't look regretful that I heard what she said about the board position.

"Diem, Peter, this is my cousin, Rhys Spencer." Jerrod nods in my direction. "And his assistant, Ramsey."

"Peter Archer." The guy shakes my hand, then Ramsey's.

"Diem Vega." She extends her hand. "I'm sure you know my mother, Aditi. She's on The Spencer Foundation board."

"Yes, I know her." That's all I can say because other than our brief conversation at Jerrod and Corinne's dinner party last night, I don't know much. I certainly didn't know she had a daughter that is good friends with Corinne and Jerrod.

I'd say I could attempt to make a good impression with Diem and it might get back to her mother, but Diem's body language is telling me everything I need to know. She's the female version of Jerrod. Before she even opens her mouth, I know that she's going to tell me everything that makes her great.

"I'm on the fundraising committee for Leg-Up. I worked

closely with Colette Davenport on putting the performance showcase together for tonight."

I'm not sure if she's name-dropping Colette right now, but it's odd she's using Lettie's last name as if I don't know who she is.

"Colette is my girlfriend."

"Oh." She looks taken aback for a moment but then recovers. "How long have you and Colette been together?" Diem asks.

"It's only been a few weeks. But for Rhys, that's a record. Right, bud?" Jerrod's patronizing tone lights the short fuse that I was already working with.

"We grew up together. We've known each other forever," I respond.

"That's nice." Those are her words, but her face looks like she sucked on something sour. She's likely disappointed to hear about Colette's association with me.

I need to keep my shit together. Diem is Aditi's daughter and works with Colette through Leg-Up, so before I say something I regret, I quickly excuse myself. I need a drink.

Ramsey and I make our way out to the lobby, a red and gold carpeted space filled with high-top tables draped in black linens. On one side of the room is the silent auction, while the other side has tables filled with light appetizers and desserts. A small bar is set up on either side of the room to prevent congestion.

"She's talking out of her ass. She's not on the board. Her mother is. And you said you made good headway getting to know the board members last night."

"I did." I order a whiskey neat from the bar. Ramsey's brows lift as I down it in one gulp, then order another. "But that was before Corinne and Jerrod got engaged."

"There's still time, and all this hype about their engagement will die down. Besides, the tides will turn when you propose to Lettie. You think you two dating has garnered interest, just wait until you're engaged."

"Fake engaged," I correct.

"Sure." He takes a sip of his white wine. "Oh, I see Sebastian." He lifts his arm above his head and waves his fingers fervently.

"You going to be okay?" Ramsey asks.

"Yeah. Go on, make your move."

While Ramsey greets Sebastian across the room, I find myself making my way to the silent auction table to pass the time until Lettie comes out. She's the only person that can lift me out of this mood that the conversation with Diem, Jerrod and Corinne put me in.

I'm already making a substantial donation to Leg-Up tonight, but making a bid on the silent auction items would be beneficial, too. When I reach into my pocket to produce the paddle number I was given at the registration table, my fingers brush against the velvet ring box. I start to pull the small paddle out, but the box comes with it. With my drink in my left hand, I use the fingers of my right hand attempting to flip positions of the box and paddle, so I can hold the paddle in my palm and put the box back in my tuxedo jacket pocket, but the velvet box slips from my hand and onto the ground.

I reach to retrieve it but another hand picks it up instead. My eyes lift to the man now holding the ring box.

It's Jerrod.

"Whoa, what do we have here?" he asks.

Before I can grab it out of his hand, he flips it open.

If he's surprised, he doesn't show it. He was probably prepared for it. Anything to win, right?

I'm about to snatch it out of his hand when Aditi Vega approaches us.

"Gentlemen. It's good to see you both here tonight." She turns her glowing smile on me. "Colette was absolutely magnificent tonight. She's an amazing dancer, and I know

Diem has had only wonderful things to say about working with her on this fundraiser."

It's hard for me to focus on responding when I'm aware that Jerrod is still holding my engagement ring out in the open. I'm hoping I can keep Aditi's attention on me before she notices it.

"She truly is a breathtaking dancer. She'll be happy to hear you enjoyed the performance, and that everyone is here to support Leg-Up." I motion to the silent auction tables beside us. "Have you checked out the auction items yet?"

"I was just on my way over when I saw you two and thought I'd say hello."

Fucking fantastic.

"Personally, I'm going for the luxury candle collection," I teasingly wag a finger at her, "so don't you outbid me."

Beside us, Jerrod laughs, drawing Aditi's attention to him and her gaze to what is in his hand.

"Jerrod, what's this?" she asks. "That's not Corinne's ring, is it?"

"No. Rhys was showing me the ring he got for Colette."

I press my lips together and attempt to talk myself down.

Do not assault Jerrod at this event. That's exactly what he wants.

Aditi gasps, then holds her hands out indicating she wants to see the ring. "Oh, do you mind?"

I shake my head because what the fuck else can I do at this point? While Aditi examines the ring, I attempt to keep my composure.

If Lettie says no to the fake engagement and I don't propose, then Aditi and Jerrod will know.

But Aditi doesn't know when I was planning to propose. I can do it another time.

"Oh my, it's beautiful." She glances up at me. "Are you proposing tonight?"

Fuck.

Don't say yes. You have to ask Lettie.

It's like a pinball game inside my brain right now.

Before I can answer, Jerrod turns to Aditi. "He's getting cold feet, not sure if he can make a commitment to one woman." He throws a knowing smile at me. "Classic Rhys. But knowing my own strong, steadfast relationship with Corinne, he came to me for some encouraging words." Jerrod places a hand on my shoulder. "You can do it Rhys. You got this, buddy."

Jerrod is going to be a pile of dust when I get done with him. They'll never be able to identify the body.

Aditi places a hand on my forearm. "It's normal to be nervous. It's a big commitment and a huge declaration to make in front of a crowd like this, but I'm sure you'll do great."

"Thanks." At this point, it's all I can say. Jerrod has done enough talking for both of us.

"This is all very exciting." With her fingers, Aditi makes a zipping motion across her lips. "I won't say a word." She squeezes my forearm, then hands the ring box back to Jerrod. "Good luck."

With Aditi gone, Jerrod snaps the ring box closed and hands it back to me with a smug grin on his face.

"She's never going to say yes. Date you…that was a stretch…but an engagement? I'll believe it when I see it," he says, strolling away with his hands in his pockets like he doesn't have a care in the world.

My heart is pounding, looking for a release for all the adrenaline it wants to unleash on Jerrod. With one mistake, I've been pulled even deeper into this game with him. I look around, hoping to see Lettie. To steal a private moment with her to explain everything that just happened.

And if she says no? I'm fucked.

My heart hammers in my chest at the thought of having to face Jerrod if Lettie doesn't agree to a fake engagement.

But I have to ask her or she'll be blindsided. She won't know what to say in front of everyone.

Except, I know Lettie well enough to know she wouldn't question a proposal in front of everyone and out our fake relationship. She trusts me.

There's no time and I can't take that chance. The foundation board presidency depends on it.

I know what I have to do, I just hope Lettie understands.

CHAPTER 29

Colette

As the curtain closes on me and Sebastian, the continued thunderous applause from the audience sends a thrill through my body.

"Wow, Lettie. That was—" I turn to see Sebastian, hairline drenched and temples dripping sweat. He looks like he's run a marathon, when really, he gracefully performed a pas de deux. He pulls me in for a hug. "That was perfection."

"That felt amazing, right?" I squeeze him back, his skin warm and sweat-slick from our performance, but I don't even care. "You are the best. Thank you for doing this with me."

He pulls back, holding my upper arms as we catch our breath and start to come down from the rush of the performance.

"Anytime, doll." He kisses my cheek before grabbing my hand to lead me offstage.

We accept the water bottles from the stage crew and make our way to the dressing rooms backstage.

As I go over our performance in my head, I'm still in awe. We'd decided to incorporate the challenging lift that Alexei had been working with us on this past week into tonight's performance and it had been executed perfectly.

But separate from the lift, there was something different about my dancing tonight. A tingle of awareness that made my movements less technical and more expressive. More passionate. Whatever it was, I could feel the difference, and I'm determined to chase that feeling and keep pushing for more.

And, I'll admit, I enjoyed having Rhys in the audience.

I'd felt his presence and that had done something to me. I've always danced for myself, because I love it, and want to push myself to be the best I can. But I have to say, there was something thrilling about knowing Rhys was watching me, his eyes taking in every move, that made it more fun.

When it was over, my gaze had immediately spotted Rhys a few rows back, big hands clapping and a gorgeous, supportive smile beaming up at me. I don't know what had come over me, but I'd given him a little wave, then blew him a kiss.

Now I'm realizing it was the first performance where my parents were in the audience but I hadn't looked for them. My first thought had been about Rhys.

I grab a handful of pretzels and cheese off the snack table, then quickly shower and change into my dress before making my way to the reception part of the evening.

I chose one of the dresses Rhys had sent over for the dinner party last night. It's cream with a fitted bodice, sweetheart neckline, and a chiffon midi-length skirt. I swear it's the formal, grown-up version of a princess dress I had when I was younger.

I'd asked if he wanted me to return the dresses I hadn't worn, and he told me they were mine now. I'd thought it was too much to accept them, especially once I got a look at their price tags, but when I asked Ramsey to return them, he pretended like he didn't hear me and continued organizing them in my closet.

My parents are here, Hannah and James, Hunter and

Sophie, the Cartwrights, Hunter and Hannah's parents, Emma and Griffin, Choe and Barrett. Rhys's grandfather, Ward, and Edith. Even Jerrod and Corinne made the effort to come, which I know Rhys wasn't thrilled about, but they're another affluent couple that can help raise funds for this special cause. It makes me happy to see such a great turnout for the event.

I spot Rhys and a beaming smile breaks out on my face. Weaving through the crowd of guests, I rush over toward him. It's only when I'm a second away from throwing myself into his arms that my brain reminds my body that he's not that kind of boyfriend. Being around Rhys and not wanting more with him physically is starting to become a challenge. My body easily forgets itself in his presence, and my brain has to reel it back in.

But Rhys quickly eliminates the few inches I've left between us and pulls me into his arms. A squeak escapes from my throat when he lifts me off the ground.

"You were wonderful," he whispers against the shell of my ear.

"Thank you," I say. As he slowly lowers me to the ground, I feel every inch of his body against mine and it makes my core ache.

Our relationship is fake, but the way I'm starting to feel toward Rhys, the fondness, the attraction, the *desire* is starting to feel very real.

He leans back to take in my dress.

"And you look absolutely stunning."

"You look pretty good yourself." I reach up to pinch his bow tie between my fingers.

His tux is classic and black. He looks gorgeous, so I feel guilty when I realize I'm wishing that he'd have worn something more unique. The way he does when we're hanging out together at home. A fun pop of color or a wild pattern that only he can pull off. That's the Rhys I've grown fond of.

Classic black tux Rhys is sexy and all, but there's something passive about him that dims his otherwise self-assured smile. Some people are more comfortable fitting in, but Rhys thrives on standing out.

"Are you hungry? Can I get you a drink?" He asks.

"Yes, and yes."

Rhys leads me to the food table and I get the biggest thrill from the way he holds my hand, firm and protective.

I load my plate up, while Rhys gets me a drink from the bar. Then, we make our way over to the balcony staircase where Mila, the director of Leg-Up, is giving an introduction for the evening. She gives an overview of the program and encourages attendees to peruse the silent auction.

"We've been so fortunate to be contacted by an anonymous donor who will be matching all donations tonight up to ten million dollars."

My jaw drops. "Oh my god." I turn to Rhys. "Did you hear that?"

"Yeah," his lip curves up, but his eyes don't match his smile. "That's great."

Mila finishes her speech, giving recognition to me and Sebastian for our volunteer performance and the silent auction sponsors, but I'm only half listening. I stare at Rhys's profile while he lifts his drink to his lips. Something's off with him. I lift my hand to his cheek.

"Hey, are you okay?" I ask.

"And now, I'd like to recognize Colette Davenport for being a champion of this project. She's generously donated her time and her talents to our program. Colette, would you come up and say a few words?"

Rhys turns to me, a half-smile on his face. "Yeah, you need to go."

I set my drink on the table nearby and make my way up to the front of the crowd. Mila gives me a hug, then hands me the microphone.

The speech I practiced comes out somewhat coherent, and when I'm done, everyone claps.

That's when I notice Rhys walking toward me.

"Rhys?"

"May I have your attention?" Rhys says into the microphone, then laughs. "I guess I have your attention just by way of radio frequency."

"What are you doing?" I whisper.

"As we celebrate all the dancers in the showcase tonight and raise money for Leg-Up, I want to give a much-deserved applause to my beautiful girlfriend, Colette Davenport. Her dedication and determination to putting on this showcase and making this evening possible is unmatched. This woman has danced away with all our hearts, but especially mine."

Rhys turns from the crowd to face me.

"What—" I start but he cuts me off.

"Colette, in a vast expanse of night sky, where countless stars twinkle, you are the one constant that guides me. The beacon of light that illuminates my darkest hours."

That's a little much. I'm going to have to tell Rhys he needs to tone it down or it won't be believable.

And then, my heart trips over itself as Rhys drops to one knee and pulls out a small velvet box.

Wait. *What?*

"Colette Elaine Davenport. I'm the luckiest man in the world to have you by my side. Marry me?"

I can't tell if those last two words are a statement or a question.

There are several gasps from the crowd around us, or maybe that was me. It takes a moment for me to remember how to breathe. To recover from the shock of his words. *His proposal.*

I know my eyes are huge as I stare at Rhys, searching for a clue about his intention.

What are you doing? I ask him silently. Pleading with my eyes for him to help me understand what is happening.

If his eyes were a magic 8 ball dice, they'd read *reply hazy, try again.*

So, I give up and shift my gaze to all the faces around me. Staring at me, waiting for an answer.

I should be used to this. All eyes on me. I'm a performer after all. But this is different. When I'm dancing, I know the steps, I've practiced them a thousand times before the curtain goes up. Rhys's proposal is catching me completely off guard.

I look around at everyone's expectant faces. Down at Rhys, who has no business looking that handsome in his suit. All the thoughts whirling in my head. *What is happening right now? This isn't real, right? Why didn't he talk to me? My mom and dad are here. And Rhys's grandfather. Our friends and family. What do I say?*

"Lettie?" Rhys lifts his brows in encouragement. I see it there now. The way his eyes widen. Rhys's usual bravado slips ever so slightly, allowing a touch of vulnerability to edge its way in.

Please. Those hazel eyes of his plead and my breath catches.

It's part of a scheme. But it wasn't part of *our* deal.

Anger flares in my belly. Rhys is fake proposing to me in front of our family and friends, banking on the fact that I will just go along with this plan he told me nothing about.

With dating being such an unfamiliar concept, I haven't thought much about what it would be like to get engaged. To have a man I love kneeling on the ground and telling me I'm his world. But I know it wasn't supposed to be Rhys Spencer with an obnoxiously large diamond asking me to fake an engagement for our already fake relationship.

No, this has gone too far.

And I'd trusted him. I'd seen a different side of him. The man who'd finished the tutus for the children's hospital while

I slept, ordered all my favorites so I didn't have to grocery shop, picked me up from practice with my favorite snack, and helped me with my anxiety around dating. Over the past few weeks, we'd become good friends…maybe more?

God, I'd loved the way his touch lit up my body and the way his kiss made me forget my surroundings.

I'm such an idiot.

Because while I've been thinking there might be more to Rhys, he's been plotting ways to one-up Jerrod. It's not a coincidence his proposal is on the heels of Jerrod and Corrine's engagement. Rhys wants to win and he doesn't care about anyone else.

I should say no. Tell Rhys he's insane and expose our arrangement.

My lips part to speak but nothing comes out because my brain is running through the aftermath of this moment, desperately trying to run a pros and cons analysis of each scenario while I feel the heat of hundreds of pairs of eyes on me.

One thing is certain. We can't pretend to *date* if I reject his very public marriage proposal.

If I say no, everything ends. Right now, I'm not prepared to make that decision. Under duress, which has been placed upon me by my beloved fake boyfriend.

My eyes scan his face. His stupidly handsome, ridiculously gorgeous face.

The bead of sweat rolling down the side of his face is a momentary distraction until he says my name under his breath and I realize I haven't responded yet.

I need to go along with this. *For now.*

I need to accept Rhys's proposal. *For now.*

I force a smile and focus on keeping my feet still so I don't reflexively kick him in the shin.

"Yes." I do my best to not make it sound like a question and throw in a nod, hoping that makes it more convincing.

Rhys places the giant rock on my finger, then stands to scoop me into his arms. He presses a demanding kiss against my lips, then he's hugging me again.

I'll play the part right now, but if he thinks this is all well and good, he's so wrong.

He holds me against him, and through a clenched smile, I pretend to nuzzle his neck so I can lean in and whisper, "I'm going to kill you.

CHAPTER 30

Rhys

After a million congratulations from family and friends, and fundraiser guests, Lettie grabs my hand to pull me toward a dark hallway, which I find leads to the dressing rooms. Once we're behind the dressing room door, she drops my hand and begins pacing.

"Wha—"

"How—"

"I can't even—"

She starts and stops so many times, her anger clogging her ability to speak. Her arms cross over her chest and there's fury in her eyes. If she were a cartoon character, she'd have steam coming out of her ears.

"What the hell, Rhys? This was not part of the plan."

It only takes a brief lock of our eyes and she inhales on a gasp. She knows. My guilt must be evident.

The realization only fuels her fire more.

"Oh, I see. It was part of *your* plan." She waves her left hand in the air, the huge diamond I placed on it minutes ago sparkling beneath the dressing room's vanity lights. "I can't believe you did that."

The part of me that's competing with Jerrod, that loved

seeing the shocked look on his face when Lettie accepted my proposal, is pleased. Now, he doesn't have an advantage over me. We're even. And several members of the board were here tonight to witness it.

But as the rush of adrenaline from besting Jerrod wears off, all I'm left with is regret.

She's right. This is completely fucked up.

Suddenly, the sight of the diamond on Lettie's finger makes me nauseous. Not because I don't want my ring on her finger, but because of what it represents.

She didn't say yes because she wanted this, she felt forced into it. I blindsided her, and I did it knowing that the pressure of the situation would get me what I wanted. That Lettie would have a hard time saying no to my proposal in front of an entire room of people.

A room that included her parents. Fuck. If they didn't hate me before, I'm sure they do now.

Regret is a dull ache in my chest.

I let Jerrod do what he does best, push me to rash decisions then walk away when everything blows up in my face. But even Jerrod isn't to blame, because I'm the one that let him get under my skin. I let my fear of losing control of the situation, the possibility that I might lose control of my parents' legacy foundation, blind me to the fact that I'd taken Lettie's trust in me and broken it.

"I needed—" I start but realize there's nothing I can say right now that makes this right, but I can start with an apology. "I'm—" Before I can get the words out, she cuts me off.

"Of course, it's all about what you want. Ugh. I can't even look at you right now."

Tears fill her eyes. Her hands move up and down her bare arms like she's trying to hug herself. My arms ache to hold her and make this better.

She presses a finger into my chest. "Stay away from me."

"What about the party?" I motion out the door, back

toward where the fundraiser is still in full swing. "We just got engaged."

Her blue eyes flash with rage and I back off.

She's not herself. Gone is the even-tempered woman that wouldn't dream of making a scene. I've done that to her. If there was ever a question about Lettie's lack of passion, it's not an issue right now.

I follow her back into the theater lobby where she grabs two champagne glasses off a waiter's tray and slings them both back. Fuck. This isn't going to be pretty.

"Princess." I reach for her.

"Don't call me that," she snaps setting the glasses back on the tray and rolling her shoulders back, before disappearing into the sea of guests.

Ramsey appears at my side. "What the hell was that?"

I don't bother looking at him, intent on keeping track of Lettie as she makes her way across the room to speak with her parents.

I push a hand through my hair, then hold my hands out. "I'm engaged now." I force a smile, but Ramsey's glare tells me now isn't the time to be cute.

He shakes his head. "You didn't ask her, did you?"

"To marry me? You saw it with your own eyes." I motion to where I'd stood in front of the entire fundraiser crowd and proposed to Lettie.

"Fuck a duck, Rhys," he hisses under his breath. "I'm talking about asking her permission to propose."

I shake my head and tell him what happened with Jerrod and Aditi.

He's so annoyed with me, he can't even speak. He simply shakes his head then walks away leaving me standing alone.

It's what I deserve, but it doesn't hurt any less.

Lettie told me to stay away from her, but I also need her to keep our arrangement under wraps. I can't have her getting loose-lipped and telling people we're not really together.

As the party progresses, I keep a watchful eye on her. She talks with friends and fellow dancers. Her left hand outstretched for everyone to examine the ring I just put there.

The ring I proposed with is obscene. It's in complete conflict with Lettie's quiet grace and effortless style. I knew that picking it out, but it's even more obvious now as the large diamond causes the ring to rotate under its own weight.

Everyone is oohing and ahhing at the rock, but I can tell by Lettie's reaction to it that she's not impressed one bit.

She turns her head and catches my eyes, her lips pressing together in silent rage.

I'm about to make my way over to her when my grandfather claps me on the shoulder.

"This is a positive development. Congratulations." He pulls me into a hug. It's foreign. The feeling of his arms around me, and the approval.

"Congratulations, darling." Edith holds my face so she can kiss me straight on the lips. "This is so exciting! Another wedding to plan."

I nod. "Thank you, but I think we'll be waiting until after Lettie's fall performance run to finalize any wedding plans. She needs to focus on her upcoming evaluation and performances."

"That's understandable. You two have had such a quick courtship, it's okay to slow down. Now that you know you want to spend the rest of your lives together, you have all the time in the world."

There was a moment when I dropped to my knee, when Lettie's eyes went wide and her lips parted in surprise, that it felt real. And it made me question everything. I wish I could capture that moment and replay it over and over.

Did she notice my hand was shaking when I opened the ring box? Could she sense that her 'yes' meant something to me?

My eyes find Lettie again. She's among a group of

dancers. She told me to stay away, but I can't keep my eyes off her. Fuck. How is everything going according to plan, yet completely off the rails at the same time?

I'm about to move toward her when I run right into Hannah Cartwright-McKenzie, and she does not look happy to see me.

"The etiquette for a new engagement is a congratulatory hug but I don't know if I can give you that, Rhys."

I hold out my hand instead, but Hannah just shakes her head.

"What is going on?" she asks.

Hannah's always been good at sniffing out bullshit, even when we were kids. I stuff my hands in my pockets and do my best to look nonchalant.

"What do you mean?" I ask.

"I know about your fake relationship, Rhys. Lettie told me last night. I would expect this to be part of your agreement, but every time someone says congratulations, she looks like she's going to burst into tears. It doesn't make sense."

"She said yes, didn't she?" I bite back like a wounded animal unwilling to accept help.

Hannah's eyes narrow.

"If you hurt her in any way, they'll never find your body." The threat falls easily from Hannah's lips.

I'll admit the loyalty is endearing. It reminds me that's the kind of person Lettie is. She's sweet and giving, kind and trustworthy. She's got amazing friends that would do anything for her. The only people here tonight for me are my grandfather and Edith, but they're more apt to side with Lettie in the event of our breakup, which is inevitable.

"Good to know."

"I'm serious, Rhys."

"I don't doubt it for a second."

With one last flash of her brown eyes, she walks off.

My eyes immediately scan the room for Lettie but come up empty.

From his place next to Sebastian, Ramsey must see my panic and feel sorry for me.

He motions toward the door. "I just saw her headed for the exit."

With an unintelligible goodbye, I rush toward the exit in search of my fiancée.

CHAPTER 31

Colette

Slugging back two champagnes within a span of twenty seconds was not the smartest idea.

Now, I'm tipsy. Tipsy and engaged to Rhys.

I've spent the better part of the night in a silent fury. I still can't believe it happened. And not in a good, *oh wow, I'm super shocked my loving boyfriend proposed to me* kind of way but more of a *I can't believe how selfish he is.*

My only solution had been to keep drinking, hoping it would help me deal with the stressful situation of being ambushed by his proposal. And the hurt.

Once the anger subsided, that's what bubbled to the surface.

I'm hurt that he didn't bother talking to me. I hate that he didn't trust me enough to include me in his plans. And I'm angry with myself for the split second of hope and excitement I'd had before I came to my senses and realized it was all a sham.

I don't want to analyze why I thought his proposal might be real. That's a problem for future-Colette.

My heart aches, a tiny shard of betrayal lodged inside it.

I'd thought I could trust Rhys. I thought we were in this

together and then he pulled the rug out from under me. And I was starting to develop feelings for him. Real feelings. And his proposal assured me he not only doesn't share those feelings, he hadn't even considered mine.

My friends were surprised and concerned. Join the club, I wanted to tell them. It's called *Bamboozled by Rhys Spencer*. We'll make t-shirts.

My parents were oddly enthusiastic, especially my mom, who got the same gleam in her eye that she does when she's starting a new design project. *Look at all the possibilities!* My dad was quiet, which isn't like him. I know they talked to Rhys. I saw them at the bar together. Rhys's smile and his handshake with my dad only fueled my anger more. I wanted to march over there and tell my dad not to shake his hand. None of this is real. But my desire not to make a scene at this important event has kept me silent.

As for Rhys, I'd told him to leave me alone, yet I'd felt his gaze on me the rest of the night. Now, he's in a heated conversation with Hannah. To think I had defended him to her last night when she'd questioned his integrity. It makes my stomach hurt. Or maybe that's all the carbonated alcohol I've consumed.

My feet hurt, and I'm too tired to wait for the winner of the stand-off, so I start walking toward the exit.

I'd planned to make an effort of thanking everyone for coming before I left. I would have liked to make a final round to chat with guests and encourage donations to Leg-Up, answer any questions they may have about the program, but no one wants to talk about Leg-Up right now. They only want to talk about the big fat diamond on my left hand and I can't stand to be here a second longer.

I push through the gold-plated doors and into the warm night air. After the air-conditioned theater had started to give me a chill, the temperate air feels like a warm hug. Before descending the stairs, I glance toward the street, and wonder what the odds are of finding a taxi right now.

When I wobble on the first step, my body nearly pitching forward and sending me into a free fall down the stairs, strong hands grip my waist, pulling me upright.

I don't even need to look up to know it's Rhys. His alluring scent gives him away. Also, those firm hands and long fingers I've become accustomed to touching me.

"Oh, look, it's my fiancé," I grumble. "A sneak attack from behind, how original."

Rhys doesn't say anything, only holds me around the waist and helps me down the stairs. I could fight him on this, it's what my ego wants, but between the alcohol I consumed and my tired feet, these heels are starting to give me trouble. And he's delivering me from this nightmare of an evening and closer to getting home, so I allow myself to be guided to a black SUV.

Rhys tucks me into the backseat, then goes around to the other side to get in.

"Good evening, Miss Davenport."

It's Wanda. She's got to agree with me on this one.

"Wanda, we're engaged," I lean over the front seat to tell her. I'm hoping for some commiseration, but since I've failed to give her any context of the situation, she gives me the appropriate response.

"Congratulations, Miss Davenport." She nods in the rearview mirror. "Mr. Spencer."

"No, it's not, Wanda. And remember, I asked you to call me Lettie."

"I'm sorry, Miss Davenport, it's a habit."

I know I'm a mess, but I can't help it. This night has been a rollercoaster. From the high of nailing my performance showcase with Sebastian, to Rhys's sneak attack proposal and having to pretend everything is peachy in front of friends and family. Now, I'm fake engaged and my phone is buzzing with texts from my mother who is already throwing out wedding venue ideas.

"Lettie." With both hands wrapped around my waist, Rhys pulls me backwards. The quick motion and my inability to get my muscles to function properly finds me landing helplessly in his lap.

I expect him to move me aside, but instead, he wraps his arms around my waist, holding me to him. It's like the night of Hannah and James's wedding when we took Aunt Maggie home and there wasn't room for both of us to sit so he pulled me into his lap.

For a moment, I forget that I'm mad at him and nestle my head into the space between his shoulder and chin. His warm, solid body beneath me sends a familiar ache between my thighs.

Traitorous vagina.

It's a sensation I've become familiar with over the last few weeks with Rhys. Lust. Desire. Want. But tonight, I find it surprising that despite my anger with him, my body still reacts to his.

I carried that emotion with me as I talked with friends and fellow dancers. Every congratulations fueling my frustration even more. I'd felt his eyes on me. When I reached for another glass of champagne, our gazes caught across the room and a wave of lust had crashed into me so hard, I'd nearly reached for the waiter's arm to steady myself.

It was like a taut thread, opposite emotions pulling from either side. Anger and lust battling it out. Watching that thread snap would be so satisfying. I'd never understood the concept of hate sex. How you could want to be intimate with someone who you disliked so much. In this moment with Rhys, I get it.

I press my ass against him. His hands tighten around my waist. I can't tell if he's holding me away or to him.

I extend my left hand out. "Look at how it sparkles."

Rotating my hand, the diamond on my finger shimmers with the lights of the city as we make our way down Broadway. "I feel like a little girl playing dress up."

The diamond is obnoxious. A show piece. As if Rhys thought the larger the diamond the more believable this ruse would be.

"It's almost like you're compensating for something, Rhys. Large diamond, small—"

Wanda opens the door. "Goodnight, Miss Davenport, Mr. Spencer."

I wasn't even aware we had stopped.

Rhys shifts me off his lap, then helps me out of the car, before Wanda shuts the door behind us.

"Goodnight, Wanda. Goodnight, you." I wave in Rhys's direction. Wanda gets back into the vehicle and drives off, but Rhys stays put. "If you think I'm going to let you up, you're sorely mistaken, pal. And it's past Mrs. Donahue's bedtime so you better not try to wake her up."

I glance to the other side of the street, expecting to see my apartment building but instead it's the walkway leading to the Seventy-Ninth Street Boat Basin.

"I wanted to go home," I announce, but Rhys starts leading me toward the dock.

"This was easier. And you shouldn't be alone like this."

"Like what, Rhys?" I raise my arms in challenge, nearly sending my clutch flying into the Hudson. "Enraged? Incensed? Horny?"

Probably could have left that last one off.

"It's not because of you. That's the alcohol talking. You know, champagne goggles and all that."

"It's beer goggles. Not champagne goggles."

My eyes flare at his audacity to correct me. He lifts his hands in surrender.

I could order a ride share, haul it back to my apartment and let Rhys have a peaceful night. He might like that. Guess

I better ruin his night like he's ruined mine.

I start down the dock, but with unsteady legs on top of these heels, Rhys's hands move into place to guide me.

"I don't need you to help me. I can walk by myself," I say before nearly crashing into the railing on the side of the dock.

"Sure," he mutters right before his large hands encircle my waist and he steers me in the opposite direction I was going.

"You know what, Rhys? For a guy who sprang a fake proposal on his fake girlfriend and she—I—said yes to save your butt, I don't appreciate your tone." I take another step but it's as unsteady as my last. For a professional dancer I've got zero body control. "It's the heels. They're impossible to walk in."

He slings me over his shoulder so he can remove my heels, then carries me the rest of the way to his boat. A minute later, he sets me onto a cushioned seat in the breakfast nook then gets a glass of water from the kitchen and hands it to me.

"Drink."

"Bossy much?"

"You're going to feel like shit if you don't."

I sulk at the table and drink my water. When I lift the glass to my lips, the ring shifts on my finger.

It doesn't feel real.

That's because it isn't.

Rhys smacks two ibuprofen onto the table beside my glass. "Take these."

My attempt at sassily mimicking his bossy tone becomes muddled under my breath. His brows lift with authority, and I stick out my tongue at him. But I do take the ibuprofen because I don't want to feel bad tomorrow and if anyone knows about post-drinking remedies it would be Rhys.

"Are you hungry?" he asks.

I shake my head. "No."

"Then let's get you to bed."

I contort my arms to reach for the zipper of my dress but have no luck. Rhys steps in behind me, his fingers easily releasing the zipper down my back. The warmth from his finger pad gliding down my spine makes me shiver. He's helped me unzip my dress before, but tonight feels different.

That clench from the car ride is back. Every nerve ending is on high alert.

It's like my body doesn't understand that Rhys is enemy number one right now.

I don't bother to turn around, but simply drop my dress and step out of it. I'm used to being half naked in form-fitting tights and leotards and the alcohol has made me care even less.

I have zero fucks left to give.

I wander into Rhys's closet. He doesn't follow. Apparently, he's still giving me the space I asked for, but his silence is starting to infuriate me. I want more of that back and forth he'd given me outside, if only so I can argue with him and hold this engagement over his head.

My hands make contact with a t-shirt in the drawer. Not bothering to see which one it is, I grab it and walk back out to the bedroom.

That's when it hits me and I start to giggle uncontrollably.

"What's funny?" Rhys calls from the other room.

"You were right. You said I would be using all the four-letter words once you were done with me. I was just thinking about how I could give zero fucks right now. Fucks is technically a five-letter word, but it counts, right?"

I start to pull on the t-shirt, but the darkness makes it impossible to find the head-hole. Now I'm wandering around the room lost inside Rhys's shirt.

Suddenly, hands yank the shirt downward and my head

pops through. My eyes blink open to find Rhys standing in front of me.

He stares at me blankly, clearly not amused with me, which is annoying because I was mad at him first.

Without a word, he moves past me to the bathroom.

"I've got a toothbrush you can use."

"Is it new? I don't want to be using a toothbrush that other women have used before."

"It's new," he says, extending the still packaged toothbrush in my direction.

"Thanks." I accept it. After a minute of me clumsily pawing at the package, Rhys takes it out of my hands and removes the toothbrush. Like he doesn't trust me to do anything myself, he spreads toothpaste on the toothbrush, then runs it under the faucet.

"Oh my god!" I gasp in horror.

"What?" he asks, taken aback by my disgust.

"You're a toothpaste *then* water kind of tooth brusher?"

He glances around the bathroom, likely searching for a witness to commiserate with. *Is it me or is she nuts?*

"Is that a problem?" he asks.

"Yes! You're supposed to wet the bristles, then put the toothpaste on. Otherwise, you could rinse the toothpaste off while you're wetting it down, which results in an inadequately wet toothbrush and a waste of perfectly good toothpaste. Everyone knows this."

Rhys stares down at me with knitted brows. "How drunk are you?"

"I'm not drunk. I'm right."

He simply shakes his head, refusing to engage further in the wet bristles before toothpaste debate.

He leans casually against the door frame, watching me. It's like he thinks taking care of me is his job now that he's my fiancé.

That's not true. He took care of me before. I push the memories of all the kind things Rhys has done for me away. They're tainted now. Maybe he was always planning this fake engagement and just wanted to butter me up.

My fiancé. It's a joke, but I'm not laughing. The anger I felt earlier, the frustration with Rhys for not including me in his plan, bubbles back to the surface. My hand grips the toothbrush tightly, my gums taking the brunt of my anger in this moment.

When I'm finished, I drop the pink toothbrush into the cup on the counter next to Rhys's and push past him. I'm exhausted, yet not tired at all.

"What do you want, Lettie? What will make this better?" he asks. "You're mad. I get it, so tell me what to do and I'll do it."

I lift my arms over my head and fall backwards with a pfft against his navy blue bedding, soaking in the feel of his luxury mattress beneath me.

What do I want from him?

For him to apologize.

To beg on his knees for my forgiveness.

And to kiss me and relieve this ache between my thighs.

Huh, my brain is a confusing place to be right now.

"Is this how it starts? Do the women just fall into your bed?" I ask, stretching out on the navy comforter.

"I've never had a woman in my bed," he says quietly.

That gets my attention. I lift, propping myself on my elbows.

"How's that possible?" I ask.

He shrugs. "I don't fuck in my bed."

For some reason that makes me laugh.

I study him. He's gorgeous. His carefree attitude and rebellious nature making him even more fascinating. How does someone just not care what other people think?

But Rhys does care. He cares about what the foundation

board members think and his grandfather's opinion of him and his stupid competition with Jerrod. Just not about me.

I swing my legs over the side of his bed and stand before walking over to him.

I stop right in front of him and his eyes drop to mine.

"Then where do you fuck, Rhys?" His nostrils flare and a surge of pride rushes through me. After the night I've had, I like the idea of knocking *him* off balance. Tilting his world off its axis like he did mine with that proposal.

"Anywhere but here."

"Hmm."

My hands slide under his tuxedo jacket, and up the front of his body. Beneath my palms, I can feel his chiseled abs contracting through the luxurious fabric of his shirt.

I've seen him without his shirt. I know what's underneath but exploring him this way is fun, too. My fingers tease their way up to the knot in his bow tie. I'd straightened it earlier tonight when I first saw him, but now all I want to do is yank it off.

I find the flattened ends and pull. The knot releases, and I tug the fabric from around his neck and toss it aside.

Why is that so satisfying?

Being angry and turned on is a heady combination.

I start to undo the buttons of his shirt.

Rhys stands there, letting me do what I want. He knows the engagement stunt was crossing the line. I want retribution. I want to cross some lines, too. When the buttons are undone, I yank his shirt out of his pants and move to push it off his shoulders. I've forgotten that he's still wearing his jacket. I grunt at all the material bunching up until he assists me with their removal.

When his magnificent shoulders and torso are exposed, and his glorious tattoo is uncovered for my perusal, he lifts his hands out to the side in a 'what now' gesture. It only serves to annoy me. Getting naked doesn't affect Rhys. He's not nervous or embarrassed. He doesn't feel the pressure of my eyes on him like I felt everyone's eyes on me tonight when he dropped to one knee.

This might be harder than I thought. He looks unimpressed. It hits me in this moment, that's Rhys's default setting. It's a defense mechanism. To avoid caring too much, he pretends to not care at all.

But I want a reaction from him. I want to see him come undone.

My fingertips explore his tattoo, loving the feel of the raised ink beneath them.

I recall his question. *What do you want, Lettie?*

At his shoulders, my fingers dance over the ink there before slowly sliding down to his chest. With my teasing movements, Rhys's nipples tighten.

I've never explored a man's nipples before. Are his nipples as sensitive as mine are?

Beneath the soft cotton of Rhys's t-shirt, my nipples are hard points, sensitive and achy. I imagine how good it would feel to have Rhys's mouth on them.

I drop my mouth to his chest, pressing a kiss over his left pec. At the same time my thumb teases over his nipple.

Above me, a muffled groan escapes his throat.

It's faint, like he managed to smother most of the sound on its way out and shove it back down, but it still causes a tug in my lower belly, the needy ache between my thighs to intensify.

The alcohol that was making me bold is starting to lose its effect and I'm wondering if I have the courage to keep going. But all I have to do is draw on the frustration and hurt from earlier tonight and my confidence soars again. I know what I want from Rhys and I'm going to seize this moment just like he did when he fake proposed to me tonight.

I take his hand from his side and place it over my breast.

His jaw clenches, followed by the bob of his Adam's apple.

He's not squeezing me, but I can feel the tension in his fingers. His entire body is coiled tightly.

"Show me, Rhys."

CHAPTER 32

Rhys

"Show me, Rhys." Those three words are now seared into my brain.

Feeling Lettie's breast under my palm sucks the air right out of my lungs. It seems impossible that's what she wants when she's angry with me about the proposal. She has every right to be, but this, right now, feels different.

The palm covering Lettie's breast is burning. I'm trying to shut my brain off. To stay in this moment without feeling anything. Without feeling *her*. But the more I try to distance myself, the more I'm aware of every sensation.

Lettie's body is lithe and muscular. As a professional athlete, she's in phenomenal shape. Underneath my palm, she's so fucking soft. The hardened peak of her nipple teases through the cotton of the shirt she's wearing. *My shirt*. I didn't realize seeing her in my old NYU shirt would be such a turn on.

This isn't part of the plan, but neither was an engagement.

Lettie's palms rake over my chest, her finger pads teasing their way down my abs.

"Or should I show you?" she whispers.

She quirks her lips to one side, her cheekbones lift with

the movement. She's heartachingly beautiful. I'm spellbound by the sight of her, yet there are alarms going off in my head.

Do something. Take control.

But I can't. I've lost the ability to steer this ship. Lettie's a siren pulling me toward the shore and all I can do is stand here and watch.

She slowly drops to her knees. The ring I put on her finger earlier catches the light from the lamp as her hand reaches for my belt. The alarm is getting louder, yet I'm too captivated by the sight of her looking up at me to react. I'm frozen as I watch her eyes drop to where her hand is lowering my zipper.

It's a game of chicken. How far will I let her go? How much restraint do I have?

She's the one on her knees, yet the sight of her there makes me feel powerless.

Slowly, she lowers the waistband of my boxer-briefs to expose me.

There was never a question if I'd be hard for her, but her eyes widen like she's fascinated by the sight.

On our first date when she'd learned I had a piercing, she'd been flustered, but I also saw curiosity in her eyes. She's got the same look on her face now as her thumb circles around my crown before dropping to the metal barbell below.

With the fingers of one hand still exploring my piercing, her other hand wraps around my length to apply more pressure before she strokes me. My hips jolt forward.

Fuck me.

"*Lettie.*" I groan, knowing I shouldn't let her do this. Afraid she'll find out just how much power her touch wields against me. How easily I could lose control with her.

If her name was a warning, she doesn't take it as such. With her chin tilted sideways, her determined eyes still holding mine, she flattens her velvety tongue against me and licks the underside of my cock.

Fucking hell.

My jaw clenches. I should stop this.

I'm going to do it right now. Any second, I'll pull away.

But my intentions get lost when her tongue slides along the length of me. She's warm and soft. Her hand pumps down toward the base of my cock and this time when her mouth descends, my crown slips past her lips. Insider her hot, silken mouth, her tongue flicks against the end of my piercing.

Jesus Christ.

My fingers ache to tease into her hair, to wrap it around my fist so I can control her movement. Instead, my hands find the doorframe, bracing myself there.

Lettie's lips wrapped around my cock is a fucking vision, but still, I fight against the pleasure she's giving me. Guilt making it impossible to enjoy her mouth like I want to.

I will my conscience to quiet, to not make me wake up from this dream. She sucks me good and deep. My balls tighten with the euphoric feeling of being in her warm, sweet mouth.

"Am I doing it right?" she asks, before sucking me back into her mouth, her dark lashes fanning over her hollowed-out cheeks.

Gone is the sultry vixen whose anger and frustration stripped me of my clothes.

It's Lettie. She's too good. Too perfect. And she's making me lose control.

I don't deserve this or her. I can't take pleasure from her when I know she's angry with me.

I grip her chin. Her eyes lift to mine.

"No," I tell her, yanking my cock out of her mouth and tucking it back into my pants. She drops back onto her heels, stunned.

My body takes over. The desire. The need to be in control. To touch her and taste her.

To worship her the way she deserves.

In the next movement, I'm gripping her at the waist and lifting her onto the bed. The t-shirt is huge and puddles around her hips, exposing the scrap of lace between her thighs.

"This," I say, moving forward to reach under her shirt and yank down her panties in one quick motion, "this is how I make a woman beg for it."

Before I can stop myself, I drop between her legs and flatten my tongue against her center.

She's drenched. Sucking my cock made her pussy slick and needy.

With the first taste of her, my eyes roll to the back of my head. Fuck. She's even sweeter than I imagined.

Above me, Lettie gasps with a sudden intake of air.

"If you don't want this, then tell me to stop, because that's the only way you won't be coming all over my face."

I wait for any indication she wants me to stop, but the room is silent except for the rustle of sheets as Lettie's pelvis rocks, undeniably searching for my absent mouth. I smile against her thigh before I graze my teeth over her soft skin.

"Lettie, I need you to say it."

"I—I want it."

"You're not drunk?" I ask, searching her flushed face for consent.

"Rhys, *please*."

It's not an answer to my question but I can't stand the sound of her pleading. I should be the one begging, not her.

I will myself to slow down, pull back from her glistening slit and kiss the inside of her thigh. I'm dying to graze my teeth against that smooth skin of hers. Mark her as mine.

"I need you to say it."

She sighs. "I'm not drunk but I'm still mad at you. Now make me come."

That's all I need to hear.

"Spread your legs wider, Princess, and I'll fuck your pretty cunt with my tongue."

Her knees drop open, creating space for my shoulders, so I dive back in and lick up her center.

"Rhys." Lettie's breathy plea sends a jolt of lust to my swollen cock.

I love hearing my name fall from her lips like that. I want to hear it again and again.

I spread her with my thumbs and lick her good. Her back bows off the bed and it's an immediate rush of satisfaction as I watch her lose her mind under my tongue. When she's wild and writhing beneath me, I plunge a finger into her tight, slick cunt.

Her walls clench around my finger, making it impossibly tighter. Slowly, I thrust in and out, waiting for her to adjust before I tease a second at her entrance.

"Can you take two for me, Princess?" I ask.

"Yes," she pants.

My eyes lift to take her in. Her parted lips, heavy-lidded eyes, the way her slender throat arches toward the ceiling. The hard points of her nipples nearly drilling holes in her shirt. *My shirt.* My cock throbs at the sight of her and she's not even naked.

In my haste, I'd forgotten to strip her bare. I'm regretting that now, but I'll be damned if I stop what I'm doing because Lettie is damn close.

When a second finger presses inside, I watch her face light with pleasure and anticipation.

"So fucking tight, Princess."

I fuck her with my fingers and suck her clit hard.

The sound of her arousal slicking in and out fills the room. On a breathy moan, with her fists balled in the duvet, Lettie comes hard around my fingers.

I pull my fingers out and move to lean over her. Her eyes are closed, her breathing heavy but starting to even out. I paint her lips with my fingers and she startles, eyes fluttering open. I let her orgasm glisten there before I drop my mouth to hers.

Her taste is now branded on my tongue. I'm fucking ruined for her. My body knows this, but my brain is still fighting the good fight, trying to put distance between my desires and my actions.

"That's how I do it," I whisper before pulling back to look at her.

She's boneless on my bed. Eyelids heavy, chest rising and falling in a slow, peaceful rhythm. Her dark hair splayed out in a glorious mess on my pillow.

In the bathroom I grab a warm washcloth to wipe gently between her legs. Finding her lace thong on the bed where I discarded it earlier, I ball the damp lace into my fist and place it in my pocket. I'm waiting for her to sit up and argue with me but her breathing stays even.

She's tired from the night and deserves to let the post orgasmic release lull her to sleep. Clearly, it already has.

I place a glass of water on the nightstand and plug her phone into the charger. Her home screen lights up with notifications of unanswered texts and calls.

Her hand reaches out to loosely grip my bicep. I lift it and press a kiss to her palm before pulling the covers over her.

"Goodnight, Princess."

The desire to slide in next to her has a weight settling against my chest. But I already know I fucked everything up, and giving in to the temptation to hold her will only blur the lines even more.

This was a mistake, not because I didn't want to touch Lettie, but because now I know how good it feels to give in. How easily she can make me forget what we're doing here.

Not trusting myself to be near her any longer, I retreat.

Upstairs, in the living room, I pour myself a whiskey and

drink it slowly, willing each sip to wash away the taste of her. I know it will be impossible, but I have to try.

Later, before I pass out on the couch, I check on Lettie.

She's curled up in my bed, hands tucked under her cheek, the diamond ring still wrapped around her finger.

When I wake up the next morning, Lettie's gone. I check for a note, then my phone for a text, anything that might give an indication as to where her head is at. I find nothing.

The shirt she wore is folded and sitting on my dresser. Her dress and heels are gone.

The toothbrush she used is still neatly tucked into the cup next to mine.

It's ridiculous the rush I get from seeing it there, but then I do a double-take.

Looped around Lettie's toothbrush is her engagement ring.

Fuck.

CHAPTER 33

Colette

This morning, I padded down the dock on bare feet, carrying my heels, cursing Rhys's name. I'd gotten a few double-takes from passersby but mostly people didn't find it odd that a woman was in a formal dress at six o'clock on a Saturday morning.

It may not be unusual for most, but it was certainly something I'd never done. And the fact that I couldn't find my underwear before I left…that made for a stressful exit from the cab.

Every time I think about last night, a new emotion surfaces.

Last night I was angry and hurt by Rhys's sneak attack proposal. I'm still angry with him, and hurt by his lack of trust, but it's not the proposal that I keep replaying in my mind. It's what happened after.

The memory of his tongue sweeping over me for the first time is so engrained that I swear I can still feel him there between my legs. Licking. Sucking. Filling me with his thick fingers. It was a vulnerable position to be in, spread open for him like that, but Rhys made it feel like the most natural thing in the world.

And the way he talked to me? It was straight out of the spicy romance novel I'm reading for Chloe's book club.

Spread your legs wider, Princess, and I'll fuck your pretty cunt with my tongue.

Can you take two for me, Princess?

So fucking tight, Princess.

I didn't know guys actually talked like that. Or that I would like it so much.

But I can't let one orgasm, albeit mind-blowing and the only one I've received that didn't require an electric charge, blind me to the fact that I'm furious with him.

When I stood over a sleeping Rhys this morning, I felt the desire to place my hands around his neck and squeeze, maybe throw a cup of water on him, but then my vengeful thoughts took a wrong turn when I was distracted by the sight of his naked arms and torso. And the top button of his pants that was unfastened.

I'm starting to wonder if all his pants' top buttons are faulty or if it's operator error?

But, god, he looked perfectly disheveled and peaceful lying there so I let him sleep and decided leaving the engagement ring hanging off the toothbrush he gave me last night would send a clear message.

We're done.

And now all these thoughts and emotions from the last twenty-four hours are swirling in my brain as I move around the practice studio.

It's Saturday and no one else is here. That's why I came, because I knew I'd have the space to myself.

The chaos in my head matches the allegro style of music piece I've selected, so it's easy to let all my emotions from last night carry me through a stylistic jumping sequence. I'm not even paying attention to the specific steps, I let my wounded heart guide me, and my feet follow its lead.

My movements feel different today.

And not because I was still a little hungover when I got here. With hydration and ibuprofen, the headache and dry mouth have subsided, yet there's still this out-of-body feeling. Less control, more chaotic energy. Like I'm letting my body dance instead of my brain.

In the mirror, I watch my image, looking for any flaws in my technique.

My lines are perfect.

As I try to pinpoint the source of uncertainty, the music crescendos and I land one last jump before holding a final position.

Two breaths later, I stand and catch my own gaze in the mirror. The woman staring back at me looks wild, uncontained.

I'd be breathless if the adrenaline from thinking about Rhys wasn't pumping through my veins. I grab a towel off a chair in the corner and dab at my forehead.

From the doorway comes a slow clap.

When I turn to find the source, it's Alexei, and he's smiling ear to ear as he walks toward me.

"There she is," he says, his accent thick as ever.

I'd ask who he's talking about, but I'm the only one here.

"A dancer with passion and fire. Wow. I don't know how you tapped into it, but Colette, whatever you've done, don't stop now."

"Thank you," I say, trying to contain my elation. His words have my pulse quickening, and my breath coming faster than it was during that entire dance sequence.

Alexei's compliment is everything I've been working for, but then I let his words sink in.

Whatever you've done, don't stop now.

Alexei squeezes my shoulder. "Whatever is fueling this, hold onto it until evaluations."

I know what is fueling this fire. *Rhys.*

I give him a weak smile. "Right."

No matter how much I don't want to admit it in this moment, especially because I'm still very angry with him, he's inspired this change. He's gotten me out of my routine in a good way, showed me it's okay to have fun, necessary even, and there's no doubt last night awakened something in me as well.

"I know you will because you're going to do everything you possibly can to nail this evaluation and get that lead role in *Rubies*."

The realization that I need Rhys if I want to stay in tune with this newfound passion in my dancing is annoying. He's not the sole reason for the change, right? I can maintain this on my own. Maybe I'll replay the video Hannah sent me of his proposal and it will continue to fuel me.

What if that doesn't work? What if the only way to ensure a more passionate performance at evaluations is to keep fake-dating Rhys? Well, after last night, I'll need to continue to be fake engaged to him.

The headache I nursed this morning is slowly seeping back in. This is a mess.

When I don't respond, Alexei smiles. "Don't stress. Get through evaluations and then you can worry about wedding planning."

I force a smile onto my face.

"Right. Thanks."

Wedding planning is not my issue.

At least not my main issue, I think, remembering the texts from my mom this morning insisting that we start looking at venues right away because they book years in advance.

What am I going to do?

I watch Alexei leave, then gather my bag and head toward the dressing room.

All the missed calls and texts are weighing heavy on me, but right now, I need to talk to Hannah. She knows us both and hopefully will be able to help me sort out this mess.

She answers immediately.

"Good morning, sunshine. How are you feeling today?"

"Hi, Hans. I'm okay. I just finished up at the practice studio."

"On a Saturday morning?"

"It helped, you know, to dance out my frustration."

"Yeah, I get it. How are you feeling after last night? About the engagement?"

"Angry. Confused. Hurt. I still can't believe he fake proposed without talking to me."

"And I can't believe he didn't ask your dad. It's tradition to ask for a daughter's hand in marriage."

"Is that still a thing?" I ask.

"It's a tradition."

"I think traditions don't apply to fake engagements."

"And let's not forget he didn't even bother to talk to me. I mean, I wasn't even consulted on the ring." She's joking, but there's still a tinge of hurt in her voice. "It's a beautiful ring, if not a bit ostentatious."

"Is that the word of the day?"

"Yes, and I'm so sorry. Do you want me to kick his ass? I mean, I won't actually do it, but I can hire someone to."

"Tempting, but no."

"Okay, let me know if you change your mind. So how did you leave it with him last night? I saw you leave the fundraiser and then Rhys followed you out. Did you two talk?"

"Yeah, and we did some other stuff."

In the silence that follows, I know Hannah's eyes are widening and her lips are pressed together processing what I just said.

"Other stuff?" she asks, her tone reaching a new octave.

"Yeah," I say, hesitantly, but then I remember this is Hannah and she's never made me feel awkward for my inexperience. "I wanted to. God, Hannah, I wanted it so bad. Is something wrong with me?"

She sighs. "No. I don't think so. Rhys's charm is pretty powerful."

"That's the thing. He wasn't coming onto me. I instigated it and then it was like he was annoyed with me, but then he ate me out like I was his last meal."

"Damn. So, it was good?" she asks.

"I don't have anything to compare it to, but yeah, it was hot. Oh, and I gave him head. Kind of. I started and then he stopped me."

My cheeks flush remembering how bold I'd been with Rhys, unzipping his pants and fisting his erection. The cool sensation of his piercing sliding against my tongue and into the back of my throat.

And then, how good it felt with his mouth on me. And how hard I'd come for him. But when my eyes opened this morning, I'd been alone in his bed, and it told me everything I needed to know.

"Jesus, Lettie. You're checking all the foreplay boxes real fast. Did you have sex with him?" she asks.

"No. And besides, it wasn't about me, he was simply proving a point. I asked him what he does to make women fall into his bed, and so he had to show me by giving me the most powerful orgasm of my life."

I had been perfectly happy being a battery-operated orgasm girlie and now I'm not sure I can go back. At least not permanently. No, I had a taste of how good it can be to have a partner that isn't made of silicone and I want more. I can add that to the growing list of reasons to be furious at Rhys.

"He's an egotistical, self-absorbed, arrogant, bigheaded asshole."

Hannah stifles a laugh. "Those words all mean the same thing."

"I know. That's how self-centered he is. I have to list the same attribute four times."

Except, before last night, before his proposal, I had started to think Rhys wasn't the guy everyone thinks he is. He was different. Thoughtful, endearing, supportive and a lot of fun to be around.

"So, what do you want to do?" she asks.

"I don't know. The whole point of fake-dating him was to help me find more passion in my dancing and I think it's happening. Last night's performance felt incredible, and just now I got some great feedback from Alexei. He sees more expression and passion in my moves. But I'm so mad at Rhys I can't even think straight."

Having Rhys help me practice dating was supposed to be safe. A way to dip my toe in the dating pond without getting burned. Turns out, the water is HOT. And our charade has already spiraled out of control.

I don't tell Hannah that I was starting to have feelings for Rhys. The surprise proposal is justification enough for my anger, so admitting that I was starting to fall for him and his proposal felt like a bait and switch isn't going to do me any good now.

"Okay, here's an idea. You can go along with this fake engagement—"

"But—" I start, because of all people, this is not what I expected from Hannah.

"Hear me out. You go along with the fake engagement but make sure Rhys knows who's the boss now. He's got a lot of groveling to do. Use that to your advantage. That way you can reap the benefits with your dancing, but also hold this shitty stunt over his head. It's a win-win."

I pick at the callus on my big toe while I think about Hannah's advice.

"I'm not the best at holding a grudge."

"It isn't a grudge. It's thinking about what is best for you in this scenario. Last night, Rhys was only thinking about himself, so maybe it's time you did the same."

I let her words sink in.

I was beginning to love the idea of me and Rhys as a team, but maybe Hannah's right. I need to focus on what I need out of this arrangement and not let those pesky feelings I was starting to have derail my progress.

Before ending the call, we chat about brunch plans on Sunday and Sophie's upcoming bachelorette party, and then we promise to look at our calendars to plan a weekend together at Lake George before the summer is over.

Then, I shower, taking my time to blow dry and curl my hair. I'm hoping the routine activity will let my brain figure everything out. When I'm done, I'm no more certain what I should do about Rhys, but at least I'm somewhat ready for my appearance at the children's hospital this afternoon.

When I walk out onto Sixty-Fifth Street, I find the man himself at the curb, leaning against a black SUV.

At the sight of him, my stomach flutters.

His shirt is unbuttoned at the top, his suit jacket and slacks tailored to perfection. His hands are in his pants pockets, his gaze down at the sidewalk, causing the longer hair on top of his head to fall forward. As if he senses me, he looks up.

Even with sunglasses on, I can sense the intensity of his hazel stare, causing that fiery passion in my belly to come flooding back. I want to ignore it, pretend it's not him making me feel this way and go home. But if I want to keep dancing like I have been, proving to Alexei that I can handle the emotional depth and passionate dancing the lead in *Rubies* requires, then I'll need Rhys's help.

But, right now, with last night's ambush fresh in my memory, I hate the thought.

"I'm sorry." Those are the first words out of his mouth as I approach.

Instead of assuaging my anger, they only serve to upset me more. I'm so mad, I can't even find the words to express it. It's funny, I didn't know I had a temper until Rhys Spencer became my fake boyfriend. Now fake fiancé.

Maybe I'm not ready to talk to him. I'm probably going to start screaming at him right here on the street and cause a scene. I change directions to start walking home, but he follows.

"Lettie, did you hear me? I said I'm sorry."

I whip back around, my emotions bubbling up inside of me. "What exactly are you sorry for, Rhys?"

"Last night I fucked up. I shouldn't have proposed without talking to you first."

"Maybe sorry isn't good enough," I shoot back before starting to walk off again.

"Lettie, please. Not here." He reaches for my elbow, pulling me against him before pressing me back against the car. It's a Lettie sandwich. I'm stuck between the hard plastic of the car door and Rhys's firm, muscular body.

Just like last night, lust and rage are battling it out. My body is already caving into the feeling of him against me, loving the way his luxurious scent makes my nipples pebble beneath my tank top.

My head spins. I'm sure it's dehydration from a strenuous practice session. I just need some electrolytes and I'll be fine.

Finally, my brain takes the lead.

My hands move to his chest to push him off. "What are you—"

That's when I see several men on the sidewalk with cameras. Rhys isn't trying to make a move on me, he's shielding me from the photographers.

Rhys drops his forehead to mine. "There are photographers watching us."

I can see the struggle on his face. He wants me to know

he's taking our argument seriously but also trying to put on a happy façade for the nosy photographers.

"I see them," I whisper, my arms instinctively wrapping behind Rhys's neck to pull him closer. "How do they keep finding us?"

"I don't know." He pulls away slightly and I can see a worry line forming between Rhys's brows. It only makes him more handsome. "It's their job, I guess."

I'm still mad at Rhys, but in this moment, all my frustration is redirected toward the paps that are trailing us.

They might have already captured Rhys and me arguing, but if they're still lurking here, that means he wants to see how the argument ends. If I yell at Rhys and walk off, that will be a juicy tidbit for the media to run with. I refuse to give those photographers what they want.

Before I can change my mind, I lift on my toes and seal my mouth to Rhys's.

He's surprised, but he catches on quickly, matching my determined kiss with hot, hungry kisses of his own.

Rhys's hand wraps around my waist. Possessive and firm. Just how his tongue had been between my thighs last night.

At the memory, I moan into Rhys's mouth.

I might be embarrassed but I'm going to play that one off as being a really good actor. And the fact that he can't say shit to me right now because he's in hot water and I'm saving his ass.

Look at the newly engaged couple sucking each other's faces off.

Rhys breaks the kiss. "Get in the car," he rumbles against my ear.

The moment we're safe in the backseat of the SUV, I scoot away from him. The need to pretend out there thoroughly confused my body and now I need some space.

"Thank you." He presses his lips together. They're still wet from our kiss, and I can't stop staring at them.

I nod, then look away, staring at the leather seat in front of me, willing my breathing to calm so it doesn't sound like I'm hyperventilating.

"What can I do? What will convince you to keep our arrangement?" he asks.

"Last night—" I begin.

"I shouldn't have let things go that far between us. Not when you had been drinking."

I scoff, because how dare he take credit for my bad decisions.

"I wasn't drunk. And you didn't force me onto my knees."

Our eyes lock and the memories come rushing back. My hand stroking his thick cock. The weight of it on my tongue. The warm saltiness of his pre-cum as I sucked him to the back of my throat.

His throat bobs as he swallows. "It doesn't matter. It was a mistake on my part. And I won't touch you again," he says adamantly. "Only in public. Like we agreed. When necessary for appearances."

I open my mouth to argue. To tell him that's the last thing I want.

But his stance on the subject makes me hesitate. Either he regrets touching me or he thinks I regret it. Admitting I want more feels like a risk my sensitive heart can't take right now.

I search his face. The chiseled edge of his jaw, the sharp points of his cheekbones. Still hidden behind sunglasses, his eyes are unreadable.

I reach over to remove them. Beneath his shades, there are dark circles under his eyes I hadn't noticed before.

"I fucked up. I'm sorry I ambushed you with the proposal. I shouldn't have let Jerrod goad me into it. I should have talked to you."

"Trust is important to me. Maybe it's rooted in me as a dancer. I put trust in those around me. Last night, during our performance, my face was inches from the floor after dropping from Sebastian's shoulders. I didn't even flinch because I knew he would catch me. I trusted him to do that." My eyes dampen as unexpected emotion creeps up on me. "I trusted you. I thought we were friends."

"We are, Lettie," he insists. "I fucked up. I didn't think it through. Jerrod proposed to Corinne and then the article with their engagement announcement made me feel like my parents' foundation was slipping out of my grasp. There still have been comments about our relationship and whether it's real, and I thought an engagement would make it more believable. I had planned to talk to you about it, but then Jerrod and Aditi saw the ring, and I panicked."

He swallows thickly. "And I was afraid you'd say no. I took the risk and hoped for the best. I shouldn't have and I'm sorry."

I can see he's sincere.

"If you would have trusted me with the truth and talked to me, I would have said yes. I would have planned it all with you."

I'm surprised by how passionate my words come out.

Rhys must be, too. His eyes widen in disbelief. His jaw goes slack.

"I didn't know if you'd understand. If you'd take that leap with me. I'm sorry."

His fingers slide along my palm before interlacing with my own.

"I let this competition with Jerrod fuck with my head and I wasn't thinking. Again, I should have talked to you."

"Yeah, you should have." I squeeze his hand. "I need to be able to trust you, Rhys. Fake or not, relationships don't work without trust."

"You can. I'll prove it to you."

I nod, pressing my lips together.

"And I'm sorry for making the Leg-Up fundraiser about the proposal. You worked really hard making last night special and I hate that I messed everything up for you."

"The fundraiser was actually a success, but I appreciate your apology."

We're quiet for a few minutes. I'm not sure what we're practicing now. Being awkwardly silent when a relationship goes off the rails?

Finally, I speak. "I've got the children's hospital 'Dream with a Dancer' event today."

He studies me a moment, then looks away before settling his gaze back on mine.

"Can I come with you?" he asks.

My brows lift, shocked that Rhys would want to come with me to the event. Then again, he did make all those tutus and he does need to do damage control. A children's hospital event would be perfect for an image boost and to make amends with me.

I know he's got ulterior motives, but I'm also curious to see how he'll do.

"Yeah, okay, but I need to stop by my apartment to change first."

While Rhys directs the driver to my apartment, I lean back into the leather seat. I've forgiven Rhys, and agreed to move forward with this new arrangement, but I'll need to be vigilant about guarding my heart.

CHAPTER 34
Rhys

After a quick stop at Lettie's apartment so she could change, we're on our way to the children's hospital.

"The tutus we made were delivered to the hospital earlier this week. When we arrive, we'll meet with the program director so she can introduce us to the nurses on the floor we'll be visiting."

I'm quiet as Lettie explains the process for the children's hospital event.

As Lettie talks, I'm half listening and half berating myself for our earlier conversation.

Yes, I needed to apologize and tell her I'd fucked up, but had I really promised to not touch her again? *What the fuck was I thinking?*

In the moment, it seemed like the right thing to do. To backpedal us out of the gray area we crossed over into last night. To redraw the lines we originally set. The rules Lettie was determined we establish and I agreed upon.

What I really wanted to do was apologize, then beg her to let me touch her again.

For me to work off my atonement between her thighs. As

many orgasms as it takes for her to forgive me. That's what I should have done.

But she did forgive me. Or at least she's tolerating me enough to let me come with her to this event. And she agreed last night was a mistake, so we need to find our way back to the 'friends only' side of this arrangement.

But fuck, the way Lettie responded when those photographers were watching us in the middle of our argument. How right that kiss felt even when the issues between us were unresolved.

My eyes drop to the smooth expanse of leg exposed by her sundress. It's a soft shell-pink with a fitted bodice and flared skirt and Lettie looks like a fucking dream in it.

She's a virgin.

Until last night, I'd done my best to block the thought out. But after tasting her, feeling how tight and slick she was, I wondered what it would be like to be the man that pushed between her legs for the first time. To be the man that deserved that honor.

You're not the one. She deserves better.

I can't argue with my brain's response.

Even if I hadn't been the man to trick her into a fake engagement, my reputation and history with women are enough to keep me out of the running.

When Lettie's done practicing with me, she'll find the real thing with a nice guy and none of this will matter. Our fake engagement will become something wild and crazy she once did.

"We're here." Lettie motions to the building we've pulled up to.

I blink, realizing she's right. We're already at the children's hospital.

I help her out of the car, then follow her inside.

Just as Lettie had said, we meet with the program coordinator who then introduces us to the nurses on the floor we're visiting.

The large box of tutus that we made a few weeks ago have been placed behind the nurses' station. Deciding I need to pull my weight here, I pick it up and motion to follow Lettie to the first room.

When we walk in the door, I stop in my tracks.

Sitting on the bed is a young girl in a blue nightgown holding a scruff-looking teddy bear. She's thin and pale, and her head is bald.

This is a children's hospital and the nurse, Brittney, did give us an overview of the children's conditions. But I wasn't prepared for this.

I watch Lettie walk over to the girl.

"Hi, Madelyn, I'm Colette from The City Ballet." Lettie nods to the guest chair. "May I sit with you?"

"Yes!" She pumps her arm enthusiastically. "You're finally here! I was waiting all morning."

Lettie smiles. "I'm sorry to keep you waiting."

"You're a dancer?" Madelyn asks, her brown eyes openly perusing Lettie's frame the way I would like to.

"I am. I dance ballet."

"Do you go on your toes? Does it hurt?" Madelyn asks.

"I do and it did when I first started, but now, I'm used to it. Do you want to see a picture?" Lettie asks.

Madelyn nods eagerly and Lettie pulls out her phone to find pictures to show the little girl.

"That's so cool. My mom says I can start ballet after my treatment."

"That's amazing. I'm excited for you."

As if Madelyn finally notices I'm standing there, she points at me. "Who's that guy?"

"This is Rhys." Lettie motions for me to come closer but I barely move. I'm frozen in place.

I'm not good with kids, so I imagine I'm going to be even more awkward with a child that's sick. My only way of coping is to tease and joke, but there's nothing funny about cancer.

"Hi." I lift the box since I'm not able to wave.

"Reece like Reese's pieces?" Madelyn asks.

I exchange a look with Lettie to acknowledge the nickname she gave me when we were younger.

"It's spelled differently. R-H-Y-S."

Madelyn shakes her head. "That doesn't sound like it spells Reece. That sounds like rice."

I shrug. "That's how it's spelled."

"Hmm. Are you a dancer, too?" Madelyn asks, her eyes giving me a discerning look.

"No. I'm not." Finally, I step closer and set the box down on the floor next to the bed. "I'm here to help Colette."

Lettie smiles. "He's the official tutu passer-outer."

Madelyn's gaze snags on my arm. Where my sleeve is rolled up exposing my tattoo. "I like your tattoo."

"Thanks." My eyes drop to the friendship bracelet on her wrist. "I like your bracelet. I'm a Swiftie, too."

"My friend Leah made me this one. She went to the concert, but I couldn't go." Her eyes dart to mine. "Wait. You like Taylor Swift?"

"Yeah, I do."

Madelyn's eyes narrow in disbelief. "What's your favorite song?"

I chuckle at her skepticism. "You can't ask me that. It's impossible to choose."

"Fine. Favorite album."

"I'm partial to *1989* but *Reputation* is a close second."

"I love *Reputation*! *Lover* and *Red* are top three for sure."

"Solid choices." I nod toward the tutu box. "All right, I didn't make any black ones with snakes on them, but there's a pink, blue and gold one that's giving *Lover* vibes."

Madelyn squeals with delight. "Oh my gosh, yes! I love it!"

Lettie helps Madelyn pull it over her gown, then Brittney comes in the room to take a picture.

I move to get out of the way, knowing this is Lettie's gig, not mine, but Madelyn insists I be in it. After the picture, Lettie and Madelyn chat some more before we say our goodbyes.

On our way down the hall to the next room, I catch the smile on Lettie's face. The hint of fascination as she glances at me.

"What?" I ask.

"I didn't know you were a Swiftie."

"You going to add it to your flash cards?" I ask.

She tosses a playful glare in my direction. "No, I've retired those. Threw them in the trashcan this morning."

"So, we'll have to do it the old-fashioned way?"

"And what way is that?" she asks.

"Spending time together."

Her eyes never leave mine, but her lips push out in a slight pout. God damn, I have the strongest urge to grip her by the back of the neck and kiss that scowl right off her. Never mind the fact we're in the hallway of a children's hospital oncology wing.

"When absolutely necessary."

If that's the case, then I'll be adding as many appearances and events to the calendar as I possibly can.

For the next two hours, we make our way down the hall, visiting with the children in each room, passing out tutus. It's more fun than I thought it would be. The good news is most of the kids love Taylor Swift, pink, and fashion, so I've got plenty to talk with them about. I end up with a few friendship bracelets and promise to come back with some of my own to exchange next time.

Outside the last room, Lettie places her hand on my forearm. "Don't make promises you're not going to keep."

I broke her trust and now she's concerned I'll do it with the children here.

"I plan to keep it. I've already texted Ramsey to pick up a bracelet making kit. I've got a million ideas."

She nods and presses her lips together.

"Thank you for coming today."

"I had fun."

"Me, too." Lettie smiles and my whole world gets brighter.

"We done with this?" I motion to the empty box.

"No. I'll keep it and start making tutus for another visit."

It hits me then. This doesn't end. There will always be children here that Lettie can visit. That she wants to visit and try to make a bright spot in an otherwise challenging and scary time in their lives. I wish I had half the good heart Lettie does.

In the elevator, Lettie stands on the opposite side and it feels like she's a million miles away. I thrust my hands into my pockets and my fingertips brush against the cool platinum band of her engagement ring.

I pull the ring out of my pocket.

To start building back trust with her, I need to be honest.

I hold the ring up in front of me and Lettie's eyes drop to the large diamond.

"I hated the moment I found this hanging on your toothbrush this morning. Not because I knew it meant you didn't want to play this game with me anymore, but because I thought I'd lost you as a friend."

Her eyes lift to mine as she sucks in a sharp breath.

"You've easily become my best friend over these last few weeks, and I hated the thought that I hurt you and I might have lost you. I was an idiot letting this thing with Jerrod get out of control, and again, I'm sorry I blindsided you last night. My parents' foundation is important to me, and I let my fear of Jerrod getting the board position cloud my judgment."

I'm searching her eyes. This moment is more intimate than my proposal in front of everyone last night.

"Lettie, will you—"

She extends her left hand out to me, fingers spread so I can place the ring on her finger.

"Yes, Rhys," she sighs, "I accept your fake engagement proposal."

I wait for the relief. The moment that the weight lifts off my shoulders knowing I've patched things up with Lettie and she's agreed to continue our fake engagement.

It doesn't come.

The car ride to Lettie's apartment is quiet, and all too soon we're pulling up to the curb outside. I hold the car door for her, then walk her up the stairs.

"Do you have plans tomorrow?" I ask, trying to find a way back to the easy companionship we'd shared before I blew everything up last night. "Do you want to hang out? I can bring over Mo or we can go out on the boat?"

She gives me a tight smile. "I'm busy."

She doesn't elaborate. I'm desperate to ask what she's doing, but unfortunately, even the title of fake fiancé doesn't give me the right.

Even though our arrangement is continuing, and she's accepted the ring back, everything between us is different now and I fucking hate it.

"Have a good night." She gives me a quick wave before slipping inside her front door.

With Lettie gone, I glance at my watch. It's three in the afternoon, what the fuck am I supposed to do with myself for the rest of the day, and tomorrow for that matter?

Those thoughts alone have me groaning inwardly. This is why I've avoided relationships and kept things casual. Before

Lettie, I would never be so wrapped up in a woman that I needed to be with her constantly. Somehow in the last two weeks, I've become reliant on our friendship, and seeing Lettie every day. Lettie and I are friends, nothing more, so why does the fact that she's pulling away bother me so much?

CHAPTER 35

Rhys

A curtain of raven hair surrounds me. Soft lips press against the shell of my ear.

"Show me, Rhys," Lettie whispers as she sinks down onto my cock. "Please make me come."

She leans back and I take in the sight of her straddling me. Her small tits with tight rosy nipples bounce as she lifts herself up and down. I watch where my cock splits her slick pussy. She's drenched, and each drag coats me in her wetness. So wet. So tight. So fucking perfect.

My hands grip her hips. My fingers digging into her toned ass, shifting her forward so her clit rubs against the base of my cock.

"Oh, fuck. Yes, Rhys."

I open my mouth to respond, but nothing comes out.

"I'm coming," she moans.

Like a clenched fist, her pussy clamps down around my cock. The pulse of her orgasm has me spilling inside her.

I reach for her, but she climbs off me and starts collecting her clothes.

"Thanks for that." She pecks me on the cheek before getting dressed. "I knew you'd be the perfect man for the job."

Then she's gone.

My eyes fly open on a strained pant. My hard cock is in my hand, my cum in a puddle on my stomach. Lettie's image is gone, vanished into the depths of my mind.

That's how I wake up now.

Every. Fucking. Day.

I grab a t-shirt off the floor and wipe myself up, then toss it into the hamper on my way to the bathroom.

"Stop," I tell my reflection, but it doesn't matter.

The memory of Lettie spread out on my bed, her pussy wet and needy. The taste of her on my lips, the pulse of her climax when she came all over my face, are now core memories that my subconscious has been using to torture me.

The torture isn't the sex dream and waking up to know it wasn't real. I would gladly have that dream about Lettie every day.

No, it's when dream Lettie thanks me for fucking her and then leaves.

Sure, there are variations.

"Thanks for practicing with me, Rhys."

"That was fun. I knew you'd be a good time."

I never respond. I just watch her pull on her clothes and leave.

The worst one is when I ask her to stay. She laughs and pats me on the cheek. *"You thought this meant something? Oh, that's sweet."*

What kind of fucked up shit is that?

It's messing with my head and I want it to stop.

It doesn't help that I haven't heard anything from Lettie all week. I've sent her a few text messages but she hasn't responded.

Mo pushes through the bathroom door and hops up on the counter.

"Hey, buddy." I stroke his back before picking him up and carrying him out to the kitchen.

I reach for my pack of cigarettes and pull one out. Holding

it between my index finger and thumb, I roll it like I always do. It's my morning ritual after all. A ritual that I haven't been able to enjoy since my visit to the children's hospital last weekend. I've tried like hell to light up and not picture those kids' smiling faces, their heads covered in peach fuzz, some covered in hats, others adorned with headbands. Their slender arms hooked up to machines as they received their treatments.

I lift the cigarette to my mouth, lighter in the other hand, hoping today will be different. But it's no use. The memory floods my vision.

They'd been so fucking happy to see Lettie, hell, to see me, even after they found out I wasn't a dancer. Meeting Lettie and receiving a tutu from her was a dream come true.

And fuck, if she hadn't looked perfect in that pink dress. Sweet and innocent, yet spirited and determined. It's the last time I saw her.

My hand drops the lighter. I place the cigarette back in the pack, then pitch it in the trash can.

Fuck.

I want to be angry that she's ruined another guilty pleasure. That she's seeping into my every waking thought, but I can't because I fucking ruined everything when I ambushed her with that proposal.

To everyone else, we're happy and engaged, but the reality is I'm miserable and alone.

Don't text her again.

I reach for my phone anyway. Find another funny cat meme and send it.

I watch the screen, waiting to see if she responds. Nothing.

"Why isn't she responding, Mo?" I ask, because talking to my cat is all I have now.

Then, my phone starts buzzing with an incoming call.

Holy shit.

It's *her*.

"Hey, Lettie," I answer casually.

"You know you don't have to send me a cat meme if you want to talk. You can just call me."

Am I that transparent? I guess so.

I ignore the twitch of my cock that hearing Lettie's voice brings to life. That's not going to be helpful in getting my friend back.

"Oh, right." I should have called her. What a novel concept. "Well, I was here talking to Mo and he wants to come over and see Maxine." Fuck. I didn't realize how stupid that would sound until the words are out of my mouth.

"Oh, yeah? How can you tell?" I can hear the amusement in her voice.

"I think he's lonely. Not because I'm not a good time, because I am. But you know, it's a cat thing. He wants to be with another cat." What the fuck am I rambling about? "It's because he misses her whenever they're not together."

"I see. Well, I'm going to be heading out soon. I've got a thing this afternoon."

"A thing?" I ask, nearly groaning because what the fuck do I have to do to get on this woman's priority list? *Not blind-side her with a fake marriage proposal, idiot.*

"The Leg-Up community open house and painting party."

Earlier this week, Ramsey had mentioned it was on Saturday, but without Lettie to structure my days, this whole week has been one continuous string of hours that bleed into the next. My spirits lift because as a major donor, I was invited.

"They're going to announce the results of the fundraiser and we're going to paint the main studio. It'll be a perfect Saturday afternoon."

My idea of a perfect Saturday afternoon would be my face between Lettie's thighs but since that can't happen again, the Leg-Up open house sounds like the next best thing.

"I was planning to go, too. Can I pick you up?" I ask.

She's quiet a moment, then finally responds. "Okay, but on one condition."

An hour later, per Lettie's request, I pull up to her apartment on my motorcycle. It was the one condition she insisted on. Obviously, Mo wasn't a fan because it meant I couldn't bring him to hang out with Maxine, but I told him I'd do everything in my power to get him more time with her. Then, I realized I was talking to my cat again, so I rushed out the door, with Ramsey laughing in the background before he called out to tell me he'd meet me at the Leg-Up open house later.

By the time I get my helmet off, Lettie's already coming down the stairs to the sidewalk. She's dressed in cut-off denim shorts and a tight black body suit that cuts low on her chest. Lettie doesn't have large breasts, but what she does have is being hugged tightly and put perfectly on display.

"Hi." She beams up at me and I'm sure I look like a fool standing here on the sidewalk gaping at her.

"Hey." That's all I get out. Clearly, it's been a long week and I've forgotten how to talk to a woman I find attractive. I swallow thickly. I have to remember what we're doing here. That she's my friend, and the woman I am relying on to help me win favor with the foundation board. I need to consider that and stop ogling her.

I hand her a helmet and help her climb on.

On our ride, Lettie wraps her arms around me and it feels so fucking good to have her near me like this again. To even be in her presence. I didn't know that it could feel like this.

At Leg-Up, Lettie walks me through the building, pointing out each studio room and explaining how they will be transformed. I already know about the plans for the new Leg-Up Dance Academy. I took a tour when I reached out to them about the gaps they had in their funding. They sent me the school's detailed plan, then I pledged ten million dollars over ten years. But Lettie's tour is far more animated than the one I got before. Her enthusiasm is infectious and I'm enjoying listening to her. The expressions she makes talking about her passion for the program are adorable. The urge to pull her into my arms and kiss the hell out of her is making it hard to focus.

"Are you bored?" she asks, turning to glance at me with a sheepish smile on her face.

"No, not at all." I follow her across the room. "Why would you say that?"

She leans against the barre, her hands wrapping around the splintered wood.

She shrugs. "You're being awfully quiet."

"I'm taking it all in. Practicing being a good listener." *Thinking about kissing you.*

I close the space between us, my fingers pressing beneath her chin to lift her gaze to mine. I can't help myself, I need to touch her in some way, to breathe her in. It's been a week, but that's too fucking long since I've felt the calm from her presence. That satisfying dream-like haze I get from her proximity.

"I'm never bored when I'm with you, Lettie. I could watch you paint a wall and it would be the most entertaining thing I've ever seen."

The inhale between our lips is sharp. I can feel the warm puff of air from her mouth as she exhales. I want to capture her perfect lips with mine.

"I'm glad you feel that way," she says slipping out from where I nearly had her pinned against the barre, turning at the last minute to grab my hand and pull me along with her. "That's exactly what we're doing today."

I follow her into the main studio where everyone else is gathered. Paint and supplies are positioned against one of the walls. There's a table set up for volunteers to sign in, with snacks and drinks laid out on another.

When I made the donation to Leg-Up, it was clear we didn't need to have a community volunteer day to paint the studios. My donation could pay to paint this place a thousand times over and still have millions left in the bank, but I had insisted that we keep it. It's what Lettie would want.

Her passion for making tutus, visiting the children's hospital, and now painting this once underfunded dance school, are moments that give her the satisfaction of connecting with the people and spaces she wants to support. While money is what a lot of programs need, the impact of showing up and getting your hands dirty to make a change is even more satisfying than writing a check. It's one of the things I remember about my parents' involvement with their foundation, and now I'm experiencing it firsthand during the time I've spent with Lettie.

Lettie moves closer to the front of the group while I hang back for a moment.

"Before we get started, I wanted to make an announcement." Mila, the program director, addresses the small crowd. Ramsey's gaze shifts from my profile to Mila. "While our fundraising this year has been a struggle, we've had a very generous anonymous donor step in at the last minute." Her eyes meet mine for a beat before moving on. "This very generous donation has allowed us to move forward with the renovation and all our planned programming, but has also given us the opportunity to build a sustainable future here and start dreaming of even more ways to serve our students and this community."

My gaze drops to Lettie as she dabs at her eyes.

Ramsey appears beside me, he and Sebastian having just arrived. "I still don't get why you wanted to be anonymous. Your connection to The Spencer Foundation could bring in more donors."

"There's no need for other donors now. If they need more money, it's theirs."

Ramsey smirks. "Sounds like the start of The Rhys Spencer Foundation."

I throw him a look, but he just shrugs.

"Wouldn't telling her about the donation help things between you two? Make for a smoother engagement?"

I considered it. For the exact reason Ramsey is pointing out. I could easily buy Lettie whatever she wants or donate to every charity and passion project she has, but I don't want her to think I'm doing it because I want something in return. Or that I'm trying to push her to make up.

"Probably, but I want her to see who I am, not be influenced by the fact I used my money to help Leg-Up." I shove my hands in my pockets, watching Lettie on the far side of the studio passing out paint brushes and trays.

Once the supplies are handed out, everyone is assigned an area to paint.

I pour the paint into the tray so Lettie can place her roller into the soft gray paint. She glides the roller over the wall and I can't help but snap a photo of her in action. Her hair's pulled back into a ponytail now and she's wearing a pair of baggy coveralls that were supplied to her, yet I've never been more attracted to her.

"Should we get a picture together?" she asks. "You know, for your socials."

"Yeah, that's a good idea." I pull her into my side, then with one arm wrapped around her waist, I snap a photo. We're both in baggy coveralls and there's already a streak of paint on Lettie's forehead, yet it's my favorite photo of us so far.

"Community activism alongside your fiancée. The board will be impressed." She smiles up at me before turning back to continue painting the wall.

That's what I would have thought weeks ago. It's the

entire point of me and Lettie being together, to show off our relationship to prove I'm worthy, but now, I don't even want to post the photo. I want to keep it for myself. The photo brings me joy not because of what anyone else thinks but because of the woman I'm here making the memory with.

She's the only one I care about.

As the thought enters my brain, I wonder if I should be concerned about how badly I want Lettie's approval. For her to think the best of me. I've always prided myself on not giving a fuck what other people think but now that Lettie's a part of my life, that's quickly changing.

CHAPTER 36

Colette

"Strawberry, banana, peanut butter and spinach protein smoothie." Rhys hands me the drink, before taking a seat on the patio across from me, then takes a sip of his own.

"Thank you." It's my favorite smoothie from my favorite smoothie shop and I didn't even have to tell him.

That's the thing that has been so confusing with Rhys. Outside of blindsiding me with the proposal, he has been thoughtful and sweet. While I took space from him this week, the reality is I've missed him.

Painting with him at the Leg-Up community day earlier reminded me how much fun he is to be around. How much I missed his playful grin and the way his laugh emanates in his chest, so deep and full of warmth. But then, it also reminded me how badly I want his lips on mine. How achy I get between my thighs whenever his warm skin touches mine, whenever his firm grip pulls me in close and holds me to him.

"What kind did you get?" I ask.

"Guess." He holds up his drink which I can see through the clear plastic is pink.

"Strawberry."

"With?" he prompts.

"Nutella, of course." I shake my head, but can't help the smile that pulls at my lips.

"I'm a sucker for anything with chocolate and hazelnuts." He grins.

I take another sip of my smoothie and pretend like his smile isn't the best thing I've seen all week.

Even after our talk last Saturday, I was frustrated by his actions and taking time away from him this week was what I needed to clear my head. Now that I've had time to process, I understand why he didn't ask me about the proposal. It's not that he didn't trust me, it's that he didn't trust himself.

I've realized Rhys doesn't have anyone in his life that has made him believe he's worthy of trust, of friendship, of love. That he can ask for help and it won't be judged as a weakness or not being good enough to handle something on your own. Since his parents died, he's been in competition with Jerrod for attention from his grandfather and Edith. It makes sense that he would struggle to communicate his needs.

"What do you have going on this week?" he asks, setting his already empty smoothie cup on the table between us.

"Training as usual. I've got one month until evaluations. I also volunteered to fill in for Mila this week to oversee some maintenance at Leg-Up while she's out of town. Oh, and Sophie's bachelorette party is Friday. It's a spa day and a ladies' sleep over."

His eyes meet mine.

I see the vulnerability there. The question. *Do you still need me?*

"Sounds like a busy week. Should I get you home?"

"Actually, I need to find a dress for Sophie and Hunter's wedding." I let him take my empty cup and place it in the recycling bin. When he turns around, I place my hand on his forearm. "I was thinking we could go shopping."

The corner of his mouth pulls up. "Yeah?"

"I mean, if you want to. If you're not busy."

"I'd love to go shopping with you, Princess."

At the sound of the nickname I haven't heard since the night he proposed and he pressed his thick fingers inside me, my core clenches and I'm taken back to that night.

I just know I'll never be able to erase the memory of it. It's my go-to when I touch myself now. I pretend it's Rhys's fingers filling me up. Even if I'm treading carefully now, still annoyed with the way he handled the proposal, I can appreciate that Rhys is skilled in other areas. If I had the nerve, I'd tell him he could make it up to me, over and over, with his head between my thighs.

We leave the smoothie shop and start to walk back to where he parked his motorcycle. As we walk, Rhys takes my hand. There's something about hand holding that fascinates me.

I'm appreciating the way his hand feels wrapped around mine when I hear a familiar click and it draws my attention.

"Photographer," I say, taking notice of the man in the green baseball cap.

"Where?" Rhys asks, glancing around.

"By the brick building." We stop on the sidewalk by his motorcycle. "I thought that's why you were holding my hand."

He drops my hand to take the helmets out of the storage compartment. "I fucking hate photographers."

I'm surprised by his reaction. "Isn't that what you want? Pictures of us as a happy couple?"

With my helmet in his hands, he steps between me and the photographers—because there are two now—blocking them from their shot. Rhys stares at me for a long moment. I'm expecting him to kiss me the way I'd kissed him the morning after our engagement when there was a photographer outside the practice studios. His piercing hazel gaze settles on my lips. Just when I'm certain he's going to pull me to him, he pushes the helmet in his hands down onto my head.

"It should be."

That's all he says before he puts on his helmet, straddles the motorcycle, then helps me on.

I'm not sure why he didn't take the opportunity to give the photographers what they wanted. If anything, he might have looked angry for how tight his jaw was clenching.

We spend the rest of the day shopping. I've never been shopping with a boyfriend, or fake fiancé, so another new experience checked off. Yay, me!

Rhys knows a good amount about fabrics and fit, and what styles look good on me. Even Ingrid, the personal shopper that helps us at Bergman's, is impressed by his knowledge.

In the dressing room, I pretend I can't get a zipper down so that Rhys will help me. I don't know what I'm doing. Trying to recreate the friction that was between us last weekend, but for some reason, Rhys isn't meeting me halfway. He gently pulls the zipper down to where it stops above my bottom, then excuses himself. He doesn't even comment on my black lace thong that I know he saw because I can see it peeking out from the unzipped dress in the mirror. It's really quite rude.

I settle on a deep teal backless dress, then help Rhys pick out a matching tie from the swatches Ingrid brings over from the men's department.

"It's like we're going to prom," I tease as Ingrid hangs my dress on the rack in the private dressing room.

"Who did you go to prom with?"

"We didn't have prom at the ballet academy."

"They figured no one would dance?" He cracks a wide smile.

"Funny. But no, it just wasn't a thing. We were all too

focused on spring performances and auditioning for the company."

"What would you have done if you hadn't made it into the company?"

"Probably teach. I'm loving the class I teach at Leg-Up."

He nods, then drops his gaze to my feet.

"She needs shoes, too," he tells Ingrid.

"I've got several pairs that would work perfectly with this dress," she says.

When she's gone to find these so-called perfect shoes, I pout. "I hate shopping for dress shoes. Everything hurts my feet."

"You can't go barefoot. It's a wedding."

"Yeah, well, when I get married, it's going to be on the beach. Footwear optional."

He looks at me pensively. "Do you think about that? What your wedding will be like?"

I laugh. "Not really. That's the only thing I've got so far. Barefoot on the beach."

"Sounds nice." He reaches over to brush a piece of hair off my face.

It's a sweet gesture, but the way his finger pads lightly graze my face has my thighs clenching and my heart thumping wildly in my chest.

"I'd invite you but it might be weird having my ex-fiancé there." It's a joke. Something to lighten the mood, but Rhys is having none of it.

"Fuck that." He growls. "I'll be there. Front row."

I don't know what to say to that, so I quietly try on the shoes Ingrid brings and let the two of them debate over which ones look best. Ingrid doesn't bat an eye at my battered feet.

"I've seen worse," she says comfortingly.

I doubt that, but I'm not going to argue.

Rhys buys me a pair of Jimmy Choos. I insisted he not, but after those were the clear winner as far as comfort, he sneakily had Ingrid ring them up without me knowing. They cost more than my dress, but Ingrid insisted the latte color was classic and I'd be wearing them for years to come. Not if I can help it.

After shopping, we grab an early dinner at a bistro near my apartment before Rhys insists we get a cupcake at Magnolia Bakery.

"I don't know how you live down the street from this place." He takes a huge bite of his salted chocolate peanut butter cupcake. I'd been surprised he didn't go for the Nutella one, but he insisted he needed variety in his life.

"I'm not a big sweets person, but clearly you would be a frequent visitor."

He moans around the cupcake, then licks frosting off his lips, which elicits another erotic sound.

I glance around. "Stop making that sound, you'll scare the children."

"What sound?" he asks, but I can tell he's playing innocent.

I give him a wide-eyed stare. "You know."

"I'm not sure which sound you're specifically referring to. I'll make it again so you can clarify." His eyes widen in challenge, as his mouth opens to take another bite.

I grab the cupcake from him and take the last bite. It's either that or listen to him make moaning sex noises in public. He attempts to look outraged, but I think he secretly likes that I ate it.

He walks me down the block to my apartment, and I let us inside the downstairs foyer.

"We should do this again sometime," I say casually, doing my best to practice giving off chill girl dating vibes like he's instructed me to do.

"Tomorrow?" he asks eagerly and a laugh nearly bursts

past my lips. He might need a little work on his chill guy dating vibes.

"I've got plans at Hunter and Sophie's tomorrow night."

"Like dinner?" He asks.

I'm about to confess it's to babysit their twin girls, but I hold back. I decide I'll use his eagerness to hang out to my advantage.

"Yeah. Do you want to come?"

"You bet. What time?"

"Six."

"Cool. I'll pick you up."

"Sounds good."

He starts down the stairs, but I call out after him.

"If you want to bring Mo over to hang out with Maxine tomorrow while we're gone, I know she'd like that."

"Yeah?" He smiles at the thought.

I nod. "Yeah, she's been missing him, too."

CHAPTER 37

Rhys

All I want to do right now is relax with Lettie on the couch with the cats curled up beside us, but we've got dinner at Hunter and Sophie's tonight. A dinner party, even if it's with friends, is the last thing I want to do. But, if Lettie's going to be there, then that's where I'm going to be.

Hunter opens the door and immediately envelops Lettie into a hug.

"Thank you for doing this," Hunter says, guiding us into the entryway of the penthouse.

"Of course." Lettie bounces excitedly. "We wouldn't miss the opportunity."

I give Hunter a nod, but he pulls me in for a quick hug, too. I have to admit it feels good to be welcomed back into this friend group. I know it's because of my relationship with Lettie, but spending time with Hunter, James, Barrett, and Griffin has been cool. When Hunter releases me, I hand him the bottle of wine I brought.

"Thank you for having us."

Chuckling, he takes the bottle of wine. "You might not be saying that by the end of the night. They're a handful."

"They?" I turn to question Lettie, but she's already slipped off her shoes and disappeared down the hallway.

"Come on," Hunter says, waving me to follow him.

We step into the kitchen where Hunter pulls two wine glasses from the beverage center and sets them on the counter.

"How's wedding planning going?" I ask. It's not typically a male topic, but after shopping with Lettie yesterday for the event, it's what's on my mind.

"Sophie's taken on the majority of it, but I've been helping where I can." He chuckles. "Where she'll *allow* me to."

I think back to me and Lettie's conversation yesterday about her wedding.

Barefoot on the beach.

The moment she'd said those words, I could imagine her there. White flowing gown fitted in all the right places; dark hair pinned back loosely as the ocean breeze blew through it. Bouquet of tropical flowers in her hand as she made her way down the aisle to me.

The vision in my head had evaporated when she made the comment that as her ex-fiancé, I likely wouldn't even be invited. It was like a punch to the stomach.

He reaches for the corkscrew, then pauses to look at me.

"You okay?"

"Yeah, I've got a lot on my mind."

He nods. "I saw the article about Jerrod and Corinne, and the board voting in a new president for The Spencer Foundation. I didn't realize you and Jerrod would be competing for the position." I watch as he effortlessly pulls out the wine cork, then pours two glasses of the pinot. "That's got to be challenging for your relationship."

I try to keep my laugh light, but it comes out sardonically. "It's exactly on par for our relationship. We've been competing since we were kids."

Hunter considers this. "I don't know much about the

inner workings of a foundation like your family's but if you ever need to talk, let me know."

"Thanks, man. I appreciate it."

I expect him to hand me one of the glasses but he leaves them on the counter, opens the refrigerator, and hands me a seltzer water from inside.

I stare at it confused, before following him into the living room.

There, we find Lettie on the floor, legs wide as she lifts a giggling baby up in the air. Heels click down the hallway and Hunter's fiancée, Sophie, appears in a black cocktail dress. I look back at Lettie in leggings and a tank top. Did she not get the dress code for this dinner?

"Rhys, good to see you again." Sophie pulls me in for a hug.

"Yeah, thank you for having us."

She laughs. "We'll see how you feel at the end of the night."

Hunter hands Sophie the extra glass of wine and kisses her neck.

"You look gorgeous," he says.

"Thank you." She returns his adoring smile, then takes a sip of her wine. "Oh, I texted you the event center address and hotel concierge number in case of emergency."

"We'll be fine," Lettie assures her, then blows a raspberry on baby number two's belly.

"I thought we were having dinner," I say, still confused as to what is happening.

"Oh, there's a pizza in the freezer you can heat up," Sophie offers. "Or you can order in. They'll bring it right up."

"Sounds great," Lettie says, not bothering to glance in my direction.

Everything suddenly becomes clear. This isn't a dinner party, and we're not dinner guests, we're the babysitters.

"We've been having some separation issues with the girls,

so we're going to just go," Hunter whispers, then nods toward the door.

"We'll keep them distracted," Lettie singsongs to the smiling babies like she's not trying to cover up their parents' escape.

Sophie looks torn, but she must decide it's for the best because she allows Hunter to usher her out the door.

The front door softly clicks shut, but the babies don't notice a thing. They're too enthralled with Lettie. She's making silly faces, scrunching up her nose and sticking out her tongue. Even with those goofy expressions, she looks gorgeous.

"What happened to all that talk about being honest?" I ask.

"Oh, I'm sorry, did I surprise you with a change of plans? Hmm, that is awfully neglectful of me to not keep you up to date on all the current happenings. Must have slipped my mind."

"I get it. You're still mad about the proposal."

She whips her head in my direction, eyes narrowed.

"I will probably always be mad about the proposal."

My gaze falls to her left hand. "You're still wearing the ring."

"Sometimes I use it as a paperweight. It comes in handy." She shrugs. "If I told you what we were doing tonight, you wouldn't have come."

"That is an accurate statement," I tease before chugging the seltzer water, the lie easily rolling off my tongue.

Am I excited to be babysitting two infants? No. But I would have come even if Lettie had told me we were getting our nose hairs plucked out. That's how badly I want to spend time with her.

"Oh, come on. This is fun." With her legs still stretched out, she's made a circle with the babies across from her, rolling a ball to one, then the other.

"We have a very different idea of fun, apparently."

She rolls her eyes at me, then turns back toward the babies to cheer at their ability to drool all over the balls they're gnawing on. The pillow dam she's built behind them comes in handy when one of them suddenly tips backwards.

"I think Uncle Rhys is a party pooper."

Uncle Rhys.

She doesn't mean it literally. I'm not related to Hunter and Sophie's girls, but that title awakens something in me. It's connection. A sense of belonging.

Does that make her Aunt Lettie?

I push the thought aside.

She lifts the tipped over baby back onto her butt, then takes each of their free hands, shimmying their upper bodies as she chants, "He's a party pooper, he's a party pooper."

I watch the scene with fascination and anxiety. I've never been around babies before. Lettie, on the other hand, looks like a natural.

Lettie pats the ground next to her. "Come on, Rhys. You can do it." It sounds like she's talking to a dog. I shake my head, staying firmly planted on the couch where I can safely observe.

"What are we having for dinner?" I ask.

Lettie pins me with a look.

"What? I was under the assumption we were being served dinner."

"You heard Sophie. We can order something once the girls are down for the night."

I glance at my watch. "And when will that be?"

"First, we need to feed them, give them a bath, then read them a book."

"Read them a book? They can't even talk."

There's that look again. If this is a test, I'm failing. Lettie is giving me another chance and I'm fucking it up.

"You're right, they can't talk, but they can listen to us. It's good for brain development."

Watching Lettie with Poppy and Finley, she's a natural.

"Do you want kids?" The question leaves my mouth before I can reconsider.

She's quiet a moment. "I think so. I want to dance for as long as I can, though, so that will take priority, but yeah, I can see myself having a family." She turns to find me staring at her. "What about you?"

"Do you even have to ask?" My sharp remark comes out just as easily.

A smile tugs at her lips. "You were good with the kids at the hospital."

"Yeah, but this," I motion to the helpless babies cooing on the floor, "is terrifying."

"Because you don't want to have a family or because you don't know what to do?"

I shrug. "I don't know, maybe both."

"You're not going to learn anything sitting up there."

"Fine." I lower to the floor, trying to stretch out my long legs, but every position is uncomfortable. "Adults are not meant to sit on the floor. I've got tight hip flexors."

Lettie easily leans forward, her ass lifting behind her.

"That's not natural." I motion to her. "No one but you and other elite athletes with highly flexible hips can do that."

A loud farting sound comes from one of the babies.

"Oh my goodness. Was that you?" Lettie coos, tickling the baby's belly. "Smells like someone needs a change."

Lettie scoops up the baby in question. I have no idea which one is which or how to tell them apart.

"You need to watch Finley while I change Poppy."

She motions toward the remaining baby.

"Is it going to move?" I ask.

Lettie blinks at me. "*She* is Finley and she doesn't know how to crawl yet."

I nod. "Okay."

Lettie's still talking as she walks down the hallway.

The baby that was left in my care must have good intuition. She quickly realizes she's been left in the hands of an unqualified caregiver. Her eyes that had been tracking Lettie and her sister leave the room shift to take one look at me and her bottom lip begins to tremble. Her big blue eyes turn glassy. From the looks of it, those tears are going to be huge.

"No, no, no, no." I attempt to head off the meltdown but I think my deep voice only serves to scare her more. Her mouth opens but there's no sound. Then, a moment later, the crying starts.

"Lettie!" I call, but I doubt she can hear me over the wailing. "Shit."

I lift to my knees in front of the baby and reach for a stuffed toy. I bounce it up and down in front of her hoping it will be a distraction.

"Look. It's a giraffe." I stare at the giraffe, trying to think of silly things to say about it. "It's got a long neck."

The giraffe does nothing so I toss it aside.

"Look, I don't know what you need, but they'll be back soon and Lettie will figure it out, so let's stop crying while we wait."

She only cries harder. Her tiny hands balling into fists, her face turning bright red.

"Okay, should I pick you up? Is that it?"

With my hands encircling her sides to lift her, I sit back down on the couch and set her on my knee. She's stiff in my arms and the crying continues.

"Fuck. I wish you could tell me what's wrong." I remember how Lettie had held one of them in his arms earlier and bounced up and down, producing a giggle. "Do you want to bounce?"

There's no answer, only crying.

"Okay, here we go."

I bounce her up and down on my leg.

"We're bouncing now. You can stop crying."

Her cries start to ease up and are slowly replaced by a vibrating giggle.

"Buh-buh-buh-buh-buh."

I'm entranced by the gurgling laugh that escapes.

"We figured it out, didn't we?" I smile and I swear she smiles back. "Maybe this isn't so—" I don't get the words out before the baby projectile vomits all over me.

I sit there, baby vomit sliding down my neck and chest. It's warm, and thick, like somebody dumped a bowl of oatmeal on me.

"Lettie!"

"Yeah?" she calls, coming down the hallway toward us. "Oh, what—"

"It threw up on me." I inhale, then gag on the scent of baby vomit.

"Oh, no, you poor thing," Lettie says, her soothing voice making me feel a little bit better.

Except Lettie doesn't fuss over me; instead, she scoops up the vomit baby, so she's holding both babies now, and starts back down the hallway.

"What about me?" I say to the empty room, my arms extended, palms to the ceiling, the vomit starting to dry on my skin.

It's clear nobody cares, so I stand and follow Lettie to the babies' room. She's there with one baby sitting in a seated contraption while vomit baby, who barely got a drop on herself, gets a full outfit change.

"We'll get you all changed up. Nice and clean," Lettie coos to the baby.

"And what am I supposed to wear?" I ask, motioning to my soaked shirt. "This is vintage Valentino."

"You shouldn't have worn it to babysit."

"I didn't know we were babysitting." Lettie tricked me

into being here. Well, joke's on her, she's got three babies to take care of now.

"Grab a t-shirt out of Hunter's closet."

I don't make a move.

"What?" she asks.

"That seems weird."

"You're being silly. It's just a t-shirt. Besides," she wrinkles her nose, "do you want to smell like vomit for the rest of the night?"

I move slightly to the right and get a big whiff of baby vomit from my shirt. "No."

Lettie makes a waving motion for me to get moving.

In Hunter's closet, I find his t-shirt drawer and wade through the selection, finding several Princeton crew shirts before I settle on a light gray Lake George t-shirt.

In the bathroom, I clean up, wipe the now dry spit-up off my body then put on a clean shirt. I attempt to rinse the vomit off of my vintage Valentino polo with water, then pray that the dry cleaner will be able to get the smell out.

When I return to the babies' room, I find Lettie there with both girls sprawled out on the carpeted floor.

"Better?" she asks, nodding at my shirt.

"Yeah." And because I'm already epically failing at this so I might as well go all in, I reach for the toes of the baby wiggling around on the floor and give her my best rendition of *this little piggie* before blowing a raspberry on the bottom of each foot.

Hearing the baby's high-pitched giggles and squeals of delight is surprisingly rewarding.

I look up to find Lettie watching me closely, a huge smile spread across her face. And if the baby's joyous laughter wasn't enough, that smile right there makes my night. Maybe I'm not so bad at this after all.

CHAPTER 38

Colette

After I lay Poppy down in her crib, I quietly exit the room to check on Rhys and Finley.

Even when we put the gas medicine into her bottle as Sophie instructed, Finley was still fussy, so Rhys took her into Sophie and Hunter's bedroom so her crying didn't disturb Poppy. I'd offered to take Finley, to let him put Poppy down since she's easier going, but he shook his head and told me he could handle it. It was a far cry from the helpless man who got thrown up on.

Rhys had not been pleased when he found out we were here to babysit, but I figured if he didn't want to be here, he could leave at any time. But he stayed. And when he tapped into *this little piggie* and his foot massage skills, he really turned a corner.

I crack open the bedroom door to find Rhys in the middle of the room cradling Finley in his arms. He wasn't even comfortable holding her two hours ago, but now he's softly humming to her and holding her snugly against his chest. Something about the contrast of his black ink tattooed arm against the pastel pink of her pajama onesie makes my stomach flutter. Or is that my ovaries? It's hard to tell. They're kind of in the same vicinity.

I know I shouldn't even be having these thoughts, but watching him rock her to sleep is one of the hottest things I've ever seen.

Don't you dare swoon over Rhys Spencer, I chastise myself. We're just friends. Friends who are fake engaged.

But it's moments like these that I see a glimpse of the gooey center he's got hidden beneath his rough edges. The more I seek these moments out, the more I find the treasure trove of hidden gems.

I push the door open farther, and the light from the hallway filters in. Rhys lifts his head in my direction, a finger to his lips to indicate Finley is asleep, or very close to it.

He carefully walks her across the hallway and lays her in her crib.

"You're a natural," I whisper, once he's closed the door to their room.

"If I was a natural, you wouldn't have found it so entertaining to torture me with this little surprise tonight," he says as we move down the hallway and out to the kitchen.

"Torture wasn't my incentive, more like introspection." And payback.

"You've made your point."

"Have I?" I ask, my lashes lowering.

I'm flirting with Rhys. I'm not even doing it on purpose, it's become second nature. I didn't think it would be this easy. Part of our comfort with each other since we've been in this fake relationship. I should see it as an achievement, but instead, I find myself panicking a little.

Will I ever feel like this with someone else?

Do I want it to?

"Yes. You're cut out for this kind of thing and I'm not. You'd be sweet, doting Aunt Lettie that does everything right and I'd be wildly inappropriate Uncle Rhys that swears too much and gets everyone drunk on their twenty-first birthday."

"You don't give yourself enough credit."

"What do you mean?" he asks.

"You'd be fun, yet dependable Uncle Rhys. The guy who picks you up when you fall and carries you the three miles home. The one who sneaks you fudge popsicles when your parents said no because you didn't eat your vegetables. And you'd be the guy they go to for shopping advice."

"Neither of us have siblings so I don't have to worry about it."

It takes me a moment to realize what he said.

Does he mean that hypothetically for our fake engagement we don't need to worry about being married and having no siblings to make us an aunt or uncle? Or that even if we were really together there's no chance of being uncle and aunt because again, we don't have any siblings?

My phone buzzes on the counter. "That's probably the food. I asked them not to ring the doorbell since the girls are asleep."

"That's for sure something Aunt Lettie would do." He winks at me. "I'll get it."

While Rhys goes to get the takeout, I think about our conversation. Rhys is fun and goofy and charismatic and playful, but he's also thoughtful and generous and sweet. Everybody is allowed to want a certain life for themselves, family or not, but it's wild to me that he doesn't see how much he has to offer someone.

I wonder if our fake relationship will change him, and he'll be interested in being with only one woman, or if he'll return to whatever it was he was doing before we started this arrangement.

For the first time since this started between us, the idea of seeing Rhys with another woman makes me nauseas. Which is not great for all the food we just ordered.

Rhys is back a few minutes later and he starts unpacking the food.

I watch as he distributes the various dishes onto two plates. He starts picking off mushrooms from one of the dishes and putting it onto the other plate.

"What are you doing?" I ask.

"They forgot to hold the mushrooms in your Moo Goo Gai Pan so I'm picking them out."

"You don't have to do that. I can eat around them."

"I got you, Princess." He winks and that simple flash of his eyelashes sends a shockwave through my body. I feel it deep. All the way down in my bone marrow.

This right here. Rhys being this sweet, thoughtful man, is going to be trouble.

CHAPTER 39

Rhys

"Okay, that's about all I can take of that show. It's my turn to pick." I motion for Lettie to give me the remote control. We're two episodes into this show and it's starting to give me an eye twitch.

She shakes her head, a sly smile pulling at her lips. "*90 Day Fiancé* is a classic. I think you could learn a lot from it."

"*Lettie,*" I warn. There's an edge to my voice, but she's not fazed at all.

"What are you going to do?" she asks. "Take the remote away?"

When I don't respond, her lips twist in amusement. "For such a bad boy, you're actually quite a softie, Rhys Spencer."

She's goading me. Sitting there cross-legged in her leggings and cropped t-shirt. Her hair piled high on her head, face free of makeup. She looks like a fucking dream. An angel with a wicked smile that has every muscle in my body on high alert. The way she's defiantly pursing her lips and cocking her eyebrow, she's exactly like dream Lettie that has been wreaking havoc on my subconscious every night.

Testing my resolve, I learn forward, letting her warm,

feminine scent wash over me. My fingers slide under her chin, tilting it up until her blue eyes are level with mine.

"For such a good girl, you're awfully disobedient."

"Thank you. I'll take that as a compliment."

She pulls away and my fingers immediately miss touching her. Then with that beautiful grin pulling at her lips, she side-eyes me while slowly lifting the remote toward the screen.

"It's cute that you think you've won." I stretch my arms toward the ceiling before casually placing my hands behind my head. "If I want that remote, I will take it from you."

Her lips press together and her chest starts to vibrate with the laughter she's holding in.

"Yeah? I'd like to see you tr—" her words are cut off when I suddenly lunge toward her. She shrieks, scrambling toward the other end of the couch, but she's not quick enough. I'm on her so fast, my larger frame covering the space between us and easily pinning her beneath me. Her hand holding the remote is now tucked beneath her back.

"I'm sorry, what was that you were saying?" My finger pads find the smooth skin exposed by her cropped shirt and tease her there. A laugh bursts out of her as she squirms from side to side trying to get away from my torturous fingers, but I'm relentless.

"Wait, Rhys. Please." She's breathless as she pushes her free hand into my chest. "Did you hear that?" My fingers are still on her skin as she turns her head toward the monitor sitting on the coffee table. I follow her gaze there. While I'm looking at the video feed of Finley and Poppy's room, searching for anything but two peacefully sleeping baby girls, Lettie shoots out from beneath me.

That little sneaker.

But she's not quick enough. I grab her hips to pull her backwards.

"I was going to take it easy on you," I flip her onto her

back, pinning her lower body down with mine, "but now you're really going to get it."

My fingers resume their mission to make her squirm.

And I do.

Peals of laughter escape but I can tell she's trying to be quiet, holding back so she doesn't wake the babies. Her body thrashes from side to side, but even with her jerky movements, I can't miss the soft skin beneath my fingers, the way her pelvis rocks against mine.

"Rhys!" she whisper-screams through her laughter. "Oh, god!" She gasps for air as tears from her laughter cut a path down her face.

I can only imagine one other scenario where I want to hear my name falling from her lips in that way. The thought has my fingers easing up on her ribcage.

"I'll be good." She pants, relieved the tickling has stopped. "You can have it." Her fingers release the remote, dropping it by her side.

Her now empty hands lift to her shoulders in surrender.

But I couldn't care less about the remote. There's nothing I want to see more than Lettie smiling and panting beneath me. I'm fascinated by the view. The feel of her there. Her chest rising to meet mine, then falling away, a rhythm that slows as her breath evens out. Being this close to her is the same euphoric rush I get when I'm out on the open water.

Ignoring the remote, my hand lifts to wipe at her damp cheek. One side, then the other. My thumb following the path of the tear before circling back to trace the line of her jaw.

Before I know it, I've found Lettie's bottom lip. With a gentle pressure, I slowly trace the ridge where her lips meet the groove above her chin.

"This mouth of yours is going to get you in trouble, Princess."

She inhales a deep breath, and swallows. I swear I can hear her heart racing.

"Maybe I like trouble," she whispers against my finger.

For a moment, we hold each other's gaze.

We're back in this place. Teasing each other until someone takes it too far.

Once again, my eyes zero in on Lettie's mouth and every thought I've had to stop myself from touching her again must have taken the night off because there's no hesitation before I drop my lips to hers.

The moment I capture her plush lips with mine, I know I'll hate myself for this later.

It's a reminder of how sweet she tastes.

How good it feels to be this close to her.

And gives me another memory that will haunt me the moment I close my eyes tonight.

But I can't stop. And Lettie doesn't pull away.

Instead, she dips her tongue into my mouth, and with that invitation, I go fucking wild.

Diving deeper, claiming her mouth as my own.

I've still got her wrists pinned with one of my hands, I'd held them there to keep her beneath me. Her lips are telling me she wants this, her mouth meeting mine for every hungry kiss, but I want to feel her hands on me, to confirm her body is as lost to this moment as mine is.

I release her pinned hands and they immediately find my hair, fingers curling as she holds me against her. Her hands on me are another layer to this addiction and her touch only feeds my desire. Gentle strokes of her fingers down my neck have me shuddering, goosebumps lifting from the surface of my skin.

I think I'd be perfectly happy kissing her like this forever, but then she grinds her hips and presses her center against my cock. *Fuck.* I groan into her mouth. My hands find her hips, sliding along the waistband of her leggings, under her shirt, until I'm palming her over her bra. It's her turn to moan as I thumb her hard nipples through the thin fabric.

Kissing Lettie is like a drug. She gives me the highest high; it's exhilarating, but I'm terrified that I'm addicted now. And dreading the withdrawals when this is over. Because once she comes to her senses, this will be over.

I push the thought away. I don't want to think about that now. All I want to do is ride the wave of pleasure that kissing Lettie gives me.

I want to strip her bare right here. Put my head between her pretty thighs again. My cock strains against my zipper just thinking about having her on my tongue, lapping her up until this hunger is satiated.

I'm so lost in Lettie; it takes me a second to register the voices in the hallway. Even then, I want to ignore them, stay in this moment with her, but the quiet click of the front door has me pulling back. Lettie must not have heard them because she whimpers with protest, her fingers still finding purchase in my hair as I lift her off the floor and set her back on the couch.

Lettie's hair is a mess and her lips are swollen. Her eyes scan me, widening at the impressive bulge in my jeans.

She's half laughing when she tosses a pillow at me to cover my erection.

"Watch it," I say, turning to fend off the overstuffed pillow with my thigh to protect my balls.

"Oh, I am. Trust me, it's all I can see right now."

Sophie and Hunter enter the room and I casually hold the pillow to my front.

It's clear from their smirks that we were caught.

It shouldn't matter.

Lettie's my fiancée. I can kiss her anytime I want.

Except I can't. Since the night I proposed, after I tasted her and made her come hard, I told her I wouldn't touch her again. Not unless we needed to for appearance's sake. So what was that kiss?

"H-hey, how was your night?" Lettie asks Sophie while sweeping loose hairs from her bun.

"It was good, but I'm exhausted." She grabs a blanket from the back of the couch and wraps herself in it. "How were the girls?"

I watch Lettie compose herself, going from make-out bandit to responsible adult in seconds.

"They were angels. Finley didn't eat as much as Poppy but she seemed happy and they both went to sleep pretty easy."

"I should check on them," Sophie says, swinging back the blanket she just finished wrapping around herself.

"I got it," Hunter says. "You relax."

Hunter rubs Sophie's shoulders, then places a kiss at her temple.

"Thank you," she says, squeezing his hand before he moves to leave the room.

Maybe I'm still recovering from kissing Lettie, but watching Hunter and Sophie together, their open affection and adoration has me feeling envious.

I stand there, caught in a trance as Sophie and Lettie talk. Their conversation is only noise as I take in Lettie's easy smile. She reaches up to her bun, pulling it loose to let her hair down, absently shaking out the dark strands.

Sophie's yawn brings my attention back to their conversation.

"We'll let you get to bed," Lettie says.

"Yeah, the girls will be up early. Thank you again for filling in tonight."

"Anytime! We truly had a blast."

"I bet you did." Sophie's eyes are tired, but her lips twitch with amusement.

"I can't quite match Lettie's enthusiasm. I won't be volunteering to be on your babysitting call list, but your girls are adorable."

"Thank you. You two have a good night."

"You ready?" Lettie asks.

"Yeah, let's go."

CHAPTER 40

Colette

Rhys holds the door open for me but doesn't make a move toward my building. He's been unusually quiet since we left Hunter and Sophie's place.

I'm not ready for the night to end. I want him to kiss me again. To see what might have happened if we hadn't been interrupted. My body is still tingling with the thought.

He walks me in, up the elevator and to my apartment door, but as soon as I get the door open, he starts backing up.

"Do you want to come in?" I ask.

"No, thanks. I'm tired."

"Oh, yeah, that makes sense. First babysitting gig can really take it out of you."

A smile pulls at his lips. "I did have fun tonight, minus the baby vomit."

Now I'm analyzing if he's talking about rocking babies to sleep or kissing me. Maybe it's both. I hope kissing me is somewhere up there with smelling the baby's heads.

"Me, too."

He nods, backing away toward the elevator. "I'll talk to you later."

"Okay." I try to not sound too disappointed, then throw out a *goodnight* just as he's getting on the elevator.

Once I'm inside my apartment, I lean against the door, giving him ample time to change his mind so I can fling the door open and rush into his arms.

I'll give him one more minute. Okay, two minutes tops.

Maxine stares at me from across the room. If cats could give side-eye, that's what she'd be doing now.

"What? Just because Mo is obsessed with you doesn't mean you need to gloat."

Rhys had brought Mo over earlier today to hang out with Maxine while we went for a walk around the park. I wish Mo was still here so Rhys would have had a reason to come in my apartment.

A few minutes later, I push off the front door and make my way to my room. I change into my pajamas, then start to brush my teeth when my phone buzzes on my nightstand.

Rhys: *I shouldn't be telling you this, but I was dying to come into your apartment tonight.*

I blink a few times to make sure I'm reading that right. Rhys sending a flirty text isn't new, but all the other times they had been because we were practicing.

Should I ask if that's what this is?

Part of me doesn't want to know. I don't want to ruin it.

I spit out my toothpaste and rinse before grabbing my phone and hopping into bed. Maxine saunters in and jumps up to join me.

Lettie: *I wanted you to.*

Rhys: *Why?*

Lettie: *You tell me first.*

Rhys: *I wanted to kiss you again.*

I swallow thickly, letting the words on the screen sink in. He wanted to come up to my apartment and kiss me. I imagine what it would be like if he was here now, and I wonder if he'd let himself do what he wanted.

Lettie: *Why didn't you want to tell me?*

Rhys: *It's against the rules.*

Lettie: *Rules schmules*

Rhys: *That doesn't sound like you at all. Now I'm wondering if I'm texting the right person.*

Lettie: *The old Lettie can't text right now.*

Rhys: *Why?*

Lettie: *Because she's too turned on*

I don't think I would be able to tell him that to his face. Texting gives me the confidence.

My thighs squeeze together as I wait for his next message, but nothing comes. Those three dots indicating he's typing appear, then disappear. Oh, god. I'm starting to second-guess everything. Maybe I went too far.

Rhys: *What are you going to do about it?*

My body shivers in response to his reply.

Lettie: *Touch myself*

Rhys: *Is my ring on your finger when you touch yourself?*

Lettie: *See for yourself*

I snap a photo of my left hand, fingers teasing into the waistband of my sleep shorts, my engagement ring winking up at the camera.

Rhys: *Damn, Princess. Are you wet?*

Seeing my nickname on the screen loosens the grip on my chest. I slide my hand under my panties and dip a finger into my center. I'm drenched.

Lettie: *So wet*

Rhys: *If I were there, I'd lick that pretty cunt*

Lettie: *If you were here, I'd probably let you*

My phone starts buzzing with an incoming call from Rhys. For a moment I'm debating not answering it, but I need to be an adult about this.

"Hello?" I answer, my voice barely a whisper.

"Probably?" His husky voice tickles my ear through the phone. "You'd *probably* let me?"

"Oops, it just came out that way. I guess I'm not very good at this." I put the phone on speaker and set it down near my pillow.

"Are you kidding? I couldn't get my zipper down fast enough the moment you started texting me."

"Really?" I like the idea that Rhys was so turned on by my words that he had to touch himself.

"Are we doing this?" His voice is strained, like he's holding himself back.

"I don't want to stop," I sigh, letting my fingers slide over my slick flesh. "I want you to talk to me like you did the night you proposed."

A deep growl echoes over the speaker. I close my eyes.

"Tell me what to do, Rhys."

"Slip your fingers inside, Princess. Imagine they're mine and stretch that tight cunt for me."

A breathy moan leaves my lips as I do what he says, letting my fingers slick over my seam then push inside.

"Are you touching yourself?" I ask.

"Yes. I'm stroking my cock and imagining it's your hot little mouth."

I imagine him there on his bed, his beautiful, thick shaft with a bead of precum oozing from his tip, rocking his hips as he thrusts into his hand. His piercing glinting under the bedroom light with every stroke. I bite down on my lip and circle my clit.

Call it insecurity from the night we hooked up, but I can't stop myself from asking.

"Am I good at it? Do you like the way I touch you?" I ask.

"You're so fucking good, Princess. You have no idea how good you make me feel."

My fingers work faster.

"Fuck. I can hear how slick you are." He groans, and the rough, guttural sound sends me over the edge.

"I'm coming," I pant.

I lie there breathing hard and the same sounds are echoed back to me over the line. We're both quiet for a minute, letting our panting even out.

"Rhys?"

"Yeah?" he huffs, still recovering from his orgasm.

God, I wish I could have seen his face. Watched him come apart. *Touched* him as he did.

"I really liked what we just did, but I'm not sure what it means."

"Me either." The sound he makes is a half groan, half sigh.

Suddenly, I'm drained from the day, my orgasm, and the feelings I'm desperately trying not to acknowledge. "We don't have to figure it out tonight, right?" I stifle a yawn.

He sighs. "No, we don't."

"Okay, then I'll talk to you later."

"Tomorrow," he corrects. "I'll talk to you tomorrow."

"Okay. Goodnight, Rhys."

"Goodnight, Princess."

This time our goodnights are final.

I drift off to sleep, Maxine curled up next to me, not disturbed in the slightest by what she just witnessed. I have no idea what we just did means for our fake engagement, for our friendship, but I'm worried the feelings I'm developing for Rhys are becoming all too real.

CHAPTER 41

Colette

Rhys: *Have a good dinner with your parents. Tell them hi for me.*

Lettie: *Thanks. I will. I hope your dinner with Sandeep goes well.*

Rhys and I have been texting all day, with no mention of what we did over the phone last night. I'm not sure if that means we're planning to pretend it didn't happen or if we both still need more time to think about what it means for our fake relationship that little by little seems to be edging into something real.

I'm good with tabling it for another night.

Clutching the bottle of wine in my hand, I tuck my phone away and walk over to my parents' apartment. I'm excited to spend time with them tonight, *both* of them, as it's been nearly impossible to catch them together lately.

When my dad greets me at the door, I throw my arms around him.

"Hi, sweetheart." His tight squeeze causes emotion to bubble up. With everything going on with Rhys and the engagement, I didn't know how much I needed it. To be at home with them, just the three of us, like it's always been. "It's great to see you."

"You, too. It feels like we haven't had time like this in forever."

My mom walks into the room and takes in my watery eyes.

"Why are you crying?" She glances to my dad, an accusing expression on her face. "Did you already tell her?"

I wipe at my eyes. "I was telling Dad it feels like it's been so long since we had a family dinner, and I've missed it, that's all." My mom's question finally sinks in, and I glance between my parents. "Tell me what?"

They share a look, and it makes my stomach drop. It's not a typical look they share, filled with affection or warmth, understanding or passion. It's a look of defeat.

"What is it?" My mind is whirring. My subconscious kicking into high gear, thinking up every possible scenario. They're moving. My dad lost his job. One of them is sick. Like *really* sick.

My mom plasters a smile on her face. "Should we eat first?"

She has a plan and she's trying to steer us back on course, but there's no way I can sit through dinner when they've clearly got something important to tell me.

"I won't be able to eat. Please, tell me now."

"I really think it's best—" she starts, but my dad cuts her off.

He nods toward my panicked face. "We should tell her."

My mom sighs, motioning toward the living room. "Fine. Let's sit."

I sit down on the couch next to my mom, then glance around the space for clues. It looks exactly like it did when I was here last. Or maybe it looks completely different but I can't tell because my brain is overloaded trying to guess what my parents' news is.

"Honey—"

"Sweetheart—"

They both start talking at once.

"Just tell me. I'm a big girl. I can handle it." If I say it, maybe that will make it true. Because the reality is when it comes to my parents, my family, I'm a pile of mush.

"We're separated," my dad says.

I blink. His words are a punch to the gut. My chest caves in and I can't seem to breathe.

That possibility hadn't even crossed my mind.

My parents. *Separated?* Not a thing.

Even my brain, which is desperately trying to grasp the concept, comes back with an error message. *Does not compute.*

There's a hundred-year-old tree at Lake George where my dad carved in Mer & Tom 4EVA.

Except, maybe it does. It would explain why I haven't seen them together much lately. Even at events where they were both in attendance, they weren't *with* each other. And how difficult it's been to reschedule our family dinner night.

"Since when?" I finally ask. "How long have you been waiting to tell me?"

"Since January," my mom replies.

"That long?" I swallow back the lump in my throat.

My mom stands from where she's sitting next to me. "We were waiting to tell you after your spring show wrapped. Then you were busy getting ready for Hannah's wedding, and then your relationship with Rhys and your engagement. We couldn't find the right time. And we didn't want to hurt you."

Six months.

Had I been so involved in my career, lost in my own world, that I hadn't seen my parents' marriage falling apart?

"It was going to hurt no matter when you told me but…" My words trail off, my stomach lurching as the news starts to sink in. "I can't even process this. What happened? Why are you separated?"

"We grew apart. It happens in relationships. We've been taking some time to figure things out."

"Okay, so how are you fixing it? Are you going to counseling?" My eyes dart between them, searching for answers.

I watch their wordless exchange. Their relationship may not be intact anymore, but they still speak the same language.

Should we tell her now?

I think it's best.

A laugh exits my throat, but it's humorless. I can see it written on their faces. "You're not just separated. You're getting a divorce."

"We met with our lawyers last week. We wanted to get all the information before we said anything."

"We tried counseling. We did." With his elbows on his knees, my dad pushes his hands through his hair before clasping them under his chin. "What's happening between your mother and I isn't something we can fix."

"You mean it's not something you want to fix."

"It's amicable. We still care for each other deeply, and we will always be a family. We're at a point in our lives where we want different things." It sounds like my mom is reading a blanket statement written by someone in PR.

How will we always be a family if we're broken? We'll never be the same from this moment on.

For them, this is a relief. A change that they want, a decision that they've been mulling over for six months. Maybe longer.

They're not happy together.

I know it's about *their* relationship, but for me, it's the end of my family as I know it. The end of the one thing that I could always count on. My support system. My place of belonging.

With tears streaking down my face, my mom wraps her arms around me.

"I'm sorry, baby. If I could stop your pain, I would, but these things are painful. For everyone."

I wipe at my face, then glance at my dad. His eyes are red and glassy.

He reaches across to place a hand on my knee. "We love you so much. That will never change."

I pull my gaze from him and glance around their apartment. The place I grew up. Where every memory is seeped into the walls.

"What is happening to the apartment?" I whisper.

My mom rubs soothing circles on my back as she responds. "Your dad is moving closer to the university, and I've found an apartment in Midtown."

With her answer, another shard lodges itself in my heart.

People move all the time; I try to rationalize it. Besides, I haven't lived here for six years. I'm on my own now.

I'm trying to be an adult about this, because I am, technically, but the little girl who helped paint her bedroom walls pink is crying and screaming about leaving this place.

That's when it occurs to me, if they're selling their apartment, what does that mean for our other family property?

"What about the Lake George cottage?" I sniff.

They exchange another look, and I know what's coming even before the words leave my mom's mouth.

"We're going to sell it."

Something inside me splinters. Hearing the fate of our beloved Lake George cottage sends me over the edge. It's the final straw, and I can't be here anymore.

I bolt upright, breaking the gentle hold my mom's arms had on me.

"I have to go," I announce in a rush, furiously wiping at my face to stop the tears, but they're persistent.

"Colette, please stay," my mom pleads. "We can talk more."

"We know this is overwhelming." My dad wraps his arms

around me, his soft baritone warm and soothing near my ear. "We'll get through it together."

There's no more together, though.

Not here. We're broken. Our family, the family we once had, doesn't exist anymore.

And I can't stand to be in this heartbreaking moment any longer.

"I've got to go," I sob, moving toward the front door.

"I'll walk you home," my dad insists.

I don't bother answering as I rush out the door.

On the short walk to my apartment, we don't talk. His presence is somewhat comforting, but also a reminder of what just took place.

At the stairs to my building, he waits on the sidewalk while I let myself inside. I can't look at him without bursting into tears, so I give a quick wave, then go straight up to my apartment.

By the time I get inside, I'm completely numb.

I know they'd wanted me to stay for dinner, but after their news blew up my life, I couldn't stomach it. Food or watching them tactfully exchange pleasantries. I'm not ready to navigate that yet. The news is too raw. I can't go from the idea of my parents together and happy to knowing they're divorcing and witnessing the aftermath in less than an hour. No, that's going to take time.

Maxine ambles over to where I'm sitting on the couch, so I scoop her up and bury my face in her fur. As the tears start to flow again, her fur turns damp, and she wiggles out of my arms.

I look around my empty apartment. I'm alone now, but I don't want to be. Maybe I should have stayed at my parents' place. The thought has my stomach clenching.

I reach for my phone.

I expect my fingers to navigate to Hannah's name, but they don't. They scroll to Rhys's name.

He answers on the first ring. "Hey, Princess."

Just the sound of his voice has the emotion taking over. My throat tightens, making it difficult to talk.

"I—I need you." That's all I can get out before I crumple to the floor and burst into tears.

CHAPTER 42

Rhys

My dinner with Sandeep has been insightful. I'd arranged it as part of my plan to have one-on-one sit downs with each of the board members to get to know them better with the sole purpose of swaying their vote to me instead of Jerrod, but we've been having a good time getting to know each other, and the topic hasn't even come up.

He has two children in college now and the shit he's telling me about parenting puts my baby vomit incident last night into perspective. It was nothing compared to what he's been through.

"Sometimes we take ourselves too seriously," he lets out a jovial laugh. "Especially in arenas like board rooms, where everyone is trying to put on a front to make everyone else think they're important. If you want to be humbled, be a parent."

Our conversation reminds me of babysitting with Lettie, which gives my brain a clear pathway to thinking about what we did last night on the phone. I've been thinking about it all day.

I had no intention of texting her when I got home, but I

was so keyed up from kissing her that my fingers went rogue. And the way Lettie responded? So fucking hot.

Once I called her, it was clear she was far more comfortable texting, but I knew I had to hear her voice. To tell her exactly what I wanted to do to her and soak in the sounds of her breathy moan when she came on her own fingers.

My phone buzzes on the table and I reach for it.

"Sorry," I glance at Sandeep to gauge his reaction, "I thought I put it on silent."

He responds with a casual wave. "It's fine."

When I see the screen, Lettie's name is there.

"I apologize, but I have to take this."

I stand so I can take the call somewhere private, but slide to answer as I'm walking.

"Hey, Princess."

There's silence, then a sniff before I hear her. "I—I need you."

"Lettie? What's going on?" I ask. When I'm met with silence, I glance at the screen to see the call has already ended.

I call her back, but she doesn't pick up. I try again. Still, no answer.

Rushing back to the table to grab my suit jacket, I call her again.

It rings and rings.

"I'm sorry, but I've got to go," I say, pushing my arms into the sleeves of my jacket.

"Is everything okay?" he asks, the skin between his brows creasing with concern.

"I'm not sure. It's Lettie. She sounded upset, then the call ended but now she's not picking up and I'm worried." My words are leaving my mouth so quickly, I'm tripping over them.

"I've got this." He motions to the table. "Just go."

"Thank you." I run for the exit, nearly crashing into a

waiter. "Sorry," I mumble, half out of my mind wondering if Lettie's okay.

Thankfully, Wanda is nearby and in less than thirty seconds, I'm on my way to Lettie's apartment.

"Wanda, I give you permission to break any traffic laws you need to get me there as fast as you can. I'll pay for it. I don't care how many tickets you get, I'll make it right, I'll expunge your record, just please hurry."

"Mr. Spencer, I will do my best, but if we detour to the hospital, that's going to slow us down."

"I know. You're right. Drive safe, but fast."

"Is everything okay with Miss Davenport?" she asks.

"I don't know." I rub my fingertips against my chin. "I don't know."

Seven minutes later I have my answer.

I find Lettie curled up in a blanket on the floor in her living room. Maxine is lying next to her and at my arrival, stretches her front paws out toward me.

Lettie didn't answer when I buzzed at the door, so I tried Mrs. Donahue and she let me in. Lettie's apartment door was unlocked, which I hate for security reasons, but right now when I needed to get to her, it was helpful.

"Lettie, baby, I'm here."

I scoop her up into my arms and pull her into my lap. She throws her arms around my neck and buries her face there. Her only response is to cry harder.

"Can you talk to me, Princess?" I stroke her hair. "I'm worried. Did someone hurt you? Did someone—"

I can't get the words out. The thought of anyone touching Lettie, hurting her, clogs my throat with emotion. I'm preparing myself for her response, and the fact that I'll be going to jail after I'm finished with said person.

"N-no." She breathes in shakily between sobs. "It's n-nothing like that."

My body sags with relief.

"I—I can't—" She tries to get the words out but a fresh sob wracks her body.

I don't know what happened, but as long as she's not physically hurt, I'll hold her until she's able to talk.

"Shh, it's okay. I've got you."

We stay like that for a long time. It's nearly an hour until Lettie's sobs subside and her breathing evens out. With her still clinging to me, I stand up and carry her into her bedroom. Carefully I help her into her pajamas, an oversized shirt and cotton sleep shorts, doing my best to ignore the glorious sight of her half naked, then carry her into the bathroom.

I set her on the closed toilet lid, then prepare her toothbrush. Water, then toothpaste. Just how she likes it.

"You remembered." She hiccups before taking the toothbrush from me.

"You were very passionate about it, so yeah, it's locked in my brain forever now."

As she brushes, she motions toward the cabinet. "There's an extra toothbrush under the sink if you want to use it."

I hesitate. I want to be here for Lettie, but I don't know if spending the night is a good idea. My eyes drift back to her.

She's got her knees pulled into her chest; one arm wrapped around her legs while the other hand holds her toothbrush. Her toes, those beautifully bent and battered toes of hers, are curled over the side of the toilet seat. She's staring at a spot on the floor, her eyes completely glazed over.

She catches me staring. Her eyes drop to the packaged toothbrush that's still in my hands.

"Please," she says, her mouthful of toothpaste spraying when she talks.

I nod, knowing there's no way I can say no to her right now. Even if I wait for her to fall asleep, then move to the couch, I'll hold her as long as she needs me to.

She rinses her mouth, then goes to lie down in her bed. I

brush my teeth and take off my dress shirt, then hang it on the back of the bathroom door. My hands reach for the button on my pants, but decide that sleeping in my pants is the better option. The safer option. Not that Lettie is in any condition for something physical to happen between us tonight, but we've never slept in a bed together and I'm trying to determine what's the best protocol.

I climb into bed and Lettie immediately scoots closer. Her hands find my bare chest, and my arms wrap around her back, cradling her to me.

"Can you tell me what happened? My mind is going crazy right now."

Her fingers tickle my collarbone. "My parents are getting a divorce."

It's sad news, but part of me is relieved that it's not something worse.

Illness. Injury. *Death*. My mind had been going wild trying to think of what could have put Lettie in such a broken state.

But while the news of Lettie's parents' divorce may come as a relief to me, compared to all the terrible things that could have happened, I know it's breaking her heart. She's always been close with her parents. The end of her parents' relationship and a change in their family dynamic is devastating. And that, in turn, is crushing mine.

"I'm so sorry." I press a gentle kiss to her forehead.

"It's always been the three of us. I can't imagine my life without them together. Without us as a family. What will holidays be like now?" she whispers. "Will we still celebrate together or separate? What happens when either of them meets someone new?

"And they're selling the lake house. I thought we'd have it forever. I thought I'd spend summers there with my kids, creating memories in the house I loved so much as a child. It's strange. I hadn't even known that dream was in my head until I realized it wouldn't be happening."

I cup her cheek, my thumb brushing away a freshly fallen tear. Imagining Lettie visiting Lake George with her kids, a family of her own, does something to me. Now, the idea that she won't have that, I hate it.

"I don't have the answers right now but your parents love you, and we'll figure it out."

In the dark, she blinks up at me. Looking into her crest-fallen face, seeing those blue eyes filled with such hurt, I wish I could make everything better.

She swallows.

"I should be grateful they're still—"

"Don't." I brush my thumb against her lips. "My parents not being here doesn't minimize the pain you're experiencing with your family."

She sighs. "You're right. I just feel—"

"Lost," I finish for her.

"Yeah." She nuzzles closer.

"That's okay." I stroke her hair, letting my fingers glide over the smooth strands.

After a while, Lettie's breathing slowly evens out and finally, she's asleep.

I lie awake, loving the feeling of her in my arms, and the unexpected contentment that being needed like this brings me. And soon, I drift off, too, the sound of Lettie's soft snore against my chest lulling me to sleep.

CHAPTER 43

Colette

I'm drooling on my pillow.

I'm in that state of consciousness where I'm aware something is happening but my sleep-soaked brain can't do anything about it. Signal to close my mouth? Nope. Hand to wipe the excess saliva away? Absolutely not.

That's fine. I'll just focus on how good it feels to lie here on my pillow.

My warm, muscly, skin-like pillow.

At that description, my brain becomes fully alert.

Pillows aren't skin-like. Or muscly.

I blink, then my eyes fly open to find the man-chest my head is resting on.

Rhys.

That's right. I'm not drooling on my pillow. I'm drooling on Rhys's chest.

Careful not to wake him, I slowly lift my head, then with the precision of a neurosurgeon, I peel back the covers and slink out of bed. I tiptoe to the bathroom to grab a washcloth —something to remove the evidence from his chest.

Being held by Rhys was exactly what I needed last night.

He didn't press me for what was wrong, he only held me, rocking me gently, until I was calm enough to talk.

The way Rhys comforted me, held me while I cried, even the fact that he remembered how I like to put my toothpaste on my toothbrush, was everything to me. It's the reason I called him.

I needed him. And he showed up.

There wasn't a trace of the flaky playboy with the bad reputation. Last night Rhys was the sweet, soothing man I've come to rely on. He's the one I wanted to be comforted by.

And I paid him back for his kindness by drooling all over his chest. There's nothing I can do to change it, but what I can do right now is wipe it off before he finds out I slobbered all over him.

I grab a washcloth but, on my way back to my bedroom, a glance in the full-length mirror on the back of the door tells me that drool is not the only off-putting problem I have this morning. I've got red, puffy eyes, dry patches on my cheeks, likely from the skin there being soaked in salty tears, and a mass of wild, unruly hair.

Last night, the hurt and heartache from my parents' announcement made me a sobbing mess, but I hadn't cared what I looked like. Now, in the light of day, with Rhys lying in my bed, I'm more concerned.

Damn. I look rough.

I splash water on my face and attempt to finger-comb my hair before making my way back to my bedroom.

On my way back to my bed, my eyes are drawn to the sight of Rhys lying there. His head is turned to one side with a few strands of his dark hair falling over his forehead. There's a bit of scruff on his square jaw and his left arm is bent and tucked under his head, making the bulge of his bicep bring my attention to the dark ink covering it. There's something about seeing him there, the contrast of his golden skin covered in black ink against my dainty pink and white floral bedding that's so alluring.

He's sexy and hot and all the other adjectives that come to mind to describe a sinfully attractive man, but as much as I'm attracted to Rhys physically, I also know his heart.

Under my heavy gaze, he stirs. Crap, I need to clean him up before he wakes.

I start with a gentle swipe but immediately his eyes open to find me hovering above him.

"Hey, good morning." His eyes drop to where I'm wiping. "Whatcha doin'?"

"I drooled on your chest," I announce, hoping that acting like it's no big deal will relieve the anxiety building in my chest.

His lips curve up into a gorgeous smile.

"It was kind of hot."

"What?" I shake my head, confused. "Drool is not hot."

"No, I mean temperature-wise, it was warm on my chest." He motions to the spot where I'm still wiping.

"Oh, sorry." I finish cleaning him up.

"I didn't mind. You can drool on me anytime you want."

My chin wobbles at his sincerity.

"Hey. Come here."

He wraps me in his arms again and I love the feeling of him holding me. It's the only thing that made last night bearable. Fresh tears sting my eyes at the tenderness with which he rubs my back.

Find yourself a man that holds you when you cry and doesn't think you drooling on his chest is gross. I'm not sure what category this type of caretaking falls under. We're not in public so he doesn't have to be my fake fiancé right now, but he's going way above and beyond as a friend. It's exactly what I need, even if it only adds to what is becoming a very complicated fake relationship.

I sniff, pulling back to finally take in his pant-clad legs. "You slept in your pants?"

He shrugs. "Yeah."

They're expensive and designer, I'm sure, and right now they're a wrinkled mess, but he doesn't seem to care. Maxine jumps up on the bed, pushing herself between the two of us, with the hopes of getting double the pets. Now his pants will be covered in cat hair, too.

Rhys strokes a hand down her back, but keeps his attention on me.

"What do you want to do today?" he asks.

It's Monday. For the first time ever, my calendar hanging in the kitchen feels overbearing.

I can't recall a day where I've woken up and not gone through my planned schedule in its entirety. I've also never felt like this. So raw and frayed at the edges. Like I'm barely being held together.

And right now, a workout and studio time feels foreign to me. I want to yank the calendar off the wall and throw it out the window.

An unfamiliar idea forms in my head.

I need a day off.

"Absolutely nothing," is my response.

Rhys smiles and it eases everything inside me. "You're in luck. I'm the master of doing absolutely nothing."

But we don't do absolutely nothing. We do something *different.*

I shower and get dressed, then we head over to Rhys's boat, picking up breakfast sandwiches from one of my favorite local delis which I never go to because it's not typically on the schedule.

We bring Maxine because according to Rhys, Mo has been

desperate to see her, which he demonstrates when they're reunited by spooning her and sweetly licking her head. With another stroke of Mo's rough tongue, Maxine's eyes close, and I swear her cat mouth is stretched into a relaxed smile.

"Until this moment, I hadn't thought about it, but a cat's head is one of the places they can't reach when they give themselves a bath. Maxine always licks her paw then rubs it around her ear." I demonstrate by waving my hand over my head in the motion I've seen her make. "I guess it's handy to have a friend who can lick you in places you can't reach."

Rhys bursts out in a laugh, and I realize how that sounded.

"A cat friend, that is."

When my eyes finally meet his, Rhys's gaze is full of heat.

"Mmhmm. Sure," he teases. "I guess Maxine is lucky to have a good friend like Mo to take care of her like that."

"Yeah. He's a good friend," I say, easing past Rhys and the electric charge that just ignited between us, before walking out onto the deck to get away from the tension I just created inside.

Rhys had Ramsey call an engineer, the person legally required to drive the boat, since Rhys isn't licensed. And the three of us, plus the cats who don't bother leaving the couch, spend the day out on the water.

It's exactly what I need. Sunshine. The breeze in my hair. And stillness.

"This is nice." I sigh from where I'm lying on the lounger, soaking up the sun.

"Being out on the water is my favorite thing. It's calming."

I turn to look at him. He's heartachingly handsome in navy blue swim trunks with brightly colored roosters all over them, which upon donning them, he asked me and Ramsey if we liked his cocks.

"Doesn't being on the water, on a boat, remind you of your parents?" I ask.

"Yeah, it does." His sunglass-covered eyes glance out to the ocean. "But it's comforting. It's the place I feel closest to them because I remember how much they loved it, too."

"I've got drinks." Ramsey appears carrying a tray with glasses.

"Thank you, Ramsey," I say, selecting a fresh mojito from his tray.

"You're welcome, sweetie." He gives me a conspiratorial wink.

I take a sip and close my eyes. It may not be a beach vacation, but this is what I needed today.

While the sun's warmth feels good, I'm aware my skin hasn't seen much of it lately and I need to be careful or I'll burn. "I think I need to put more sunscreen on," I say, glancing at my shoulders.

"I can help you with that."

I grab my sunscreen and move to sit between Rhys's open legs.

With each stroke of his hands, I melt. And the way he inches his fingers underneath the straps of my top and the waistband of my bottoms to be thorough is everything.

"I like this suit." He lifts the thin strap of my top. "You look amazing in it," he announces before placing a kiss on my bare shoulder. I feel that kiss in every cell of my body.

I'd dug out this old black bikini which nearly had cobwebs on it from lack of use. It had reminded me that I haven't been to Lake George yet this summer and that once my parents sell our house there, we won't be going there as a family anymore.

My mom had texted earlier, to check in on me, but also to mention that it would be good for us to go to Lake George this weekend to pack up our personal belongings so that they could get the house staged and listed to sell.

"My parents and I are going to Lake George this weekend to pack up the house. Do you want to come?"

Behind me, I can feel him tense. Other than once to help his grandfather clean out their house, I don't think he's been back to Lake George since his parents died. But if he doesn't mind being on the water, then maybe he would want to come. I know I could use another person to help deflect the awkwardness I'm feeling with my parents right now.

And if I admit it to myself, not just any person. *Him.*

"I can't."

It's a simple answer with a far more complicated reason behind it.

I nod in understanding.

"Do you need a ride? I can have Wanda drive you," he offers.

"Actually, that would be great. My mom wanted to leave on Thursday, but I have a class at Leg-Up on Friday morning that I don't want to miss."

He smiles. "I'll have Ramsey set it up."

"Thank you."

I'd rather have Rhys there, but I understand why he doesn't want to go. That while being on the water makes him feel close to his parents, being at Lake George where they died is still too hard.

We enjoy the rest of the day on the water before Lucas, the boat's engineer, sails us back to the slip.

"Do you want me to stay with you tonight?" Rhys asks.

My brain is offline, but my heart, which is still in tethered ruins from the last twenty-four hours, instructs my head to give a confirming nod. *We need this. We need him. Don't argue with us. Let it happen.*

Rhys gathers some clothes, and Mo, then Wanda drives us back to my apartment.

We watch mindless television, order in tacos, then Rhys gives me a foot massage until I fall asleep. It's exactly what I needed today.

CHAPTER 44

Rhys

Princess: *Thank you for having Wanda drive me.*

Rhys: *I'm confident you're in good hands with her. Have a good weekend.*

Princess: *You, too.*

I miss her already. We've spent every day together this week.

After Lettie's day off on Monday, she adjusted her training schedule, scaling back on her workouts and studio training for the next few weeks until she needs to start focusing intently on preparing for evaluations.

We've spent afternoons walking in Central Park or shopping on Fifth Avenue—mostly for me—and evenings curled up on the couch with the cats, watching television. And every night in her bed, cuddling. I'm in a permanent state of blue balls that even stroking myself to the thought of Lettie every morning in the shower can't cure, but all I want to do is be there for her, even if it requires nearly rubbing myself raw from all the self-love.

We never discussed our make-out session at Hunter and Sophie's or what happened on the phone that night. I want to kiss her, touch her again, but maybe it's safer that I don't. I've worked my way back to a solid friendship with Lettie, fuck, if I'm being honest, she's my best friend, and I don't want to ruin it.

Now she's gone for the weekend and I don't know what I'm going to do with myself. She wanted me to come with her to Lake George, but I couldn't.

Lake George is the last place I remember being truly happy. I had my parents and my friends. Lettie was there. My life was perfectly content.

And while it holds that place in my heart, I don't know that I can go back. I only want to remember it how it was. A place and time where I felt understood and loved. But I know Lettie is struggling right now. She's facing a huge change in her life with her parents' impending divorce, and their plan to sell their lake house is crushing her.

Still, I told her no.

Then, after she taught her class at Leg-Up this morning, I helped her load her suitcase in the SUV and watched her and Wanda drive off. It's been an hour since she left and I'm already bored.

Maxine is staying with me on the boat while Lettie's gone, which I love for Mo, but watching the two of them playfully bat at each other, then curl up and nap together only makes missing my girl worse.

My girl.

Lettie's always been someone special to me, but I've never thought of her as mine before. Even when I placed that giant rock on her finger, I never allowed myself to contemplate what it would be like to claim her. Now, I can't get the thought out of my head.

The way she'd told me what she was doing to herself. Her strained voice and soft panting. How those full pink lips must have parted when she came. I know, because I've seen it, and it's so fucking beautiful. But, more than all of that, I love that she was comfortable enough with me to let herself go. She trusted me to do that with her, and that's the most important thing.

I'm recalling that night with Lettie when Ramsey finds me moping out on the sun deck.

He drops into the chair beside me. "You want to take the boat out?" he asks.

"Nah."

"Play ping pong?" he suggests.

I shrug, not even bothering to answer that one.

"Well, you're a ray of sunshine today."

"I know. I'm in a crappy mood."

Ramsey sticks out his bottom lip in a teasing pout, then picks up one of the friendship bracelets I made earlier.

I motion to the box filled with bracelets. "I started making them one night and couldn't stop. It was fun."

"This only confirms my suspicions that inside you truly are an eight-year-old girl."

"Fuck off, you know you love this shit, too."

He grins. "You're right, but is there a reason you made this many?"

I shrug. "I told a few of the kids at the children's hospital that I'd bring them sometime. They make them, too. I said we could exchange them."

"All right. Let's go." Ramsey starts to gather up my collection of bracelets.

"Where?"

"You need to clear this funky energy." He waves a hand around me as if there is an actual substance clogging up the air.

I want to argue with him, but he's right. I need something to take my mind off Lettie and my inability to be there for her.

Taking the bracelets to the children's hospital immediately lifts my spirits. Seeing the smiles on the children's faces when I stop by their rooms is priceless.

"Thank you for coming back," Brittney says.

I'm lucky she was on her lunch break in the lobby and recognized me.

"Thanks for letting me back in the building. I was nervous the security guard was going to throw me out."

After I make the rounds, I realize there's one last room I want to stop by.

Brittney smiles, but then it drops. "Madelyn's having a rough day. Do you want to leave a few bracelets with me and I'll give them to her later?"

"Sure." I nod, even though disappointment hits me that I won't get to see the little girl who inspired me to make them.

I pick out a few that I had made for her based off her favorite albums and songs, then hand them to Brittney.

I'm on my way toward the elevator when movement catches my eye. Standing in the doorway to her room is Madelyn.

"Hey." Not certain that she wanted to see me, I give her a small wave.

"You came back."

"Yeah, I said I would."

"Sometimes adults break their promises."

There's no point in arguing with her. "Yeah, they do."

"My mom promised me I was going to get better soon, but now I have to do another round of chemo."

At Madelyn's news, my stomach plummets. What I want to say has a few expletives but I can't swear in front of her.

"Damn. That sucks. I'm sorry." I can't even wrap my head around what Madelyn and the other children have to go through with their illnesses. And at eight years old? "You're incredibly brave. I wish I could be like that."

"I thought adults were brave."

"No, you can be an adult and still be scared to do things. Trust me. I would know."

"Yeah? What are you scared of?" she asks.

I consider her question. *What am I scared of?*

So many things.

Snakes. Using too much wasabi and getting that nose burning sensation. Accidentally walking in on Ramsey shaving his balls. It happened once and I was traumatized.

But that's not what Madelyn means.

The reason I didn't go to Lake George with Lettie is because I'm scared of what I might feel when I'm there. The memories that will likely surface by being in that magical, yet heartbreaking place.

And the fact that I'm starting to have real feelings for Lettie, and I have no idea what I'm going to do when our fake engagement has run its course, only made the idea of going to Lake George with her more worrying.

"It's okay if you're not ready to share."

I give her a small smile. "Thanks for understanding."

We exchange bracelets. Madelyn instructs me not to look at mine until after I leave.

Before I go, we talk about Taylor's upcoming album and all our hopes and dreams for it. Ramsey is going to be so mad he missed this conversation. Then, I check out with Brittney at the nurses' station.

Leaving the children's hospital, a few photographers swarm toward me as Ramsey meets me at the entrance.

"Where's Colette?" one photographer asks. "Have you set a wedding date yet?"

"Rhys, why are you here?" another one asks. "Do you have a secret love child?"

What the actual fuck? I'm angry at their prying questions and even more at their audacity to show up here.

Since news of me and Lettie's engagement, I've noticed an increase in media coverage. I've tried to embrace it, because it's good press, but just like the increasing posts about Lettie, it's starting to make me uncomfortable.

Even with the annoying photographers, I'm in a far better mood than I was earlier.

Ramsey greets me in the car with a huge grin. "I guess the hospital was the best place to get that stick up your ass removed."

"Funny." I smirk, but he's right.

When I pull back the sleeve of my shirt, I find the bracelet that Madelyn gave me.

There, between purple and white beads is a single word: Fearless.

I know what I need to do.

CHAPTER 45

Colette

Our lake house is far smaller than the Cartwrights' and Spencers'. Nestled along the western side of Lake George, it's a charming white house with navy blue shutters. Or at least, it was. I mean it still is, but as I stand out in front of it, I'm wondering if the new owners will paint the shutters or if they'll have young kids that will use the tire swing still hanging from the large maple tree on the side of the house.

Finally, I give up and let myself into the house.

My mom, being an interior designer, has impeccable taste. The décor is rustic, yet modern, white shiplap walls and ceilings, with a large wooden beam separating the sitting room and kitchen. Cream-colored couch with navy blue anchor pillows. Even the throw I love to wrap up in and sit on the porch when the night turns cool is draped over the back of the couch. Everything inside looks the same, yet the feeling I have walking into the house is completely different. I can't get the magic back. The happy memories made here are just that. Memories.

A moment later I hear footfalls on the stairs. I turn to find my mom dressed in navy chinos and a white short-sleeved blouse.

"Oh, there's my girl." My mom wraps her arms around me and kisses my temple.

"Hi, Mom." I return her embrace, forcing myself to swallow past the lump in my throat.

"I didn't realize you'd arrived. I was upstairs packing."

"I just walked in."

She pulls back to study me, a soft smile on her face.

"I'm so glad you came."

"Me, too." I'd thought about not coming, letting my parents pack everything up and pretend the loss of this place didn't matter, but the idea of never setting foot in this house again only made me feel worse.

She takes in my leather weekend bag by the door. "Is it just you?"

"Yeah." I understood why Rhys said no. Coming here would be hard for him. And with the added stress of my parents' situation, it's not exactly a fun weekend getaway.

"Your father will be here tomorrow. I thought we could do a little packing, then relax on the porch and watch the sunset with a glass of wine."

"Sure." I walk toward the large living room windows overlooking the lake, and she follows.

"Hey," she squeezes my hand, "I know change is hard. You've never been a fan. But it's progress toward something amazing."

Deep down, I know she's right. And I do want my parents to be happy, but I also want them together. I wish those two things weren't mutually exclusive.

I give her a tight smile, it's the only one I can muster, then follow her upstairs.

In my room, I take in the comfort of the wallpaper with light blue grass design, and the white curtains with blue dots. The heart and unicorn stickers my mom was upset I stuck onto my gold-trimmed vanity's mirror, but my dad insisted gave it character. On a hanging shelf are framed photos from dance academy over the years, as well as one of me, Hannah, Hunter, and Rhys together on the Spencers' boat.

Sitting on top of the blue and white comforter is Whiskers, the stuffed cat Rhys gave me after his failed attempt at rehoming the Jenkins' cat. I pick up the fuzzy gray cat and hug it to my chest.

My room looks exactly how it always has, with the addition of a pile of deconstructed moving boxes leaning against the wall.

I'm not ready for any of this. I don't even know where to start, but it's not in this room, so I set Whiskers back into place, then leave my room, shutting the door behind me, so I can keep everything how it is for a little bit longer.

After a few hours of packing up the kitchen, my mom and I enjoy a quiet dinner on the small screened-in porch, then go down to the dock with our glasses of wine to soak our feet in the lake while we watch the sunset.

"I'm sorry I haven't been there for you like I should."

"What do you mean?" I ask.

"I've been so caught up with everything happening between me and your father, that I haven't been very involved with what is going on in your life. You and Rhys are engaged, yet we haven't talked much about your relationship."

When I meet her eyes, I see the guilt there. She takes a sip of her wine and I clear my throat.

"Don't feel bad, everything between us has happened pretty fast."

Suddenly, I want to tell her everything about me and Rhys. I want her guidance and advice.

"Mom—" I start but she interjects.

"As your mom, I wondered if I should be concerned about his past relationships, or lack thereof, and how quickly you're moving, but then I saw a photo of you two from the Leg-Up community day and it all made sense."

My eyes snap to her face. "What made sense?"

"How much Rhys adores you. He looks at you like you're his whole world, and you appear to be as in love with him as he is with you."

Her words stun me into silence.

"Seeing you with Rhys, knowing you're in love and happy, made telling you about the divorce both harder and easier. I didn't want you to second-guess your relationship because mine and your father's is over, but also knowing you have a partner you can lean on during this difficult time has been reassuring."

Me and Rhys *in love*? It's what we've been working to convince everyone of so the foundation board would take him seriously. I should be happy that we've managed to convince my mom as well. With a renewed sense of hope dancing in her eyes, there's no way I can tell her none of it is real now.

We watch the sunset in contented silence, then return to the house with our empty wine glasses.

Later, while I'm lying in bed, Hannah texts me.

Hannah: *I've been thinking about you today. If you need me there, just say the word.*

She'd offered to come when I told her about this weekend, but I know she and James have a wedding to attend tomorrow, so I insisted she not.

Hannah: *I barely even know the couple. It's James's boss's daughter. I'm there if you need me. Just say the word!*

I laugh out loud at her insistence.

Colette: *It sounds like you're trying really hard to get out of this wedding.*

Hannah: *Just want to be there for my bestie.*

Colette: *I appreciate you. Have fun tomorrow and I'll call you when I get back.*

Hannah: *I love you!*

Colette: *Love you too*

I'm about to plug my phone in when it buzzes again. It's a text from Rhys.

I turn out the lamp but settle back into my bed.

Rhys: *How was today?*

Before I can respond, he sends another text.

Rhys: *That's a stupid question. I know it must have sucked.*

Lettie: *It was hard. My dad's coming tomorrow. It's going to be weird.*

Rhys: *I'm sorry. I don't know what to say. Maybe this will make you smile?*

An image comes through. It's a picture of Maxine and Mo both fighting for space on Rhys's lap. Maxine, the clear winner, is curled up squarely on his lap, while Mo is hanging halfway off, but still happy to be near them both.

I smile at the photo, then type out a response.

Colette: *You made your own cat meme. And it did make me smile, so mission complete.*

Rhys: *I love your smile. Send me a pic.*

I snap a selfie with me smiling, then send it to him.

Rhys: *I almost forgot how beautiful my fiancée is*

Colette: *I've been gone for nine hours*

Rhys: *I miss you when you're gone for nine minutes*

I suck in a deep breath, trying to control the giddiness I feel reading his text. I'm not sure where we stand anymore. What is real, what is fake. Right now, with everything going on with my parents, I don't have the energy to figure it out. All I know is what is happening between us feels good.

Colette: *I wish you were here, but I understand why you're not.*

The three dots appear, then disappear. Then finally a text comes through.

Rhys: *Goodnight, Princess*

Colette: *Goodnight*

I plug in my phone and roll over onto my side to get comfortable. In such a short amount of time, Rhys has become the person I rely on the most. Maybe it's our arrangement, the fact that we've got a common goal, but it's starting to feel like more than that.

I stare at my phone. It's nine-thirty. The latest I've slept in years.

My dad will be here any minute, but I don't want to get out of bed. I can't seem to face the thought of the three of us saying goodbye to this house. Spending one last night in it before it's listed for sale.

My mom swings open the door, nearly scaring the hell out of me. "Your dad's here."

I pull the pillow over my head and groan.

"Get up, sleepy head," she sing-songs. Man, she's awfully chipper to see her soon-to-be ex-husband.

I hear the door click shut and I'm thankful she's leaving me to wallow in peace.

But then the edge of the bed sinks and I realize she didn't give up that easily.

"I'm getting up. I just need—"

A warm hand settles on my back.

A large, firm hand.

Why, Mother, what large hands you have.

I'm about to tease her with the line from one of my favorite books as a child when I peek out from under my pillow and realize it's not my mom sitting there.

It's Rhys.

CHAPTER 46

Rhys

Lettie leaps into my arms, knocking me off the bed and onto the floor. Unfortunately, my arms were already reaching for her, so I end up taking her with me. With a loud thump, I land on my ass, with her straddling my lap.

"You came." She wraps her arms around my neck and fuck if this isn't the exact welcome I was hoping for.

"I rode up with your dad."

A huge grin spreads across her face. "Wow. You must really like me. Four hours in a vehicle with an economics professor with marital problems couldn't have been easy."

"No, it wasn't, but after listening to *The Economist* podcast for hours, I'm caught up on my world politics and business news."

She laughs and the sound is all the reward I need for waking up at the crack of dawn this morning.

A moment later, the door swings open. "Everything okay, I heard—" Lettie's mom starts but her eyes widen when she finds us tangled up on the floor and she shuts the door as quickly as she opened it.

I groan. "Your mom thinks we're going at it on the floor right now."

"Who cares? As far as she knows, we're engaged. At least somebody's going at it in this house."

It's meant to be a joke, but I can tell it reminds her of why we're here.

"Hey. We'll do this together, okay?"

She nuzzles into my neck. Even though I hate the thought of her being sad, I love that she looks to me for comfort.

"How can I help?" I ask.

She pulls back to look around the room. "I'm supposed to pack up my room. They want all personal items out so they can stage it for the listing photos."

With Lettie's help, I lift her up so we're both standing.

She picks up a flattened moving box from the stack leaning against the wall, then walks over to her closet. In less than two minutes she's filled the box with the contents of her closet.

"That's it? That's all you had to do? I'm certain my help wasn't needed." I shove my hands into my pockets and grin.

"My parents are downstairs likely sorting out who gets what. Dividing up our memories." She sighs. "I want to soak up every last moment we have here today. Can we do that?"

I hesitate answering because now that I'm here, and the excitement of surprising Lettie is wearing off, I'm not sure what I'll be able to do.

She notices my hesitation.

Wrapping her arms around my waist, she presses her ear to my chest. "Thank you for coming. It means the world to me. And I know it's not easy for you."

I wrap my arms around her back, holding her to me. "You make it easier."

It's the truth. While my visit to the children's hospital yesterday and hearing Madelyn talk about facing her fears had pushed me to consider coming to Lake George, I knew once I got here, seeing Lettie, being near her would give me the confidence to stay.

When she pulls back, her gaze falls to the opening of my polo shirt.

She smiles up at me. "I like your necklace."

I release her so she can take a better look. "I went back to that boutique on Fifth Avenue we visited last week."

Lettie's finger traces the C on the chain around my neck. "Why'd you pick a C and not an L?"

"I debated, but ultimately I went with C. Lettie is the girl I grew up with, but Colette is the woman you are to me now."

"It's a nice touch. Really committing to the role of doting fiancé by putting my initial around your neck." She smiles and it's so fucking bright, I know I'll be able to face anything as long as she keeps looking at me like that. "It's very Taylor Swift of you."

Should I tell her that I'll wear it even when we're done pretending because she owns me now? And that I'm hers, even if I don't deserve for her to be mine.

"Did you bring trunks?" she asks.

"Yeah."

"Then you should get changed."

"It's not even ten o'clock."

Lettie laughs, pulling away so she can grab her swimsuit out of her luggage.

"You know the rope swing will be packed in less than an hour."

After spending the better half of the morning in the water, we grab lunch at the yacht club where we sit out on the dock just like when we were kids. Except we're adults now, so we find two Adirondack chairs facing the water. Lettie ordered a Mediterranean bowl with grilled chicken, while I opted for the classic New England lobster roll.

"I remember the first time I ordered one of these. I think I was seven, and my dad was certain it was going to be too much food for me, but I thought lobster was fancy and cool, so I wanted to try it. He told me I could order it, but that I would be eating the leftovers at every meal until I finished it. He knew I couldn't eat it all and wanted to instill the idea that although we had money, it's not appropriate to be wasteful."

"Did you eat it all?" she asks, before loading her fork with a bite of quinoa, chicken, cumber, and chickpea.

I laugh. "Eventually. I think I finished it at breakfast the next day. I remember the bun was soggy, but the buttery lobster was so good, even cold." I take a bite before offering my sandwich to her. Wrapping her hands around mine to hold the sandwich steady, she takes a big bite.

"So good. Want to try mine?" She offers me her fork with a pre-loaded bite of food and I take it.

She looks at me expectantly, and as I chew, I twist my hand back and forth in a so-so gesture.

"It's okay." That lands me a playful swat on the arm. "Hey, it's hard to compete with lobster."

"You're right. Give me another bite." She motions for me to hand over my sandwich but I hold it away from her. She takes the bait, setting down her bowl so she can climb over my lap and gain access to the sandwich.

"You want my delicious lobster roll so bad, don't you, Princess?" I wiggle my brows and give her the cheesiest grin.

At my words she burst into a fit of laughter.

"Your *lobster roll*? Is that a euphemism for your dick?" She shakes her head, still laughing.

When she reaches out to push my shoulder, I catch her wrist and pull her down into my lap. We're so close now, we're breathing the same air. My hand drops to her jaw, and I let my thumb sweep over her cheek.

Lettie's eyes close. I know she's expecting me to kiss her. We're even in public right now so technically it would be okay, but with everything going on with her parents, I don't want to put any added pressure on her right now. So my lips drop to her forehead instead.

"Should we head back?" I ask.

Her eyes flutter open, like she's coming to after being in a daze.

"Oh, yeah. Sure." She nods, then disentangles herself from me. When I stand up from the chair, I have to use what's left of my lobster roll to momentarily hide my erection. Then, I offer the rest of my sandwich to Lettie and she happily eats it.

Later, on the way back to her house, we find ourselves walking the worn path which passes by the dock below my old house. The house is still technically mine, passed down to me by my parents' estate, but the condition it's in makes the 'old' part true.

"We don't have to go in." I feel Lettie next to me. Her fingers thread through mine. I turn to look down at our hands, then back up at her. I'm so fucking grateful for her.

She's right. And maybe someday I'll go inside, but today, standing here is enough.

"I miss them, too. I think about how your mom was so different than my own. It's like I had the best of both worlds. Hannah's mom, too, but Abigail's love of dance always connected us. And with my mom working a lot, it was nice your mom was always around."

"It's been fifteen years. They've been gone for as much time as I had with them. Isn't that wild?"

"Yeah, it is when you think about it like that. They'd be proud of you, Rhys."

Her words are sincere, but I have a hard time accepting them.

"For what? Fake-dating you so I can regain my rightful place as foundation board president? Something I should have been appreciating this entire time?"

"I think they would have wanted you to experience all the twists and turns of life so that you could have perspective when you found your place. Look at me. I've been doing what I thought I was supposed to do. Staying focused. Working hard every day. But it hasn't been enough. I was missing out on everything else around me."

I nod considering her words.

"I tried to do what I thought was right. To be the man they wanted me to be, but the pressure got to be too much. It felt like Jerrod was always breathing down my neck."

"I never knew why you left New York. Was it because of Jerrod?" she asks.

I nod. "After graduation, I got a business analyst position with Harper & Benson. Jerrod announced his job at Martin, Breaker, Short the same day and I knew everything would continue as it was. Our competing wouldn't end with our academic career, it would transcend it, spilling over into our professional lives. The comparison would always be there. When I got my first trust fund installment at twenty-five, I quit. Not because I didn't want to work but because the joy was sucked out of everything in my life. Nothing was my own. And I had no one telling me I was doing okay. It was always *'how does it compare to Jerrod'* and I hated it. I still do. I did my best to be opposite of him in every way. I'm not proud of all the partying and the women, the reputation I built, but it was mine. Does that sound crazy?"

Her comforting smile is all I need.

"No. Not at all. In fact, it makes a lot of sense now that you've explained it."

"But I don't want to live that life anymore. And I'm worried that it's too late. That I've fucked everything up."

"Do you want to be president to beat Jerrod or because you want the position?"

"It started out as wanting to beat Jerrod. Our old rivalry got to me. But it's more than that now. I like connecting with people and their nonprofits, learning about their missions and what motivates them. I didn't realize I'd enjoy it so much."

"That's great, Rhys."

"It's because of you." I tell her.

She shakes her head. "What?"

"Seeing your work with Leg-Up and your passion not just for ballet and dance but to help others. And, of course, your visits to the children's hospital. You inspired me."

"So, what happens if you don't get the president position? Can you still sit on the board?"

"Under Jerrod?" My jaw tightens, but Lettie's hand on my arm eases the tension there.

"If that's the only way to be involved?" she asks.

"I don't know."

"I think it's okay to not know."

"Really? You have everything planned out."

She laughs. "If I had everything planned out, I would have been promoted to principal two years ago."

"You're a phenomenal dancer. You'll get there even if the timeline is different."

"Thanks."

She shivers.

"You're freezing." I wrap my arm around her shoulders. "We should go in."

"Yeah."

As we walk past my parents' lake house, I can't help but think that while I'm here for Lettie, today was a good step toward healing my own family wounds.

CHAPTER 47

Colette

Watching my parents awkwardly fumble around each other at dinner was exhausting. It was like watching a first date but in reverse. People who knew each other like they knew themselves turning into strangers that barely talk.

I'm over this day, but also wanting it to linger. When I wake up tomorrow and walk out of this house, I'll never be back here again.

"How's your book?" Rhys asks as he turns the bathroom light off and walks into the bedroom, shirtless, a pair of gray lounge shorts sitting low on his hips. Those deep muscular Vs on either side of his pelvis taunting me from across the room.

"Good." It is a good book. A good distraction from what is going on in my life. This sad weekend saying goodbye to a lake house I love and cherish, trying to navigate the new dynamic with my divorcing parents, and my growing feelings for the man that just climbed into my bed.

That's right. A small detail I didn't consider when Rhys showed up earlier today. With everything going on, it wasn't until my mom retired to her bedroom, and my dad started making up the couch, that I realized the only place for Rhys to sleep would be with me. My parents didn't even flinch. We're engaged after all.

My eyes dart back to the pages where I'm working on my poker face. The goal is to read about the sweet, sunshiny girl getting railed by the tattooed bad boy and not give anyone around me, especially Rhys, a clue as to the contents.

"I saw it on your nightstand the night we were making tutus and you fell asleep."

"Oh, yeah?" I turn the page. Next to me, Rhys slides into the bed and settles against the pillows.

Out of the corner of my eye, I see his tattooed arm reach for an e-reader he put on the nightstand earlier.

"What part are you on?" he asks, tapping the device to wake it up.

"Um," I squeeze my thighs together, trying to ignore the throbbing between my legs, "what do you mean?" I ask, distracted by said throbbing.

I'm spending the last night in my family's lake house before it's sold, and my parents are splitting up, yet I'm lying next to Rhys reading a spicy romance novel and I'm incredibly turned on. What in the world is happening?

He turns his e-reader toward me, and there on the screen is the cover that Chloe had shown us at the restaurant. The tattooed bad boy, devilishly handsome and winking at me.

"Xander just picked Jessa up for the party. She's trying to make her ex jealous."

"What?! Why are you reading this book?!" I practically shout.

He shrugs. "I'm taking an interest in your interests. Isn't that what boyfriends do?"

"Sure, but you're my fake boyfriend—er—fiancé, and you're not in book club."

"Actually, I talked to Chloe and she said anyone could join. That you'd welcome a male perspective."

I'm turned on, and now I must sleep next to Rhys who is

reading the exact same book as me? He knows all the dirty talk and explicit sex that is happening in this book. And that I've read it.

My poker face is slipping.

And with everything else going on, there are too many emotions for me to process. I thought Rhys was on my side. I was overjoyed when he arrived earlier today, but now, it feels like he's poking fun at me, and I don't like it.

I toss the book on the nightstand and turn off my light.

"Do you mind if I keep reading?" he asks.

"Go for it." I roll to my side, putting my back to him.

"Goodnight, Princess." His fingers tease in my hair. It's sweet and comforting, and I'm so turned on that it makes me angry. It's irrational and I know it, but I can't help it.

Today has been overwhelming in both the best and hardest sense.

I want to take it out on someone, and Rhys is the closest in proximity.

My hand grips the throw pillow next to me and a moment later there's a loud thump as it makes contact with Rhys's face.

"Don't call me that," I growl. *Now who's the one growling?* I preferred it when Rhys did because I sound like a maniac.

He laughs. "I thought you liked that nickname."

"No, you like it." I spring to a sitting position, turning to face him, ready to fight. "Why do you call me that? I'm not a princess. Far from it."

Rhy sits up, and the covers fall to his waist. He turns toward me, his muscles contracting with the movement. I swear his abdominals wink at me. Now, I'm even more annoyed that he's sitting there looking like a delicious snack while we're trying to have a serious conversation.

"I'm using it ironically," he says.

"Meaning?" I keep my eyes trained on his face, even

though my body is well aware of his half-naked one within arm's reach.

He looks away for a moment, before turning back to me.

"As a dancer you make it look effortless. Your appearance is graceful and demure, maybe even mild-mannered, but if someone really knew you, the way I know you, they'd see all the hard work and commitment you have signed up for. You're a fucking badass, Lettie. You're dedicated to your sport and your career, putting in an insane number of hours for practice and training. Diet, conditioning, sleep, and recovery in addition to teaching and the philanthropy roles you've taken on. You're the most dedicated person I've ever met, and I want to give you a space to be spoiled and cared for. You're not a princess, Lettie, you're *my* princess. Maybe it was a joke at first, but for me the nickname is my way of telling you that it's okay to relax and let me be there for you." He swallows hard, his eyes searching mine. "It's a way of letting you know I've got you, just like you've got me."

I'm stunned by his response. There are no words.

"I thought you were poking fun at me or teasing me, like I'm soft or super girlie."

He shakes his head. "Quite the opposite."

"Oh." That's all I can manage as I process Rhys's far more eloquent words.

I slink back under the covers, embarrassed at my outburst, while Rhys turns back to reading.

It doesn't feel like that's what should be happening after that passionate speech, but I'm not sure what else I can do but lie here and pretend like I'm not dying for him to touch me.

An eternity later, Rhys turns out the light, but I'm still wide awake. I won't sleep a wink under this kind of duress.

I roll over for the millionth time, putting my back to Rhys again. A second later, his strong forearm wraps around my waist and pulls my back to his front.

"You're more keyed up than Mo when I get the laser pointer out."

"Maybe that's what I need. To chase a red dot around the room."

"Why can't you sleep?" he asks. His words are warm against my ear as his palm splays out against my belly.

"I'm not tired. I thought I would be after the emotional day we've had, but I—I can't fall asleep."

He presses his nose into my hair. "Is there anything I can do to help?"

I press back into him, closing the millimeter of space that was between us. I feel it there now. Rhys's erection pressing against my cheeks. The fresh wave of lust pooling between my thighs makes me dizzy. I squeeze my eyes shut, hoping it will stop the head rush.

"Touch me." My words are spoken so softly, I'm second-guessing if I said them aloud. I'm also wondering if he heard me.

A moment later, his fingers dip under my shirt, those warm finger pads grazing under the swell of my breast. "I am touching you."

I bite my lip in frustration, fighting a low moan that's being slowly drawn out of my throat by the way Rhys's thumb is tracing circles around my belly button.

Is he really going to make me say it?

He confirms as much when he whispers against my ear. "How should I touch you?"

I'm an anxious ball of need, so I skip all pretense when I tell him, "I want your mouth on my clit and your fingers inside me."

He smiles against the back of my neck before placing a kiss there. Then his hand moves lower until it's cupping me over my sleep shorts.

"Is this what you want, Princess? You want me to take care of you tonight?"

I arch into his touch, my ass pressing farther back into his erection before I simply answer, "Yes."

As quick as a shot of lightning, Rhys flips me onto my back.

"Lettie—" he starts, but I cut him off with a kiss. I don't know what Rhys was going to say, and right now, I don't care. All I want is to feel. His tongue on mine, his hands all over me. I want to forget what is happening with my parents and the fact that tomorrow when we walk out the front door, my memories at Lake George, in this house with my family, will be just that.

Above me, Rhys's hard body presses me into the mattress. My frantic hands reach for his waistband, but he pins them over my head.

"This is about you, Princess." He yanks my shirt up, then kisses down my stomach. With his free hand, he works my sleep shorts and underwear down my legs.

Once they're free, I bend my knees and spread my legs for him.

"Fuck," he groans, pressing his thumb against my already swollen clit, before dragging it through my center.

"I need more," I tell him.

Lifting my legs over his shoulders, Rhys settles between them.

He swipes a single finger down my center, but it's gone too quickly.

"You're dripping, Princess. Was it the book? Did it make you wet to read about Xander fucking Jessa with his tongue?"

The book, yes, it turned me on, but only because I was imagining Rhys doing those things to me. Remembering how good it had felt to have his tongue on me, his fingers stretching me.

His tongue licks up my seam. "God damn, you're sweet."

"Rhys, *please*."

"You know I'm going to take care of you, Princess." He

places a gentle kiss against my clit before swirling it playfully with his tongue. "This sweet pussy belongs to me, and I take care of what is mine."

With that, he presses his finger inside me and goes wild.

His skilled tongue devours me.

Licking.

Sucking.

Swirling.

Thick fingers thrusting inside me, filling me up so full and tight. The perfect combination that has me spiraling out in a matter of minutes.

By the time the rush of my orgasm subsides, he's already cleaned me up and pulled my underwear and sleep shorts back into place.

He doesn't say another word, but simply turns out the light again before pulling my back to his front and wrapping his arm around me.

As I settle back against him, he presses a kiss to my hair.

I close my eyes and let my breathing even out.

The orgasm let my body relax, but if I don't watch out, all the possessive things Rhys just said could have me overthinking what is happening between us. I think about what my mom said. That we appeared to be in love.

Could the bad boy really fall for the good girl? Or does that only happen in romance novels?

Eventually, my heartbeat falls into a rhythm with Rhys's and we both fall asleep.

CHAPTER 48

Colette

Hannah's picking me up for Chloe's book club tonight. I got home from the practice studio late, so I'm scrambling to get ready. I toss the book and my phone into my bag when I see a missed text from Rhys.

Rhys: *Have fun tonight, Princess.*

On my way downstairs, I type out a reply.

Colette: *You too!*

Before I can change my mind, I add a kiss emoji to my text.

Rhys: *I'm still going to finish the book*

Colette: *You should. It had a happy ending.*

Rhys: *I'll come over later and give you a happy ending <wink emoji>*

That's me, just a regular girl flirt texting with her fake fiancé.

Rhys is going out with the guys tonight. Even though he'd teased me about Chloe inviting him to book club, when it came down to it, he decided to hang out with the guys at a bar to play pool instead.

When I step out onto the sidewalk, Hannah's already there in a black SUV.

"Hey, thanks for picking me up," I say, climbing in.

"Of course. It's good to see you and I'm happy to have a moment alone to catch up."

We've been texting, but it's the first time I've seen her since before my last weekend at Lake George.

"How are you feeling after the weekend?" she asks.

"I'm okay. It was hard to watch my parents, how different they are around each other now, but it was nice to have Rhys there."

"I was shocked when you said he showed up. Not because he wouldn't want to be there for you, but because he really hadn't been there since his parents died."

"I know, but besides the melancholy of packing up our house, it was a good weekend." I swallow and give Hannah a sly smile. "We hooked up."

"Oh my god. Really?!"

"Yeah. I was worked up from reading this book." I motion to the paperback peeking out of Hannah's Berkin. "And also sad about my parents, which maybe hooking up is a weird thing to want to do when you're sad, but it was a lot of emotion and I just wanted to get lost for a moment."

"Good for you. I think it's great that you're getting that experience with him. I think it will make pursuing future relationships easier."

I let her words sink in. Since this arrangement with Rhys started, I haven't given any thought to future relationships. I had originally planned for this to be a jumping off point to get experience, but now I'm having a hard time imagining not being with him. Even though we're fake engaged, the conversations, the kisses, and the orgasms are very real. The thought of dating someone else makes my stomach hurt and the skin on my chest start to tingle.

"Yeah, maybe." I lick my lips, pressing a hand to my chest to calm the itchy skin there.

"At first I thought this arrangement was crazy, but now

I'm seeing that it's been beneficial for you. You just needed a guy like Rhys who's all confidence and smooth charm to ease you into the world of dating."

"Um, I think I want to have sex with him," I blurt out.

The driver stops at a red light and we both lurch forward.

"*Oh*." Hannah straightens, but I can't read her expression behind her oversized sunglasses. "I'd say if that's what you want to do, then you should go for it."

"Yeah?" Had I been expecting her to be against it? To try and talk me out of it?

"I think Rhys will be the perfect guy for your first time. He's experienced, and I'm sure he'll make it memorable. My first time with Ryan Haskins in the back seat of his car was not great. And at least with Rhys you two can agree on what the expectations are."

While we'd agreed to keep our touches and kisses to public appearances only, over the last week, that rule has gone out the window. Now we're kissing and touching simply because it feels good. He held me all night when I learned my parents were getting divorced and the fact that he had his head between my thighs on Saturday night made it seem like we'd abandoned those rules altogether. Besides, Rhys had said I could make the rules and he'd follow along.

But that doesn't mean he was offering to have sex with me.

I bite down on my lip. "Do you think I just ask him?"

She turns to me, angling her body in a conspiratorial way before lifting her sunglasses to the top of her head.

"Okay. This is Rhys, right? I think if this is only about sex and you losing your virginity, then you should focus on that."

"As opposed to?"

"Feelings. Don't talk about feelings. That will only freak him out."

I consider this.

The problem is, I do have feelings for him. He's the only

man I want to take this next step with, but if I admit my feelings will it send him running? Will he deny me because he doesn't want to lead me on?

Maybe Hannah's right. The only way to approach this is to make it casual. That's what Rhys is comfortable with.

I send him a quick text.

Colette: *Dinner Friday night?*

Rhys: *What did you have in mind?*

Hannah lifts her head from my phone screen to catch my eyes.

"Oh, you should go to Raoul's and have oysters. It's dark and got a sexy vibe. It'll set the mood."

Colette: *Raoul's at seven*

Rhys: *Cool. Will you wear that blue dress with the flowers and ties?*

I'm surprised Rhys knows my wardrobe. But also, who am I kidding? He probably knows it better than I do.

Colette: *Sure. If you wear those new loafers I picked out.*

Rhys: *You bet.*

My stomach twists with anticipation because it's settled. I'm going to ask Rhys to take my virginity.

CHAPTER 49

Rhys

Once I'm inside the restaurant, I shake my damp umbrella and fasten it. Looking around the crowded bar area, I spot her familiar dark waves. Perched on a barstool, Lettie's impeccable posture is easily recognizable in a row of hunch backs.

She's wearing the dress I requested. Pale blue with flowers and those delicate ties at her shoulder that I've dreamt about pulling loose and watching the material fall from her body.

When she texted me about tonight's date, I had mixed feelings. Of course I want to see her, but I've spent the better part of the week replaying our time together in Lake George. The conversation we had out on the dock. And that night, how good it felt to touch her again, to taste her, and know she was as desperate for my touch as I was to give it.

But for the first time in my life, I feel the need to slow down and understand where we stand. To not rush into anything. Or maybe that's the part of me that's terrified Lettie doesn't feel the same.

"Hey." At the sound of my voice, she rotates toward me.

"Hi." Her face splits into a sunny smile.

She hops off the bar stool and wraps her arms around my neck before pressing a kiss to my lips. My hands slip around her waist, bringing her into me until her body is aligned with mine.

Fuck. I could get used to this.

I already am.

"They're backed up on reservations, so the hostess said we can wait at the bar."

"That's okay. This is good." My eyes drink her in, long dark waves, and the delicate blue sundress I'd requested she wear. "You look beautiful."

"Thanks." She glances down, a huge grin on her face as she takes in my sky blue Ferragamo loafers. "I like your loafers."

"Thanks. I haven't had a chance to wear them yet."

"They look good."

"You have good taste."

"Yeah, but you're the one who can pull those off. Not many could."

I tuck my umbrella underneath the bar and take the empty stool next to Lettie, trying to ignore the thrill I get from the fact that her dress matches the color of my shoes.

"Do you want a drink?" she asks.

I nod at the glass on the bar top. "What are you having?"

"Um, a ginger ale."

"I'll have one, too, then."

The bartender takes my order. Once he's gone, I turn toward Lettie.

"How was your week?" I ask.

It's a simple question, but after a loaded weekend in Lake George, I'm trying to keep things light. We haven't spent nearly enough time together this week. Mainly exchanging texts and late-night phone calls.

"It was good. I'm feeling confident about evaluations. I think taking a step back and giving myself time to rest was a good idea. I practiced a long sequence after my Leg-Up class today and my body felt fresh. I'm on track for where I need to be so that's good."

The bartender sets my ginger ale down in front of me and I reach for it.

"What about you?" she asks.

"I've got a meeting next week with a few current board members to discuss my goals for the foundation."

"That's great."

It's easy, casual conversation, yet as I watch Lettie's leg bounce beneath the bar top, I'm wondering what the reason is for her nerves. It can't be that we're on a date. I thought we moved past this. And we're sitting at the bar, not even across from each other.

But then, I realize I'm nervous, too. Maybe she's sensing my nerves and it's making her feel on edge. I need to suck it up and put myself out there.

"Can we talk—" I start.

"Rhys, I want you to fuck me." Her words are loud enough for the guy sitting next to her to look over. The way one side of his mouth pulls up as he scans her body makes me want to knock his teeth out.

I lift my chin in his direction. "You got a problem?"

He meets my death glare, then quickly shakes his head and turns away.

Over our time together, I've seen Lettie begin to loosen the reins, allow herself indulgences and breaks. After our weekend at Lake George, things shifted between us. Or at least I thought they did. And now she's asking me to *fuck* her.

My stomach sours.

I slam back my ginger ale, wishing it was whiskey.

"Just once," she continues. "It doesn't have to be a big deal."

Months ago, I wouldn't have hesitated, but I'm not the guy I was then. And Lettie's not some random woman in a bar I'm picking up.

Had I been mistaken to think there was something more going on here? That she might want more from me than a one-night stand?

My jaw tightens.

"You want me to fuck you? Just once?" I can barely get the words out.

"You know, to get rid of my V card."

The more she makes it seem like a casual affair, the more my skin prickles with irritation.

Take the offer. That's the only way she wants you.

If I do it, then what? I fuck her, we continue to pretend to be engaged, then she walks away when she's done?

Why does the thought of it make my insides ache?

"No." The single word falls from my lips, yet I'm still not certain it's the right one.

"Are you serious?" She rears back like I've slapped her. "You've had sex with like a thousand women and I'm asking you to do this with me and you're saying no?"

Her assessment of me stings. I haven't fucked a thousand women. And if I had, is that the only reason she's asking me? Because, what's one more fuck when you've already had so many?

For a moment I'm afraid she's going to cry, but her hurt morphs into anger.

"You know what? Fuck you, Rhys." She slams her glass down on the bar, the fizzy ginger ale sloshing over the side, then she spins off the barstool so fast, I don't have time to react. She's already headed for the door when I fumble for my wallet. Throwing some bills on the bar, I rush out after her.

I'm two steps out the door when I'm greeted by a torrential downpour. The light rain from earlier is now a monsoon. I step back under the restaurant's awning, swiveling my head to see which way she went. Already halfway down the block, walking in the pouring rain is Lettie, and even from this distance I can tell she's completely soaked.

My umbrella.

It's tucked under the bar. *Fuck.* If I go back for it, I'll lose sight of her.

So instead, I plunge myself into the deluge.

The second I step out from underneath the awning, it's like someone has tossed a bucket of water on me. My hurried footsteps on the sidewalk are drowned out by the sound of the rain hitting the pavement. It's thunderous in my ears. The water blurs my vision, but I manage to keep sight of her. I keep running, closing the distance between us. By the time I catch up to her, my button-down is plastered to my skin and the weight of my pants has tripled.

"Lettie!" Her skin is slick from the rain, and my attempt to grab her elbow comes up empty.

She doesn't even look back to see that it's me.

"Leave me alone, Rhys," she says calmly. It's a complete contrast to the chaos of the storm beating down around us.

"In case you haven't noticed, now's not the time to have a tantrum."

She doesn't break stride. "What's the matter, Rhys? Getting your loafers wet?"

The only reason I care about the loafers is because she helped me pick them out.

"I'll get a new pair tomorrow. Why are you being such a stubborn ass?"

That gets her attention. She whips around. "*Excuse* me?"

The stormy day's low light shows everything exactly how it is. If Lettie was beautiful before, the water cascading down her features has only made her more breathtaking. Beads of water slide down her porcelain cheeks. Her dark lashes are wet and stuck together. Crystal blue eyes, the same color as the hottest part of a flame, stare back at me.

"You heard me."

"Well, you're being a prick," she spits, her soft pink lips spraying the rainwater that has settled there.

The urge to capture her plump bottom lip between my teeth is immeasurable. It's a constant battle. My desire to be around her. The desperate yearning. The insanity that is thinking I'm worthy of having Lettie beneath me. And now it's the very thing she's asking for and I'm going to lose my fucking mind no matter what I do.

We glower at each other, getting even more soaked by the second, until I guide her under a nearby overhang to get a break from the rain.

Her chest is heaving, the skin under her eyes now dark with smudged mascara.

With my hands braced against the wall by her head, I lean in close. The rain is loud enough to drown out the city noise around us. Like the steam created by the rain on the once scorching asphalt, our body heat mingles in the small space between us.

"This is what you want?" I ask, barely restraining myself. "Because if we do this, there's no more saving yourself for the perfect man, Lettie. For *love*." My fingers move to grip her chin. "I'm not that guy. It won't be like that with me."

I'm testing her. Trying to gauge how desperate she is. If she wants her virginity gone so badly that she doesn't care what the circumstances are. That she doesn't care that it's with me.

Her blue eyes bore into mine. Any moment now she'll come to her senses.

"That doesn't matter to me," she says quietly. "It doesn't have to be special. I just want it done."

Those words pierce my heart. Further evidence of how I feel about her. And what she thinks of me. A man for the job of taking her virginity but with nothing special to offer.

I thought things had changed in Lake George. The things we'd confessed. The way we'd been there for each other. I thought we could be more, but it's clear this is all she wants from me.

I should walk away right now. Leave her here and be done with this arrangement. Maybe then I could sleep without thinking of her. I know that won't be the case. Blissful or torturous, she's now a permanent fixture in my dreams.

My gaze lifts to the sign over the door. The Moxy Hotel. I glance to the street. It's stand-still traffic caused by the storm. With the rain still coming down hard, and no potential for a ride anytime soon, I grab Lettie's hand and pull her inside.

The lobby of the hotel greets us, the cool air making our drenched bodies shiver.

"A room, please," I tell the man working the front desk.

He perks up from what appears to be an uneventful evening. "We can offer you a standard king room with a city view."

"That's fine." I toss my black card on the desk.

Through the check-in process, Lettie stands next to me quiet and shivering. I'm waiting for her to call this off. To tell me she's changed her mind. I'm relying on it at this point.

We get our room key and take the elevator to our floor.

A few minutes later, the door clicks shut on room 715 and still no objection.

I set my wallet and the keycard on the table by the door. Peel my drenched jacket off and place it on a hanger in the closet. It's dripping, already soaking a spot on the carpet below.

I watch as Lettie slips off her shoes, neatly tucking them against the wall at the entryway to the bedroom.

Like the check-in clerk said, it's a standard king room with a small sitting area, nothing special or luxurious.

I recall Lettie's words on the street. *It doesn't have to be special.*

That's what she said, but that doesn't sit well with me.

She deserves for it to be so fucking special.

"I want you to be my first."

First. That indicates there will be others. My jaw tightens at the thought of Lettie with other men. My reaction to seeing her with Sebastian all those weeks ago, is nothing compared to the sour churn of my stomach now.

She's already given up the notion that her first time needs to be special. If I don't do this with her, she'll eventually find someone else. Selfishly, I want Lettie to stay in this place. Untouched by anyone but me. The thought that she'll move on when our time is up is eating at me. It's starting to chip away at the walls I've built around myself.

Lettie walks into the bathroom, her wet dress clinging to every inch of her body. As she moves, I take in her toned back, her perfect ass, and muscular legs. Lettie's body is perfection, not just because she's sculpted like a dancer, but how she carries herself, graceful and with purpose.

She turns to find me staring. Those blue eyes of hers have me treading carefully. They're like an undertow, and if I'm not vigilant, I'll be drowning in them.

I watch as her hands drop to the hem and starts peeling the material upward. A moment later, the wet dress drops with a thwack onto the tile floor. Underneath, her soaked light pink thong and bra are see-through. Every inch of her is on display. Her rosy nipples, the dark strip of hair between her thighs that I've claimed as mine.

If I fuck her, then she's mine. I'll have touched every inch of her body. I'll have every piece of her.

That's not the truth. I'll have claimed everything except what I desperately want.

Lettie reaches behind her back to unclasp her bra, then hooks her thumbs in her panties and steps out of them. She tosses them into the pile of wet clothes. Her hands are by her side, her middle finger pads grazing the pads of her thumbs with nervous elegance.

The sight of Lettie standing there, naked and waiting for me is a sight to behold. She's fucking perfect. I've touched her, felt her come on my tongue, the tight squeeze of her around my fingers, but this is different. With someone else I could turn off my body, go numb and barely feel anything, but that's going to be impossible with Lettie. I'm not even touching her and I already feel too much.

"Rhys?" She's five feet in front of me, but her voice sounds miles away.

I don't realize I'm bracing myself in the doorway. My hands too numb to notice what should be the sharp sting of my fingers gripping the wooden frame.

I hear the words echo off the bathroom walls before I realize I've said them.

"I can't."

Then, I'm rushing out the door.

CHAPTER 50

Colette

The click of the hotel door sends a blast of cool air against my wet, naked body.

I'm stunned.

Moments ago, I was standing in front of Rhys, stripping my wet clothes off, expecting him to make a move, when he bolted. Now, I'm shivering and humiliated.

What the hell just happened?

A violent shudder wracks my body. My eyes drop to the pile of wet clothes on the floor. There's no way I'm putting those back on right now, so I move toward the closet to see if there's a robe I can put on. As luck would have it, there are two cotton robes hanging next to Rhys's wet jacket.

I wrap myself in the thick cotton robe, sighing with the relief that its warmth brings. It doesn't make the sting of Rhys's rejection hurt any less but at least now I'm warm.

I move into the bedroom area. It's simple. A king bed with white bedding, two bedside tables with lamps, and a large dresser with a flat-screen television sitting atop it. I pull back the covers and slide in. The room is paid for, so no reason to waste it.

After being cold and wet, the robe and comfortable bed

allow my chilled muscles to relax as they warm. I stare up at the ceiling and wonder where Rhys went. If he trudged back out into the storm, deciding he would rather be out there than anywhere near me.

I want to block everything out, but when I close my eyes, I see Rhys standing in the bathroom doorway, a look of horror on his face.

I roll to my side, facing the window and let the sound of the rain outside calm me.

Then, too tired to get out of bed and find my phone, I use my smart watch to call Hannah.

That's right. I hadn't been completely naked in front of Rhys. I'd still had my smartwatch on. Why does that visual make me feel even more mortified?

"Hi! How's it going?" Hannah's voice echoes under the thick covers.

I look around the empty hotel room. "I'm lying in a hotel bed."

"Wait. Aren't you supposed to be with Rhys tonight? What happened?"

I take a deep breath in. "Rhys and I were going to have sex but because of the storm there was traffic downtown and this was the closest place with a bed."

"Oh my god, Lettie! Did you have sex? Is he there with you now?" she asks.

"No, we didn't have sex. And I wouldn't have called you if he was here."

"Good point."

"When I took off my dress and practically threw myself at him, he bolted."

"What?!" Hannah's screech is so loud, I lift my arm out of the covers to save my ears. "I'm going to kill him."

"Get in line." I want to rage along with her, but when I speak, my voice comes out wobbly.

"I can't believe it. Well, this is Rhys we're talking about, so maybe I can." She's quiet a moment, before adding, "Why would he do that?"

"I don't know. It seemed like we were on the same page." I think back to Rhys's demeanor when we came into the hotel. "He might have been a little annoyed that I was asking him to be my first, but I told him it didn't have to change anything between us. I assured him it didn't have to be special; I just want to have sex for the first time so I can move on. I did exactly what we talked about. But he still freaked out."

Reliving the moment by telling Hannah only makes me feel worse.

I never thought getting rid of my virginity would be this challenging. I'd assumed guys were usually up for getting laid and Rhys would be no different. I thought it would be an easy yes for him.

"I'm sorry, love. I can't believe he did that. I'm sure it had nothing to do with you. You're gorgeous and kind, and caring and amazing. He's an idiot. Plain and simple."

She's trying to make me feel better, but my brain is not convinced standing naked in front of a guy and having that guy run away from me as fast as he can has nothing to do with me. I rally my anger at the situation, it's what seemed to work the night of his proposal.

"I don't need that donkey dick anyways. I mean, why did the universe give the cockiest man alive a huge penis?" I ask.

"I think you answered your own question. Do you want me to come back to the city? It'll be late, but I can come if you need me."

"No, it's okay. I think I'm going to rent *Center Stage* and order an insane amount of room service on Rhys's card while I wait for my wet clothes to be dried."

"Aww, I love that movie and I'm not even a dancer."

"It's kind of ridiculous but the shoe preparation montage gets me every time."

"I love you and I'll call you tomorrow."

"Okay. Love you, too."

After I end the call with Hannah, I lie there for a few more minutes thinking about what I said.

I told Rhys my first time didn't have to be special because I thought that's what would put him at ease.

The truth is, with Rhys, my first time having sex would have been special.

Because it's *him*.

I desperately wanted it to be him.

I left the hotel an hour ago.

After I warmed up, I called down to have my dress and undergarments cleaned, then watched *Center Stage* while I waited for them to be dried. I ordered an obnoxious amount of food from room service and charged it to Rhys's credit card, but even that wasn't satisfying. My two-hundred-dollar bill won't even be a blip on his statement.

Then, I felt guilty for not eating all the food, so really the whole thing backfired.

The weather finally cleared, along with the traffic, so I took a cab home.

I've barely greeted Maxine, who is lounging on the luxury cat nap pad Rhys bought her last week, when my door buzzes.

I told Hannah not to come, and even if she had left right after we talked, she wouldn't be here yet.

"Hello?" I answer, my voice soft, but wary.

"Lettie," the deep husk of his voice has my stomach turning itself inside out, "it's me."

Rhys.

This is what I hate about the intercom system, I have to answer before I can find out who it is...there's no option to pretend I'm not home once I've answered.

I'm quiet, not sure what to say. I knew we'd have to talk at some point; I didn't expect it to be this soon.

I sigh into the speaker. "What do you want?"

"I need to talk to you. *Please*."

My emotions are raw. And while that might be good for my dancing, right now, it sucks and my heart hurts and I don't want to deal with any of this.

"Now's not a good time."

I release my finger from the keypad and wait for his response, but it's quiet on the other end. When a minute ticks by, I wonder if he already left.

But then, there's a knock on my door.

I yank the door open to find Rhys standing there. I should have expected it but seeing his devilishly handsome face makes my stomach twist.

He's changed since the hotel. He's effortlessly cool in a black button-down shirt and black slacks, and his hair is doing that thing I like where one unruly strand falls over his forehead. His shirt sleeves are rolled up beneath his elbows, exposing his tattoo.

I hate that he looks good. And I hate how my body reacts to him. Tingling all over, while my heart matches pace with a hummingbird's wings.

His hazel eyes drink me in. Lips parting in awe as he peruses every inch of my body like he hasn't seen me in years.

"How'd you get in?" I ask, crossing my arms over my chest to hide the fact that my nipples are pebbling beneath my dress.

"Mrs. Donahue was on her way in."

He swallows thickly, and there's a hint of uncertainty in his hazel eyes, but he doesn't have the decency to look regretful about his unauthorized entry.

"I guess I need to work on looking through the peephole

before I answer the door. Too many jerks showing up unannounced."

I glance next door to find Mrs. Donahue there, her overloaded keychain clanging against the door as she works her key in the lock.

"You really need to get that buzzer fixed," she calls.

"My buzzer isn't broken, Mrs. Donahue," I call back.

She waves me off. "No need to thank me, I brought him up for you."

"Oh, Mrs. Donahue, you shouldn't have."

She doesn't pick up on my sarcasm, or her hearing aid is down so she can't hear me. It's a toss-up.

"He's charming and so handsome, you really are a lucky lady."

"Serial killers are charming, Mrs. Donahue."

I get no response, only more praise for Rhys.

"You really are a beautiful couple. Your babies will be adorable." Her black-rimmed glasses are so thick, I don't know how she can make out our faces.

"That would require sex, Mrs. Donahue."

I shouldn't look at him, because the moment I do his nostrils flare and his eyes darken. He looks like a beautiful dragon, and I'm the one he's going to scorch.

But I'm too tired to care.

She gives us a little wave. "You kids have a good night."

"Goodnight, Mrs. Donahue." It isn't her fault she was charmed by Rhys. She's a sweet old lady, so I won't hold it against her.

I turn back toward Rhys. "I can't believe you used Mrs. Donahue to get in here."

"I'm sorry, but I needed to talk to you."

"What do you want to talk about, Rhys?" I prompt, my sneaker-clad foot tapping vigorously on the hardwood floor. He opens his mouth to start, but I thrust my finger at him. "Wait. No, I don't want to talk. Actions speak louder than words and you were loud and clear back at the hotel, so I'm good."

I move to shut the door in his face, but he reaches a hand out to stop it from latching.

"Please, Lettie." His voice catches and I hate that it pulls on my heartstrings.

The desperation in his voice has me pulling the door back, but only a sliver so I can see him. I realize that was a mistake because the pain in his expression immediately makes my anger melt. The urge for me to reach out to comfort him is overwhelming. But then the moment in the hotel room replays. The ashen look on his face as I stood vulnerable and baring myself to him has my anger returning. If not with him, with myself for letting him affect me this way.

"I fucked up. I'm sorry I left. I needed to clear my head."

I yank the door open.

"Do you know how humiliating that was? I was naked, Rhys. *Naked.* You could have said something. Anything would have been better than you running off."

"I felt trapped. Overwhelmed. You were adamant that I fuck you right then and there. And I just...I couldn't." He clears his throat.

Oh.

It occurs to me that maybe Rhys has a problem with the functionality of his man parts. Which is odd because he was hard as a rock when I gave him that twenty-second blow job a few weeks ago, and he had an erection when I brushed my butt against him last week at Lake George, but maybe it's a thing that comes and goes.

My eyes drop to his crotch.

"Are you getting help for this problem?" I ask.

His eyes narrow at me. "My dick is not the problem. It's *never* been the problem."

I shrug innocently. "There's a first time for everything."

"Well, that's not the issue here."

I want to be happy for him that his dick isn't broken but that just means he didn't want to have sex with me.

"I'm sorry you felt forced into it. I didn't realize it would be such a chore for you."

"That's not it at all." He runs a hand through his hair. "Fuck. Can we do this inside?" He motions to my apartment behind me.

I cross my arms over my chest again. "No."

"Okay." He drops his arm to motion down the hallway. "Will you come with me so we can talk?"

"No."

His hands find his hair and he lets out a frustrated growl.

"I fucked up…again. I panicked. And I'm sorry, but now I need you to let me make things right."

"You want to make things right?"

"Yes."

"Okay. I think it's only fair if I let you experience what I did at the hotel."

"What do you want me to do?" he asks. "Name it and I'll do it."

An idea pops into my head and I press my lips together to smother the smile that's trying to break through.

"Take off your clothes."

He searches my face, his lips pinned down in a frown, but then he nods. "Okay, if that's what you want." He moves toward me, toward my apartment, but I put a hand out to stop him.

"No. Here." I nod to where he's standing outside my apartment door.

He looks down the empty hallway, then back to me.

Mrs. Donahue is tucked safely inside her apartment for the night, but Ricardo, my neighbor across the hall, is unaccounted for. For all he knows, Ricardo could be throwing a party tonight and the guests are scheduled to arrive any minute.

He gives another glance behind him at Ricardo's door.

Ricardo is visiting family in California. He'll be there for two weeks and I'm watering his plants while he's gone, but Rhys doesn't need to know that.

I lift my brows in question. *Is this happening or not?*

He doesn't say anything, just gives me one last heated glance before he starts to unbutton his shirt. It's off in a matter of seconds, followed by his shoes and socks. Next, he undoes his belt and drops his pants.

There's a moment, right before he reaches for the waistband of his boxer-briefs that I'm tempted to stop him, but then he's stripping them off and tossing them at me. My hand snags the fabric out of the air, before I look back to find Rhys standing gloriously naked in my apartment building hallway.

"Does this make it better?" He lifts his arms out to his sides, completely exposed to me.

My eyes scan his body, taking in every inch. Broad, muscular shoulders tapered to a narrow waist. Chiseled abs and strong arms. His thick cock juts out between his muscular thighs. Semi-hard and quickly swelling under my gaze. Under the hallway light, the barbell piercing below his crown winks at me.

At the sight of him, my breath catches. My heart hammers in my chest, as a mix of longing and need courses through my veins. Damn it. It's not as satisfying as I thought it would be.

He's exposed, just like I was at the hotel. But only because he's trying to fix things between us, not because he wants to present himself to me the way I was blatantly offering myself to him. Rhys is gorgeous and I'm wildly attracted to him, but where he's trying to salvage this arrangement, I want to change everything between us.

"You can get dressed." I toss his boxer-briefs back at him and move to shut the door.

"Wait." He rushes forward, covering his erection with his

boxers. "I can explain why I left, but it would be better if I show you."

I'm exhausted. Tired of this back and forth between us. I thought being clear about what I wanted would help, but now I feel even worse. Raw, exposed and emotionally drained. It's all but a guarantee my dancing will be absolute fire after this rollercoaster of emotion.

But I'm starting to wonder if it's worth it.

What could he possibly show me that would make things right between us?

"*Please*, Lettie."

Still naked, he drops down to his knees.

He looks so defeated, my heart aches.

How many chances does he get?

I take in a resigned breath before looking at my watch to note the time. "You have one hour. You should get dressed."

All of them, apparently.

He nods, rushing to stand and pull his clothes back on while I grab my purse, and his now dry suit jacket off the hook and lock up my apartment.

We're quiet on the drive and I'm thankful Wanda isn't working tonight. With her boisterous personality, she'd have me laughing and it would be hard to hold onto my anger, my hurt. As we drive, I assure myself that there's nothing Rhys can do to fix this, but when I catch him looking at me, his hazel eyes filled with hope, I feel as if I'm lying to myself.

The car pulls up to the Seventy-Ninth Street Boat Basin. Rhys opens my door and extends his hand to me.

This time, I take it. Once my hand is in his, he holds it firmly. After a silent walk down the dock, he's guiding me onto his boat, through the living area and down the hallway to his master stateroom.

I start to pull my hand from his. "Rhys, what are—"

I don't finish my question because he opens the door and I gasp.

Candles are everywhere; lining the sides of the room, covering the built-ins and framing the bed. When I look closer, I realize they aren't real burning candles but electronic, which is probably a good thing because if one tipped over it would be a fire hazard.

Gone is the navy bedding and dark comforter, replaced with white sheets and a fluffy white duvet. Light pink rose petals are arranged in the shape of a heart on the bed, with vases of a variety of pink flowers placed around the room.

I pick up a vase of flowers and breathe in their dreamy fragrance.

"What is this?" I ask, setting the vase I was inspecting back in place.

He meets my eyes and I see the hope there again. "Something special."

I shake my head, confused. But then I remember what I said to him when we were decorating Hannah and James's wedding night suite. *Something special.* Rhys had argued that it was unnecessary and lame.

They're just going to fuck, he'd said.

"Rhys, I told you it didn't have to be. I don't need any of this. I just want—"

"I know." He swallows thickly, his hands on his hips as his eyes dart nervously around the room before landing back on mine. "But I do."

"What—" I'm confused when he slides a hand around my waist, pulling me to him.

His forehead presses against mine, one hand gently cupping my jaw.

"I can't fuck you, Lettie, because that's not what it would be. I've been losing my mind trying to understand what this is. Trying to push my feelings for you away. Because that's what I have. *Feelings.* It's overwhelming and terrifying. And when you said you didn't need your first time to be special, I realized that's all I wanted. For it to be special. For you. With me."

I'm stunned by his confession, my bottom lip dropping at the very moment he runs his thumb over it.

He pulls back to look over at the bed.

"Are the rose petals too much? I couldn't decide if they were romantic or cheesy."

Seeing Rhys unsure and second-guessing something is what I imagine a baby foal looks like when it first tries to stand and walk. It's endearing.

"They're sweet."

He nods, his confidence visibly boosted by my approval.

But in the next moment, he's swallowing hard and looking at me like I've got his heart in my hands.

"When you were standing there naked, I couldn't take my eyes off you, you were perfect. But the setting was all wrong."

"It was a nice hotel room," I argue.

"It wasn't just about the room. Something was off and I couldn't pinpoint what was wrong until after I'd left. I was a dick for leaving, I shouldn't have done that, but I needed time to think."

"And you decided to do all this?" I motion to his bed.

"I wanted your first time to be a first for me, too."

I know he's not talking about sex. He's had plenty. I shake the thought, refusing to let images of Rhys and other women into this moment.

It hits me then.

He's referring to his rule of never having a woman in his bed. I'll be *his* first.

Our eyes lock and the intensity of his stare has my breath catching in my throat. In that moment, he's telling me everything without saying a word.

My eyes drift back to his bed and the dreamy white bedding.

"I've got to be honest; I don't think white was the best choice."

He shakes his head, a tiny smirk playing at the corner of his mouth.

"I've seen your toy collection. I think you'll be fine."

"I've seen your cock and I'm certain I won't be." My core clenches, a mixture of desire and anticipation at the thought of him inside me.

He shakes his head. "We don't have to do anything tonight."

I search his face. All the tension from before is gone. His eyes are filled with warmth and certainty now.

I'm still blown away by his confession.

But it only makes me more certain that I want to do this with him.

"I'm dying to be inside you, but we can wait." One large hand strokes my back gently while the other squeezes my hip. "I can lick you, make you come on my fingers. I'd do that anyway because I can't stop thinking about how good you taste, but it doesn't have to be sex. Even if I just hold you all night, I'll be happy."

He presses a tender kiss to my lips, and it confirms his sincerity.

"What do you want, Princess?" The nickname is whispered so reverently, my heart squeezes.

I'm quickly falling for him. I imagine sex will only make my feelings more intense. Am I ready for that?

Yes.

"No more waiting. Rhys Spencer, you will put your dick inside me tonight. Pinkie promise." I lift my pinkie up between us.

With an amused smile, Rhys hooks his pinkie in mine.

CHAPTER 51

Rhys

With the hook of our pinkies, our fate is sealed. I'm going to have Lettie tonight and it's going to mean something.

It's going to mean *everything*.

My heart thumps wildly in my chest.

Fuck. I'm nervous.

I can't remember another time I've been nervous to touch a woman. It's always come easily. Smooth. But ever since that night I first touched her, after I proposed, something has shifted.

Because you care about her.

It took me nearly an hour after I left the hotel to pinpoint why I ran. Once I realized it was because I wanted more with Lettie, I knew an apology and an explanation wouldn't be enough. I needed to show her.

I spent the last two and a half hours shopping, and transforming my bedroom into a place worthy of Lettie.

My arms tighten around her, pulling her close until our bodies are flush.

"Again, I'm sorry for earlier." I turn, burying my face in her hair to suck in her familiar scent. Fuck. I love that I can do that now without an excuse.

"I'm sorry, too." Her voice is soft.

I pull back to look at her. "For what?"

"For making you strip naked in my hallway."

"No, you're not."

"You're right. I'm not." A laugh bursts from her throat, but in the next second, she's serious again. "I am sorry for pressuring you. For assuming that because of your history you would have sex with just about anyone who asked."

"You're not *just anyone*." I kiss along her jaw.

Her hands find my hair. I expect her to guide me to her mouth, but she uses her grip to pull me back until we're staring into each other's eyes again.

"And you're not just a guy to lose my virginity to and get it over with. You're Rhys. *My* Rhys." Her fingers dance along my cheek. "I want it to be you, because of *you*, but I didn't know how to say it. I thought if I made it a big deal, I'd freak you out."

I smile at her confession because it strips away the insecurity of her only seeing me as a guy good for this task, not as the man she truly wants.

Lettie's virginity isn't a conquest. Something I want to win and carry around like a trophy. It's more than that for me and that's what's terrifying. I want to see the look on her face when I enter her for the first time, knowing I'm the only man who's had the privilege of being there, and keep that memory sacred.

"I didn't want you to think I'd been doodling Colette Spencer in my journal or anything. That I was infatuated with you. It wasn't like that."

"No? That's too bad. I kind of like the sound of it. Colette Spencer." I guide her left hand to my chest. The large diamond of her engagement ring presses into my palm. There's satisfaction that even while she was angry with me earlier, she didn't take it off. "You've already got the ring."

I wait for the sense of dread, the heavy weight on my

chest at the very real thought of tying myself to another person descend on me. But it doesn't.

My lips drop to hers again.

I love that she's still in the blue dress from earlier. It's dry now, almost like we rewound time, to before the chaos of the storm, and our time at the hotel didn't even happen.

But it did happen and I know I need to be careful with her.

To show her I want this.

Want her.

For real.

With Lettie in my arms, I drop to the edge of the bed, and settle her into my lap. The skirt of her dress billows around our hips.

My fingers tug on the end of one tie at her shoulder, watching with satisfaction as the bow shrinks until two separate strings fall, leaving her shoulder bare. I replace the bow with my lips, then repeat on the other side.

Lettie's hands reach for the hem of my shirt and I help her pull it off. As I toss it aside, her fingertips caress my skin, stopping to trace the ink on my left arm until they come to a rest on my chest.

With a hand behind her neck, I kiss down the smooth column and along her collar bone.

My lips suck against the sensitive skin above her breasts and she gasps.

Licking.

Tasting.

Worshipping.

I could spend all night kissing every inch of Lettie's skin to see her reaction.

I increase the suction of my mouth, drawing more of Lettie's delectable skin into it.

"Is that going to leave a mark?" she asks.

"Do you want it to?"

She bites her lip but nods, eyes flashing with curiosity. "Yes."

"I want to mark you everywhere."

I suck her again, this time grazing her with my teeth.

A breathy sigh escapes her, before she holds my head in her hands, directing my eyes to hers. "Maybe only places people won't see. I can't have a hickey for evaluations."

"Mmm, they'll only be for me. I like that."

Guiding the top of her dress down, I let the material slide over her breasts.

She was naked at the hotel, but I never *saw* her. I was too concerned she was thinking sex with me would mean nothing to appreciate the sight of her bared to me.

Now, I'm focused on every detail and discovering every new part of her is the biggest turn on.

"So fucking pretty." With her rigorous training, Lettie's breasts are small. I've known their shape since she wore that dress without a bra on our first date. Now, they're under my palms and the perfect handful of soft flesh, with the most luscious rosy nipples. My mouth waters just looking at them.

I brush my thumb over one nipple, loving how it pebbles even further under my touch. My head dips to suck one into my mouth.

"I thought you were a tits man."

"I am." I flick her nipple with my tongue and she moans. "And yours are the prettiest I've ever seen." I cup them, letting my rough fingertips squeeze them. When I do, Lettie's hips rock against my erection.

I capture her lips again, loving the feel of her tongue against mine with no pretense. The way our mouths dance, how easily our kiss turns molten and wild; I begin to wonder if there ever was.

"I need more." Lettie groans into my mouth. "Can we do foreplay later?"

I chuckle. "The point of foreplay is to make sure you're

ready for sex."

"Trust me, I'm ready."

She slips my hand under her dress and places it against the crotch of her panties. She's soaked them through.

A low rumble rises out of my throat.

"So fucking wet."

She beams, treating my declaration like a pat on the back for a job well done.

Lettie wins top prize for the slickest pussy.

I can't hold back my grin.

She matches my smile. "It's good, right?"

"So good, Princess."

I tease a fingertip against the wet fabric before slipping it underneath to feel her.

She's slick and warm.

When I dip my finger inside her, a groan escapes my lips.

And so fucking tight.

While I assured her that her toys may have prepared her for sex, my cock is going to ruin her if I don't make sure she's ready to take me.

I withdraw my finger and she pouts.

"I want you naked," I say, before lifting her dress overhead.

Her long, dark hair spills over her shoulders in messy waves.

I drop to my knees in front of her. Pushing my hands into the backside of her underwear, I massage the firm flesh of her ass before dragging the material down her legs.

Her hands find my shoulders to steady herself while I unhook them from her ankles.

In a quick motion that elicits an airy laugh, I swoop Lettie into my arms and lay her out on my bed. She settles against the pillows. The flickering candles around us bathe her in a soft yellow light. She's stunning. Spread out on my bed, her dark hair cascading over the white pillows beneath her.

"What now?" she asks.

Her eyes track my movements as I strip down to my boxer briefs, then kneel on the bed, spreading her legs until I have room to settle between them.

"I'm going to lick that sweet pussy until you come for me."

Hooking her legs over my arms, I press kisses to her inner thigh. The desire to nip the soft flesh there is strong, but I hold back. Tonight isn't about my desires. It's about Lettie. Making it good for her.

"I've been dying to taste you again."

I lick up her center, and she whimpers.

"So fucking sweet."

I devour her. Eating her pussy like a starved man because that's what I have felt like this last week. I dip my tongue inside her to lap up all that sweetness.

I play with her. Teasingly light strokes down her center. My thumb circles her clit then I flick it with my tongue.

When she's dripping, from her arousal and my mouth, I thrust a finger inside her.

Pretty soon she's writhing on the bed, hands clutching the duvet.

"More, Rhys."

I give her a second finger.

My fingers stroke her, pumping in and out, stretching her.

My cock oozes with precum. I'm desperate to be inside her. To mark her as mine.

She's close. Her walls are shrinking around my fingers, making it impossibly tighter. When I crook my fingers inside her and suck hard on her clit, she cries out, her orgasm making her clench around my fingers.

I love seeing her like this. A little disheveled, a little wild, and completely exposed.

All for me.

CHAPTER 52

Colette

With a euphoric sigh, my back bows off the mattress and I come hard around Rhys's fingers.

When my orgasm wanes, his head lifts from between my thighs, a satisfied grin pulling at his lips.

Good lord.

If I thought the other times he went down on me were life changing, then that orgasm just altered the entire universe. But then his smile slips.

"Fuck," he groans, and I open my eyes to find him reaching over to look in his bedside table.

My stomach drops. "What's wrong?"

He pushes a hand through his hair. "I don't have any condoms."

My eyes widen at his confession. "What?"

"I got rid of them, and even with all this preparation for tonight, I forgot to buy some." He shakes his head. "How did I forget the most important thing?"

"You got rid of them? Why?"

"I was trying to clean up my reputation. Then when we started fake dating and I found out you were a virgin, I threw them out."

I crack a smile. "You were trying to not have sex with me?"

He sighs, nodding.

"I thought I was removing the temptation." Leaning back over me, he lazily skims a finger down my center and I shiver.

"Clearly it didn't work." His fingertip teases inside me again. "I can run out and get some." He moves to extract himself and I catch his wrist to glance at his watch.

"It's eleven o'clock at night," I protest.

He presses his lips to mine. "I'll be quick."

But I don't let him go that easily. Before he can reach for his pants, my hand snakes beneath the waistband of his boxer briefs to palm his erection. His eyes close on a groan as his hips rock into my hand. My fingers wrap around his shaft while my thumb circles his crown, playing with the piercing there.

"Fuck, baby, that feels good."

With my free hand, I push his boxers down farther until his erection is free. My pussy aches at the sight of him. The need to be filled up by Rhys is almost painful. I can't wait any longer.

"I'm on the pill," I whisper, still stroking him.

Rhys's eyes open to meet mine.

"I got tested when I came back to New York. I'm good."

That's all I need to hear. I've waited long enough. Right now, all I want is Rhys inside me. My hands are busy touching his body, so with my knee bent up toward my waist, I press my foot against the waistband of his boxers, guiding them the rest of the way down his legs, until they're at his shins. He uses his feet to kick them off completely.

He places his hand over mine where I'm still stroking him.

"I want this to be perfect for you." He nudges my jaw to the side with his nose and sucks the sensitive skin there. "Tell me what you want, Princess."

His lips ghost over mine, licking into my mouth before they graze down the other side of my jaw.

"Suck my nipples."

He did it earlier and I really liked it.

I feel his smile against my skin. A moment later his mouth is making its way down the column of my throat. His hands find my breasts first. Large and warm, he palms the weight of me, groping and playing. He squeezes my breast, extending the hardened peak toward his greedy mouth. When he flicks it with his tongue, I cry out.

"You look beautiful like this. Are you ready for me?"

He slides a hand between my legs and presses two fingers inside me. I'm dripping, but his fingers are still a snug fit. His cock is going to be a challenge.

But the longer we wait, the more desperate I become.

"Rhys, please."

"You don't have to beg, Princess. I'm going to give it to you."

That's when I feel the pressure at my entrance. The crown of his cock nudging against me.

Okay, maybe I am nervous, afraid of the pain, but I also want this so badly.

"Wait." I push a palm to his chest. "Is it possible it won't fit? Like I'm too small and you're too big?"

"We'll make it fit, Princess. I promise."

I nod, his words not only making my core clench, but causing another flood of arousal between my thighs.

"Relax, baby. Take a deep breath."

I'm trying to focus on his words, to take a calming breath, but the feel of him pushing against my entrance is distracting. Rhys rolls my nipple between his fingers, bringing awareness there and allowing the muscles constricting him to ease.

"You're too big. It's not going to fit." I start shaking my head, panicking at the thought that my options are for Rhys to rip me in two or that I'll still be a virgin after tonight. Neither of them sound appealing.

"You need to breathe, Lettie," he says, his voice calm and reassuring. "I don't want to hurt you."

I focus on my breathing again, but when he presses between my legs, I start to feel a burning sensation. He rocks into me, and my muscles clamp down hard. I can see the strain on Rhys's face. It's not easy for him either.

"I'm convinced it's going to hurt no matter what, so maybe just do it quick." My hands are gripping his shoulders, my nails clawing into his bronzed skin. "Like a band-aid, you know?"

A small smile pulls at his lips, and he nods knowingly. Then, he drops his mouth to mine.

His kiss is sweet and gentle. His thrust between my thighs is not.

That burns.

Another subtle shift of his hips and he presses in farther.

"Let me in, Lettie. I want you to feel every inch of me."

"I feel every inch. There's no way there can be more. I'm so full. And it's so tight, if I orgasm, I'm going to break your dick."

He chuckles lightly. "*When* you orgasm, you're not going to break anything."

His words relax me. I thought I had been relaxed but I was still holding tension between my legs.

"Jesus fucking Christ." He pants.

"Oh, no. Did I break your dick?"

"No, that's my way of communicating that being inside you is the best fucking feeling in the world."

He huffs.

It takes a minute, but once I've adjusted to him, he starts to move. I expect it to be long strokes in and out, but it's more of a deeper press in, a roll of his hips as he finds and moves against the most tender spot inside me, fucking me so gently that I know I'm going to come fast. It's not only his cock worshipping me, but his hands caressing every inch of my skin, his mouth licking and teasing me, all of it perfectly orchestrated to bring me to the edge.

"Rhys."

"Let go, Princess. Let me feel you come on my cock."

His words have me climaxing hard. I clench down as my orgasm pulls Rhys's cock deeper inside me.

"God damn." A moment later, Rhys pulls out of me, and with a final stroke from his hand his cum paints my stomach. I stare at the warm, opaque liquid, fascinated. When I shift to sit up, a bead starts to slide down my side.

"Hold on. I'll get a washcloth to clean you up."

I watch Rhys leave, his still-hard cock jutting up toward his stomach and his firm glutes contracting with every step.

That's when I spot the pink splotches on his new white duvet.

"Told you white wasn't a good option," I say when he walks back into the room, wet washcloth in hand.

He picks up a rose petal.

"That's not you. That's the rose petals."

"Oh."

Rhys gently wipes the warm washcloth between my legs, and it feels wonderful. While everything after the initial thrust had felt good, I can tell I'm going to be sore.

When he's done with me, he uses the washcloth to clean himself up.

"Now, that's you."

He lifts the cloth up for me to see a few red-tinged streaks.

I wince. "Sorry."

"Don't be. I like it."

"You like me bleeding on you?"

"I like the fact that my cock has been the only one inside you and that's the evidence. So, yeah, it's hot."

My cheeks heat but my stomach flutters because secretly I

like that he's into it. He pulls on his boxer-briefs and picks out one of his t-shirts for me to wear.

"You hungry?" he asks, as I pull the shirt over my head.

"No, I ordered the entire room service menu at the hotel." My lips twitch. "Just a heads up for when you get that bill."

Like I knew he would, Rhys doesn't even flinch.

"That's my girl." He shoots me a lazy grin before dropping his lips to my forehead. "Let's get ready for bed."

I follow him into the bathroom where I find my toothbrush still in the cup next to his.

While we brush in silence, the dopamine starts to dissipate and my overthinking brain takes over.

We hadn't talked about what would happen after tonight. What it means that we have feelings for each other and what we plan to do about it.

Will we go back to being fake engaged until after the foundation board votes? Then, what?

I tell my brain to quiet. For once, I don't want to think about every detail. I want to be in the moment. Not worry about the *what ifs*.

Tonight was a big night. There's no need to pile on with a discussion about the future.

I glance over at Rhys, who's gloriously shirtless and adorably foaming at the mouth.

He winks at me.

That's what I tell myself, but I wonder if I'll be able to follow through with it.

CHAPTER 53

Rhys

Watching my bare cock move inside Lettie's pussy has altered my brain chemistry. I'll never be the same after tonight and that's fine with me.

I glance over at Lettie brushing her teeth. Her hair is a mess and she's wearing my shirt. She's stunning.

Her eyes meet mine and I give her a wink. She smiles around her toothbrush.

She's *mine*. It's the same primal urge I felt when I saw the streaks of blood on my cock from being inside her.

My eyes drop to her engagement ring.

It's a symbol of the arrangement we had before tonight, but it doesn't work for me anymore. While our fake relationship status is still necessary, out of the public eye, I want to do things right with her. I've got to ask my fiancée if she'll date me.

I drop my toothbrush back in the cup and turn to Lettie.

"Lettie, will you go out on a date with me?" I ask.

"Um, I didn't think there was anything planned until the foundation dinner next week."

"There isn't. I'm asking you out on our first official date."

"Oh." Her eyes widen, but then her face breaks out into a smile. "Then, yes. Of course, I will."

I fist the extra material of the shirt she's wearing and pull her toward me.

"You like me, huh?"

"I didn't say that. I was just hoping to get more free food out of the deal."

I reach to tickle her, but she yelps and leaps out of my arms before I can pin her to the wall.

When she runs back into my bedroom, I stalk after her, finding she's crawled beneath the covers. She thinks she's safe in there. She has no idea the things I'm going to do to her.

But I can be patient.

On my way over to the bed, I lay her dress over the chair in the corner of the room. Then, I grab her panties from where they've been discarded and place them in my drawer. When I turn around, Lettie's watching me.

Her lips twitch with curiosity. "What are you doing with my underwear?"

"They're wet because of me, so I get to keep them."

She scoffs. "That's not how it works."

I shrug. I want them, I'm not going to analyze it.

She's quiet a moment, before her mouth drops open in understanding. "Wait, did you take my underwear the night we hooked up here? I couldn't find them the next morning."

There's no point in keeping it a secret now.

The corner of my mouth lifts. "Yeah, I did."

She shakes her head, confused. "What for?"

"You really want to know?" I ask, pulling back the covers and climbing in next to her.

"Um, *yeah*."

My hand wraps around her back so I can pull her closer to me. Then, I look her straight in the eyes.

"I've been using them when I masturbate."

Her eyes widen, then her lashes start fluttering, like they're trying to help her understand. I wonder how long I should let her mind run with that.

Not long.

"I wrap them around my dick while I stroke myself and think about you."

"Oh."

She places a hand over her mouth. Her cheeks are two patches of pink now, and my smile widens. I love that she's thinking about me doing it now.

Her hand drops from her mouth to my chest. "I have so many questions."

"Ask away."

"Have you done that before? Like do you buy women's underwear to pleasure yourself with? Or was it because they were mine?" Her eyes widen again. "*Oh my god.* They were wet…with my," she clears her throat, "…wetness. Did you wash them before, you know, you *used* them?"

I chuckle. "No, I didn't wash them. That was the point. They smelled like you. But then I got my cum all over them and they needed to be washed." I tease a hand up her shirt and she wiggles when I trace my thumb over her pelvic bone. "And no, I couldn't just go buy new women's underwear. The point was that they were yours. That's the only reason I wanted them."

"Fascinating."

"Come on. Didn't you think about me when you were touching yourself? Using that vibrator of yours?"

"Maybe."

"You can admit it. It's natural, and it only turns me on more."

She presses a kiss to my lips, then blinks up at me. "Yeah, I did."

"See, that wasn't so hard."

Lettie's hand reaches between us to palm my erection.

"Speaking of hard." She strokes me over my boxer-briefs.

Her seductive smile breaks into a yawn. Her glazed-over eyes telling me what she won't.

She's tired.

I could easily sink back into her silky heat, but that's not what she needs right now.

I lift her hand, kissing it before I roll her over. With her back against my chest, I hold her close.

"You better rest while you can, Princess. I'm going to want you every second I can have you."

It's the middle of the night, but I can't sleep. With Lettie next to me, I'm too alert. Too aware of her scent and her warm body pressed up against mine. Also, my cock has been like granite for the better part of the night, making it impossible to relax.

I shift again, trying to calm myself down enough to fall asleep again.

"Rhys?" Lettie whispers.

Shit. I didn't want to wake her up.

"Go back to sleep."

She rolls toward me, her arms reaching out to wrap around my neck.

"I can't."

"Why's that?" I whisper against her jaw where my lips are already moving toward that sensitive place on her neck.

"Mmm, I had a dream about you."

"I'd imagine that would make you want to go back to sleep. Try to pick up where you left off."

"It was a nice dream. You were very attentive in it." She moves my hand between her legs. "But I want the real thing."

I bite back a groan. She's swollen and so fucking slick.

"Is that for me, Princess?"

"Yes," she murmurs as I shift her under me.

I press two fingers inside her. "See, this is why I should keep all your underwear. There's no need for them when you're in my bed."

She reaches for my waistband, her eyes still heavy with sleep. "I want you."

She doesn't have to tell me twice. I'm already shedding my underwear and positioning my head at her entrance.

Sleep-warm and so fucking sweet, Lettie is going to be the death of me.

"You sore, baby? I can go slow."

"Yeah."

I inch in, giving her a little at a time, so she can adjust. Watching her sweet cunt take me inside is the hottest thing I've ever seen.

Once I'm fully seated, she sighs.

"It feels better when you're inside me. It takes away the sting."

My hands grip her waist as I work her over the length of me. The feel of her surrounding me is intoxicating.

"Rhys, Rhys, Rhys," she chants.

I groan because I love hearing my name on her lips, but it's also the sign that she's close. I've been holding back my orgasm, pushing to get her there. Our fingers tangle in each other's hair, our kisses turning frantic and wild, matching the pace of my thrusts.

"Oh, fuck. Yes. *Rhys*!"

I smile at how unfiltered she is during sex. How the sensations she's experiencing make it impossible for her to hold back. And she feels safe to have those moments with me.

When her orgasm peaks, her pussy grips me so fucking tight. It feels like she's trying to bend my dick in half.

Damn.

I'll never get tired of watching Lettie come. She has the

prettiest O face. It's like watching her fight with me before she gives in to the ecstasy.

Once Lettie's pussy relaxes enough for me to move again, I lean back on my heels and tilt her pelvis upward. From this angle, I can see where we're joined, how her muscles contract around me with each thrust, and it's the most stunning sight.

"Fuck, Princess. You should see this." I huff. "How good you're taking me."

My eyes lift to hers.

"Come inside me," she whispers.

Those three words have me spiraling to my climax.

When the familiar heat builds at the base of my spine, I ride the euphoric wave and thrust my cock deep inside her tight cunt.

A moment later, I groan as my cock pulses, the liquid heat of my orgasm spilling inside her.

Dizzy from my release, I take a deep inhale, my eyes dropping to where my cock is still buried in Lettie. Her pretty cunt slick and stretched full of my cock. I'm already addicted to the sight.

I slowly pull out.

Before Lettie, I'd never had sex without a condom. Last night, I wasn't sure if I should come inside her so I pulled out before I came. But just now, when she'd given me the okay, I'd been into the moment and let myself go.

The sight of my cum leaking out of her entrance gives me a head rush.

That's new.

Seeing the evidence of claiming Lettie this way is so fucking satisfying.

She moves to sit up.

"Wait." With my palm on her stomach, I gently press her back to the mattress. The movement causes her core muscles to contract and a stream of my cum floods out of her pussy.

"Damn," I groan, my cock thickening at the sight.

"What is it?" she asks, her blue eyes wide with concern.

"I like watching my cum drip out of you." I press the crown of my cock at her entrance again, letting the tip inch in slowly. Satisfaction pools in my chest as I watch my cum slip back inside her. "Almost as much as I like fucking it back inside."

Slowly, I give her my full length again.

"*Rhys.*" She flutters around me. "Ahh, that feels so good."

"Good, because I like giving you everything you need."

Our bodies are still fused together. She reaches up to cup my jaw.

"I just need you."

I press my lips to her palm. "And trail mix. Don't forget trail mix. That's very important."

"You're right. It's a toss-up for first place. Stay on your toes or trail mix might edge you out."

When she laughs it's airy. It's the laugh she has when she's at ease. I love it and I want to hear it more often. I want it to be associated with the way I make her feel. Light and cared for.

She kisses my neck before leaning back into the pillow with a sigh.

"Sex is messier than I thought."

I chuckle at her observation. She's right, but I like it. "I like you messy and marked by me, but we should probably clean up, for personal hygiene's sake."

Still deep inside her, I wrap her legs around my waist and carry her to the shower.

Sleepy and sated, we silently wash each other under the warm shower spray.

Once we're clean, we climb back into bed and fall asleep in each other's arms.

CHAPTER 54

Colette

Evaluations are in a week, followed by the start of rehearsals. For those company members who took time off or picked up other gigs around the city, it's time to get back into the routine of things. For me, I'm back to my schedule with a few adjustments. Like I've swapped out Gyrotonics for morning sex.

Rhys and I are still fake engaged, but also officially dating. We're going on our first official date tonight and I've had zero anxiety about it. Probably because this week has been insane and I haven't even had a moment to think.

I drop my bag by the door, too tired to even hang it up.

Food. That's what I need. But I shouldn't eat before my date with Rhys otherwise I won't be hungry at dinner. He at least was open to an earlier reservation time.

There's a clanging sound in the kitchen but my adrenaline barely spikes. At this point, I've got no energy to fight off an intruder. If I'm being robbed, I'll just lie down on the couch and point out the few valuable items they could take.

But then I smell it. Garlic and herbs, something aromatic and savory. My stomach cheers. *We're saved!*

That's when I see Mo's tail peeking out from behind the

wall. Maxine, on the other hand, is matching my energy, and curled up on the cat bed by the window.

After I pet Mo, I make my way to the kitchen. For a moment I'm concerned that maybe there were burglars at some point, because the kitchen is in complete disarray. Drawers open, a bubbling pot of water on the stove top, and a countertop filled with cutting boards, vegetables, and various dishes.

Rhys is there with a white and blue checked apron fastened around his neck. He's listening to Taylor Swift *and* singing along.

"Colette, what you want, yeah, Colette what you wanna do."

I'm certain those are not the right words.

I watch, enraptured by his process, when suddenly he turns, banging his hip into an open drawer.

"Fuck," he mutters, slamming the drawer. My lips press together to stifle the laugh that's threatening to burst out.

"Hi," I say, deciding to let my presence be known.

He looks up from where he's slicing a parsnip.

"Hey, Princess."

His eyes are on me, but his hands are still working.

"Fuck." He lifts his finger from where it made contact with the knife blade.

"Oh, no." I rush toward him to assess the damage. His fingertip is red, blood starting to flow from the cut. "Sit down. I'll grab the first aid kit."

I rush back to the kitchen with the kit. Rhys isn't sitting like I instructed.

"You need to sit down. You'll get lightheaded," I warn.

"That was a thing when we were kids, I'm good now."

He removes the paper towel I wrapped around it. It's soaked with blood.

I can see the moment he's not good. His face pales and his eyes go glossy.

"Easy." I reach out to stop his fall. He's a big guy so my goal is to at least make sure he doesn't hit his head. He slinks to the floor, his back against the kitchen cabinets.

I wrap a clean towel around his finger, absorbing more blood before I put on the antibiotic cream and band-aid.

"Am I going to live?" Rhys teases, his color coming back.

"It's a small cut but sometimes those are the worst bleeders."

"Yeah, I think my pride is more wounded than my finger."

"Well, I think it was a good thing my knives are sharp, otherwise you might have needed stitches." I press a kiss to his lips. "I thought we were going out."

Even as I mention it, my body revolts at the idea of washing my hair and getting dressed to be in public. To be on display.

"I figured you'd be tired, so I was cooking for us."

"Really? I love that."

"I wanted to do something nice for you." He lifts his bandaged finger up. "I guess I'm not doing a very good job."

"This is nice."

"You playing nurse while the food gets cold?"

"You being here when I got home, but I wasn't expecting you to cook."

"I thought about all the places I could take you on our first date. All the fancy restaurants and exclusive lounges." As he talks, I slide into his lap, letting my hand wander under the collar of his shirt. "But there's nowhere I rather be than cuddled up on the couch at home with you." Maxine saunters over and puts her paw on Rhys. "Do you need some attention, too?"

She meows which clearly means yes, so we give her some love, too. A loud beep starts going off.

"I've got to get that. You want to shower before dinner?"

"I'll do it after. If I stand in a hot shower before I eat something, I'll probably pass out. Unless you think I smell and will be too disturbed by it to eat dinner?"

He lifts my arms over my head, gathering them with his hands as he leans down to smell my armpit.

"Okay, I wasn't expecting you to really get in there. I thought a general area sniff would be sufficient."

"I love how you smell. Even when you're sweaty and fresh from practice. I think it's pheromones or something."

"Great, so you're clearly not the person to ask if I suspect I have body odor."

He smirks, then swats my butt. "Go sit down."

I lift my brows in challenge, but ultimately follow his instruction. "See, this is how you do it. When someone asks you to sit down, you listen."

"You're such a good girl, Lettie. Following directions." He leans close, his lips pressing against the shell of my ear. "That'll come in handy later when I tell you to sit on my cock."

The temperature of my blood spikes at his comment. Forget food, forget the shower, my body has other needs. But then I realize I'll probably pass out during sex if I don't eat and that doesn't sound appealing, so I keep my priorities straight.

On my way to the table, I pass by the living room and notice the tulle for the tutus is pulled out.

"Did the cats do this?" I ask, but then I notice that there are a few tutus completed and one that is halfway done.

"Oh, shit. I forgot to put that away. I got distracted making dinner."

"You came over early to make tutus?" I ask.

"I figured with evaluations coming up, your schedule would get even more intense, so I wanted to help."

I'm floored. I can't believe he came over early and started making tutus.

"Thank you. That's so sweet."

Rhys shrugs. "It's nothing," he distractedly answers, while plating our dinner.

He moves to the table, setting the plated food on the placemats he's arranged there.

I can't help wrapping my arms around his waist and snuggling against his back.

"You say it's nothing, but to me, it's everything."

He looks over his shoulder at me, smiling.

"Don't tell anyone, it'll ruin my image."

I smile against his back, because I don't think the image he created for himself was ever truly him. This is who Rhys is.

"I don't have much experience but you're really knocking this boyfriend thing out of the park."

"Boyfriend?" His tone is all teasing. "Let's not get ahead of ourselves, Princess, it's only the first date."

"I've already got the ring," I wiggle my left hand in front of him, "so if anyone is getting ahead of themselves, it would be you." The engagement ring is too large to wear during practice but I always put it on right after.

"Touché."

He unwraps my arms from around his waist so he can turn and draw me in for a quick kiss. Then, he pulls out my chair so I can sit down.

My eyes drop to the plate. It's turkey meatloaf. The way my mom makes it in silicone muffin liners which are the perfect size for portioning out leftovers throughout the week. That means he called my mom and got the recipe. I stare at him, even more fascinated by this man.

He sits down across from me and sets his napkin in lap.

"Acts of service. It's your love language."

It is? Did I know that?

Rhys could buy me anything I want. He told me that, but it didn't hold much appeal. While I do enjoy nice things, having people around me that love and support me, and show that by lightening the load when I'm stressed, is what really fills my cup.

I dip a forkful of the turkey meatloaf into the cauliflower mashed potatoes, because the combo of them together is what makes it tasty, then take a bite.

Delicious. It's so good I make a little humming noise around it as I chew.

"Is it okay?" he asks, eyes watching me closely.

"It's delicious. Thank you for cooking."

"You're welcome. I actually kind of enjoyed it. Until the finger slicing incident. And the task wasn't as challenging with Taylor keeping me company."

"Should I be jealous?" I tease. "Of Taylor?"

"Nah, I prefer brunettes." He winks while he takes another bite of food.

"So, back to love languages. I should know yours."

His lips twitch knowingly. "I'm sure you can guess it."

"Let's see, what are the options? Acts of service, gift giving, words of affirmation. What else?"

"Quality time and physical touch," he adds.

He's right. I do know his.

"I'm going to go out on a limb here and say physical touch."

His grin is wide. "You know me so well."

I laugh because I do and being with him is easy. It's our first date but we're far from strangers.

I want to keep things light and easy, but I'm also curious how my mom sounded when he talked to her.

My dad has officially moved out. And even though I know this is what they both want, my mom mentioned it was starting to sink in and she was feeling lonely.

"When you called my mom, how was she?" I ask.

"She was good. Happy that I was cooking for you. That you were being taken care of."

I set my fork down, my appetite fading when I think about my parents.

"I'd love for my parents to be together and everything be good, like it has been my entire life, but they're not happy. I can't fault them for that."

"Even if you want the best for them, it still sucks."

"Yeah, it does." I scoop some mashed cauliflower onto my fork and lick it. "I'm sorry. This conversation is depressing."

Rhys reaches for my hand on the table. "It's what's going on in your life, Lettie. And I want to hear about it."

I squeeze his hand. "Thank you."

"Are you done?" he asks.

"Yeah, it was so good, I just can't eat anymore."

"I'll pack it up so you can have leftovers."

"You know how much I love leftovers."

"Why don't you go shower, and I'll clean up the kitchen?"

I smile. "You clean, too? Fascinating."

His cheeks turn rosy, a sheepish smile on his face. "I was going to have Ramsey arrange a cleaning service to come. Does that count?"

I roll my eyes. "I know what those hands are capable of. You can scrub a pan."

"That's true, but it's more fun to annoy Ramsey. He's out on a date with Sebastian right now, so I have to mess with him."

I grab his phone. "Do not call him right now."

When I look down at the screen saver, it's a picture of us. One that he took of us at Lake George, by the water. I'd expected him to share it on social media. To keep putting our time together on display for the world, but I haven't seen him post this one. It's candid, less posed than some of the ones we've taken. I'm all smiles, looking at the camera, but Rhys is looking at me.

"My favorite photo."

"From the weekend?" I ask.

"Of us."

"Why didn't you post it?"

"It was special. I wanted to keep it for myself."

"Will you send it to me?" I ask.

"Yeah." He kisses my forehead before taking his phone from me. "Now go shower."

"Are you sure?" I ask, glancing at the mess that is my kitchen.

"Yeah, I'll be in shortly."

I stand under the hot water so long, letting it soothe my tired muscles, that it starts to turn cool.

When I get out, Rhys is there with a fluffy towel. His hungry eyes devour my naked body before he wraps the towel around me.

He kisses my jaw. "You tired? Want to go straight to bed?"

It's sweet that he's asking. I might have had a different answer an hour ago, when the weight of the day and heavy thoughts about my parents surfaced, but him being here and making dinner, along with the hot shower...now, I'm a different woman.

I shake my head because there's no way I can sleep with this desire crackling between us. I need to feel him inside me. It's what I want all the time now.

He picks me up in his arms and carries me to the bedroom.

After sitting me down on the bed, he reaches for the back of his shirt and pulls it off in one quick motion. Seeing him standing there shirtless, the muscles of his torso deeply contoured by the shadows in the dimly lit room, his black-inked arm, and the bulge that's threatening to tunnel its way out of his pants.

My pussy aches just looking at him.

I drop the towel and reach for his belt.

"You're so beautiful." His hands hold my face as he places a demanding kiss on my lips.

That's when I get an idea.

I look up at him, eyelashes fluttering.

"I've never done this on a first date before. Will you still want me in the morning?"

I kind of enjoy messing with him.

His smile stretches, eyes lighting with understanding. *It's fun to pretend.*

He drops between my legs, his thumb making contact with my clit. My hips automatically rock forward, seeking out more contact.

"I'll still want you, baby. In fact, I'm going to hold you all night. And in the morning, when your pussy is all hot and slick from my cum, and your ass is rubbing against me, I'm going to rock into you from behind and make you come so fucking hard. Then, I'll get up and mix up that green sludge you like to drink. And I'll cut up a banana for your granola."

He dips a finger inside me, and my core clenches.

"Ahh," I cry out, "you're really good at first dates."

"You make it easy. I want to be good for you."

His tongue swipes up my center, and he adds another finger. He strokes in and out until the waves of my orgasm crash over me.

"Now, get my cock out, Princess. And I'll show you how to ride it."

And like the good girl I am, I do.

CHAPTER 55

Rhys

There's a sense of déjà vu when I walk into the wedding reception venue for Hunter and Sophie. It's another elaborately decorated ballroom overflowing with white flowers and huge white lanterns hanging from the ceiling, but when I look down at Lettie on my arm, it's in complete contrast to two months earlier when I showed up alone to Hannah and James's wedding. An overwhelming sense of happiness fills my chest.

"Congratulations!" Lettie wraps her arms around Sophie, who is beaming in a fitted white gown.

Hunter pulls me in for a hug. "You're next, man."

It's easy to think that this could be me and Lettie. That we could have a real engagement, and get married. Per Lettie's specifications, it will be somewhere on a beach, but that's fine with me.

The evening is perfect. Delicious food. Slow dancing with Lettie in my arms. Watching Hunter cry when he toasts his bride. I'm hanging with the guys near the bar when I get a notification on my phone. It's a text from Ramsey with an article attached.

Ramsey: *Giving you a heads up. This just came out.*

I open the attachment on my phone to find an article revealing my anonymous donation to Leg-Up. Included is a picture of me and Lettie at the Leg-Up community day. But it's the title that twists everything and makes my stomach sink.

Billionaire Funds Dancer Girlfriend's Passion Project

First off, Lettie's my fiancée, so clearly no one fact-checked this bullshit. Second, they're having it sound like she asked me to make the donation, which is flat wrong. And as an anonymous donor, I'm fucking angry my information was leaked. To make matters worse, it's shit timing with this happening when we're here at Sophie and Hunter's wedding.

My eyes lift from my phone.

While Lettie normally isn't attached to her phone, she is currently across the room taking a selfie with Sophie, Chloe, Hannah, and Emma. I've learned my lesson from the proposal, I need to talk to her before she sees the article.

On my way across the room, I keep my eyes on her. The way she's packed into the frame with her girlfriends, smiling with uninhibited joy, then a moment later laughing at something on the screen when Hannah hands her back the phone. I watch her tap her phone screen, and her eyes narrow, before the corners of her mouth slowly fall. She keeps her gaze on the screen, and the second I reach her, I know I'm too late.

Someone already sent her the article.

Lettie stares at me for a beat, those beautiful blue eyes filled with confusion, then without a word, she takes my hand. Pulling me along behind her, she exits the ballroom, marches us down the venue's plush carpeted corridor, then pushes through the door to what looks like a women's lounge, locking the door behind us.

She leans against the door, watching me. I stuff my hands in my pockets, then take a breath.

"Lettie—"

"You're the anonymous donor for Leg-Up." I'm relieved

that the words don't come out accusingly. It's more like she's fitting pieces of a puzzle together and surprised that they align. "Why didn't you—" she cuts herself off, her face lighting with understanding. "You didn't want me to think you were doing it because of our fake relationship, or so I'd forgive you for your proposal."

I nod. "I made the donation before I proposed, but yeah, I needed you to forgive me because you wanted to, not because I was generous with Leg-Up. I want to give you everything and when I realized helping Leg-Up was part of your dream, it became mine, too."

For once I can't read her face.

"Are you upset?" I ask.

She shakes her head. "No, I'm incredibly turned on." That's all she says before she pulls me down and kisses me hard.

"I'm happy you're not mad," I say, between kisses, gripping her hips to grind her pelvis against mine. I start gathering the material from her dress until I make contact with her silky thighs beneath.

"I'm not mad." She sighs into my mouth. "But I will be if you stop touching me."

"Where are we? What room is this?" I pull back to look around.

"It's a changing room for the bridal party. I came in here earlier with Hannah and Sophie."

My hand teases beneath her dress, fingers gripping the flesh of her ass, needing to feel her.

"I bet you're good and wet for me right now, aren't you, Princess?"

A single finger sweeps through her slick flesh and I have my answer. So fucking wet.

"I bet my cum is still dripping out of you."

Distracted by each other in the shower earlier, we'd almost been late to the ceremony.

I lower to my knees, taking the scrap of her lacy underwear with me.

"I want to see it."

"Rhys." It's a sigh, an expletive, and an approval all in one word.

I smile up at her. "Yeah, Princess?"

"We're at Hunter and Sophie's wedding."

"I know. I can't think of a better place to lick you."

I spread her with my thumbs, then my tongue dips inside her. It's like tasting a delicacy. The sweetness of her pussy and the saltiness of my cum complement each other perfectly.

"*Fuck*, baby. We taste so good together."

A breathy sigh escapes her throat, and her legs start to shake around my head.

I could die right here a happy man.

"Don't—don't stop."

It's like she heard my thoughts and is concerned I'll perish before she finishes. I smile against her pussy, then plunge two fingers inside her.

"More. I need more." She moans.

"Tell me what you want, baby."

"Your cock. I need it."

She's shaking with need, so I know not to argue with her. I look around again and spot a chaise lounge in the corner of the room. Extracting my fingers, I pull her over to it. Her feverish hands unbuckle my belt while I remove my suit jacket. I yank her dress up, and spin her around so she's sitting in my lap. Holding my cock at her entrance, I wrap an arm around her waist to hold her in place as I sink into her.

My eyes fall closed, as I focus on how unbelievable it feels to be inside her. Every. Damn. Time.

We both let out a satisfied groan as her arousal coats me fully, and I'm able to press in deeper.

This position isn't my favorite, which seems ridiculous because any position when I'm inside Lettie is a fucking joy, but it's because I can't see her face. But I know she loves it because my piercing finds the most sensitive place inside her.

Other than that article being circulated, apparently luck is on my side. There's a full-length mirror I didn't see before positioned perfectly across from the chaise. My gaze drops to where I'm filling her.

"Look at that, Princess." She lifts her head to find my eyes in the mirror. "Look at how perfectly we fit together."

"Oh, god." She takes in a shaky breath. *Rhys, Rhys, Rhys,* she chants, telling me she's close. And fuck, I love hearing her say my name when she's about to go over the edge.

I slip my hand down to her clit and give it a few strokes before she tenses around me. Her muscles milk my cock, pulling me in deeper, and a moment later I pulse my release inside her.

She leans back into my chest, and her hand cups my cheek.

"Rhys?"

"Yeah, Princess?"

"How do you know if you're addicted to sex? I'm starting to become concerned that I can't control myself when you're around."

She lets out an airy laugh to tell me she's not really concerned but dealing with the feelings of being physically intimate in a relationship for the first time.

I smile and turn my head to press a kiss into her palm.

"Same, baby. Same."

CHAPTER 56

Colette

After a relaxing weekend, evaluation week is finally here. During the evaluation period, Alexei and his assistant choreographer, Aszure, attend the company's morning class each day to observe us. It's a way for them to get insight into where dancers are after the break and observe the new trainees that have been asked to attend company class.

Outside of my time spent with Sebastian working on our showcase routine, I've been training and practicing alone. The energy with everyone back in the same room is what I missed the most.

The past two days, we've spent six hours, with a one-hour lunch break in the middle, learning various elements of choreography for the pieces that will be performed for the fall session. While I was able to practice and train for certain elements that I imagined might be a part of the performance or sequences that I personally felt needed work, no one can ever predict what the choreography will be. That's what makes these days grueling, but also fun.

After today's lunch break, we'll be doing the final practice in which Alexei, Aszure, and the company's artistic director,

Susan, will be observing us for the last time before decisions are made.

Right now, Isabella, Sebastian, Dimitri, and I find a shady bench outside to eat our lunch and let our bodies rest before the final practice. With Dimitri's absence during the break, we've had to fill him in on what has happened between me and Rhys.

He didn't question the quick timeline at all. He simply said you know when you know. I also have the growing suspicion that after Isabella visited him in Greece, they have a romantic thing going on now.

I watch closely as Isabella moves closer to Dimitri on the bench, and he discreetly, but clearly to my prying eyes, drops a kiss to her bare, sun-kissed shoulder.

I pull out the mixed greens, chicken, and sweet potatoes that Rhys helped me prepare last night.

"That looks delicious." Sebastian points at my food with his fork.

"Rhys made it," I say.

"A gorgeous billionaire fiancé that cooks?" Sebastian fans himself. "I'd be jealous if I wasn't already falling for his quirky and boyishly handsome assistant."

Isabella wiggles her brows. "So, what you're saying is he has more skills than just in the bedroom."

I smirk. "Rhys has a lot of hidden talents."

I smile at how Rhys has become a good cook, but also have to laugh at how messy everything is while he's making a meal. We've learned I'm a clean as you go person, while he lets everything in the kitchen become complete chaos, in my opinion, then cleans it all up at the end.

"How was Greece?" I ask Isabella and Dimitri.

"So much fun." Isabella grins. "We should all go next year."

As he eats, Dimitri's hand squeezes Isabella's thigh affectionately. There's an ease to their affection. It seems like the most natural thing in the world. Yup, there's something happening there.

Isabella's face lights up even more. "Maybe you and Rhys can get married there."

"Put it on the list," Sebastian says.

"Wait. There's a list?" I ask.

"Ramsey and I have started planning."

All I can do is laugh. Both Ramsey and Sebastian know our engagement is fake, so I'm not sure why they're starting to plan a wedding.

The conversation moves to what we did over the weekend. Isabella and Dimitri went to a friend's birthday party, while Sebastian and Ramsey had a relaxing weekend at home.

"You and Rhys were at a wedding, right?" Isabella asks.

"Yeah, Hunter and Sophie got married, and it was a blast."

As I eat another bite of chicken and mixed greens, I recall Hunter and Sophie's wedding. Rhys and I had the best time celebrating. It reminded me of how everything between us had started at Hannah's wedding, but it was even more fun dancing with him this time knowing we were together.

When the news of his donation to Leg-Up was revealed, I'd been shocked. Rhys is wealthy, so it makes sense that he would be able to give such a generous donation, but what had surprised me more was that he hadn't told me. That he was happy to give the money because it made me happy, not because he would get credit for it.

With his grandfather in attendance, he refused to wear a more colorful suit, and instead opted for a dark blue one, yet he had no problem going down on me in the bride's lounge. I told him it didn't make sense but he assured me he had his priorities straight.

We finish our light lunch, because nobody wants to finish evaluations with an overly full stomach, then pack up our things and return to the practice studio.

Before we take the floor, Isabella squeezes my arm. "You're going to do great."

"Thanks." I embrace her. "I know you will, too."

Sebastian twists his torso, his nervous energy making him restless.

That's the moment I realize I'm not as nervous as I thought I'd be. A little bit of nerves is healthy, it's motivating, but most of the session evaluations before today I was constantly second-guessing myself, getting in my head and not letting my dancing speak for itself. Everything was wrapped up in this one moment. Who I was, what my future was going to be. It's important to be prepared, but I was so far past that I was burnt out with training because the fear of not having the right role and getting promoted to principal was all I had.

But that's not true anymore.

Now there's Rhys, who I'm completely falling in love with. Through book club I've gotten to know Chloe, Emma, and Sophie better. This summer, I've become closer with Isabella and Sebastian. Speaking of Sebastian, he and Ramsey are hot and heavy now, and it's honestly the most fun to go out on double dates with them. My students at Leg-Up are everything and I'll continue to volunteer my time there as long as they'll have me.

And I've learned that while I love to dance, sometimes keeping a passion for something involves taking a break from it so you rest and recharge, and be excited to do it again. I don't want to treat my career like a list of items to check off.

While I'll always be a committed dancer and give one hundred percent effort, there is life outside of dancing. And that makes this moment less stressful.

We spend fifteen minutes warming up, then move into the sequences we've been working on this week. It's not an audition with a certain starting and stopping point, but more of a fluid observation.

As I move through the routine, I forget about the director watching. I forget all about Alexei and his comments earlier this summer, and I simply feel the dance. The heartbreak of my parents' pending divorce, the thrill of falling in love with Rhys, because no matter which way I try to spin it, that's what is happening, and with all of that comes passion and desire and heartbreak, and a million other emotions.

Before I know it, we've performed all the pieces and Alexei dismisses us for the day.

"Thank you, dancers. We'll have a decision for you shortly."

No matter what happens today, whether I land the lead role in *Rubies* or not, I know I gave it everything I have.

CHAPTER 57

Rhys

I'm on the phone with Sandeep when Colette bursts through the door.

When she hears Sandeep talking, her mouth makes an O shape as she realizes I'm on the phone.

She starts to quietly tiptoe by me, but I motion for her to stay. It's her apartment after all. I don't want her to feel unwelcome.

It's a reminder that we need a bigger place. We've been mostly staying at Lettie's apartment because the cats are more comfortable here, and honestly, so am I. I want to be wherever she is, but we need more space. I make a mental note to call Hunter when he gets back from his honeymoon.

While my brain is trying to focus on finishing my call with Sandeep, my eyes eat up Lettie in a flowy wrap skirt and cropped tank top that reveals a sliver of her midriff. Those sapphire eyes of hers are wide, and she's bouncing on her toes in her ballet flats.

"Hey, Sandeep, Colette just walked in. I'm going to have to call you back."

"Sure. We'll talk more next week."

"Sounds good."

The moment I hang up, Lettie's launching herself into my arms.

"I got it!" she exclaims, breathless with excitement. "I landed the lead role in *Rubies*!"

"Congratulations, baby." My voice comes out huskier than I planned, emotion in my throat making it difficult to speak. Her arms wrap around my neck, followed by her familiar scent. Holding her against my body, a feeling of contentment washes over me.

She did it.

Is this what it's like? Hearing the other person's good news makes me just as happy as they are. Not wanting to pull back from our embrace, I press my lips to her temple. "That's amazing news."

"I still can't believe it." She sighs, her body still clinging to mine.

"You deserve it, Lettie. You're so talented, and you've been working so fucking hard for this."

"Thank you," she whispers against my neck. "For everything."

She doesn't owe me gratitude. She did all the hard work, but I greedily accept her words anyway.

"What did your mom say? And Hannah? Did she lose her mind when you told her?"

"I haven't told them yet. I came straight to see you."

It's a good thing her head is still tucked into my neck, so she can't see my eyes turn glassy. She found out the biggest news of her career, and she came straight to see me. *What is this woman doing to me?*

I quickly realize I'd do the same with her.

I clear my throat, and once I know my emotions are at bay, I set her on her feet and pull back to look her in the eyes.

"We have to celebrate. What do you want to do?" I ask.

"Hmm, good question." Her eyes drop to my crotch, and

when they lift to meet mine again, they're filled with desire. "I was thinking I could suck your dick?"

I can't help the exasperated chuckle that escapes my chest. Lettie just accomplished a career milestone. She's earned the lead role in the fall session performance and from what I know of the inner workings of her ballet company, principal dancer is most likely to follow, yet the reward she wants for all her hard work is to give me pleasure? Make it make sense.

"That's what you want to do to celebrate?" I ask.

"Well, that, and maybe a nice dinner out?"

I shake my head, still confused this is what she's asking for. "Why do you want to suck my cock?"

"Well, you haven't let me since the night you proposed and that was barely even a taste. Is there a reason you don't like it?" Suddenly, her eyes widen. "Oh my god. Am I bad at it? Did I use my teeth? Are you afraid I'm going to bite your dick?"

I chuckle. "No, it was the best twenty-second blow job of my life."

Her lips press together in a pout. "Then why are you against it?"

"Honestly?" I ask.

She nods and makes a waving motion with her hand. "Give it to me. I can take it."

I chuckle, not sure if she's talking about my honesty or my dick.

My hand drops from her jaw to her neck. I squeeze her lightly there.

"I don't like giving up control. It's a vulnerable position to be in."

"Right. You should remember that every time you put your head between my legs." Her brows lift knowingly.

"Do you want me to stop fucking you with my tongue?" I ask.

She shakes her head. "Of course not."

"Good, because I love it. I couldn't stop even if it was going to kill me."

"I guess it's a good thing eating me out isn't a direct threat to your health." She smirks.

I want to give her everything she asks for, but if I'm not careful, I could easily let all my defenses slip away with this woman.

Haven't I already?

We're quiet for a moment, my thumb dancing over her throat while her fingers explore my waistband.

Her face lights up. "Maybe you could use me. Bind my hands and fuck my mouth. That would keep you in control." She smiles, satisfied that she's found the solution.

It's a scenario from the book she read for Chloe's book club.

My brows knit at her eagerness to please me. I don't deserve her. "Jesus, Lettie. When you say it like that, it makes me sound like a real asshole."

She shrugs. "I mean, you can be."

"Thanks," I say, sardonically.

"Everyone can be. It doesn't mean you're a bad person, right? We all have quirks and preferences that may seem odd to others, but that doesn't make it *wrong*." Her hand lowers to stroke me over my pants. "It kind of turns me on that you like to be in control."

"Yeah?" My thumb slides over her pulse. Beneath my finger pad, it's thrumming with anticipation.

She nods, pushing my free hand below the hem of her skirt. When my fingers hook into her panties, I find her pussy dripping wet.

I stifle a groan that only becomes more challenging to hold onto when Lettie leans forward and kisses my neck, her tongue following in a soft sweep.

"Please, Rhys?"

How can I not want this woman on her knees for me?

Wanting her lips around my cock isn't the problem. It's allowing myself to let go. To trust someone else. *To trust myself.*

But isn't that what I've been doing with Lettie all along? I've fucked a lot of things up, but ultimately, we've built a real relationship, with honesty and trust.

Her big, pleading blue eyes search mine and my defenses easily crumble.

My groan is half-hearted when I reply, "Why can't I say no to you?"

Because I love her.

I love this woman. I expected that rush of emotion to feel complicated, but nothing has ever felt simpler. But I'm not ready to tell her. While the awareness of loving Lettie has been slowly seeping into my bones, it's still too delicate to share with her yet.

At my affirmation, Lettie smiles with such elation, you'd think I'd solved the hunger crisis and created world peace, not told her she can get on her knees and suck my cock.

Once I'm settled in the chair, Lettie kneels between my legs and unbuckles my belt. I've been hard since she walked in the door, but the sight of her there, on her knees, the way her tongue darts out to wet her lips, has my cock throbbing. By the time she's got me in her hand, there's precum leaking from my tip.

She strokes me, her thumb circling my crown before teasing below to the sensitive ridge above my piercing.

"Does that feel good?" she asks.

"Everything you do feels good."

Her eyes lift to mine. She's looking for approval, making sure I'm good with her continuing. I nod, and she lowers her mouth.

The warmth of her breath teases me before the slide of her tongue has me lifting my hips. I remember how perfect she looked the night of our engagement. A little tipsy, a lot angry.

How she channeled her rage and desire into testing me. Now, she's all soft eyes and sweet mouth and I'm going to fucking come before she even gets me in her mouth.

"Oh, should I put my hair up?" she asks.

I thread my fingers through her soft hair, gathering the dark strands into my fist and giving it a playful tug. She smiles in approval.

"That works, too."

She offered to let me fuck her mouth, to have her hands bound, but the reality is I want her touching me, *and* I want to be in control. I want my cake and I want to eat it, too.

I'm fascinated by her. The curious look on her face, almost like she's determining her plan of attack. She licks her lips, then swirls her tongue around my head before flicking my piercing with it.

My eyes roll to the back of my head. *Fuck.*

She's the one on her knees right now, but her sweet mouth and eagerness to please me are quickly bringing down all my defenses down.

Involuntarily my hips thrust and I press farther into her mouth.

She gags, but only looks more determined.

"I'm fine. I just need to warm up a little."

"Are you sure?" I ask. "I don't want to hurt you."

"I'm good. I promise."

Between my desire to protect her *and* fuck her mouth with wild abandon, I give her long, deep strokes. As she adjusts, the back of her throat opens, and she relaxes, taking me deeper.

"Look how pretty you are." I stroke her cheek. "Lips stretched; cheeks hollowed out."

Lettie hums around my cock.

"Are you touching yourself, Princess?"

She is. I can see her free arm moving, her hand working between her legs.

"I'm so fucking close." I close my eyes, then open them again. There's no difference. The blood rush to my dick is making me see stars.

"Okay. Give it to me." She licks around my crown before bobbing back down onto my shaft.

I pull my cock out of her swollen mouth.

"Hey," she pouts, "I wanted to try to swallow."

"Next time I'll paint your throat, but right now I want to fill up your pussy."

She's about to argue, but there's no time because I've already wrapped one forearm around her back and lifted her onto my lap. Pushing her panties aside, I thrust home into her perfectly sweet cunt.

She moans with pleasure, her walls clamping down hard on my cock.

This feeling, this connection with her, will never not amaze me.

"God damn, Princess. You spoil me with this tight pussy."

She's warm and slick, just like her mouth, but the primal need to fill her with my cum has become my obsession. I've never felt anything like it.

I've still got her hair wrapped around my hand. I use it to angle her head back so I can nip at her neck.

My teeth graze her collar bone and her startled gasp makes her pussy clench down tighter.

"Behave," she warns playfully. And I love her even more for it.

"That's impossible when you're riding my cock so well, Princess."

And she does. So fucking well.

Her movements aren't rushed or hurried. They're graceful, exactly like her. She takes her time lifting and lowering, letting my crown and the piercing beneath it nearly come all the way out before she rocks her hips, pulling my cock back inside her.

"I love how it feels when you spread me. I want it over and over." She lifts all the way up then a moment later, she slowly lowers down onto me again.

Fuck. If she keeps talking like that, it'll be impossible to last.

"I love that, too, baby." I grunt, trying to hold my shit together.

Letting her hair go, I pull her tank top off, then wrap my hands around her ribcage before lowering my mouth to feast on her tight nipples. With my tongue lashing at her nipples, her hands dig into my hair holding me to her, and she begins to pick up her rhythm. I slip one hand beneath her skirt and rub her clit over her panties. I can feel how soaked they are, how they're now stretched out to one side to make room for my cock.

I have to see it.

I lift her skirt and drop my gaze between her legs. It's one of the hottest things I've ever seen.

"I love that you're still wearing your panties while I'm balls deep inside you, Princess."

A whimper floats past her lips.

If there's one thing I know about my girl, she gets off on dirty talk.

"These pretty blue panties are ruined now, baby." I slide a finger underneath the edge of them and tease her clit, it's slick and swollen, and begging for my touch. "Soaked by your pussy. Stretched out by my cock."

Her muscles spasm around my length and I know her orgasm is right there.

"Is that something a good girl does? Lets me pull her panties aside so I can fuck her?" I pinch her clit between my fingers and she cries out.

"You're not a good girl, are you, Princess? You're a filthy fucking girl who loves getting railed by my cock."

"Oh, god. Rhys. Yes." She moans before she pulls my face

to hers and claims my mouth. Kissing Lettie is like breathing, exhilarating, and absolutely fucking necessary. Beneath all the heat and lust is so much more. Too much to verbalize, so I let our bodies do the talking.

You feel so fucking good.

I'll never get enough.

I'm in awe of you.

You're it for me.

"That's it, Princess. Come on my cock."

A moment later, she shatters around me, her cries muffled inside my mouth as she squeezes me so fucking tight, I'm gasping for breath. Then, I'm right there, too, my orgasm spilling deep inside her.

Lettie collapses into my chest, wrapping her arms tight around my neck.

It takes a moment to catch our breath. The skin beneath our clothes sticking with the sweat that has gathered there.

I stroke her back and soon our breathing evens out.

"Do you have any idea what you do to me?" I whisper, my voice husky and raw.

Lettie pulls back, then after studying my face for a moment, she kisses the corner of my mouth.

"Make you really horny?" She makes a silly face and we both laugh, but then I slide my thumb across her lips and she inhales.

"You make me happy." Through the opening of my button-down shirt, I place her hand against the left side of my chest, on top of the ink that covers the skin there, and I let her touch, gentle yet determined, ease the loneliness and heartache that have lived there for years.

CHAPTER 58

Colette

After we clean up, Rhys takes me to Nobu to celebrate me landing the lead role in *Rubies*.

We're tucked into a small table toward the back. Having worked our way through all my favorite dishes, Rhys orders a chocolate namelaka. It's so sinfully delicious, I eat it up. That, and it's fun to tease Rhys by licking the spoon suggestively.

When the waiter leaves our table, I find Rhys staring at me, a knowing smile on his lips.

He lifts his glass like he's about to give a toast, so I playfully snag the last bite of dessert.

"What?" I ask innocently, trying not to laugh. "I worked up an appetite earlier."

"Order anything you want. I like watching you eat."

"That could be interpreted in different ways, considering what happened before we got here."

I lick my lips seductively.

"You're right. To clarify, I love your mouth. I love the words and sounds that come out of it. And I love watching things go into it, whether that's food or my cock."

"Was that part of your toast?" I ask.

"No. You distracted me." His lips twitch. "Lettie, you are an amazing dancer, and most importantly a beautiful human inside and out. I'm so fucking proud of you, Princess."

"Thank you." I have to mouth the response because his words have brought tears to my eyes.

We clink glasses. Rhys takes a drink of his cocktail, then leans back into his chair, his eyes full of amusement as they dance over me.

"Now, what am I going to do with you?" he asks.

"Keep me forever," I tease, but Rhys's expression turns stoic, the playfulness from a moment ago gone.

Whoa, Lettie. Too much.

"We should talk about how to handle the engagement," he says.

"Oh, right." I nod, the pit in my stomach now making me regret my comment and that last bite of food.

"What were you—"

"Did you—"

We start at the same time. I laugh nervously, struggling to get the words out. Earlier, when he asked me how I wanted to celebrate tonight, I had no issue telling him I wanted to give him a blow job. But putting myself out there, letting him know about the very real feelings I have, is harder. But we promised to be honest with each other.

"I want—" I start again.

"I don't want this to end," Rhys rushes out before I can speak. He shakes his head. "Fuck. I'm bad at this." His eyes finally lift to meet mine. "I want you, Lettie. For real. These last few weeks of dating, real dating, have been the best. Any time I get to spend with you, I keep thinking how did I get so damn lucky? I want to keep doing this."

My heart is beating rapidly, but I give him a reassuring smile. "Same." My hand reaches for his under the table. His palm is warm, if not a bit clammy. While I hate showing my nerves, it's endearing to see Rhys's on display.

He's a confident rebel. A bad boy who tries to hide his soft side, but the more I've seen it, the more I know that's his true heart.

Like when I talked with Brittney last week about coming in for a visit now that the entire dance company is back from break, and she mentioned Rhys had come on his own a few weeks back. He'd brought friendship bracelets for all the children and spent hours hanging out and talking with them. The coolest thing? Like the Leg-Up donation, he didn't tell me about it. He did it because it felt good, not because he wanted me to know he did it.

That alone made me fall harder for him.

I know we have feelings for each other, that what is between us is real now. But I also don't want to rush things. Right now, I'm enjoying our time together. Dinners out, running in the park and soaking up the sunshine on his boat. Our quiet nights reading the next book club book on the couch with the cats snuggled up around us. And of course, the sex.

I love Rhys's dirty talk. I get off on it. But it's the combination of his playful delivery and gentle, yet commanding touch that makes sex so empowering. I'm curious about trying new things, and he's very supportive. Like the other day when I asked him about pegging, he only looked mildly terrified as he contemplated it before I burst into laughter and told him I was joking.

I will say, Chloe's romance book recommendations are opening my eyes to so many possibilities.

"Yeah? Okay, good." His smile is cocky, but I can see the relief in his eyes. "After the board votes, we don't have to pretend to be engaged. I know you didn't want to be. It was too soon and I don't want to rush us into that kind of commitment right now."

My eyes drop to the ring on my left hand. He's right. I thought his proposal was crazy at the time. This ring was too much, it still is, but I like what it means. That we belong to each other.

"Tonight's about celebrating you," he says. "We don't have to figure everything out right now."

I nod in agreement.

For the first time in my life, not knowing what the plan is gives me comfort.

CHAPTER 59

Rhys

Tonight, my grandfather and Edith are hosting a dinner for the foundation board members at their home. The board votes in two weeks, so it's likely the last time I'll see all the board members before then.

Unlike the evening of Corinne and Jerrod's dinner, I'm feeling confident tonight. Across the room, Lettie is talking with Aditi, Corinne, and Ayesha, Sandeep's wife.

I catch Lettie's eye and she winks.

I return it and raise her a huge fucking grin because I am in a fantastic mood tonight.

Sandeep hands me one of the Manhattans the bartender just made, then follows my gaze to Lettie. "Ah, young love. Looks like everything is going well for you two."

"Yeah, it's fucking great." The curse slips out before I can correct it. "Sorry, but yeah, I'm crazy about her."

He laughs. "You were right the first time. And there's nothing better than having a supportive partner by your side."

I know he's right. While Lettie's assured me that I would have found my footing with the board and proven myself to be a good fit for the president position even without her in my life, I know her support and encouragement have been key to my transformation.

She's across the room right now, but I still feel her calming presence like we're connected by an invisible string.

Two of the foundation board members, Keiko and Jason, walk over to join our conversation. After we catch up on everyone's weekend plans, I shift the conversation toward the business end of this evening.

"Has anyone had a chance to review the investment policy I sent over for the foundation?" I ask the group.

"I think the risks and asset allocation were refreshing. A different direction than what we've done in the past," Sandeep says.

Keiko nods in agreement. "I particularly thought the impact investments you outlined were interesting. Having The Spencer Foundation seek out companies that are in need of crossing a certain threshold before they can compete in the marketplace not only fulfills our charitable support but also boosts companies that are on the verge of technology and discovery to better the world."

"I couldn't have said it better myself." Jason agrees with Keiko. "Great work."

I'm ecstatic to hear their feedback. I've spent the last few weeks working on the investment policy guidelines I'd like to adopt as board president. Every free moment I've had, I've spent researching and catching up on current policy. I wanted to have something concrete to show the board, to prove that I don't just want to be the face of the foundation, but I'm here to do the work.

A hand squeezes my shoulder and I turn to find my grandfather beside me.

"Rhys, I need a word."

"Sure." I nod to the rest of the group. "Excuse me."

My eyes seek out Lettie's, but her back is to me now, so I follow him into his study where Jerrod is waiting for us. I've been able to avoid him most of the night, so my mood is soured the moment I see him leaning against the bookcase with his arms folded across his chest.

"What is it?" I ask, my voice laced with irritation. I can't help it. That's what Jerrod's mere presence does to me.

My grandfather leans against his desk. He's positioned himself between me and Jerrod like a referee. "It's been brought to my attention that you've made a substantial donation to Leg-Up, the community dance studio that Colette was fundraising for."

"Ten million dollars," Jerrod adds.

I want to roll my eyes. He's like a parrot on my grandfather's shoulder, chiming in and annoying the fuck out of me.

"It was supposed to be anonymous." My eyes flick to Jerrod. "But somehow my information was leaked."

His eyes hold mine for a beat before he blinks and looks away.

Mila, the director of Leg-Up, had been profusely apologetic when I talked to her about it this week, and assured me that all my financial information was confidential, but clearly someone on the Leg-Up board had dropped my name and it spread from there.

I glance back at my grandfather.

"The donor leak doesn't even matter now. So, what's the problem?" I ask.

"That's a large donation for such a small non-profit," Jerrod squawks from his perch. It's clear he's the instigator of this inquisition. That he brought this information to my grandfather, and my grandfather is doing his own due diligence. Making sure I haven't done something dishonest that would tarnish the Spencer name and make being voted in as board president a PR crisis.

My grandfather nods. "Was the donation an incentive for Colette to say yes to a proposal after only a month of dating?"

"No. We've known each other our whole lives. We were

friends. And now, we're more. Lettie had no idea I made the donation to Leg-Up. She was just as surprised as everyone else when my anonymous donation was leaked. And Leg-Up won't be small now. They've got funds for years of programming and maintenance. It's an organization that I'm passionate about as well as Lettie. I'm personally excited for them to explore some mobile programming that they can take to facilities outside the studio, like children's hospitals and activity centers that don't have dance programs."

Jerrod's eyes narrow at me. "This is an interesting turn of events. Rhys Spencer actually cares about other people? Shocking." His words drip with derision.

I take a step closer to Jerrod. "And it's an interesting coincidence that you and Corinne are friends with Diem Vega who's on Leg-Up's fundraising board."

His appearance, shoulders back, hands casually in his pockets, projects confidence, but upon closer inspection I see the distress in his eyes. That underneath his cool exterior, his nerves are frayed and he's losing control of the situation. He didn't anticipate I would be this much of a threat, but now that I am, he's worried. And all his digging into my finances and relationship with Lettie is his way of trying to take back the reins.

Jerrod steps forward to match my movement. "What are you accusing me of, Rhys?" he asks.

My brows lift in challenge. "What are you accusing me of, Jerrod?"

"Gentlemen." My grandfather raises his hands between us. "I'm all for a healthy competition but this is getting too heated." He looks to me, his eyes wary. "Is your relationship with Colette bogus?"

"It's not." I'm relieved I can answer truthfully.

"He bought her a house on Lake George," Jerrod argues.

"What the fuck, Jerrod?" I growl. Lettie doesn't even

know about the sale of her parents' lake house yet. I wanted to make sure it was a done deal before I told her about it.

"Language." My grandfather looks to me. "Is that true, Rhys?"

"Her parents were selling it as part of their divorce, and yes, I purchased it, but that has nothing to do with the foundation. It's my money and I'll spend it how I see fit."

Jerrod opens his mouth to speak, but my grandfather raises a finger to quiet him.

"I've seen positive changes in you, Rhys. These past few weeks, you've found your place with the foundation. The board is impressed."

His words make my chest expand. I suppress the grin that wants to escape and instead give a curt nod.

My grandfather turns to Jerrod. "Financial affairs are a private matter, so if something is not directly related to foundation business dealings, then it's not for discussion."

Jerrod opens his mouth to argue, but nothing comes out. His eyes flash to mine briefly and before he strides past me and out the door, I catch the look on his face. It's one that has matched the one in my mirror for the last five years.

Frustration, defeat, apathy.

Except I know Jerrod, and he doesn't sit well with those things. Unlike my tendency to withdraw, he will only dig deeper, push harder.

For the first time since this whole thing started, I wish we could fix things between us. That we could get to the root of the animosity and pluck it out like the rambling weed that it is. I want to be board president and I want to end this feud with Jerrod. I hope both are possible.

CHAPTER 60

Colette

After searching nearly every room in Ward and Edith's brownstone, I find Rhys on the third floor, a large open space that appears to be used as a sitting area and library. His large frame is spilling out of an overstuffed chair in the corner, a lowball glass, with an amber liquid and one large round ice cube in it, dangling from his fingers.

"There you are." I ascend the last step and move toward him.

"Here I am," he responds playfully, but I can hear the strain in his voice.

"I was beginning to think you left."

His eyes follow my movements, his gaze lifting as I draw closer.

"I wouldn't have. Not without you."

His response makes my heart soar. Is this what it's like to be in love? To have another person, *your person*, to depend on.

When I reach him, I step between his spread thighs, then reach to take the glass from his hand. He's still watching me, hazel eyes burning with curiosity.

I lift the glass and take a sip of the chilled spirit, my throat constricting as it burns its way down.

The liquor tingles the back of my throat and I can't help but cough.

He smirks. "Still not a fan?"

I shake my head.

"Are you okay?" I ask, setting the glass down on a nearby table, then slowly intwining my hands into his thick hair.

"Better now," he says, leaning forward, his hands wrapping around the backs of my thighs as he rests his chin against my chest to gaze up at me. The tease of his fingertips on my bare skin sends a shiver down my spine. I'm still fascinated by how quickly my body comes alive under his touch.

Rhys's hands explore me, rubbing my legs and caressing my ass before they settle at my front, dangerously close to where my panties are already damp.

While I'd love to feel those fingers dipping beneath my underwear, and I know he would welcome the distraction, there's a reason he's up here alone. My hands find his face, and I tilt his chin up until our eyes are connected again.

"I saw you leave with your grandfather earlier."

Rhys's jaw visibly tightens.

"Yeah, Jerrod accused us of faking our engagement. Saying the donation I made to Leg-Up was a way of compensating you for saying yes to my proposal."

I'm surprised, but also not. The engagement was originally fake, I guess it still is, but Rhys didn't even tell me about the Leg-Up donation, so it had no influence on my relationship with him. Fake or real.

"What did your grandfather say?" I ask.

"Ultimately, that we shouldn't be digging into each other's personal finances."

Rhys pulls me down until I'm sitting in his lap.

"Something like that was bound to happen. This whole thing was crazy, right? You and me, engaged. I'm surprised more people aren't calling us out."

His words bring awareness to the thrumming of my pulse.

"I don't think it's that surprising, is it?" I ask.

"The beautiful and talented Colette Davenport taking up with an unreliable guy like me?"

I can't tell if it's the whiskey or the conversation with Jerrod and his grandfather that have him second-guessing our relationship.

"We've already established you're not as much of a bad boy as you think you are."

"And you're not as much of a girl good as I thought." He slides his hand under my dress and grazes his thumb over the bite mark on my inner thigh. He gave it to me this morning when he ate me out in the shower, right before he bent me over the bench and fucked me from behind.

He's right. We're not the people we thought we were. Or we've grown together to be different, I'm not sure which is true.

"Your proposal was romantic and heartfelt. I don't know why people are questioning it."

The corner of his mouth lifts in a sexy smirk.

"Really? You were furious when I proposed."

One hand wraps behind his neck while my other hand toys with his collar.

"What can I say? You've grown on me."

He chuckles, then with his hands on either side of my face, he pulls me in for a kiss. In true Rhys fashion, he steals my breath. A minute later, when we finally come up for air, I slide my thumb along his lower lip to remove the lipstick color he now has there.

"This feels right."

"It's perfect."

CHAPTER 61

Colette

After a busy week of rehearsals for the lead role in *Rubies*, I'm ready to have fun and celebrate Rhys tonight.

His birthday party is being held at Brandy Library, a swanky Tribeca lounge that Sophie's friend, June, helped me plan.

I'm not dressed for the party yet. I was in the middle of trying on the lace crotchless bodysuit that I got as a birthday present for Rhys when I hear the front door click shut.

"Lettie?" Rhys calls out. Both cats leap off the bed to follow the sound of his voice. A moment later, I hear his footsteps moving toward the bedroom.

"In here!" I yell before scrambling into my closet, searching for something to throw over the lingerie. I'm dying to get Rhys's reaction, but I don't want to spoil the big reveal. I'm also incredibly turned on just wearing it and thinking about his response.

"Where are you?" His voice is closer now.

"The closet," I call. "Sit on the bed, I'll be right out."

There's a deep chuckle from the other side of the door, but it seems he's following my directions and not just yanking open the door to find me half naked.

I shove my arms through the silk robe and fasten the belt into a knot at my waist, then pull open the door. Sitting on the bed looking gorgeous in a dark gray suit, Rhys scans me from head to toe as I approach. The hunger in his eyes grows with every step.

He's got both cats snuggled up in his arms, but as I walk toward him, he gently sets them down on the floor.

"Happy birthday." I settle into his lap, wrapping my arms around his neck, before placing a sweet kiss on his mouth.

"Mmm. Is this my present?" he asks, rubbing his hands along my sides before gripping my hips over my silk robe. His nose runs along my jaw until his mouth is against the shell of my ear. "Because I'd like to unwrap it now."

He reaches for the robe tie, but I swat his hand away. "Not yet."

I grab the small wrapped box off my nightstand and present it to him.

"Here."

I watch him unwrap the paper, then flip open the box. My stomach flutters with nerves. Will he think they're silly?

"Cat cufflinks." His smile grows with the reveal, then he looks closer. "Wait, are these Maxine and Mo?"

"Yes, they're personalized. I sent in pictures and the artist designed them then made them into cufflinks. I figured you have the C necklace and when you wear these, too, it'll be like we're all with you."

"I love them, Princess." He presses a soft kiss to my lips. "They're perfect. Thank you."

I love you.

The words get caught in my throat. It's his birthday, and while he might like the sound of those words, I wouldn't want to put any pressure on him to say them back. And if he doesn't feel the same, then I'll be self-conscious all night. So, I hold onto them for another time.

With all the moving around, the knot on my robe has loosened. I move to tie it again, but Rhys catches my wrists. "Wait. Just one peek."

"Okay." I sigh, pretending like I'm not dying for him to touch me.

Rhys splits the robe apart.

"Fuck," he groans, running a palm over my lace-covered breasts. "You're so beautiful. You know you're torturing me, right? Showing me this and not letting me touch you until after the party."

"I never said you couldn't touch me *before* the party. I just wanted to give you your present first."

His brows lift, a sexy grin pulling at his lips.

"So, I can play with you right now?" he asks.

"I was hoping you would." I take his hand and guide it between my legs. "I'm so wet for you."

He bites his lip, groaning as his fingers tease me and I rock against his hand.

"No crotch? Christ, baby. You're going to kill me."

In one swift move, he's got my robe peeled off and my back is on the mattress.

"This little outfit of yours is extremely convenient." His large hands press my thighs apart, revealing me to him. Without any preamble, he drops his head and gives me one long lick up my center. "How do you get sweeter every time I taste you?"

It's a rhetorical question as he continues to flick my clit and tongue me hard, but my response is a breathy moan.

In a matter of minutes, I'm writhing against the bed, my legs quaking with the need to come.

Between my thighs, Rhys's head lifts to stare up at me. His gaze is drunk with lust and adoration, his lips already wet with my arousal. *Does he know what that does to me?*

When he drops his head again, I feel the sharp nip of his teeth against the sensitive skin of my inner thigh just as his fingers pump inside me.

"You like that, don't you, Princess? My sweet Lettie likes being marked with my mouth."

I sigh in response, feeling both incredibly turned on and in awe of how much he loves going down on me.

He massages my breasts, his fingers teasing my nipples through the lace, while his wicked tongue continues to fuck me.

I was so ready for him, it's not long before I'm riding out my orgasm against his face.

I'm still catching my breath when he lifts himself off the bed and starts to undress. I lie there recovering, my muscles relaxed and my body satiated, while piece by piece his suit is discarded. Somehow, I find the energy to prop myself up on my elbows to watch him. With each newly exposed section of skin, my heart rate starts to pick up again. There's something so sexy about the way he casually strips. Shirtless now, I watch fascinated as his biceps contract beneath the ink of his tattoo, causing some of the trees to be cast in shadow like a cloudy day at Lake George. His fingers unbuckle his belt and drop his zipper. Even the way his fingers deftly take off his watch is arousing.

He crawls over me, his hands and fingers exploring my hips, waist, and breasts along his journey.

"This is hot, baby. You look amazing in this. You should wear it every fucking day," he yanks at the thin straps, peeling them down my shoulders, "but right now, I need to see all of you."

Once he's discarded the lace onesie, he drops to his elbows and sucks one nipple into his mouth. He nips and teases me there, before making his way to my other nipple.

When I can't take it anymore, I beg. "Rhys, please. I need your cock."

"Yeah, Princess?" He kneels over me, stroking himself. "How badly do you need it?"

I lift myself up, and pressing my hands into his chest, I push him onto his back.

"This badly," I say, placing him at my entrance and lowering onto his shaft in one swift movement.

"Fuck, baby." A moan emanates from his chest, low and rich. "I love watching you take what you want, especially when it involves my cock."

His hands grip my hips, but he lets me set the rhythm. With my hands on his chest, I lean forward to grind my clit against the base of his cock.

"I'm so close." I pant. "Oh, god."

"Show me, Princess. I want to see that pretty O face." He presses his hand against my belly, and with the rock of my hips, everything tightens at once. A second later, my orgasm splinters through my body. Pleasure radiating from that sensitive bundle of nerves out to the farthest reach of my toes.

I've barely caught my breath when Rhys sits up, and keeping my legs wrapped around his hips, he drops his feet to the floor and holds me in his lap. His fingers trail down my back, making me shiver.

"I love this position because I can hold you and fuck you at the same time."

"And I love it because you can play with my ass while you're inside me."

We've been trying new things, and I like when he teases a fingertip inside my butt. When he first did it, I thought it was weird, but when I let him really explore the second time, I realized I liked it a lot.

Rhys reaches behind me and collecting wetness from where I'm dripping around his cock, he drags it backwards, lubing me up.

His teeth graze my neck, as he slips a single digit inside my back entrance. "I love that you're going to walk into the party tonight still dripping. No one's going to know how much my good girl likes to be filled with my cum."

He's right. I love the warmth of his orgasm releasing deep inside me.

"Would you ever let me fill this ass?" he asks, hooking his finger inside and giving me exactly what I need.

"Yes." I sigh as I rock against him, my clit throbbing with the need to come again. I want to try everything with Rhys. I want everything with this man.

He kisses me with such fervent desire, a moment later, my orgasm rips through me. I clench down hard, and with a primal groan, Rhys follows me over the edge, pulsing deep inside me.

We stay like that for a while. Kissing. Caressing. Basking in the afterglow of our intense orgasms.

Later, once I've cleaned up and put on a fresh pair of panties, I shimmy into my dress. Rhys steps behind me to zip me up. He's gorgeous in his baby blue suit and white dress shirt with the top buttons undone. If I look closely, I can almost see the dark edges of his tattoo. I'd comment that his hair looks like we just had sex, but it's the way it always looks, so there's no reason to bother with fixing it.

"Oh, I've got to run an errand before the party," I say, touching up my lipstick.

His arms wrap around my waist, then he presses a kiss to my neck.

"That's fine. I'll come with you."

"No can do. It's for your birthday. It's a surprise."

"Then I'll wait in the car."

I laugh. "Nope. This is not a negotiation."

He threatens to bite my shoulder, and my eyes go wide.

"That would not be a good idea for many reasons." I don't want him to get in the habit because performance costumes are typically revealing. I've already had to tell him to tone down the bite marks on my inner thighs. Pink tights are not good at covering things up, and makeup can only hide so much.

"Fine. I'm going." He squeezes my waist before he starts to back away. "To my birthday party. All alone. By myself."

I'm about to roll my eyes when he swoops back in. Wrapping an arm around my waist, he turns me to face him, and drops his forehead to mine.

"You make me happy."

My entire body bursts with joy. It's not a declaration of love, but it feels like a step toward it. Like it's Rhys's version of *I love you*.

"I can't wait to celebrate with you tonight." My hands wrap around his neck. "And you make me happy, too."

I press my lips to his, then give him a playful push toward the door.

"I'll meet you there."

"Okay. Text me when you're on our way," he says.

"I will."

With a final kiss, Rhys leaves and I finish getting ready.

CHAPTER 62

Rhys

When I arrive at Brandy Library, in Lower Manhattan, my birthday party is in full swing. Even though Lettie's rehearsal schedule has been intense over the past week, she still insisted on planning a party for me.

The venue is a classic gentleman's club with a modern twist, featuring mahogany woodwork and leather furnishings. Floor-to-ceiling bookshelves display the lounge's impressive collection of spirits and wines. There are even sliding ladders to access the top shelves.

"It's a library filled with bottles of cognac," Chloe announces. "I'm just now realizing why it's called Brandy Library."

Beside Sebastian, Ramsey laughs. "Did you think it was an actual library?"

Even in the dim lights, Chloe's face flushes pink. "I'll admit it crossed my mind. I mean, I would hold my birthday party in a library."

"It's got a great vibe." Emma takes a sip of her cocktail. "One of the brides I'm designing a dress for currently had some engagement photos taken here. They turned out amazing."

"You know what? We have been meaning to redecorate." Barrett wraps his arm around Chloe's waist. "This gives me an idea."

Chloe gasps. "Don't you dare."

I know Chloe is one of the assistant editors at St. Clair Press and as an avid reader, she would probably rather see books on these shelves.

"We have a beautiful library at home and not a single book on those shelves will be touched. Unless I'm simply moving them around like I do from time to time."

Barrett presses a kiss against her temple. "You know I would never change anything about your library, baby."

As Chloe and Barrett settle their dispute, Hannah and James join our group.

"Happy birthday, man." James nods in salute before raising his glass in my direction.

"Thanks." I nod, lifting my glass toward his.

"Where's Lettie?" Hannah asks, looking around.

I'd like to know the answer myself. I glance at my phone for the hundredth time since I got here.

"She had a last-minute errand to run. It's top-secret birthday stuff, I guess."

"How's it feel to be thirty?" Griffin asks, letting his hand settle on Emma's hip.

I shrug. "Pretty great. No complaints."

The moment I say it, I realize it's a water-downed version of what I'm feeling.

Life is fucking fantastic.

I'm surrounded by friends I truly enjoy. Good friends who don't care what's in my bank account or what party I can get them into. I'm feeling more positive about the foundation board's vote on Monday, and I'm in love with Lettie.

Why haven't I told her yet?

My eyes catch Hannah's and she must notice the change in my expression. "You okay?"

"Yeah, I'm good. I just realized I need to do something."

My phone buzzes. I pull it out of my pocket to reveal Princess lit up on the screen.

"Your ears must have been ringing," I answer with a smile.

"Rhys?" The woman sounds familiar, but it's not Lettie.

"Yeah. Who's this?" I ask.

"Rhys, it's Meredith, Colette's mom."

"Oh, hi. I thought the caller ID said it was Lettie calling." I pull the phone from my ear to check it again. Her name is there just like I put it in that first day with the tiara crown next to it.

"I'm using her phone. I left mine in the ambulance and they haven't located it yet."

My heart starts racing. "Ambulance? Are you okay?"

"I'm fine, but Lettie was in an accident."

Accident.

With one word, I'm taken back to a moment in time I've pushed to the far corners of my mind.

My chest collapses and I can't breathe. It's like someone has landed a punch right in my diaphragm and I'm wheezing.

As I attempt to recover from the emotional blow, the rest of the conversation is a blur, and I only hear bits and pieces.

"Rhys? Are you there?" Meredith asks, pulling me back to reality.

"Y-yeah. I'm here." I shake my head trying to focus.

"She's okay. A few bumps and bruises, and they're monitoring her for a concussion."

I manage to focus on Meredith's words long enough to hear which hospital she's at. Then I end the call.

"Lettie was in an accident," I say, numbly.

Gasps and murmurs surround me. Everyone talking at once.

Is she okay?

What can we do?

Do you need a ride?

"Let's go." Hannah doesn't wait for my response, probably because I'm unable to form words.

She says something to James, then grabs my arm. I follow her blindly through the party and out the front entrance.

Lettie was in an accident.

There's a black car waiting at the curb and Hannah ushers me inside.

"Which hospital?" she asks.

"Um," I blink trying to recall what Meredith had said. "Mount Sinai on Madison Avenue."

As we move down the street, this is one moment where I'd rather be behind the wheel. It would give me something to do other than imagine the worst.

She's okay. That's what Meredith had said.

Lettie's okay. My brain is trying to convince my body, but it's no use.

I look down at my hands. They're there, but I can't feel them. I ball them into fists and squeeze but there's no pressure. No sensation.

"Meredith said she's okay, right?" Hannah's voice is shaking. "Rhys?"

Hannah looks down at my hands, then back up to my face.

I see the worry there, but she must see something in my eyes that tells her I need her to be the strong one right now.

"She's going to be fine." She nods her head. "I'm sure of it."

I need to see Lettie. Then all this madness can stop. If I see her, everything will be fine.

At the hospital, we check in at the nurses' station, where we're sent upstairs to Lettie's room.

As we make our way down the hall, the sound of my shoes hitting the tile floor is thunderous to my ears.

The moment I see her there, sitting up in the hospital bed, relief washes over me and my heart starts to beat in a natural rhythm again. To the rhythm of us.

Lettie looks at me with a wobbly smile. She waves to Hannah, who's still at my side.

"Hi."

"Hey, baby." I rush to her, taking her hand between both of mine and rubbing my lips over her knuckles. "What happened?"

I know Meredith told me on the phone, but I wasn't listening. I couldn't focus, I just needed to get here. To see with my own eyes that she was okay.

"I tripped and fell backwards, hitting my head on a curb. I was pretty woozy so there was concern I had a concussion, but everything seems to be checking out okay. Just a few bumps and bruises."

Hannah goes to the other side of Lettie's bed to give her friend's hand a squeeze. "Holy shit. I was so scared and thinking the worst." She wraps her arms around Lettie, careful not to hug her too tight. "I'm so glad you're okay."

"We'll give you two a minute." Meredith guides Hannah out the door to give us privacy.

My eyes scan her from head to toe. I can't see any of her injuries. "Can I hold you? Where does it hurt?"

She nods slowly. "The back of my head has a huge goose egg. I have a few scrapes on my arms and legs from the concrete."

I press a kiss to her forehead. Her familiar scent, floral, sweet, and feminine, washes over me and my knees go weak. Reaching for the chair beside her bed, I keep hold of her hand as I pull the plastic seat close and drop into it.

I could have lost her today. I could have never felt her soft, warm skin or heard her soft snore as she fell asleep beside me. The thought has me spiraling. And knowing that I'd decided to wait to tell her how I feel, to say the words that are etched on my heart, only makes this moment feel more desperate.

Her eyes drop to my hand. It's shaking.

"Rhys, are you okay?" she asks.

Of course she's checking on me. She's sitting here in a hospital bed with a concussion and she's worried about me? I really don't deserve her, but I'm going to spend the rest of my life proving to her that I'm the man she needs.

"When I got the call, I lost it. Yes, it reminded me of the accident and losing my parents, but more than that, it made me realize I hadn't told you what you mean to me." Emotion has me choking on the words, but I persevere. "I love you, Lettie. I've wanted to tell you but thought it was too soon. Now, I realize that was so fucking stupid. It's never too soon to tell someone how you feel about them."

Her smile brightens, but her eyes stay heavy.

"Are you going to remember this?"

"Of course. When the man I've fallen in love with tells me he feels the same way, it's not something I'll forget."

"You love me?" I ask.

She nods, but then her lower lip starts to tremble.

"What is it, Princess?" I ask, tucking a strand of hair behind her ear. A strand of dark hair that has something sticky and white in it.

"I never made it to your birthday party. And I dropped your cake."

I don't care about the first part, only that she's okay. But the last part makes me smile. "You got me a cake?"

She nods. "It got ruined when I fell."

I wipe a tear that has fallen down her cheek. "How did it happen?"

"A photographer was following me, taking photos, and asking me questions. I was trying to get away, but with the large cake box, I couldn't see and I stepped off the curb too soon and nearly got hit by a biker. The biker swerved and didn't hit me, but I tripped backwards and hit my head on the curb. And the cake went everywhere." She picks up another sticky strand of hair. "It was a really good cake, too. It was Taylor Swift inspired, and pink with lots of edible glitter. The bakery was charging one hundred dollars for delivery, so I went to pick it up."

Hearing what happened to Lettie, knowing a photographer was involved makes my stomach turn sour. And knowing I could have been there to prevent it has my adrenaline spiking. I can't be mad at her, but beneath the surface of my skin, my blood is raging hot lava.

"Now's maybe not the best time to address this so we'll follow up later, but just so you're aware, in the future, I'll be covering all delivery fees. For anything you want, any time you want it."

She nods in understanding.

After the nurse gives us an update on when Lettie can be discharged, Hannah sits with Lettie while Meredith leaves to get her some clothes to change into. All she has right now is a hospital gown and the dress she was wearing for my party.

"Where are you going?" Lettie asks.

"To get you some trail mix and then I'm going to track down and beat within an inch of his life the photographer who caused this."

"Rhys!" she calls. "You can't do that."

I turn and give her a smile. "Kidding!" But I'm not.

I take a minute outside her room with Ramsey, who I've already tasked with hiring security and having him find out what photographer went after Lettie.

Lettie's okay.

The physical response to the uncertainty of her condition has dissipated. I've held her in my arms and she is in all respects okay and going to heal. But there's still unease in my gut. A knot of apprehension that didn't lessen even after I had proof she wasn't badly hurt.

I'm walking out to the waiting room when I spot Jerrod rushing toward me. His typically smug face is filled with concern. It's almost shocking to see it there in regards to me.

He stops right in front of me, his stiff body language clear that he's uncertain how to proceed. "I came as soon as I heard."

I nod. "Thanks. Lettie's resting. There was a possibility of concussion, but tests are negative so far."

Jerrod nods slowly and looks away before settling his eyes back on mine.

"Listen, man, I didn't mean for any of this to happen."

I shake my head, words forming in my brain to assure him that it wasn't anything we could have controlled, but that's when I see it in his eyes. Guilt.

My eyes narrow. "What didn't you mean to happen?" I ask, my words even and measured, nothing like the hurricane of emotion that is threatening beneath the surface as I start to process Jerrod's words.

"I hired a photographer to follow you and then once you became involved, Colette as well. But the guy went rogue. Once the media outlets were clamoring for more information, more photos, I couldn't control him."

He registers my moment of understanding and takes a step back, but I'm quicker.

I don't think, I only react.

My hands grab his shoulders, pushing him back until he's up against the wall.

"It was never—" he starts, but my forearm across his neck cuts him off.

His fingers claw at my arm, but the adrenaline in my body from his confession is too much for him to contend with. The knowledge that Jerrod hired a photographer to follow me and Lettie, and that same photographer was the one that had her running when she got hurt tonight, has me seeing more than red. I'm nearly blacked out with rage.

"You fucking piece of shit." My free fist meets his stomach. His knees buckle and I release my forearm, letting his doubled-over body collapse to the floor.

Holding his side, gasping for air, he admits, "I was trying to expose your relationship. I thought it was fake."

"Come on, Jerrod. Where's your photographer now? This is what you were after, right? You want me to look bad in front of the board, well kicking your ass should do it."

Jerrod staggers to his feet, and I should be done, but another landed punch, this one square in his face, feels too gratifying.

As blood sprays from Jerrod's nose, somewhere behind me, a woman screams. Hospital security will probably be here any minute.

He wipes at his nose. It's probably broken now. How many bones are in a human nose? The body for that matter? I have no idea, but I figure it's one down, only several hundred to go.

"Rhys!" Hannah yells from the doorway of Lettie's room. "Stop!"

I release the fist that is curled into the front of Jerrod's shirt, and he staggers backward, placing a hand on the wall to steady himself.

I'm so fucking tired. Of trying to prove myself. Of molding myself into who others think I should be. I want Lettie, and I want to be a good person, and I hate that I let Jerrod pull me into this ugly game with him.

"Stay the fuck away from me and Colette." I stagger backwards, the adrenaline from fighting Jerrod starting to wane.

"Everyone cared more about you," he calls.

I should ignore him and walk away but I find myself turning back.

"What?"

"Your parents died and everyone was there for you. My

family fell apart but I never got the sympathy you did, I couldn't compete."

"That's fucked up. It was never a competition to see who could get more sympathy."

"It wasn't only that. Your parents treated me like their own. When my mom went to rehab, and I spent time at Lake George with you, I was jealous of your family. I saw what it was like to have loving, supportive parents."

"Then I lost them."

"Yeah, I lost them, too."

For the first time, Jerrod's mask falls and I see the hurt and insecurity behind it. I'd never thought of him hurting from my parents' death. That he'd also lost their guidance and love. And even though he hadn't lost his parents, they weren't what mine had been to him.

I stare at him, now bloody and bruised. My anger has dissipated, but I'm still processing what he shared and how I feel about it.

A security guard shows up to escort me off the premises.

"Hannah, tell Lettie I'll be waiting for her outside."

She nods, still looking shell shocked, and I let the security guard show me the way out.

CHAPTER 63

Colette

I wake up around two in the morning, my back cold where it once was warm from Rhys's body.

Last night, when we got home from the hospital, after the adrenaline crash, I'd slept hard. But now, the soreness from the accident has started to settle into my muscles, and everything is tender.

Slowly, I lift myself to sitting, my head swimming a little with the motion.

The moment I do, a movement in the corner of the room catches my attention.

The dark shadow sitting in the chair moves forward and into the light coming from the open window shades, highlighting Rhys's face. The spike in my heart rate eases at the sight of him.

"You scared me. What are you doing over there?" I ask.

"You shouldn't be moving like that," is his response.

He's beside me now, guiding me back into a prone position. When he starts to move away, I reach for his forearm.

"Then come back to bed."

"I can't sleep and I didn't want to wake you."

"So, you're going to watch me sleep? While it sounds romantic in theory, in practice, it's kind of creepy."

"Fuck." He sighs. "I'm sorry."

Even in the dim light, I can make out the dark circles around his eyes. For a man who says he can't sleep, he looks exhausted.

He'd told me what happened with Jerrod at the hospital. How Jerrod had confessed to hiring a photographer to follow us in hopes of exposing old habits that he could use to undermine Rhys's character for the upcoming board vote. But instead, the photographer had fed into social media's desire to know more about mine and Rhys's relationship and he'd gotten more aggressive, like chasing me on the street.

Rhys climbs back into bed, and I settle my head onto his chest. With the lump on the back of my head, this is the perfect position to be in.

"I'm going to apologize in advance if I drool on you," I tell him.

That earns me a light chuckle, and it warms my chest to hear him at ease if even for a moment.

Rhys's hand slips under the back of my t-shirt, his fingertips dancing against my skin in soothing strokes. And with my ear to his chest, the steady heartbeat of the man I love lulls me to sleep.

The next time I wake up, it's nine o'clock in the morning but I'm alone again.

After using the restroom and brushing my teeth, I find Ramsey and Sebastian in my living room. Mo and Maxine are snuggling in the cat bed next to the window like it's a just a normal Saturday.

"Hey. How are you feeling?" Sebastian asks.

I rub the back of my head where the lump from my fall yesterday is tender. "Like I fell off a curb and hit my head."

"*Colette,*" Sebastian scolds mockingly.

Ramsey's eyes widen, but even with his lips pressed together, a pfft of air escapes.

I smile. "What? Too soon?"

Ramsey shrugs. "Humor is a form of coping mechanism."

Sebastian studies me. "I didn't know it's yours."

"I can be funny," I protest.

"Okay, you're a comedian. Now, let's get you some breakfast."

"Where's Rhys?" I ask.

They exchange a glance before retreating to the kitchen. I follow and watch as both busy themselves pulling out ingredients.

"Do you want an omelet?" Ramsey asks. "That's all I know how to make."

Sebastian pauses to give him a peck on the cheek, before turning to me. "He's cute, right?"

I'm about to ask about Rhys again when the front door slams shut, and a moment later I have my answer.

"Why are you out of bed? The doctor instructed you to stay in bed," is his greeting.

"Did she?" I ask, wondering if maybe I do have a concussion because I don't recall that information being relayed to me.

He scowls. "Maybe not in so many words, but you need to rest." His gaze drops to my tiny pink sleep shorts, and when his eyes return to my face, his stare turns molten hot. "Rhys's orders."

Rhys's orders. Hmm. I wonder if that's an untapped fantasy of mine. Rhys demanding and grumpy. It has potential, that's for sure.

"One breakfast in bed coming right up!" Ramsey calls cheerfully from his position at the range.

Rhys motions for me to lead the way to my bedroom. Once there, I turn to him. "I don't have a concussion. The doctor cleared me."

He shuts the door behind himself. "We need to talk."

"Okay." It comes out hesitantly. That four-word combination sounds ominous.

He motions to the bed. "Sit down."

Somebody is grouchy today. Makes sense when you stay up all night staring at people while they sleep.

I cock an eyebrow at him. *Let's try that again.*

"Sorry. Please sit down."

Better.

I drop to the edge of my bed and watch as he starts to pace in front of me.

He looks nervous. Hesitant. Unsure. If I wasn't feeling good about this talk before, I'm definitely not now.

My mind starts spinning. What could he want to talk about?

He barely slept last night. Every time he's looked at me since the hospital, he looks like he's in pain. And now 'we need to talk.'

Oh my god. Is he going to break up with me?

That's what the talk is.

My jaw hits the floor. How dare he kick me when I'm down. Also, I'm in love with him, so that's going to be a no from me.

"You know what." I bolt upright. "No. You don't get to do this."

"What?" He looks at me in shock.

"You're scared. That's fine. But you're not going to break up with me. No." I cross my arms in an X, then wave them out to opposite sides. "I'm not allowing it."

He stares at me a moment, then starts shaking his head. "I'm not breaking up with you."

"Oh," I say, sitting back down on the bed, now a picture of serenity. "Okay, then you may proceed."

His lips twitch as he stares at me with reverence in his eyes. "Thanks."

Rhys drops to his knees in front of me and takes my hands. His right knuckles are bruised and swollen from his fight with Jerrod at the hospital. I hate that they got physical, and I'm hoping at some point they can talk their issues out.

"You're right. I was scared. Fucking terrified when I thought something happened to you."

I lift a hand up to brush a rogue hair off his forehead. "Something did happen to me but I'm okay."

He nods. "I love you, Colette. Lettie. Princess. All the versions you are to me."

"I love you, too."

"I don't want to just see where this goes because I know exactly where it leads. You and me, together. I want a million first dates with you. In fancy clothes at a gala or wearing sweats on the couch. I want to do *us* for the rest of our lives." He pulls a velvet box out of his pocket and opens it. Sparkling up at me is a breathtaking diamond with smaller diamonds surrounding it. And it's princess cut. "When I saw this ring, I knew it was meant to be on your finger. It's the one I want to put there now and make everything about us real. I know things have happened quickly between us, but for how long we've known each other, I'd say we're moving at a snail's pace."

I laugh and with the movement of my cheeks, I feel the wetness there. I hadn't even realized I was crying.

Rhys's eyes are filled with emotion, too. Then, he leans back on one knee and takes my hand in his. "Will you marry me?"

"Yes! Yes, of course I will." I bounce on my toes, my enthusiasm bubbling over.

He places the ring on my finger, and it fits perfectly. Then, I wrap my arms around him and he pulls me in for a kiss.

"What do we do about the other ring?" I ask.

He shrugs. "Keep it. Sell it. Donate it." He kisses me again. "It could fund your tutu making supplies for decades."

"Yeah, it could."

"Oh, and I'm really glad you said yes or this might have been awkward."

He pulls a folded-up paper out of his back pocket.

My eyes widen. "What is this?"

"The deed to your parents' house at Lake George. I bought it for you."

My chest squeezes, emotion returning to my eyes. "You did?"

"Yeah."

"Oh my god, Rhys. Thank you!" Then the dam bursts and he holds me close as I cry happy tears.

"Wait. If you bought my parents' lake house and you still have yours, how will we know which one to stay at?"

His smile widens.

"We'll take turns."

"And with everyone's expanding families, it will be nice to have more space, for the next generation." Remembering our conversation when we babysat the twins, I look up at his handsome face. "Do you want a next generation?"

He squeezes the back of my neck, and with a sexy grin pulling at his lips he responds, "With you, yeah, it's a no brainer."

"And until then, you'll be Uncle Rhys. I know how much you enjoy that."

"It's a pretty good gig." He drops a soft kiss to my lips.

"I knew you'd come around."

CHAPTER 64

Rhys

When the board calls me and Jerrod back into the room after their vote, I already know their decision.

After the incident with the photographer he hired to follow me and Lettie, Jerrod told the board he was no longer vying for the president position.

I respected Jerrod's decision but I also didn't agree with it. Not because I wanted to see if I would beat him outright, but because after we talked at length about our childhoods and Jerrod's work with the foundation over the years, I knew he deserved to be a part of it.

Lettie helped me realize that if Jerrod and I could move past our issues, that he ultimately would be a great asset to the foundation.

So, when my grandfather announces me as the new president of The Spencer Foundation, I use my time with the board to politely decline.

"I'll be the first to admit I don't know what I'm doing." My eyes move to Sandeep and he gives me a supportive nod. "But I want to learn. I also think the ways of the past aren't serving us any longer." I meet Jerrod's gaze. "And I think it's important to find a new way of doing things."

I lay out my proposal to remove the president role and change the board to be led by co-chairs, so that Jerrod and I can work together, maximizing each of our expertise and handling various aspects of the foundation.

When I told Sandeep what I wanted to do, he helped me organize my thoughts and come up with a structure that would give me and Jerrod flexibility as co-chairs.

The approval is unanimous, and when the meeting adjourns, Jerrod approaches me.

"I like your suit." He nods at the Brioni suit Lettie picked out for me to wear today. "Is that mint green?"

"Pistachio," I confirm.

"Nice." He swallows thickly. "Listen, do you and Colette want to grab dinner with me and Corinne some time?"

"You bet. Send me a date and I'll check with Lettie," I say, as he holds the door open for me to exit the conference room.

"Maybe we could grab a coffee right now? I've got a few ideas on how we can maximize the foundation's public investments that I want to run by you."

When I turn around, I find Lettie there, waiting for me. She's absolutely stunning in a pink floral dress.

"Actually, I'm going to have to take a rain check on that one."

"Cool. No worries." Jerrod notices Lettie and gives her a quick nod.

"I was hoping to take The Spencer Foundation's new co-chair president out to lunch," she says, pink lips splitting into a bright smile.

"I told you to stay home and rest." My words are demanding, but I'm already smiling as I wrap my arm around her waist and pull her to me.

"I guess I'm not a very good girl, then, huh?" She almost says it with a straight face, but a tiny twitch of her lips gives her away.

I lift my hand to her face, my thumb holding her chin.

"When every mark on your body is healed, every scrape and bruise gone, I'm going to remember this conversation, and then I'm going to make some marks of my own."

Lettie's smile widens. "Promise?"

I press a ghost of a kiss over her lips, then pull away.

Her lips press out in a pout. "You're a tease."

"And you, Princess, are incorrigible," I tell her.

"Hmm. It sounds like we make a pretty good team."

"Surprising, isn't it?" I tease.

She wraps her arms around my neck and pulls me down to her. "The best surprise of all."

Epilogue

RHYS

10 YEARS LATER

Every time Hunter gets a bean bag in the hole, he does a celebration dance. His arms pump overhead in a 'raise the roof' motion while his hips seem to be moving to an entirely different rhythm. Neither of them matches the beat of the music playing from the boat house speakers.

"And I thought Emma was uncoordinated." Griffin laughs.

"Hey! I've gotten better at dancing." Emma pouts from her lounger, but it's playful.

"Dad," Poppy plants a hand on her hip and rolls her eyes at Hunter, "please stop doing that. You're not cool."

Hunter scoffs. "You have no idea how cool I am. Sweetheart," he calls to Sophie who's lounging on a deck chair next to Emma, reading a book, "tell the girls how cool their dad is."

Sophie looks up from her book and gives him a thumbs up. "So cool, baby, so cool."

The twins are ten now, tweens, which they despise being called, and one of my favorite past times is to watch them give their dad shit. I can't wait until they're driving and dating, man, it's going to be fun to watch.

"Uncle Rhys is cool." Finley motions to me with one of the bean bags.

"Thanks, Fin." With my empty hand, I offer her a fist and she bumps me back with hers.

When I turn back to Hunter, I can't hide my shit-eating grin.

"It's the tattoos," he mutters, tossing his bean bag in defeat. "Are we going to finish the game?"

Both girls run off toward the tree house. "Later," they call in unison.

"Looks like they're back." Hunter motions to the group exiting the boat at the dock. Chloe, Barrett, Jerrod, and Corrine took some of the kids on a boat ride earlier. The group makes their way up the beach and onto the lawn.

Cooper and Beckett, Emma and Griffin's eight- and six-year-old sons, run to tackle their dad.

Griffin scoops each one up and throws them over his shoulder to spin them around until they're all laughing and he nearly falls over.

"Hey, Jas," Sophie calls to her six-year-old son, Jasper, who is currently dressed like a pirate. "Will you go grab the snacks Aunt Hannah and I prepared earlier?"

Jasper puts down his sword. "Really? Do I have to?"

"Yes, you need some orange slices or you'll get scurvy."

"Ah, Mom. We were just heading over to the treehouse."

"You mean the pirate ship," Eliza, Hannah and James's six-year-old daughter, corrects him.

"We've got the snacks." Hannah calls, coming down the path from the Cartwright house carrying a tray of fruit, while James, Ramsey and Sebastian follow, their arms loaded down with a boatload of snacks.

Corinne's eyes widen at all the food, but she takes the tray from a very pregnant Hannah to set it on the table nearby.

"Aren't we having dinner in an hour?" Corinne asks.

Jerrod rubs her back. "You remember that feeding this group is a constant endeavor."

Jerrod and Corinne are child-free by choice, but they get their fill, and then some, of the wild ride that is parenthood when they hang out with all our children.

"Snacks!" Jasper pulls Bodie, Chloe and Barrett's seven-year-old son toward the table. "Come on, Bo. Grab what you can and let's go!" He raises his wooden sword uphill toward the treehouse.

"Remember to close the trap door." Barrett calls after them before popping a handful of Goldfish in his mouth. "Why are these so addictive?" He asks Chloe, reaching for another handful.

She laughs. "Because you love salty snacks."

Griffin finally releases his boys. After a quick hug for their mom, Cooper and Beckett race for the table of snacks.

Griffin rubs his back. "Man, that's getting harder to do."

Emma stands to wrap her arms around his waist, and smiles up at him. "They're getting big."

Griffin presses a kiss to her lips. "Yeah, it makes me happy and sad at the same time."

When the group has ransacked the table of snacks, they run off toward the treehouse. A few years ago, Hunter and I spent a weekend attempting to replace the old, rotting boards, but ended up hiring a crew to redo the whole treehouse. We kept it rustic, though, wanting to ensure our kids get the same experience we had.

"How was the lake?" I ask Jerrod.

"Busy, but always fun with this group." He gives me a squeeze on the shoulder, and I hand him one of the craft beers from the cooler that Griffin and Hunter stocked.

Jerrod and I are still co-chairs of The Spencer Foundation, and the organization is flourishing. While we still work with many local nonprofits in NYC and around the country, we've expanded our reach to work globally with developing countries on water sanitation and hygiene projects, as well as working with a large corporation on expanding digital health community. After our grandfather retired, he and Edith moved to Florida, but they visit so frequently it feels like they still live in the city.

"Look who's up from their nap," Chloe coos at the appearance of the wobbly, dark-haired toddler walking across the lawn. It's my two-year-old daughter, Millie, who is now sneaking up behind Sophie's chair a playful smile on her lips.

"Who's that behind my chair?" Sophie asks in an exaggerated voice.

Millie lets out a spirited scream and runs straight for my legs.

"Dada, Sophie get me." She looks up at me with her big blue eyes, laughing.

I swing Millie up into my arms and give her a squeeze. She wraps her arms around me and it's the best feeling in the world. I never knew having a tiny human clinging to my chest calling me 'dada' would be the peak of my existence. It's fucking awesome.

"That's because she wants a snuggle." I squeeze her tight. "And you give the best hugs, Millie Rose."

After another tight squeeze, she gives me a kiss on the lips then wriggles free to wander over to where Harper, Barrett and Chloe's four-year-old daughter, Rowan, Hannah and James's three-year-old daughter, and Maxwell, Sebastian and Ramsey's three-year-old son, are playing at the water table. That group is too focused on how many buckets of water they can fill up to even bother with snacks.

I turn to find Lettie coming down the path with our newborn son cradled to her chest. I greet her with a kiss, then take Wesley from her.

"I was just coming to get Millie up," I tell her.

She gives me a sleepy smile. "We napped together so I was already there."

She tosses the burp cloth over my shoulder. "He just ate and I didn't get a good burp from him yet."

I rub soothing circles over his back and give him a few gentle pats. "You know burping is my specialty."

"Yes," her lips twitch, "you've come a long way in that department."

Her smile lights up her blue eyes. It's been nine years since she walked down the aisle to me on that beach in St. Thomas, yet I find myself falling more in love with her each day that passes. And seeing Lettie as a mom has only made my love for her deepen.

After fifteen years with The City Ballet, seven as a principal dancer, Lettie retired from dancing professionally three years ago, and we immediately got pregnant with Millie. A few months ago, Wesley was born, and this weekend is his first visit to Lake George.

"What can I get you, Princess? A drink? Something to eat?" I wrap an arm around her and she curls into my side.

"Nothing right now." She stares out at the water. "This is perfect."

After Lettie retired, she took the director role at Leg-Up and has continued teaching a few classes a week because she loves it so much. Madelyn, who has been taking classes at Leg-Up for the last eight years, just graduated from high school, and is interning at Leg-Up this summer to help with their mobile dance program. We're both still big Taylor Swift stans and Millie is becoming one too.

This is how it is now. Unfinished games of cornhole, two hours to herd everyone onto the boat, and countless mugs of abandoned coffee scattered between the three lake houses. And don't even get me started on how many bottles of sunscreen we go through.

All our lives are busy, but as a group, we plan out two weekends every summer to spend together at Lake George.

The Harts and the St. Clairs, along with Jerrod and Corinne, stay in my old family home, the Cartwrights and McKenzies in the Cartwright family house, and Sebastian, Ramsey and Maxwell with me and Lettie and our kids in the Davenports' old house, which is the Spencer house now. It's a three-ring circus but the best part is watching our kids play together and making memories as a family.

I always wondered if I could be genuinely happy at Lake George again. But what I realize now is that even though my parents aren't here with me, they gave me this gift. This place, these people, these connections, and now it has become so much more than I could have imagined.

Later, we gather at my parents' old house, because it has a large enough dining space to accommodate the group for dinner. With fourteen adults and twelve kids with one on the way, it's complete chaos. By the time we sit down, no one's food is hot anymore, but we shovel it down anyway so we're not running on fumes.

With Millie bouncing on my lap, I'm in the middle of my conversation with Ramsey, Hunter, Griffin, and Jerrod when the lights go out. I'm thinking a breaker needs to be flipped, but a moment later, Lettie and Corinne come out of the kitchen holding cakes with flames dancing above them. Eighty candles in total.

With Maxwell in his arms, Ramsey fans his face. "Good lord, that's a lot of heat."

The group gives their best off-key singing of Happy Birthday and finally, when the cakes are placed in front of me and Jerrod, I hold Millie's hands back so she doesn't reach for the flames, then blow the candles out.

This is forty.

I turn to look at Jerrod and he shares the same shocked expression. How did we get here?

The real question is, how did I get so damn lucky?

Much later, after I've given Wesley his late-night bottle, then rocked him to sleep, I quietly make my way back to our bedroom. Mo and Maxine are curled up on their cat bed in the corner. Mo is living his best life with Maxine curled around him. I pull back the covers and climb in, trying to not wake Lettie, but she rolls over to face me.

"Hey. What time is it?" She moves to look at the clock, panic starting to rise in her voice.

"It's three and I already fed him."

She yawns. "Really? I didn't even hear him."

"Good. That was the point. I turned your monitor off."

I wrap a hand around her lower back and pull her in close, then inhale her familiar feminine scent.

"Did you have a good birthday?" she asks, her voice a whisper.

"It was my favorite."

She sighs dreamily, like she's nearly asleep. "You said that last year."

I press a kiss to her forehead, appreciating the feel of her in my arms. "That's because every year with you is my favorite."

THE END

Thank You

Dear Reader,

Thank you for taking the time to ready my book. There are so many books to choose from, so thank you for spending your precious time reading mine. If you have a minute, please consider leaving a review for Surprisingly Us. Reviews help indie authors so much!

XO, Erin

Acknowledgments

I can't believe the series is over! Is it too soon for a next gen series? Ha! I don't know if that will ever happen but it's fun to think of the possibilities. Thank you to all the readers who discovered and read my books over the course of this series. Those who shared their love for them and told friends to read them. Your enthusiasm for these characters kept me encouraged when I had so many doubts as a writer.

Thank you to my family and friends for your unwavering support. Especially to my husband, Eric, and my three children, who gave me the time I needed to get this book to the finish line. I love you with my whole heart!

Thank you, thank you, thank you to my PA, Taylor. For letting me send you excessively long, rambling audio texts and talking me down when I was certain I'd never finish this book. You are a gem and I'm so happy to have you on my team.

Thank you to Becca Hensley Mysoor for our chats that encouraged me to figure out who these characters were and kept me moving forward.

Thank you to my beta reading team for not giving up on me even when I didn't have my poop in a group: Allie @allie_rambles, Ashley O'Dell, Isabella, Laura, Molly, and

Shea. I'm grateful for the feedback you were able to give and promise to be better next time.

Thank you to my copy editor, Chelly Peeler for putting up with me and my ever moving timelines. I appreciate you so much!

About the Author

Erin Hawkins is a spicy romcom author who lives in Colorado with her husband and three young children. She enjoys reading, working out, spending time in the mountains, reality TV, and brunch that lasts all day.

Printed in Great Britain
by Amazon